D0481294

NOV 0 9

the

doom

machine

the

doom

machine

a novel by

MARK TEAGUE

THE BLUE SKY PRESS

an imprint of scholastic inc.

new york

FOR LILLIAS AND AVA
—M.T.

THE BLUE SKY PRESS

Copyright © 2009 by Mark Teague

Library of Congress catalog card number: 2009014262
ISBN-13: 978-0-545-15142-9 / ISBN-10: 0-545-15142-2
10 9 8 7 6 5 4 3 2 1   09 10 11 12 13
Printed in the U.S.A.   23
First printing, October 2009
The art was created using acrylic paint.
Designed by Kathleen Westray

contents

....

. . .

PART ONE: EARTH

. . .

PART TWO: ARBORIA

. . .

PART THREE: SKREEPIA

part
one...
earth

. . .

1. VERN HOLLOW, 1956

THE MORNING of the invasion, Jack Creedle got up early, as usual. He dragged his newspapers onto the porch, then slipped into the darkness to get his bike.

Jack lived at the Pines with his mother, who ran the place, and his uncle Bud. It was a boardinghouse, and not a fancy one. He had another uncle who lived across town, and three others he didn't know very well because they were locked up.

Jack had been locked up, too, until recently. When he came

home, his mom got him the paper route. "It'll keep you out of trouble," she said. But trouble always found him, like it found all the Creedles — mixed up in things that were illegal or just plain stupid. They were a trouble-prone family.

Jack's own problems had started a year earlier when he was caught trying to swipe a math test from the filing cabinet in Mrs. Mousewemple's room. What made it so bad, from a legal point of view, was that it happened at three A.M. on a Sunday morning. That meant it wasn't just theft, it was breaking and entering.

What made it stupid was that he didn't even care about math. He'd done it on a bet with an eighth grader named Ray Falco. Only it turned out Ray was in cahoots with Jack's arch-enemy, Grady Webb, and the whole thing was a setup. As soon as Jack wormed his way through the classroom window, the light went on, and there was Mrs. Mousewemple — with Sergeant Webb, Grady's dad, standing right behind her like a TV cowboy, his feet wide apart and one hand hovering over the butt of his revolver. They'd sent Jack to Millbrook for that one.

He liked the paper route, the freedom of moving alone through empty streets, but even there, trouble was always lurking. There was the newspaper war, for one thing — *Sentinel*s versus *Courier*s. Jack was a *Sentinel*. His boss, Mr. Anastasio, had given him a route that straddled *Courier* territory all the way.

Grady Webb was a *Courier*.

Jack moved quietly up the driveway. The trick was to get his bike out of the barn without waking up Milo, the rooster. They had been friends once, but not anymore. Growing up had made the chicken mean. He was a typical Creedle in that way. They all got worse with age.

When he opened the barn door the hinges yelped, but Milo didn't stir. Jack grabbed his bike and hurried back to the house. Milo was a pretty sorry rooster when you thought about it. Dawn was the time he was supposed to crow his tiny head off, but the chicken didn't care—it was too cold.

Jack thought wistfully of his own bed. Bundled up under two sweatshirts and a corduroy jacket, with the earflaps on his hunting cap pulled down, he still felt chilly. His newspapers were already folded and stuffed into canvas saddlebags, so he straddled the bike, pushed off with one foot, and pedaled away.

On the far side of the train trestle he turned onto Church Street and sat up straight, burying his hands in his armpits to keep them warm. Here and there a porch light was on, but most of Vern Hollow was still asleep. Smedley Trowbridge claimed that weird stuff was more likely to happen when everybody was sleeping. He said it was only "the power of conscious thought" that kept things normal most of the time.

Jack wasn't sure about that. Smedley also claimed he saw a pterodactyl once, flying over the Wanookie River just before dawn. Smedley was a *Sentinel*.

He threw his first newspaper into the Olafskys' birdbath, cursed, and got off his bike to retrieve it. In the distance he could hear the stuttering of Mr. Vandestar's Hudson. It had been in Uncle Bud's shop once, though it probably wouldn't be back. Mr. Vandestar said Uncle Bud was a crook, and the car had more problems after he got it back than it had going in. That was technically true. Uncle Bud *was* a crook, but he didn't wreck the car on purpose. He was just distracted lately.

Jack knew the car's problem was in the master cylinder; he could tell by listening to it. He thought about how he would repair it, the tools he would use and the parts he would need, if only Mr. Vandestar would give the shop a second chance.

Folks in town didn't know it, but nowadays Jack did most of the engine work they thought was being done by his uncle. The arrangement worked out well for both of them. Jack got to do more interesting jobs, the garage was getting a better reputation, and Uncle Bud could spend more time in his workshop, doing whatever it was he did in there.

From down the block Jack heard the hum of bicycle wheels. He crouched behind the Olafskys' DeSoto, listening as a couple of *Courier*s slid by like ghosts in the darkness. The one in front was Grady Webb. Jack could tell by the voice.

"I told him if he didn't give me the sandwich I'd bust him in the mouth."

"Did he do it?" The other voice was Gordon Smathers.

Grady laughed. "What do you think?"

The bikes drifted away. Someday Jack would get Grady Webb. He made the vow often, not really believing it. Grady was a year older and twice his size.

He made some poor throws trying to warm up. Folded newspapers were awkward in flight. If they didn't spin like helicopter blades, they tended to fall like wounded ducks. Jack's throws skidded across driveways and belly flopped into piles of wet leaves. At the Gundersons' house his toss caromed off the back of Mr. Gunderson's supply truck, hit a maple tree, and fell neatly into an open garbage can. Jack admired the throw for its rarity. It was the kind of shot you couldn't make once in a hundred times, if you were trying. He wiped the *Sentinel* off on his jeans and carried it to the front porch.

As he was turning around he heard an odd sound, hollow like a Wiffle ball, sailing in from somewhere overhead. He looked up to a point just above the Belknaps' garage where a bright green star appeared and quickly expanded as the noise grew louder and almost musical—like the sound a wet finger makes on the rim of a glass.

The star became a glowing turquoise disk, spinning like a Ferris wheel turned on its side. As it approached it sloughed off a gauzy mantle of pale smoke, which continued to swirl in its wake.

The saucer moved unhurriedly from horizon to horizon directly above the town. When it had traveled some distance over the unlit bulk of Dutch Woods, it stopped, hovered, and then quickly dropped. In an instant it was gone.

Jack watched the spot for several long moments, blinking. All over town dogs began to bark. Somewhere on the next block a man shouted. Jack adjusted his newspapers so the weight was evenly distributed, got on his bike, and pedaled away.

• • •

2. VISITORS

ISADORA SHUMWAY first heard about the alien invasion on station WBZT in Fenwick Grove. For some time she had been fiddling with the car radio, trying to find something her mother would approve of. It wasn't easy. What Dr. Shumway wanted to hear was a news station, yet when Isadora finally found one, her mother switched off the radio. "Really," she complained. "Such nonsense."

"I don't know why you say that, Mother. Your own research proves advanced space flight is possible."

"My research has nothing to do with flying saucers. You of all people should know that true science cleaves to a higher standard."

"I thought it was interesting." Isadora wished she had heard the rest of the story.

Her mother squinted at the slice of road visible over the station wagon's wide steering wheel. She had a low tolerance for foolishness, an attitude easily seen in her upright posture, the elevated angle of her chin, and the sensible way her dark hair was pulled into a bun.

Isadora had some of the same features, though not, in her opinion, the very best ones. Her chin was not so strong, and horn-rimmed glasses hid her eyes. Her skin was dark brown, like her father's, and her frizzy hair, though pulled into a ponytail, remained unruly. Maybe her mind was unruly, too. It provided her, unbidden, with the image of a flying saucer skimming low over treetops like a skipped stone. It wasn't a particularly scientific image, but despite what her mother said, it *was* interesting.

The car belched, not for the first time. It had been mak-ing noises since they left the Chemical Society Conference in Utica. Isadora peered out nervously. Wherever they were, it was remote. Cornfields stretched to low ridges dominated by cop-pery oaks. From time to time they passed a white farmhouse, a red barn, a silver-capped silo. "I hope we don't break down out here," she said. "We'd have a long walk to find help."

"The engine is running poorly, although, not being a mechanic, it's hard for me to make a diagnosis." Dr. Shumway was a rarity—a female scientist, and a highly respected one at that. Though Isadora did not understand the work in detail, she knew her mother had been experimenting on materials that generated as little friction as possible. Without friction, an object could travel at enormous speeds, and a machine could work almost endlessly from a small initial input of energy. The trick was overcoming resistance. Dr. Shumway hated resistance.

The car belched again. With relief, Isadora spotted a town in the distance. Brick buildings and white clapboard houses gathered beneath church steeples and a water tower. She was a city girl, and open country made her uncomfortable.

They drove in. A sign welcomed them to Vern Hollow, THE HAPPIEST TOWN IN THE WANOOKIE VALLEY.

"I wonder how a town can be happy," Isadora said.

"I suppose it refers to the general disposition of the inhabitants."

Isadora hadn't seen so much as a stray dog. "Where *are* the inhabitants?"

The station wagon made a strangling noise, backfired, and died. They coasted downhill, listening to the popcorn sound of gravel beneath their tires. Ahead were some small stores and a gas station. "You see? We're in luck." A battered sign read BUD'S GAS AND REPAIR. "I'm sure we'll have this fixed in no time."

The garage was as shabby as its sign. They rolled to a stop beside a pair of fire-engine-red gas pumps. Dr. Shumway beeped the horn, and they waited for an attendant. A minute later, a door opened on one side of the building. A small man in blue overalls and a baseball cap blinked owlishly at them from behind thick glasses, then ran away across the adjoining vacant lot. At the edge of the lot he hoisted himself over a stockade fence and disappeared.

"Well," said Dr. Shumway.

When they got out, it was cold and windy. Isadora followed her mother to the front of the building, smoothing the pleats in her skirt. Suddenly a boy stepped out of the garage, rubbing his hands on a filthy rag. His name, Jack, was stitched on the chest of his stained coveralls, and a motor oil skid ran from the bridge of his nose to his bristling hairline.

"Sorry to keep you waiting," he said. "I can't hear much when I'm under a car." He glanced shyly at Isadora. They were about the same age. "Say, I don't suppose you've seen my uncle Bud?"

Isadora frowned. There was something utterly familiar about him—his gapped teeth, his close-set eyes, his ears like small handles stuck to the sides of his head. She blinked, and the feeling began to fade.

"Is your uncle the gentleman we saw scaling that fence?" asked Dr. Shumway.

"That was him, all right. Don't take it personal, though. It's the aliens. They've got everyone upset."

"Aliens?" asked Isadora.

"Sure. I'm surprised you haven't heard. It's been all over the news."

"As a matter of fact," said Dr. Shumway, "we did hear something on the radio. A thoroughly idiotic report—"

"—about a flying saucer!" Isadora cut in excitedly.

"That's the one."

"Is it true then?"

"Of course it isn't true!" snapped her mother. "And at any rate, it's irrelevant. We have a mechanical problem. We need to see whoever is in charge here."

"I guess that's me until Uncle Bud gets back."

"Indeed. And when might that be? We are expected in Boston this evening. It's urgent we find a mechanic."

"Well, you're in luck there," Jack said, grinning. "I can fix just about anything on wheels."

Isadora interrupted. "Are you certain about the invasion? Is that why the town is so deserted?"

"You better believe it. One look at those aliens and practically everyone skedaddled."

"Please!" said Dr. Shumway. "If you *are* a mechanic, take a look at our vehicle."

By way of an answer, Jack pointed and clucked his tongue. Then he headed back into the garage.

"He's peculiar, don't you think?" said Isadora.

Dr. Shumway pursed her lips. "He has the manners of a hoodlum."

• • •

JACK SORTED through his toolbox. It was amazing how much Vern Hollow had changed in a week. In no time at all the town was practically empty. Most of the people ran off when the monster showed up on television, but some had gone even earlier, when they first heard about the invasion. Jack supposed he was partly to blame, the way he'd described the flying saucer to anyone who would listen. But he wasn't the only one talking. Heck Van Gundy, whose property bordered Dutch Woods, had been on his way back from milking when he saw the saucer fly over. Old Mrs. Travellini saw it, too, and she told everyone at the Big Chief Diner. She had been walking her dog, Pinky, when the thing sailed by, all lit up like the new supermarket down in Fenwick Grove. But what really made the story take off was when Chief Whopper weighed in. Everyone trusted the chief. He'd been in his prowl car when he saw it. He was driving across open fields out on Route 7, so there couldn't be any mistake. After that, the story spread like crazy, and people started to leave. Knowing there was a saucer in the woods scared the pants off everyone.

• • •

DR. SHUMWAY tapped the steering wheel impatiently while Jack poked under the hood. Beside her, Isadora watched a fat man in a gray suit hurry up the sidewalk. When he reached the gas station, the man leaned against one of the pumps and wiped his forehead with a handkerchief. "Welcome to Vern Hollow!" he panted. "I'm the mayor, Gus Handy."

Dr. Shumway shook his hand and introduced herself and Isadora.

"A lady scientist!" he exclaimed, whistling. "That's something you don't see every day. You must be here because of the invasion." He lowered his voice. "I tell you, it's the sort of thing every mayor dreads: an alien attack, a town overrun by monsters."

"We've yet to see a single monster," said Dr. Shumway drily. "And we're certainly not here to investigate this dubious story. As you can see, our car has broken down."

"Nothing serious, I hope? You don't want to be lingering, under the circumstances."

Jack looked up, wiping a greasy sleeve across his face. "Hello, Mayor. I gotta tell you, it's a real mess! Look at it. The carburetor is sticky, one of the cylinders is bad, and it's leaking oil. And that isn't even what caused it to break down." He reached as far as he could into a narrow opening and pulled out a grimy hunk of metal and porcelain. "This is."

"What is it?"

"Beats me. Some kind of valve thingy. They go bad on these '53s. It'll take me a day to fix, long as I can find a replacement over at the junkyard."

"That is completely unacceptable!" Dr. Shumway protested. "We must get back to Boston. I refuse to stay overnight."

"Mom runs a boardinghouse," said Jack, slamming the hood. "So you could stay with us. It's on the other side of town, by the railroad tracks."

"There has to be some way for us to get home," Dr. Shumway insisted, turning to the mayor.

"I can't think of one. But you know, you *can* get a hot meal at the Pines." The thought of food seemed to cheer him up. "In fact, I think I'll join you. My car is right down the street."

• • •

3. THE PINES

AS THEY DROVE away in Mayor Handy's Studebaker, it began to rain. The darkened windows downtown were as expressionless as shark eyes.

"You'll like the Pines," said Jack. He paused for a moment, as if trying to decide why they would like it. "We have lots of empty rooms."

Isadora found that easy to believe. Abandoned homes lined every street, though occasionally they passed one where light blazed defiantly from the windows.

"The aliens are afraid of light," Jack explained. "Or at least that's what people think."

They dipped under a train trestle and came to the Pines, a hulking Victorian house with broad, sagging porches. The carcass of an old Packard sedan rested in the front yard.

After gathering their luggage they hurried up the steps in

the rain. A stout, red-haired woman met them at the front door. She wore a white apron over a flower-print dress. She looked suspiciously at the Shumways, then at the mayor, then at Jack.

"Why'd the mayor bring you home? Did he catch you swiping something?"

"Naw. These people need a place to stay, is all. They're scientists from Boston."

"Scientists, are ya? Come to see our flying saucer, I suppose?"

"Certainly not." Dr. Shumway put down her suitcase. "Our car suffered a mechanical failure. We are left with no choice but to seek shelter here."

Mrs. Creedle snorted. "That's usually how it is when folks come to the Pines—no choice. But you're welcome to stay, long as you can pay for your rooms. Anyone with a lick of sense took off after the aliens got here."

The rooms were small and musty. Each contained a bed, a nightstand, and a wooden chair. The beds had a swaybacked, dispirited look. There was a bathroom at the end of the hall.

"Come down for dinner," Mrs. Creedle called. "I got meat loaf cooking."

Jack met the Shumways again in the dining room. His face and hands were red from scrubbing, though black crescents of grease still clung to his fingernails. Mayor Handy had already taken a seat at one end of the table, and he rose when the Shumways entered. At the other end sat a scarecrow-thin man wearing a frayed brown suit and a shirt the color of old newspapers. The man was picking his teeth with an enormous bowie knife.

"There you are, ladies!" The mayor sounded relieved. "Joe,

these are the visitors I was telling you about. From Boston. Dr. Shumway is some kind of scientist, if you can believe it."

Joe jammed his knife into the table, stood up, and bowed. "I can believe it." He grinned, as if they were all in on the same joke.

"I was just asking Joe what brought him to our humble town."

"Same thing as these scientists, I guess. I come to find out about the spaceship."

Mrs. Creedle bustled in with the meat loaf, ketchup, and bread. "Dig in," she ordered. "This ain't the Waldorf Astoria."

"For the record," Dr. Shumway said crisply, "we did not come to investigate your *flying saucer*. However, as it continues to come up, I am inclined to ask you, Mayor, what exactly happened here?"

"An alien invasion is what happened," Jack interrupted.

"Let the man talk," growled his mother.

"Thank you, Laverne. Now let me say right off the bat that I personally didn't see a thing. But those who did claimed they saw a flying saucer. Of course I was reluctant to believe them—"

"I'm glad to hear it," said Dr. Shumway.

"—and I said so." He gave Jack a stern look. "We have worked hard for a long time to give Vern Hollow a good name, especially after the sea monster hoax of '48. Nothing is more important to a town than its reputation. Even so, there were those who *insisted* a spaceship landed nearby. Chief among them was, well, Chief Whopper. He claimed he saw it go down in the direction of Dutch Woods."

"I saw it," said Jack. "That's exactly where it went down."

"I said the idea was foolish," the mayor continued, "but folks *like* the chief. So I enlisted Whopper and some others, and together we formed a search party. We stomped through the woods for a good long time without finding a blessed thing. After that, most of us were ready to put the matter to rest."

"So why did everybody leave?" Isadora asked.

"I'm getting to that."

"They showed up on television," said Jack.

"Who showed up?"

"The space monsters. Or at least one of them did."

Mrs. Creedle pointed her fork at him. "I told you to stop interrupting."

"You claim to have seen this?" Dr. Shumway was incredulous.

"Not me," said Jack. "Uncle Dwayne stole our television."

Isadora put her fork down. "I don't get it. Why would a space monster appear on television?"

"Nobody knows," said the mayor. "Or at least nobody would tell *me*. They were in too big a hurry to leave."

"Don't you think it *significant*," Dr. Shumway said, "that those in town who watched television departed, while you, who did not, remained? Someone undoubtedly used the local airwaves to spark a panic. I'm sure it was depressingly simple."

"Do you mean it was a prank?" The mayor froze.

"A clever teenager with access to the transmitter could have pulled it off."

Isadora hated it when her mother talked like this. "What if you're wrong?" she asked, surprising herself with her vehemence. "What if there *are* aliens? Shouldn't we be trying to prove it, one way or another? And what about the evidence? Don't we care about that? Jack saw *something*. And should we assume everyone else in town is mistaken? Maybe they were smart to leave."

Mrs. Creedle banged the table with her fist. "That's what I

keep saying! Anyone who sticks around after a space invasion should have his head examined. I'd leave in a minute, if I had two dollars to rub together or any place to go."

The room lapsed into an uncomfortable silence. Joe speared the last slice of meat loaf with his fork. "Who says there's any place to go?" he asked softly. "Could be these monsters plan on conquering the whole world."

Dr. Shumway gave her mouth a final pat and stood up. "Please excuse us. As you can tell by my daughter's outburst, we have had an exhausting day."

Jack led the Shumways back upstairs. He flicked on the hall light. "I guess you're pretty worried about the aliens. Just remember, if anything happens, my room is upstairs in the attic."

"That's a comfort," said Isadora. She pushed her door open.

"At any rate," he continued, "the storm is a good thing. I'll be surprised if the monsters attack in this weather."

Dr. Shumway waited until he was gone. "Please remember we are scientists, dear. It is imperative that we be strictly rational. Good night." She patted her daughter on the shoulder.

Isadora closed her door. Maybe her mother was right. Surely the world was peculiar enough without adding space monsters to the equation. Outside, the rain came down in sheets. A drop of water fell from her ceiling and plunked into a metal pail beside the window. *And if Mother is wrong*, she thought, *then hopefully Jack is right. Hopefully the monsters have an aversion to rain.*

She climbed into bed without taking off her clothes and fell asleep with the light on.

. . .

4. ALIEN PLANET

COMMANDER XAAFUUN scurried on nimble feet through the darkened streets of Vern Hollow. The rain was falling heavily, and she was eager to return to the ship. These alien worlds were uniformly repulsive. She had tried to convince herself that rain on *Uurth* was not so different from a gruzzle storm on Skreepia, but it *was* different—thin, cold, wet, and insubstantial. It filled her with dread. Certainly it wasn't dangerous, the way a chunk of gruzzle could be, but there was something *unruly* about it, something wild that she could not accept. To think the Exalted One considered this heavy world to be a viable replacement planet! *All praise to her superior enlightenment,* but the Queen had never been here.

She found shelter in an unlocked garage and lifted the communicator from her utility belt. Ensign Phoony was searching the far side of the settlement. "Progress, Ensign?"

"Yes, Commander. A shelter full of flightless *buurds*!

Feathered, mind you, but flightless. I only ate two. The rest I can take to the ship."

"That is not our mission!" Xaafuun said sharply.

"There's still one more, hiding at the back of the shelter. Very hostile, but you must see its plumage!"

"Never mind the feathers, Ensign. Only the Special Assignment matters now."

Phoony wasn't listening. "They shimmer, even in the dark. And the colors—"

Xaafuun gnashed her teeth and rolled her multiple eyes. Phoony tried her patience, though he had a reputation as a talented Finder. She thought he would have located the Item by now, but that, apparently, was a forlorn hope. "Very well. Grab the *buurd*. But be quick about it." She returned the communicator to her belt. The Queen *did* have a passion for feathers. On earlier missions to *Uurth* the skreeps had taken practically nothing else, unless one counted the odd fighting beast. Truly there was very little on the planet worth having. Until now. Now there was the Special Item.

For the thousandth time, Xaafuun wondered what, exactly, it was. She had only one tiny pulse—and Phoony's instincts—to guide her. The Exalted One was cagey on the subject, refusing to describe either the Item's appearance or its function. When Xaafuun asked, cautiously, how she might locate a device so thoroughly shrouded in mystery, she was only told she *would* find it, and she would know *when* she found it, because it was unlike any other item on *Uurth*.

The commander watched the rain dancing on the driveway. She considered contacting Zin Zin and Bork. They were searching, too, somewhere on the other side of the native settlement, but really, what was the use? Since her unfortunate television

broadcast, the mission had degenerated badly. Not that she had been *wrong* to deliver the threat. She had simply grown impatient, knowing the Item was nearby and somebody was hiding it.

The idea of defiance from lesser creatures galled her, especially when the creatures in question were *ooman bings*. Xaafuun had a particular loathing for *ooman bings*. She ran a finger across the ropy flesh of her scar, remembering the TV broadcast and its aftermath. She had hoped the *ooman bings* might be bullied into seeing reason, but it turned out they were as unpredictable as they were stupid. Instead of giving up the Item, they had panicked, running off in great numbers to every point on the compass. Watching them scatter had filled her with despair. Surely the Special Item had gone with them. She'd slipped into despondency. The Queen did not accept failure on such a level. Xaafuun tried not to contemplate the punishment awaiting her on Skreepia.

Then, during the unpleasant, overlit period of the planet's most recent star cycle, the pulse came back, a faint echo, like a tiny hitch in time. It was far too quiet and erratic to track, but she had no doubt that it came from within the settlement. The only question was, *where?* She had no idea. Completing the mission under these circumstances would require effort and patience. Xaafuun hated effort, and her supply of patience was running low.

She stared into the night's dreary, aggressive wetness. To think it would come to this, on *Uurth* of all places, tracking an item made by *ooman bings*. Commander Xaafuun was an explorer by trade but not by temperament. She despised space, the cramped ships, the long, groggy voyages. More than that, she hated every single planet she had ever seen. Vile places, these outposts at the edge of the universe, booby trapped with unpleasant surprises (like rain) and stocked with an endless array of savages, all stupid, all unworthy, all—every one—ungrateful for the blessing of skreepish power. And yet none of them, in her opinion, was quite so repulsive as *ooman bings*—*Uurth*'s own little homegrown tyrants.

She had encountered them on her first expedition through the Medwig Gulp and had found them to be conceited, foolish, and violent. They were not strong, or intelligent, or particularly well made, and yet it was an *ooman bing* who had given her the scar that left her blind in one eye. It so marred her beauty that she could no longer aspire to a life of glamour within the Exalted One's court. She touched the ropy flesh once more. The Queen (*may her own youthful beauty remain boundless*) did not tolerate facial blemishes among her courtiers. And so, because of a single, treacherous *ooman bing*, the commander had been left with no other option than to wander endlessly through space.

If there was any hope at all, it lay in the Special Assignment. Commander Xaafuun had never seen the Queen so eager. Apparently the Item was a thing of extraordinary value. How might the Exalted One reward the captain who delivered such a prize? That was the question that kept her going, through the cold, and the wet, and the heaviness of excessive gravity. No *ooman bing* would stop her this time. She felt a vibration and lifted the communicator from her belt.

"Commander, I have it!"

Xaafuun felt a momentary surge of excitement, which she dutifully suppressed. "What is it, Ensign Phoony, the Item?"

"No, Commander, I have the *buurd*! It attacked me, the little monster, but I have it now. Its feathers are glorious. Won't the Exalted One be pleased!"

. . .

5. SENTINELS

ISADORA WOKE to the sound of someone tapping on her door. Darkness still pressed against the window, but the wind had stopped, and she could no longer hear the rain. She got out of bed fully dressed and opened the door. Jack stood in the hallway wearing a hunting cap and a heavy coat. "I thought you might want to come on my paper route," he said.

"Why on Earth would I want to do that?"

"I thought you wanted to investigate."

She yawned. She *had* said something like that. "But it's pitch black outside."

"It'll be light soon. The monsters don't come out in daylight, if that's what you're worried about."

She scowled at him. "I'm not worried."

"You can use my old bike, but put on some warm clothes. It's cold out there." He closed the door behind him.

She looked at her bare, unappealing room, the wet ceiling, the half-full water bucket on the floor. There wasn't much hope of falling back to sleep now. And she *was* curious about the aliens. She rummaged through her suitcase and put on her wool tights and a heavy sweater. Then she scrawled a note to her mother, slid it under Dr. Shumway's door, and went downstairs.

On the front porch she found Jack loading folded newspapers into saddlebags. She stood over him, rubbing her cold hands together. "I'd like to see the woods where the ship went down. Can you take me there?"

"It isn't far. But just so you know, I doubt if you'll actually *see* any monsters. They ain't like tourists."

"I understand that," she said irritably, "but maybe we'll find evidence." She followed him to the bottom of the steps.

"Stay here while I get the bikes. The chickens have been pretty quiet since the aliens got here, but you can never be too sure about Milo."

"I have no idea what you're talking about."

"My rooster. He's mean." Jack slipped quietly into the darkness. A minute later he reappeared, wheeling a pair of bicycles. One was rusty, with a missing handgrip and a cracked seat, but the other was spotless. It gleamed in the porch light. She eyed them critically. In truth, she had very little experience with bicycles, but she imagined she'd catch on soon enough.

"No Milo this morning," said Jack. "I guess he's sleeping in. How do you like my new bike? I just got it." He'd picked up lots of new things since the town emptied out, including a baseball mitt, sneakers, and a crate of red licorice.

"It's very nice."

Jack hoisted the saddlebags over his head, straddled his bike, and gave her the thumbs-up. They began pedaling into town.

She wobbled at first, then steadied as she gained momentum. An onrush of cold air stung her face and hands. It wasn't pleasant, exactly, but it *was* exhilarating. Jack whizzed along beside her. He veered onto Church Street, and she followed, leaning shakily into the turn.

He began tossing papers. Every time a *Sentinel* splashed into a puddle, he cursed under his breath. "I'm a little off today," he said after a particularly bad shot nearly decapitated an ornamental gnome.

"I'd like to try," she said.

He laughed. "You would? No offense, but I never met a girl who knew how to throw."

"How much knowledge does it take? It's obvious all you do is swing your arm around. Any idiot can manage that."

"I doubt it," said Jack. "But if you really want, I guess I could let you try the Wooleys' house over there." He handed her a paper and pointed to a yellow bungalow. "It's a simple one, and besides, they're out of town."

Isadora held the newspaper lightly. As she neared the driveway, her arm slid back in a fluid motion, then whipped forward, as supple as a rubber band. Her wrist snapped, and the paper spun off in a graceful arc, dipping under the porch roof on its way to a soft landing near the front door.

"That was pretty good."

She smiled, enjoying the tingle in her arm. "Can I try another one?"

He handed her a paper and pointed to a house where the porch was partially screened by a lilac bush. A collection of papers, soggy from the rain, lay scattered around the lawn like fallen soldiers. "The Hindemans are gone, too. In fact, most of the people on my route are gone, so I guess it doesn't really matter if you screw up."

Isadora wondered why Jack bothered to deliver newspapers to an empty town. Then she turned her attention to the throw. The bush made things tricky, but she saw how the paper had to go. In her mind's eye she saw how it *would* go, and her arm responded with the same easy motion, a jointless windup punctuated by a quick *snap* at the end. The newspaper curled over the lilac bush with inches to spare and struck the doormat with a faint *pop*.

"I think you're getting the hang of it," said Jack.

"I never get to do this sort of thing at home. Mother isn't very interested in physical activity."

"Don't you have gym class at school?"

"I don't go to school. Mother says they promote imbecility."

He stared at her in wonder. "You're kidding me, right?"

"Why would I kid? Mother tutors me. So do some of the other scientists at the lab."

"I wish I didn't have to go." Jack threw another paper and watched it sail over the Taggarts' fence. "I hate school. It's closed these days, on account of the aliens, so that's good. Hey, have you heard about the pill they're working on that will make you instantly smart? It isn't ready yet, but when it is, all you'll have to do is take it a few times, and you'll be so smart you can learn whatever you need to know for your whole life in a day or two. Math, science, you name it. They say it will put an end to school."

"Who says?"

"Smedley Trowbridge. Isn't it true?"

"Of course not. It's completely idiotic."

He handed her another paper. "I was afraid of that. You never know with Smedley. I wasn't going to talk about it, but a couple of weeks ago we had to give oral reports in class. The subject was 'Progress, and Why It Is Beneficial.' Kids talked about atomic power and modern farming—stuff like that."

"What's your point?"

"Well, I'd been meaning to prepare a report. I'm very much in favor of progress, but I couldn't think of anything to say. So the next thing you know, I started talking about the pill that makes you smart. The kids liked the idea, so I made up more and more. I swear, if I'd had some pills with me I could've sold them all. I was actually enjoying myself until Mrs. Barge started asking me questions."

Isadora plopped a newspaper squarely in front of a door.

"She asked me where I got the information," Jack continued. "And of course I couldn't say 'Smedley Trowbridge,' so I told her I'd read it in the newspaper. That was a mistake. She said I had to bring in the article the next day, but I couldn't, because there wasn't any article, so she had me right there. Later I asked Smedley where he got the story, and he said it was common knowledge. But now I know that isn't true, either."

"What did your teacher do to you?"

"Detention. I'm in detention all the time. Mrs. Barge says I'm one inch away from going back to reform school."

Isadora thought about school. Maybe if she went to one like Jack's she would hate it, too. Her mother always said she would. Even so, sometimes she wished she could try it. She was terrifically well educated, particularly in science, yet there was something dreary about the Bricklemoth Center, with its buzzing fluorescent lights, its lab rats clawing at the glass walls of their cages, and its somber-faced scientists. *At least their discoveries will make the future better,* she thought. Isadora liked imagining the future—a time when the blessings of science would deliver prosperity and leisure throughout the world and make the exploration of space possible.

Space was her passion. It was why she found the UFO story so intriguing. One day she hoped to participate in space exploration. And when that day came, she knew she would be grateful for her early education in science. She only wished that occasionally she could do ordinary things. She took another paper from Jack's outstretched hand. When it hit the doorstep, thirty feet away, it made a sound like a kiss.

Gradually the darkness softened. Jack continued to make graceless throws, while Isadora made perfect ones. Finally he stopped giving advice and merely handed her the papers, pointing to each new house as they came to it.

When they rounded a corner, the sun rose, and their shadows raced ahead of them as if they were trying to escape. "Now we can see where that saucer went down," said Jack. "The woods are just ahead."

· · ·

IT WAS HARD to believe in flying saucers on a sunny, clear morning. Nevertheless, Isadora *did* want to see where the ship had supposedly landed. She could understand why her mother disapproved of the story, but still, *something* had scared away most of the town.

They turned onto Mannerly Place and stopped where the pavement ended in a no-man's-land of weed and rubble. Beyond that, a thick wall of trees marked the beginning of Dutch Woods.

"There it is," said Jack.

Isadora adjusted her glasses. The forest stared at her without a hint of welcome. She felt a tingle at the base of her neck and mentally pushed it aside. She would behave like a scientist. There was nothing to be afraid of.

Jack got off his bike and walked into the vacant lot. In the mud was a footprint unlike any he had ever seen—long and pointed, with three toes, but extremely narrow. A few feet farther he saw another print, and beyond that another, creating a broken spot in the weeds. The prints faded away in the direction of the woods. He waded into the tall grass, and at the fifth footprint found a long feather, shimmering green with crimson highlights.

"What is it?" asked Isadora. "You have a funny expression on your face."

He held up the feather. "I think it's one of Milo's."

• • •

6. THE OUTER SPACE DIVISION

DR. SHUMWAY sat on the porch of the Pines, sipping a cup of coffee. She read the note again: *Delivering newspapers with J. Back shortly.* Clearly Isadora should have asked for permission. Still, what really bothered her was her daughter's unpredictability. Why would she *want* to deliver newspapers with Jack Creedle? That and the car's failure gave Dr. Shumway an unpleasant feeling that circumstances were out of her control. She wasn't used to it, and she didn't like it.

Mayor Handy drove up. He climbed the steps and removed his hat. "Beautiful morning, isn't it? Mind if I have a seat?"

"Be my guest."

"I see you're an early riser like myself."

"I am. And today my daughter rose even earlier than I, and accompanied the Creedle boy on his newspaper route."

"I'm not sure that was such a good idea."

"It wasn't my idea, I assure you."

He turned his hat over in his hands. "Well, I wouldn't fret too much. Truth is, I've been thinking about what you said last night—about the aliens being a hoax. It makes sense, when you take a hard look at it. Now I'm almost sorry I called the army."

"The *army*? You can't be serious."

"I am. Or at least I was. Not to worry, though. It doesn't look like they're coming. They transferred me to their Outer Space Division, where a lieutenant took my story and promised to investigate. That's the last I heard. Still, I'm disappointed they haven't responded yet. Wouldn't you think the U.S. Army would want to know if space monsters were running amok in the Wanookie Valley?"

"I am not aware of 'the Outer Space Division,'" said Dr. Shumway skeptically.

"I never heard of it, either. But this is the space age, after all, and I guess the government has to be ready for anything."

• • •

ISADORA AND JACK pedaled up the driveway.

"Thank you for your note," Dr. Shumway said in a cool voice. "As you are no doubt aware, your decision to leave without discussing the matter was highly inappropriate."

Isadora lowered her eyes. "I didn't want to wake you."

"We think the aliens might have got my rooster," Jack interrupted.

Isadora ignored him. "I wanted to see the place where the flying saucer landed. I wanted to investigate *scientifically*."

"And did you?"

"I saw the woods." She knew the answer was insufficient. "I couldn't tell for sure if anything was there."

Jack hooked a thumb in the direction of the barn. "I'd better go check on those chickens." He rode off.

Dr. Shumway's expression softened. "I cannot fault your impulse to seek evidence. Science, after all, is wholly dependent on proof. However, the notion that space creatures have invaded this community is hardly a credible hypothesis. What we are witnessing here is a case of mass hysteria."

"I guess so. But we did see something unusual—"

"They're gone!" Jack yelled, running back. "All of them! And there's more of those weird footprints."

"Who's gone?" asked Mayor Handy.

"The chickens! The monsters got 'em! I didn't think they would come out in a storm like that, but I was wrong." He handed Dr. Shumway a *Sentinel*. "You should see what they did out there! There's hardly a feather left in the coop."

"We found some strange footprints in the woods," Isadora added. "Extremely long and narrow, perhaps three inches by twelve, with three toes, slightly splayed."

"Footprints are the flimsiest sort of evidence. Think of the Abominable Snowman and Bigfoot." Dr. Shumway unfolded the paper. "Oh, for heaven's sake," she said and handed it to the mayor.

His eyes widened as he read the banner headline. "'Army to Take on Aliens!'" He whistled softly. "Well, what do you know? They're coming after all."

"Hot dog!" said Jack. "Now we'll see some action."

Dr. Shumway closed her eyes. "Isadora, please go inside and get some breakfast. And young man, it's my car that requires action."

"You bet." Jack tipped his hunting cap at her and followed Isadora through the front door.

He tossed his last *Sentinel* onto the dining room table. Isadora picked it up and sat down opposite him, putting a piece of cold toast on her plate.

"You'll notice there ain't any eggs," Mrs. Creedle announced. "That's on account of there ain't any chickens anymore, neither."

"Monsters got 'em," said Jack, slurping his coffee. "I saw the footprints."

"Well, everyone else steals from the Pines, so I don't see why they should be any different."

Jack watched Isadora pore over the *Sentinel*. That was a novelty, in his opinion—a kid who read newspapers. In fact, a lot about her was unusual, especially for a girl. "Hey, what do you think about the army coming to town? That's something, ain't it?"

"This report claims the army's Outer Space Division is on its way to Vern Hollow to confront 'an alien threat' in Dutch Woods. It says the Outer Space Division is top secret." She raised her eyes. "It's hardly a secret if they talk about it in the newspaper! What sort of paper is the *Sentinel*, anyway?"

"Tell you the truth, I never read it. All I know is that it's better than the *Courier*." He took a piece of toast. "A *sentinel* is someone who guards the town, right? But a *courier* is just some weaselly guy who runs around delivering messages and kissing up. That's where the old expression about 'couriering favor' comes from."

"The term is 'curry favor.' It has absolutely nothing to do with being a courier."

"Well, maybe you're right." He decided to change the subject. "You know, I feel pretty bad about those chickens. Especially Milo. He wasn't the best bird you ever saw, but he was tough."

"Perhaps he got away."

"You think so?"

"To be honest, I have no opinion whatsoever about your rooster." She tapped the newspaper with her finger. "If there is any truth to this article, then we are about to be caught in the middle of a battle. Doesn't that seem unreasonable? If there really *are* aliens in the woods, we know nothing about them. We don't even know if they're hostile."

"How friendly can they be? They stole my chickens. And that monster on TV wasn't exactly Santa Claus." Jack drained his coffee and stood up. "Let me know when you're ready, and we can head over to the junkyard."

Going with him hadn't occurred to Isadora. "I guess I could come," she said hesitantly. "But I'll have to check with Mother first."

•   •   •

"THE JUNKYARD?" Dr. Shumway put down the book she was reading. "Why would you want to go to a junkyard?"

Isadora had prepared her argument in advance. "Jack needs that missing part, and it's the only way to keep him focused on fixing our car." She decided not to mention her interest in the aliens.

"You have a point. Certainly the boy is unreliable. But please be quick about it. My patience is wearing thin."

Jack appeared in his grimy coveralls and they started up the embankment. "Aren't we going to ride bicycles?" Isadora asked.

"Not to the junkyard. We're hoofing it. Hemp's is a straight shot down the tracks, and that's the quickest way to get there."

•   •   •

THEY WALKED the railroad tracks in silence. The air was as clear as spring water. Faint breezes carried drifting leaves and the cidery aroma of fallen apples. "I checked out the footprints by the chicken coop," Isadora said. "They *are* curious, but I think we need more compelling evidence. Mother says a dog could have made them."

"Weird dog." Jack scratched the back of his neck. "To be honest, I'd be satisfied if those monsters left town. It was okay at first, when the school closed, but now it's starting to get creepy."

Far ahead, the tracks curved around a rocky outcropping. "Just out of curiosity," Isadora said, "how do you know a train won't come along and kill us?"

"Not enough speed, is why. Trains have to slow way down when they come around that ridge. It's called Bum's Bluff because it's so easy for hobos to catch a ride there."

"Hobos? I've read about them, but I don't think I've ever seen one."

"Sure you have. Last night at dinner. What do you think Joe was?"

"He said he was here to investigate the flying saucer. Surely a hobo wouldn't do a thing like that?"

"Oh, they'll say anything. We get loads of 'em at the Pines. Mom usually runs 'em off if they don't have money. But sometimes she lets them stay anyway, if it's stormy outside. Even a tramp deserves that much."

"I wonder if we'll see him again?"

"Joe? I doubt it. Not unless we run into him up here at Bum's Bluff, waiting for a train."

Isadora peered ahead. Someone *was* there: a solitary figure in dark clothes, perched like a crow on top of a boulder. "Do you think that's him?"

He squinted. "No, that's Uncle Bud."

"Your uncle? Why would he be out here?"

"It's a good question, but that's him all right." As Jack spoke, the figure scrambled over the rock pile and out of view. "He probably thinks we didn't see him."

When they rounded the bluff, they spotted Jack's uncle

crouching behind a cottonwood tree. Jack waved and shouted until Uncle Bud came out onto the tracks. He was narrow-chested, wearing thick glasses, a short-brimmed fedora, and a suit that was at least two sizes too big for his slight frame. A small mustache sat on top of his lip like a caterpillar. "Well, sonny, I didn't expect to run into you out here."

"I can see that." A cardboard suitcase was partially hidden behind a rock. "Where are you going, Uncle Bud?"

"Going?" He took off his glasses and began rubbing them with a yellowed handkerchief. "To tell you the truth, I'm not sure. Crowderville, maybe farther. Could be as far off as New York. All's I can tell you is it ain't safe for me here, under the circumstances."

"Space monsters," said Jack. "You know, they stole the chickens! They even got Milo, which surprised me."

"Trust me, they ain't stopping at chickens."

"You speak as if you have some knowledge," said Isadora. "Is that true, or are you merely speculating?"

Uncle Bud put his glasses back on. He turned to his nephew. "Who's this dark-skinned gal?"

"Isadora Shumway," she answered stiffly. "And you needn't refer to me in the third person. I'm here with my mother, from Boston."

"They're scientists," Jack added.

Uncle Bud scowled. "She don't look much like a scientist. Anyway, it's suspicious, don't you think, them showing up just now?"

"Oh, come on, Uncle Bud. Their car broke down. You saw them yesterday for a minute."

"I didn't trust them then, either. For all I know she could be with the FBI. You know the kind of tricks *they* pull."

"Oh, for heaven's sake!" Isadora put her foot on the rail for emphasis and felt a buzzing through the sole of her shoe. "I think a train is coming!"

"Shouldn't be. It's too early." Jack put a hand on the rail. "You're right, though. That's definitely a train."

Uncle Bud scampered over to the boulder and grabbed his suitcase. He returned, peering nearsightedly down the tracks. "I should have got out when the others did. Monsters on television! Come on, we have to hide so's the engineer can't see us."

Whoooooooo! A whistle sounded, long and low.

"This here's the jumping-off point," Uncle Bud explained. "If you want to hop a freight, you have to stay hidden till you make your move. If they see you they're liable to roust you out. Those bulls can be pretty rough. So that's your first lesson in tramping. Don't say your uncle never taught you anything."

An oily cloud of diesel smoke puffed out, obscuring the engine. Uncle Bud picked up his suitcase. "Watch me and you'll see how it's done."

Jack squinted as the smoke cleared. "I don't think you want this train, Uncle Bud."

"Step aside," said his uncle. "I'll need to get a running start."

Isadora adjusted her glasses. The approaching engine was painted camouflage green and bore the insignia of the U.S. Army. Beneath the familiar white star was a smaller logo, showing a rocket and the planet Saturn.

Uncle Bud dropped his suitcase. "What in tarnation—?"

"The *Sentinel* was right!" Jack hooted. "It's the Outer Space Division!"

. . .

7. SOUPED-UP '53

THE TRAIN rumbled past, slow and heavy. Soldiers with steel helmets looked out from the boxcars. Rifles were slung across their backs. After a while the boxcars gave way to flat cars, their bulky contents concealed under green nets. Jack said to Isadora, "What do you suppose they're hiding in there? Bazookas? Howitzers?"

"How should I know?"

"Could be giant ray guns."

"Don't be an idiot." His enthusiasm annoyed her. "There's no such thing as a ray gun."

"Sure there is. You can't fight space monsters with pea-shooters, you know. You gotta have something that'll get their attention."

"They're fools if they think they can win a shooting war," said Uncle Bud, "but I guess they'll find *that* out the hard way."

The last car rumbled past. Isadora wondered what her mother would make of the Outer Space Division. "You don't suppose they're really going to start a fight, do you?"

"I don't think they're here for the fresh air," said Uncle Bud.

Jack watched the train eagerly. "Let's go see what they do."

"Not me. I'm staying right here until the next freight comes along." He put his hands in his pockets and rocked forward on the balls of his feet.

"You're not still thinking of leaving, are you?"

"I am. And if you've got any sense, you'll do the same. Mark my words, the army's about to stir up a real hornet's nest."

Isadora pulled the sleeve of Jack's dirty coveralls. "Come on, we need to get to the junkyard."

"But we'll miss the battle!"

"I *want* to miss the battle. That's why it's so urgent you fix the car."

"You won't miss anything," said Uncle Bud. "If I know the army, they'll take their sweet time setting up."

"Uncle Bud was in the army in World War II," Jack explained.

"Now, *there's* a situation where it doesn't pay to be the little guy. Officers! They were worse than the Germans."

Isadora tugged Jack's sleeve again. "We need to get the car fixed."

"But I thought you wanted to figure out this alien thing!"

"That was before I saw those cannons. Scientists don't belong on a battlefield."

"Too many big shots in this world," Uncle Bud continued, hitching up his pants. "You can quote me on that. But the girl's right. Fix that car and get out of town. Whatever happens to Vern Hollow, it's the army's problem now."

Jack sighed. "All right. But don't blame me if we miss something great."

· · ·

"I HOPE YOU didn't get the wrong idea about Uncle Bud," said Jack. The train tracks led them along the Wanookie. "He's a little rough around the edges, but he's smart. I wish you could see some of his inventions. I think you'd be interested, being a scientist and all."

"Inventions?"

"Sure. Bud's a great inventor. A few years ago, when he first got hooked on the idea of space travel, he built a rocket like you wouldn't believe."

"Your uncle is interested in space travel?"

"Who isn't? Anyway, you should have seen this thing. He wanted it to be secret, so we launched it from Van Gundy's back pasture late at night. Some secret! It made such a racket lifting off it woke up the entire town."

"Hold on," said Isadora. "Why did it have to be a secret?"

"You know how the government gets jumpy when people start firing stuff off. All they think about is atom bombs. But there was no hiding this one. It came down in Mexico two days later. Everyone was upset, particularly the Mexicans.

They thought they were being attacked. It made eighteen orbits altogether."

"It did not!"

"Did so. At least that's what Uncle Bud calculated. We weren't absolutely sure because the transmitter broke down after orbit number seven."

"Jack, nobody has ever been able to put a rocket into orbit. The best scientists and engineers in the world have been trying for decades."

"Which is why the Feds got so upset with Uncle Bud. They took away most of his rocket stuff, and then they sent him to the Dalton Pen."

"Wait! Are you saying your uncle was sent to prison because the government didn't want him building rockets?"

"No, they didn't want him robbing banks. Building rockets is expensive. It took about three robberies to pay for the fuel alone. He still won't tell me what the fuel was, by the way."

• • •

JUST BEYOND a soot-blackened foundry they came to the junkyard, an open lot littered with wrecked cars. It was surrounded by a rusted fence topped with barbed wire. A sign on the front gate read BEWARE OF DOG!

Isadora stopped. "Do you think it's safe?"

"Sure it's safe. Hemp and his dog ran off with the rest of them a few days ago." Jack reached into a pocket and came out with a collection of small, pointed tools on a metal ring. He sorted through them until he found the one he wanted, then inserted it into the padlock. After a moment's jiggling it popped, and he pushed the gate open.

"I don't feel right about breaking in."

"Oh, come on. You want to get your car fixed, don't you?" He grabbed a wooden milk crate and began filling it with engine parts, strolling the aisles of junk as if he were shopping at a grocery store. Isadora followed at a distance.

"It appears to me you're *stealing* these parts. Am I correct?"

"I wouldn't say that, no." He picked up a used carburetor and examined it critically. "That wagon of yours needs parts, and this is where they're at. I can't help it if Hemp ran off and left the stuff here." His eyes wandered over a row of smashed cars and settled on a wrecked station wagon, nose down in the weeds. "Hot dog!" he shouted. "That's a '53, just like yours. That's where we'll find your valve."

• • •

THE TRIP TO the junkyard was a huge success. The crate was filled with wonderful things—components of the dream car Jack sometimes constructed in his head. They walked up Main Street in the shadow of empty buildings. "Actually," he observed, "I don't even know if you can call it 'stealing' if a place is deserted like that."

"You're right. That would be called '*looting.*'"

"I don't know if it's so bad, is my point."

They continued in silence until they reached the shop. Jack popped the hood on the Shumways' wagon, then carefully selected the tools he would use and laid them out in a neat row. He studied the engine with a surgeon's eye. Soon his hands began to move with confidence, removing clamps and bolts and hex nuts. As he worked, he crawled farther into the engine well. "Hand me that thingy with the rubber grip," he said. "It's got a red handle."

Isadora found the tool, a nasty-looking device with serrated jaws. She examined it closely, then handed it down. "What is it?"

"It's the thingy with the rubber grip." Jack plunged the tool into a tight spot, wiggled the jaws onto a bolt, and turned it sharply.

"Shouldn't a mechanic know the names of his tools? And the parts of an engine?"

Jack held the bolt up for her to take, then asked for a screwdriver. "Who cares what a thing is called, as long as you know what it does? I learned this stuff while Uncle Bud was in the pokey, so basically I taught myself. Every part of a machine has a job to do, and so does every tool. And they all work together in a certain way. You can feel how it needs to go, if you don't think too much."

"If you don't *think*?" She peered into the darkness of the engine well as if into some terrible abyss. "I'm certain there are books you could study to learn the nomenclature, as well as various repair techniques."

"*Books?*" Jack laughed. "Mechanics don't read books." He

lifted a greasy mass from the engine, looked at it closely, and tossed it over his shoulder. Isadora watched it spatter on the pavement.

"Didn't you say every part of an engine has a purpose?"

"I couldn't see much point to *that*."

She opened the passenger-side door and sat down. The familiarity of the car felt good. Sunlight streaming through the window warmed her like a blanket. She dozed.

Wham! The sound of the hood slamming down snapped her awake. Jack opened the driver's door and plopped down behind the wheel. "Now for the fun part," he said.

"You aren't proposing to drive it yourself, are you?"

"How else will I know if it's fixed?"

She sat up straight. "But you're too young! And small. And you don't have the keys."

He reached into his front pocket. "Surprise." The key chain had a white tab that read BRICKLEMOTH CENTER, BOSTON.

"You stole those from Mother!"

"I *borrowed* them." He coaxed the bench seat all the way forward and stretched his legs to make sure his feet reached the pedals. By peering through the spokes of the steering wheel he could see the road ahead. When he turned the key, the station wagon let out an unfamiliar, deep-throated growl.

"I'm telling you, once we get on the road, you won't even recognize her." He popped the clutch, and the car bounded into the street like a rodeo pony. Isadora pitched backward in her seat as he swung the wheel over, narrowly missing a parked car.

"What have you done?"

"Not bad, huh?" Jack shouted over the roar of the engine. "Believe me, I've souped up worse jalopies than this one!"

They raced downtown, leaving twin streaks of burnt rubber on the ground as they skidded past town hall.

"I don't think Mother's going to like this!" Isadora shouted.

"She will if she's in a hurry to get back to Boston. You won't find a faster ride." As he rounded another corner, the station wagon's rear end slipped sideways.

"Slow down!" she demanded. "You're driving like a lunatic!"

He eased on the brakes and downshifted. The engine growled ominously. "I just wanted to see what she would do."

"Jack, you turned Mother's car into a hot rod!"

He grinned enthusiastically. "Don't you see? This is the best kind of car to do it to, because nobody expects it. You could win drag races all over the state in this wagon."

"The point you're missing is that my mother does not *want* to win drag races."

"You think she won't like it?"

"She'll hate it, honestly."

Jack frowned. "I guess I got so excited by all those great parts that I wasn't thinking clearly. But don't worry, it won't be a big deal to put it back the way it was. We can go to the shop right now."

"I think we'd better."

"You have to admit, though, it's fun!" He pressed the accelerator, and they took off, speeding into the next intersection. "Watch this!" he shouted, standing on the brake pedal while he spun the wheel. The station wagon slurred around, squealing dangerously. Isadora gripped the dashboard with white knuckles.

They were halfway through the turn before they saw the police cruiser. When the station wagon finally spun to a stop, it was only a few feet away. For a second, Jack had a clear view of Sergeant Webb's surprised face. Sitting next to him was Grady. Jack hit the gas.

• • •

8. COLONEL MILES

DR. SHUMWAY was still reading when she heard the train. She put down her book and stepped outside. By the time she reached the driveway it had come to a complete stop. She took the scene in slowly—the Outer Space Division logo, the grim-faced soldiers, the cannons.

Behind her the front door slammed, and Mrs. Creedle came out, wiping her hands on her apron. "There's something you don't see every day."

"Indeed."

A group of soldiers hopped from the nearest boxcar. They scrambled down the embankment and briskly marched to the Pines. Their leader was an officer in a neatly pressed uniform. The stub of a cigar protruded from his mouth.

"Colonel Miles," he announced and saluted. "First Battalion, U.S. Army Outer Space Division. I understand you have an alien problem."

"That isn't my understanding," said Dr. Shumway.

The colonel looked at her closely. "And you are?"

"Dr. Ramona Shumway. I am a scientist at the Bricklemoth Center in Boston."

"Interesting. So you do space research?"

"That isn't why I'm here, if that's what you mean. My car

broke down as I was driving through town. I'm having it repaired as we speak."

He looked at her skeptically. "An odd coincidence, don't you think?"

"I do not."

"I *do*," said Mrs. Creedle. "Things been nothing but odd around here for the last few days."

"And who are you?"

"Laverne Creedle. I run this joint."

"Well, Mrs. Creedle, I'm going to need your house for my headquarters."

"Are you, now?" She guffawed. "So you know, the rates just went up."

The colonel ignored her. "Womrath, have the radio equipment brought into the house. Murphy, tell Captain Goldfarb I want his battery set up south of here. Sergeant Price, you come with me."

Within an hour, headquarters had been set up inside the Pines, with officers in the parlors and a communication center in the dining room. The colonel sat there amid a tangle of wires from two bulky radio sets, chewing his cigar and shouting orders. Soldiers swarmed over the train, unloading equipment and moving it by jeep to camps and batteries. By late afternoon, artillery had been positioned, sentries placed, and checkpoints posted on every road leading in and out of town.

Mrs. Creedle watched with resentment as the soldiers trampled her garden and tracked mud inside her house. Dr. Shumway was upset, too. "Really, Colonel, I demand to know what this is all about. Such military activity inside a small town is outrageous!"

The colonel studied a topographical map of Vern Hollow. "I promise you, Doctor, I don't take my duty lightly."

"You don't do anything lightly, as far as I can tell," grumbled Mrs. Creedle. "You'd think a herd of elephants'd been through here."

A soldier appeared in the doorway behind her. "Sir, a man is here to see you. Claims to be the mayor."

"Send him in."

Mayor Handy bustled through the door, flustered and out of breath. "Honest to goodness, Colonel," he said, after introducing himself, "this is some brouhaha. I had no idea the army would send such a force. The thing is, I'm worried it's all a mistake."

"At ease, Mayor. There's been no mistake."

"The thing is, *I* might be the one who made it. By calling you down here, you understand. Folks told me they saw a flying saucer. I couldn't ignore them! But what if they were wrong? Dr. Shumway here says it was probably a hoax, and you know what? She may be right! You know the kind of pranks teenagers play!"

"I promise you, this is no hoax. We're not here because of your phone call. The Outer Space Division takes its marching orders directly from the president."

"You mean to say General Eisenhower knows what happened here in Vern Hollow?"

Colonel Miles lowered his voice. "The president knows many things. But tell me, Mayor, are there other civilians still in the area?"

"A few."

"You'll need to alert them to stay in their homes."

"Happy to help. But, Colonel . . . " He paused. "You're sure about the aliens?"

Colonel Miles folded his hands behind his head. "The creatures in the woods are *skreeps*. We've been watching them for a few years now. They aren't the only aliens, mind you, but from what we can gather, they're probably the worst. They're looking at our world the way a real estate developer looks at land." He jammed a finger onto the map. "It's time they learned this planet is already *taken*."

"Really!" said Dr. Shumway. "Of all the ridiculous notions!"

"They're like giant spiders," continued the colonel. "They look like spiders and act like 'em, too. Full of schemes. Always spinning little webs. It's said their own planet is ruined, but they control an empire of slave planets to plunder for resources. Maybe that's what they have in mind for us. A slave planet. Not very pleasant, is it?"

"And you've seen them?"

"You're unlikely to see a skreep unless it wants to be seen. They prefer dark places, and anyway, they're masters of illusion. But look at this." He opened a metal attaché case. Inside was a stack of black-and-white photographs. "The quality is uneven, but I think you'll see what I mean."

Dr. Shumway glanced at the photos briefly before passing them to the mayor, who gave them a closer look. Several were pictures of disc-shaped objects, some suspended in midair, others hovering over small-town skylines. The last photo was deeply shadowed and grainy, as if the image had been magnified many times. It showed a spidery creature crawling from a circular hole. From its lumpish body sprouted long, heavily bristled legs.

Mayor Handy shuddered. "Ugly brutes, aren't they?"

"They're as bad as they look. As you can see, the problem is serious."

"Photographs are easily manipulated," said Dr. Shumway. "These do little to prove your theory."

"They look real to me." The mayor handed the photos to Mrs. Creedle. "But why did these monsters pick Vern Hollow? This isn't good for a town."

"I wish I could tell you there will be no damage, Mayor, but I can't."

Mrs. Creedle put down the photos. "I wonder where Bud got to."

"And I wonder where my daughter is," said Dr. Shumway. "Surely the car should be repaired by now."

• • •

IN JACK'S OPINION, the station wagon was more than repaired; it was dramatically improved. As soon as he saw Grady Webb gaping at him through the windshield of his father's patrol car, Jack decided to put it to the test. He gave the gas pedal a stomp. The engine roared like a bear; the back tires spun a thin layer of rubber onto the asphalt, and the car shot off in a panicky run. Jack gripped the steering wheel hard with both hands and pulled himself forward. Then he shifted gears and gave the engine more gas. Isadora fell back into her seat. Behind them a siren began to blare.

"What are you *doing*?" The cruiser picked up speed. If

Isadora looked closely, she could still see the outraged faces of the Webbs.

Jack hunched over the dashboard with the intensity of an explorer catching his first glimpse of a new world. A "T" intersection loomed ahead, and they were almost there. He leaned on the gas. Isadora put her hands over her face. At the last minute, Jack slammed the brake and jerked the wheel hard to the left. The wagon shuddered and slid sideways. Just before it slammed into the curb, he accelerated. The wheels caught, and the car pitched forward.

"Sergeant Webb said he'd toss me back in Millbrook if he caught me driving again," Jack explained. He shifted gears and punched the accelerator. "That's the reform school I told you about."

Isadora looked over her shoulder. The cruiser made the same turn, only slower. It was losing ground. "So you have to go to reform school! You deserve it! I've never seen anyone with such a criminal mentality. Anyway, it's better than getting us killed in a car crash!"

Jack hung on to the wheel, staring straight ahead. "You've never seen Millbrook."

He shifted gears, and the station wagon picked up speed again, shooting onto an open road surrounded by farmland.

Isadora watched the police car recede until it was no more than a flashing red light far behind them. "Can't you see you're only making matters worse for yourself? The police know where you live, and you can't run forever."

Jack smiled. "I can try."

.   .   .

9. ARMY HEADQUARTERS

SOMETHING TICKLED her eyelids, and Commander Xaafuun woke up. The feathery antennae of her footservant, Mellis, danced before her eyes. "Get those things away from me," she snapped. He obeyed, his ugly face inscrutable. The brightness of the room told her it was too early to be awake. *Uurth*'s sun cycle was another repellent thing about the planet. The painful glare of daytime left few hiding places. She had rarely seen such unflattering light. "This had better be good."

"It's the *ooman bings*, Madame Commander." Mellis bowed. His mouth stretched wide, revealing translucent fangs. "Maybe you should look."

She followed him into her private elevator and up to the bridge. Hidden speakers blared the song "Hungry for You," but she barely noticed. She'd heard it so many times it seemed to live inside her like a parasite.

The bridge was the largest room on the ship, a circular dome dominated by a continuous ring of porthole windows. It contained the flight officer's consoles and video monitors, her own captain's dais, and above all, the holographic image of the Exalted One's head, peering down on everything like a malevolent god. At the moment it was only a canned image, preserved on memory file, but the Queen was capable of making live appearances, thanks to instant transmission through the Medwig Gulp. Xaafuun glanced at the giant head uneasily before looking away.

A knot of officers had gathered around the periscope, grappling with multiple arms as each attempted to seize control of the viewer. *At least the thing is working,* Xaafuun thought. They had stolen it from the *boolemek*, advanced creatures living on one of the Similon planets, Five or Six, she couldn't remember.

"Step aside, officers." She didn't voice the words *useless rabble*, but her tone made it clear enough. The officers scattered, bowing as they went.

Xaafuun adjusted the viewer and brought the scene into focus. A large number of *ooman bings* stood around one of the enormous vehicles they called *traans*. (Xaafuun was proud of her command of several *Uurth* languages, most of which were spoken by *ooman bings*.) They wore nearly identical uniforms and helmets like the shells of trubilo nuts. Soldiers. Xaafuun sighed. *Soldiers* meant war.

The *traan* was in the settlement that Phoony had patrolled the night before, near the place where he had stolen the *buurd*. She wondered if that was significant. Was the Item there? And did the soldiers know about it? "Bring me Phoony," she told Mellis and turned back to the viewer.

She scanned the entire length of the *traan*'s long body. It reminded her of the segmented tunnel worms that infested the Kaarkuul Mines on Skreepia. But unlike a worm, the *traan* lay utterly still. *Ooman bing* vehicles were like that. They were not really organisms at all, not even hybrids, but dead things that could be reanimated at will with the injection of certain fuels. She wondered if the Special Item was dead. She hoped so. Dead things were so much easier to manage than live ones.

Xaafuun hated living things, with their needs and expectations, their constant disloyal scheming. On a skreepish ship, almost everything was alive. As commander, it was her burden to deal with machines that were often little better than bottom-deck crew: sullen, ungrateful, and in need of constant monitoring, discipline, and abuse. She almost envied the *ooman bings* their crude devices. How simple it would be if all of one's instruments were dead!

Xaafuun made note of various weapons, especially the big ones on the *traan*'s broad back. She had seen these things before: *kaninz*, *owitzers*, and *bazookas*. Simple weapons, but dangerous nonetheless. This was bad.

Her officers watched her expectantly.

"We must act quickly and be prepared to leave at a moment's notice." Her antennae twitched in agitation. This was exactly what the Exalted One had warned against! Frightened aliens could be difficult to control. Every commander knew it. It was much easier if the natives were lulled into complacency before conquest.

Once again she regretted her television broadcast. *But*

why hadn't the Queen given her better instructions? She had to struggle to hide the traitorous thought. Her officers were observing her closely. From the corner of one eye she could see their antennae flutter. Wouldn't they love a scandal, the wretches? Wouldn't they thrill to see her hauled into the docket for a show trial, complete with public dismemberment or an encounter with a braakinhool in the Grand Arena?

Mellis popped through the floor with Phoony right behind him. The ensign scuttled over and bowed. "Madame Commander?"

"Take a look, Finder." She pushed him roughly toward the periscope. "Isn't that *precisely* where you were last night?"

He hesitated. "Well, yes. *Pretty* close. But there wasn't any *traan* last night, Madame. No big *kaninz*, no *ooman bings*. Last night there were only *buurds*."

"Fool! I'm aware the army wasn't here yesterday. Yet today the place is as fortified as the Royal Palace. Don't you find that worrisome?"

"Maybe."

"*Maybe!* If I find you left the Special Item in that building while you were gathering *buurds*, Ensign Phoony, I will personally feed you to Beast Eleven! You must find the Item *tonight*, I don't care how, and bring it to me. There will be no more *buurds*, and no more excuses."

She dismissed him and turned to the others. "We must *all* be Finders tonight. The *ooman bings* are preparing an attack." She showed her fangs. "Yes, we could kill them all easily, but we must restrain ourselves. The invasion fleet is not ready. War is premature. Therefore you must resist direct engagement. Only one thing matters now: We must find the Special Item."

• • •

JACK AND ISADORA watched the Pines from the branches of an oak tree a hundred yards away. Soldiers buzzed around the train, but the children's attention stayed fixed on the house, where Sergeant Webb's cruiser crouched in the driveway like a mean dog. As they watched, the sergeant hurried up the steps with Grady right behind.

"Those Webbs never give up," Jack whispered. "Our only chance now is to get out of town. We'll have to be sneaky, too, with all these soldiers around."

"My mother is a law-abiding person. She would never help us avoid justice."

"My mom would. In fact, you can bet she's already come up with some cock-and-bull story. She's sent Sergeant Webb packing plenty of times."

A few minutes later, the Webbs got back into their police car and drove off. "You see? Free and clear." Jack swung from his branch and plopped to the ground like a rotten apple. Isadora followed more cautiously. They hurried to the house and ducked inside.

"Hold it!" said a hard voice. A flashlight flicked on, capturing them in its beam.

"Don't shoot, Womrath," said another voice. "It's just those kids. The colonel wants them in his office."

The sentries led them to the dining room, where they stepped into bright light and a bustle of activity. Colonel Miles pointed his cigar at Jack. "Who are you?"

"Jack Creedle."

"Jack Creedle, *sir*. Who's the little girl?"

"Isadora Shumway—sir."

"The two hooligans. Your mothers are looking for you."

"That is correct." Dr. Shumway stepped through the open door. Isadora realized she must have been waiting to pounce. "So are the police. I confess I was unable to explain your behavior. Perhaps you would like to fill me in?"

"Okay," Jack began. "The first thing you should know is I fixed your car."

"Excuse me," said Dr. Shumway. "I was speaking to my daughter."

"She'll back me up."

"I figured you'd show up once old Webb took off," said Mrs. Creedle, walking in. "He was with that son of his."

"We were hiding in the oak tree. What did you tell him?"

"The usual. I said your uncle had taken you to Munsonburg for your violin lesson."

Jack whooped. "Violin!"

She turned to the others. "I thought he'd get a kick out of that."

"This is hardly a laughing matter," said Dr. Shumway stiffly. "According to the sergeant, the boy's behavior was both illegal and dangerous."

Mrs. Creedle grunted. "*The boy?* Sounds to me like your little cupcake was right there with him."

"Well?" Dr. Shumway asked Isadora. "What do you have to say for yourself? I am still waiting for an explanation."

Isadora stared at the floor. "Jack tried to fix the car. He did fix it, too, only he made it a little too *fast*. When he started it, the car took off. We were on our way back to the shop when the police showed up."

"So you decided to outrun them."

"That was my decision," said Jack.

"I consider it a poor one."

"My teacher says I got bad judgment."

"Frankly I'm shocked," Dr. Shumway told her daughter. "Your behavior today borders on the criminal."

Isadora studied her shoes miserably. "Are you going to turn me in?"

"I will not," she said finally. "I refuse to become more entangled in the affairs of Vern Hollow. But you will go to your room, and you will remain there until further notice."

Colonel Miles cleared his throat. "I hate to interrupt these *family matters*, but if you don't mind, the army has business to conduct here."

"I *do* mind," Dr. Shumway said fiercely. "I mind that you are here, terrorizing the town with your diabolical weapons. I mind that you are feeding their hysteria with ridiculous stories and falsified evidence. Aliens indeed! However, my daughter and I will be *more* than happy to leave and will do so immediately—in fact, as soon as the boy tells me where he left my car."

The colonel's face darkened. "Actually, ma'am, you won't. Like it or not, this is a war zone. Vern Hollow is sealed. Nobody leaves this town."

•   •   •

10. UNCLE BUD'S PLAN

ISADORA LAY on her bed, staring at the ceiling. She could understand why her mother was angry, but all the same, the punishment was unjust. She had not been the boy's accomplice so much as his hostage. She had objected to him driving the car. And now *she* was being punished—for the misfortune of meeting Jack Creedle! Isadora wanted to go home.

Only she couldn't! She sat upright. The full meaning of the colonel's words hit her. She was stuck in a war zone! How could she be confined to her room at such a time? She got up and paced. The situation was maddening.

Someone knocked on the door. When she opened it, Jack stood there, grinning. He held a plate containing a slab of gray meat and a peeled, wet potato. "Mom's famous steak and taters," he announced. "She boils 'em together."

Isadora accepted the plate. Hunger overcame her better judgment, and she began to eat.

Jack came in uninvited and plopped down on her bed. "Thanks for covering for me out there. The way you told the story it sounded like the car just got away from me. That was good, even if nobody bought it."

"I told the truth. I just left out the worst details."

"That's usually the best way to play it. I hope you noticed I returned the favor when I told your mom it was all my idea."

"It *was* your idea."

"Uh-huh. How long do you think your mom will keep you up here?"

"I don't know. She's pretty upset."

"It isn't such a bad spot." Jack walked to the window. "In the morning, you'll be able to see the train from here, and Dutch Woods is in the same direction. You should have a pretty good view once they start firing those guns."

She put down her fork. *"What?"*

A very faint knock interrupted them. Isadora knew it wasn't her mother. Dr. Shumway was never timid.

"Come in," called Jack.

Uncle Bud darted in, set his battered suitcase on the floor, and quickly shut the door. "We need to get out of here—pronto," he whispered. "Before the shooting starts."

"I thought you left already," said Jack.

"Ixnay. The army sealed the town, which means no more trains. I waited up at the bluff for hours before I figured it out. But it wasn't a good plan anyway. I was leaving too much behind. My new plan is much better."

"New plan?" Isadora asked. "What is it?"

"We take your station wagon."

She nearly choked on her potato. "You must be joking! Anyway, the town is sealed."

"So it is, as far as *most* folks are concerned. But most folks don't have an extra-fast getaway car, and most folks don't know a secret back road. You have the car; I know the road. Bottom line, you and your mother want out of here, and so do I. The way I see it, that practically makes us partners."

Jack's eyes narrowed. "How did you know about the car?"

"I was hiding in the front parlor when those Webbs came by. Listen, it's perfect. There's something I need to move. No need to say what, but it's more than I can carry on a train."

"What is it?"

"A little something I've been working on. By the way, you'd be smart to get out of town, too. If the aliens don't nab you, the cops will."

"I already figured that out."

Isadora gave Uncle Bud an appraising look. "I thought you didn't trust Mother and me. You seemed quite suspicious before."

"My thinking has evolved. I seen a little bit of a crooked side in the way you handled that car business this evening. That was good. You're no friend of the police, which suits me fine."

"I'm not *crooked*! And I have nothing against the police. Anyway, Mother will never go along with your scheme. She's very law-abiding."

The door swung open, and Dr. Shumway stepped in. "What exactly is going on here?" She confronted Uncle Bud. "You're the man from the gas station, aren't you?"

"Bud Creedle, ma'am." He touched the brim of his hat. "I have a proposition to make." He explained his getaway scheme.

"Very well," Dr. Shumway said when he was finished. "When can we leave?"

"That," said Uncle Bud, winking at Jack, "is what I call a woman of spirit."

"Wait!" Isadora cried. "You can't be serious! Colonel Miles told us we have to stay."

"Colonel Miles is a petty tyrant," her mother said coolly. "In seeking to confine us here, he has vastly exceeded his legal authority. If I am to report his bizarre antics—and I will—we must first leave this town. Pack quickly," she added. "And put on some warm clothes. There's a chill in the air."

• • •

XAAFUUN LED her officers across their compound, where her carefully constructed illusions hid the growing heaps of trash. One could almost believe their landing site was not part of *Uurth* at all, but a quaint skreepish village from bygone times. Creating three-dimensional illusions was something the skreeps did well. It was said the power came from unity of belief and the unquestioned authority of the Exalted One. Practice began right after hatching.

The Queen had decreed that all landing sites not only be hidden from alien intruders, but be made to look like home. To be sure, it was an idealized home, with pod shelters and gluck pools and streets made of rubbery buzzle stone. The crew set it up on every planet they visited, and it never changed. It was comforting to know that wherever they went in the universe, they would always land in exactly the same place.

They stepped through the illusion wall and into the biological extravagance of the *Uurth* forest. Trees rose all around them. Without the soothing distraction of durbo music, the unpleasant sounds of nature intruded: creaking branches, dripping water, and tiny pattering feet. Xaafuun shuddered. The forest was so repulsive even *ooman bings* avoided it. "Follow me," she commanded the others and scuttled away on six legs, her abdomen held high to protect it from the scratchy undergrowth.

After a while she stopped in the darkness, allowing her sensors to adjust. The settlement was just ahead. With her were Bambo, Ruffy, and Zin Zin, three of her more dependable officers. Most of the town had already been searched, but her Finder, Phoony, had avoided the great, horrid waterway that marked its eastern edge. Xaafuun had no intention of touching the filthy thing, either, but there were promising buildings nearby. The Item could be in any of them.

The churning sound of an engine startled her, and she scurried quickly across the street. The skreeps hid in the shadow of a hedge as the vehicle came near. It was one of the machines the *ooman bings* called *kaarz*.

Early skreepish expeditions had assumed that *kaarz* were the dominant species on *Uurth*, and *ooman bings* were their parasitic companions. The true relationship was not deciphered until much later, and even now it was easy to understand the mistake. *Kaarz* were much more powerful than the creatures that controlled them, and they seemed to have taken the best part of the planet for themselves.

The *kaar* zipped past with a roar. Xaafuun wondered if it wasn't unusually fast, but then it was gone, headed in the direction of the settlement's core.

As soon as it disappeared, she stood up. "Follow me," she told the others, noting with disapproval the flickering anxiety in their eyes. Afraid of *kaarz*! Sometimes she was amazed that the empire was as successful as it was.

• • •

11. THE REFRIGERATOR

THE STATION WAGON rumbled toward the center of town with Dr. Shumway behind the wheel. It felt like a huge dog on a short leash. Each fluttering touch on the gas pedal caused it to bolt forward, and when she removed her foot, the engine grumped.

Jack leaned over the seat. "You don't want to baby her *too* much. Those new pipes need to be aired out a little." He had offered to drive when they left the Pines, but Dr. Shumway wouldn't have it.

"Don't listen to him," said Uncle Bud. "I think you're doing fine. Left up here on Dumont, and then it's more or less a straight shot downtown."

"What he did to my car is simply ridiculous," Dr. Shumway complained. "All this power in a family vehicle!"

Uncle Bud lowered his voice confidentially. "Jack ain't but half a Creedle, you know. His daddy was a fella named Murchison. Sorry affair. His mother never was too smart when it came to men."

It would be best not to comment, Dr. Shumway decided. Already she felt uncomfortably entangled in local events. She would happily end her association with Bud Creedle as soon as he showed her his secret way out of town. In the meantime, she would focus on the task at hand. The car was packed, and there was no sign of pursuit from the army. She breathed deeply to rid herself of tension.

In the backseat Jack was not listening. Instead, he replayed the evening's events in his mind. So far, the escape was a success.

He wasn't carrying much, but it would be enough for a few days' travel: his hunting cap, jacket, and a lucky rabbit's foot. He felt bad about leaving his mom to deal with the monsters, but after all, she had the army to help her. And with Sergeant Webb on his case, it was too risky to stay.

Getting out of the house had been easy enough. Most of the soldiers were in the dining room, busy with their plans. Isadora, her mother, and Uncle Bud tiptoed down the back

stairs to the darkened kitchen, with Jack signaling for them to follow. He eased the door open. Over at the chicken coop, soldiers pointed flashlights at the ground. Jack guessed they had discovered the footprints. It was precisely the diversion they needed. They walked silently through backyards until they came to the station wagon, hidden behind a thick stand of trees on Wemple Road.

When Dr. Shumway started the car, the roar of the engine caused them all to wince, but she quickly put it in gear and headed away. They drove the first few blocks with their lights off, making a wide circle around the train. After that they turned back toward Bud's garage—to fetch whatever he had hidden there.

• • •

SILENT AND UNHAPPY, Isadora sat as far from Jack as she could manage on the wide backseat. Inside her purse she had stuffed her journal of scientific observations, a pen, nail clippers and a file, a wallet containing two dollars and forty-three cents, a folded handkerchief, and a very small stuffed dog named Foo Foo, which she'd kept since she was a toddler. She was dressed in a wool skirt and tights, with a light jacket on top of her sweater. The hood was pulled over her head.

"Don't worry," Jack whispered. "Uncle Bud has run from the law plenty of times. Nobody knows how to get out of town like he does."

Isadora gave him a brief, disgusted sneer, then stared out the window. For a second she thought she saw something move behind a hedge, something large and shadowy with legs like tree branches. She took a deep breath and closed her eyes.

When she opened them again, both the hedge and the shadowy figure were gone.

When they got to the repair shop, Uncle Bud opened one of the big rollaway doors and had Dr. Shumway carefully back the station wagon inside.

"Okay, cut the engine," he said. He pulled the iron door shut, then rapped on Jack's window. "Come on, boy. I'm gonna need some help moving this thing."

The back door of the shop had four separate locks. As Uncle Bud was opening them, Isadora and her mother watched. "That seems excessive," said Dr. Shumway.

"We ain't all so fortunate as to work in fancy research centers. Around here, I got to provide my own security." He pushed the door open. "No offense to you, ma'am, but Bud Creedle don't like to take chances." He flipped on a light.

Jack whistled.

A fireslate workbench ran the length of the far wall, cluttered with beakers, test tubes, Bunsen burners, oscilloscopes, centrifuges, and an electron microscope. Complex instruments suited to a university science lab spilled out of open cabinets. Tiny drills, clamps, saws, and pliers shared space with an assortment of meters, gauges, switches, dials, transformers, and transistors. Other items were so sophisticated and strange that Dr. Shumway was completely mystified.

"This is no ordinary garage!" she whispered.

"Best working lab in the Wanookie Valley," said Uncle Bud proudly. He flicked a hidden switch. A square panel concealed in the floor dropped a couple of inches, humming quietly. "Elevator," he explained. "My own design. You ladies stay put. Me and Jack will go down and fetch the machine."

"And what exactly is this machine?" asked Dr. Shumway.

Uncle Bud wagged a finger at her playfully. "I'm tempted to tell you, you being a scientist and all. Unlike the dunderheads in this town, you might actually understand it. But no, it's a *dangerous* invention, you see. I've been gambling the aliens wouldn't find it, not here; but now I'm not so sure that's a good bet. I reckon it'll be safer if I take it with me."

He pushed another hidden switch, then stepped onto the trapdoor. Jack hopped on, too, and the panel lowered slowly into a hidden room. Isadora and her mother peered into the shadows as the Creedles dragged something heavy across the floor.

"Easy! Take it easy, now!" Uncle Bud scolded.

"This here is a very delicate piece of machinery!" Soon the elevator started humming again, and Jack and his uncle reappeared. Their hands were pressed against a large white cabinet with rounded corners and a chrome handle. The words *General Appliances* and *Insta-Kool* were scrawled across the door in modernistic letters.

"A *refrigerator*?" asked Isadora.

"You go on believing that, missy," said Uncle Bud with a smirk. "You'll be happier in the long run."

Dr. Shumway was clearly puzzled. "I *would* ask what this is all about, but I suspect the less I know, the better."

"That's the way. And on a personal note, let me say I admire a scientist who minds her own business." Bud grabbed a handcart, and with Jack's help, the refrigerator soon lay on its side in the back of the station wagon. "Well, that's half the job done. Now all we have to do is get out of town."

. . .

COLONEL MILES put down the headset and stroked his chin. This was a critical point for his operation. He was within striking range, with all his forces deployed for battle. Now he needed to know precisely where the skreeps were hiding. "Our boys are in the woods," he told Sergeant Price. "Both units." He plotted their coordinates on his map and chewed the nub of his cigar. Radio static crackled in the background. His reconnaissance teams were the best in the business. Right now they were slipping into Dutch Woods from the north and east.

Womrath stepped into the doorway. "Excuse me, sir, but there seems to be a problem with the civilians."

"What sort of problem?"

"They're missing, sir. The lady scientist and her daughter. Also the boy."

"For pity's sake! Didn't the sentries see anything?"

"No, sir, but O'Brien thought he heard a car. Said it was pretty loud."

"A car! If he *heard* one, why didn't he go *find* it?" Miles banged his fist on the table. "This is the last thing I need! Go get the boy's mother and the mayor. Also that cop, if he's around. On the double!"

A minute later Womrath led Mrs. Creedle and Mayor Handy into the dining room. "What's the problem, Colonel?" the mayor asked.

"Missing guests. Dr. Shumway and her daughter. Do you know where they are?"

"Maybe they ran off. The truth is, I barely know them. Peculiar people, scientists. They don't think like the rest of us."

"They ain't so stupid, is why," grumbled Mrs. Creedle.

"Your son is gone, too, ma'am."

"Well, I ain't surprised. He gets like this when the law is after him."

"Aren't you concerned?"

"Truth is, I'm glad! With them monsters around, he's smart to leave."

"I can find him, Colonel." Sergeant Webb strutted through the doorway. He was thickly built, with a wide chest and a neck as big around as the bald head on top of it. His face was flat, and his eyes were small and narrow. Grady stood behind him, leaning in to get a better view. "I can find them all. Me and the boy, that is. We know every trick those Creedles ever pulled."

"Do it, then," ordered the colonel. "And be quick about it. I can't have a carload of civilians messing up this operation."

Sergeant Webb's face twisted into a satisfied smirk. "You'll want to throw the book at 'em, I guess?"

"You do the catching," growled Colonel Miles, "and I'll decide what to throw."

• • •

12. INTO THE WOODS

WHEN XAAFUUN picked up her communicator she could hear the noise: crashes, shouts, singing, laughter. *What was going on?* She put the question to Second Officer Dreevin, who had command in Sector Four. Reluctantly he told her. Some of the crew had overturned a dead *kaar* in the upper settlement, and a strange liquid seeped out. It was harsh in the mouth but very intoxicating. A few of them had consumed a great deal.

"And?"

"It's hard to reason with them now, Madame Commander."

"Don't *reason* with them, lunkhead!" she shouted. "Arrest them! If they resist, *shoot* them!" She flicked off her communicator and glared angrily across the damp warehouse where her own small team was unpacking crates. She had never sent her entire crew on a finding mission before. This was why. How she despised them! They were incapable of following even the simplest orders.

She was running out of time. In the warehouse they had discovered nothing but large quantities of a bright red sauce. It was probably food. Xaafuun glanced through the window at the dull shine of the waterway outside. The situation was maddening. "It isn't here."

Bambo looked up, holding a bottle. Ruffy and Zin Zin looked up, too.

"It isn't *here*," she repeated. "I can feel it." She gathered bottles in each of her six free hands and shook them angrily. "We don't have time for this! We need to search somewhere else!"

"Madame Commander," Zin Zin said cautiously, "all the buildings in this sector have been searched. Phoony has been through them all."

"Phoony!" She scowled at the bottles and set them back in their crate. "Where is he, anyway? I haven't heard from him all night."

It was all Phoony's fault, of course! He was the Finder. He should be the one to take the blame. She must make sure the Queen understood that. Her communicator began to vibrate. She plucked it from her belt. "What is it, Dreevin?"

"A problem, Madame Commander." The voice hesitated. "Remember those ruffians who went crazy drinking *kaar* juice? I got them under control. The settlement is quiet now."

"So what's the problem?"

"I was taking two of them, Kleegle and Zantuuk, back to the ship, as you ordered. But something happened."

"*What* happened, you idiot?"

"We came upon a small group of *ooman bings* in the forest. Soldiers, Madame. I set an illusion screen, but the ruffians made so much noise, the *ooman bings* marched right through it."

"And?"

"One of the *ooman bing*s shot Kleegle. You know those weapons they have—big noise, very messy? He shot Kleegle in the belly. So Zantuuk . . . he was already crazy from the *kaar* juice . . . but he went *extra* crazy. He went after those *ooman bings* with his ray gun."

Xaafuun cursed. The fool! This was exactly what she had been trying to avoid! "Did he kill them?"

"Oh, sure. Killed all of them right away."

She closed several eyes. That was something, at least. No witnesses. It meant they could still get away without sparking a battle—if they hurried. But they had to destroy the evidence. "Take the bodies back to the ship," she ordered. "Feed them to the beasts, if you have to, but don't leave anything in the forest for the other *ooman bings* to find."

"What about Kleegle, Madame? Her injury looks bad."

"Feed *her* to the beasts, too!" Xaafuun roared. "And throw in Zantuuk while you're at it!" She struggled to control her rage. "Just don't let them bleed all over the place! We don't want the *ooman bings* to think they can hurt us." She clicked off. Then she sent a message to all the others. Their mission was over. The entire crew was to report to the ship immediately. They would depart as soon as everyone returned.

One by one, each of her officers acknowledged the order. All but Phoony. She bit off another curse. Where was her Finder? She switched on her tracking beam and began a wide scan of the settlement.

When she finally picked him up, on the far side of the colony, she was astonished to find him moving away from the ship. "Ensign Phoony!" she shouted into the communicator. "What do you think you're doing? I ordered you to return immediately."

"Can't!" His voice came back in a breathless gulp. "I . . . have . . . a hunch!"

"Go to the ship!" she exploded. "The mission is over!"

"A hunch," he repeated. His communicator clicked off.

•   •   •

THE NIGHT WAS dark. The Milky Way stretched overhead, vivid as a skunk's tail. Behind the steering wheel, Dr. Shumway's face was inscrutable. "You still have not told me how to find this secret route of yours."

Uncle Bud gave her a crooked smile. "Don't worry, missus, you're doing fine. Try opening up the throttle a little."

She pursed her lips and drove.

"Turn up here," he instructed. "At the stop sign. The short-cut's just ahead."

Dr. Shumway stopped the car and looked at him while it idled noisily. "And you're certain this route will not be blocked?"

"Positive." He chuckled, obviously pleased with himself. "It's an old farm road across Heck Van Gundy's back pasture. Hardly anyone knows about it, and it ain't on any map."

"*I* know it," said Jack. "It goes right through Dutch Woods."

"You've got to be kidding!" Isadora looked at Uncle Bud in disbelief.

"Last place the army will ever look."

"But what about the aliens?" asked Jack.

"There *are* no aliens." Dr. Shumway turned the corner and accelerated. The station wagon scrabbled the ground like a lizard before shooting off in a straight line.

"Anyway, the woods are big!" shouted Uncle Bud. "We won't be anywhere near where that saucer landed!"

By the time he spotted the farm road, they were nearly upon it. Dr. Shumway slammed on the brakes. Their headlights picked out a dusty track with twin ruts leading off through a field of dried weeds. She made the turn carefully, then gave the car more gas. It bucked over the ruts.

"Whoa, now," said Uncle Bud, looking nervously at the refrigerator. "That machine weren't made for hard knocks."

"I'm sorry, Mr. Creedle, but this vehicle is almost impossible to restrain." Even as she repeatedly tapped the brakes, the station wagon bounced across the fields as if on a mission of its own.

Uncle Bud winced. "Just do your best. It's all I ask."

•   •   •

DUTCH WOODS rose before them, black and grim. In a chaotic tangle of vines and branches, Isadora spotted an opening as dark as the mouth of a cave. Her stomach tightened. She hated caves. The hole widened, and they plunged inside.

The road crossed a small stream, then plowed through a thicket of blackberry and sumac. Big rocks poked out through a carpet of dead leaves. Something scurried across their path, and Isadora inhaled sharply. "What was that?"

"Raccoon," said Jack.

She gripped her purse.

The forest became increasingly dense. Trees gathered around them like eager spectators, while the station wagon's headlights cast long, swooping shadows. They drove on and on, sometimes dragging their bottom across gullies, often scraping their sides against long-fingered branches.

"Not to alarm anyone," said Jack as they slowed to avoid a fallen log, "but I just saw a really big spider."

"What do you mean?" Isadora tried to control her panic. Behind them the forest was dark.

"I mean *really* big. Like ten feet." He pressed his face against the glass. "I can't see it anymore. Must have been a trick my eyes played on me. For a minute I thought it might be one of those aliens."

"Please don't talk nonsense," Dr. Shumway said tightly. "It is distracting."

"Now pay attention," said Uncle Bud, "because there's a

tricky little section up ahead where you have to wind your way through some boulders. Don't worry. Once you're through that, you're free and clear. The town line is just beyond the edge of the woods. After that, you'll pick up the Munsonburg Road."

They half slid down a steep bank, their tires crunching on wet leaves and branches. The station wagon nearly collided with the first boulder, a house-sized rock surrounded by pines. Dr. Shumway jerked the wheel hard to the left, and they squeezed past, only to find themselves inside a narrow corridor between two more gigantic, mossy stones. They traveled slowly, the passage so tight at points they could barely get through. Isadora kneaded her purse strap, peering anxiously into the shadows, while Jack slid down in the seat next to her, playing bongo rhythms on his knees. Both of them were thinking about spiders.

Finally the road straightened and began to climb. Dr. Shumway accelerated, sending up a spray of leaves before the tires gripped, and they surged forward. Inside the car, the mood lifted.

"Another hundred yards and we'll hit the town line," said Uncle Bud.

The car picked up speed. Isadora leaned forward. The horrible woods were coming to an end.

One last, huge boulder stood at the forest's edge. Suddenly a red light began to flash from behind it. "What is that?" Isadora cried.

Dr. Shumway put her foot on the brake.

"Don't slow down!" Jack shouted. But it was too late. The police car pulled out and blocked the road. The station wagon skidded to a halt.

"This is intolerable!" Dr. Shumway complained.

Sergeant Webb stepped out of the cruiser. His right hand rested, cowboy style, on the butt of his gun. "Well, look what the cat dragged in!" he sneered, shining a flashlight through her window. "I count two Creedles and a couple of big-city troublemakers. This must be my lucky night."

Dr. Shumway gave him a frosty look. "May I ask what you think you're doing?"

"I might ask you the same, except it's plain enough. You're *fugitives*, and I caught you." He shone his light all the way into the back. "Say, what's that you got there?"

"Refrigerator," Uncle Bud mumbled.

"Refrigerator? What's it stuffed with, cash?" Webb chuckled. "Maybe I should have a look."

"You don't want to do that."

"This is a waste of time," Dr. Shumway snapped. "My daughter and I are already late getting back to Boston, so if you *must* write us a ticket, please go ahead so we can be on our way."

"A *ticket?* I'm not writing any tickets! You're all under arrest. Now I'm going to search the back there. And just so you know, if any of you move, I'll shoot you."

"Shoot us?" Isadora yelped.

"He won't shoot you," muttered Jack.

"I'd be within my rights. So don't get any funny ideas."

Jack already had one. He was fairly certain Webb wouldn't shoot. He'd done worse than joyriding, and the sergeant had never shot him before. The town line was just beyond the trees, and Webb had no jurisdiction past that line. The sergeant wasn't very fast. Jack thought about Millbrook and waited.

Webb walked around the car and opened its tailgate. As soon as the dome light came on, Jack eased open his own door. He looked at his new sneakers and slid sideways on the seat. By the time his shoes hit the ground, he was already running.

Which meant he didn't see what the others saw.

Jack sprinted past the blurred shapes of trees, hearing nothing but the sound of his own beating footsteps. Sergeant Webb's sharp "Hey!" only made him run faster.

He didn't see the nine-foot-tall spider as it came around the back of the car and lifted Webb off the ground, then quickly lassoed him with heavy, glistening threads.

The first notion Jack had that something was seriously

wrong was when he heard a garbled scream. He couldn't be sure, but he thought it was Uncle Bud. The second notion came an instant later, when he slammed into Grady Webb.

The impact was like hitting a wall. All the oxygen left his body in a single *hurff!* as Grady's arms closed around him, and they toppled backward onto the ground.

Somewhere far away the screams continued, but Grady, busy cuffing the sides of Jack's head, wasn't about to be distracted.

Jack managed to roll over, so he didn't see the monster coming. Grady didn't see it, either. "You're in for a whipping, Creedle!" he bellowed.

Jack had no reason to doubt him. He covered his face as best he could.

Far above them, something spoke. It was the strangest voice Jack had ever heard—as heavy as Grady's fists and rougher than the forest road. He didn't understand a single word.

. . .

13. OUTER SPACE

THE GIGANTIC SAUCER filled the clearing, as improbable as an ocean liner in the fall woods. It was nearly as big as one—tall as the highest trees and unbelievably wide. Its smooth skin shimmered with a pale, turquoise glow, while brighter light spilled from dozens of portholes in its spherical core. Isadora stood frozen, her mouth slack, while Jack smiled, momentarily pleased to find his story had been verified. It wasn't often he was caught telling the truth.

"You see?" he said, but before anyone could answer, the monster tugged the sticky leashes that bound them. They stumbled gracelessly across the clearing and all the way under the vast, slowly spinning rim.

The monster yanked them up a ramp that led to an open portal in the ship's belly.

The closer they came to the doorway, the harder they struggled, none more desperately than Isadora. It was no use. One by one, the spider dragged them inside.

The room they entered was dim and unpleasant. Globs of greenish light swirled within its walls like curdled milk. Two more monsters plopped out of a tube in the ceiling. They glanced at the humans but seemed more interested in the refrigerator, which the first spider carried effortlessly on its back. When the monsters saw the appliance they began to jabber excitedly.

The first monster passed the humans roughly to a second one, which gave the cords an abrupt jerk. As if by magic, a huge, spider-sized hole opened in the wall. The creature dragged the humans through, and the door winked shut behind them.

The spider shoved them one by one into a clear tube. They slid down it and landed on top of one another in a jumbled heap. Sergeant Webb cursed, and Grady aimed a kick at Jack's head, but the spider dragged them off again. The corridor twisted up, down, and around in a seemingly random way. Sodden heaps of garbage littered the floor.

When the monster finally stopped, another circular door mysteriously opened. The humans were herded into a small, nearly round cell. The monster slashed their cords, then gave Sergeant Webb a hard shove, perhaps as a warning to the

others. When it stepped outside, the doorway dilated shut, leaving no sign the opening had ever been there.

The curved walls of the cell were completely bare. The only point of interest was a porthole in the far wall, which they crowded around eagerly. Outside, they could see nothing but the saucer's overhanging rim. It had begun to spin more quickly. Beyond were the dark shadows of the woods.

Isadora leaned against the wall and was surprised when it stretched slightly under her weight. She quickly stepped away. Something about the elastic material was deeply repulsive. She wondered if everything on the ship would be this nauseating.

Jack had been right: The aliens *were* like spiders, at least superficially. Their dark, segmented bodies sprouted eight bristled legs—or perhaps they were *arms*, Isadora thought, since the monsters used them to lift and carry things. The bristles continued up the creatures' bodies and onto their heads. They wore uniforms, dark blue and shiny as the tail of a fly. The fabric stretched so tightly that every rigid contour of chest and back was revealed. Their bulbous abdomens were bare.

Isadora was proud of herself for making such careful observations. Still, her strongest impression remained her first, terrifying view from inside the station wagon when the monster bent over her, its mouth wide and slightly parted, its nostrils gaping, and its gelatinous eyes bunched together like a cluster of frogs' eggs, leering at her with greedy enthusiasm.

She shuddered and looked up at her mother. "So what do we do now?"

•   •   •

COLONEL MILES stood on the front porch. He puffed the tip of his cigar into a glowing ember. It had been fifteen minutes since he'd heard from his first recon team, and now they weren't answering. His second team claimed to have heard a rifle shot. They were on their way to investigate.

The civilians were still unaccounted for. According to his radio operator, the policeman, Webb, was no longer answering, either. Something was happening out there, but he couldn't tell what. He stood in silence, brooding and puffing. The skreeps were a slippery opponent. Maybe it was time to flush them out. He called down the steps to Sergeant Price. "Tell Captain Goldfarb to prepare the forward batteries."

"Yes, sir."

The front door opened, and Mayor Handy stepped out. Mrs. Creedle was right behind him. "Excuse me, Colonel. Another civilian is missing. It's Laverne's brother, Bud."

"The whole town's missing, Mayor. Does one more really matter?"

"It does if you know my brother," Mrs. Creedle said flatly.

"He's a peculiar fellow," the mayor agreed. "An inventor. Had some run-ins with the law."

"He builds rocket ships and such," said Mrs. Creedle.

"Rockets?"

"Big ones."

"Why didn't you tell me this before?"

"I don't recall you asking."

"It probably doesn't mean anything," the colonel said, shoving the cigar back in his mouth. "But it's funny that so much alien activity takes place around here. There's been something strange about this town for years."

"You're telling me."

"What else do you know about your brother's inventions?"

"Not much. Bud's been secretive lately. When I ask him what it's about, he tells me he's going to be a millionaire.

That's a bad sign, that millionaire thing. Whenever he gets that notion, it always means trouble."

Suddenly a column of turquoise light erupted from the darkness of Dutch Woods. A huge saucer rose to fill it, its rim spinning just above the tree line, its domed top and rounded bottom spilling light from stacked rows of yellow portholes.

A collective gasp went up from the Outer Space Division and even a few scattered cheers. The ship hovered, throwing off swirling ribbons of gas. Then, like a bubble released from the bottom of a tub, it shot straight up into the starlit sky. Soon it was no more than a star itself. Then it was gone.

In the aftermath, the town seemed even darker than before. "Looks like Bud's outdone himself, this time," said Mrs. Creedle.

• • •

"Look at that!" Isadora had never felt such wonder. Next to her, Jack whistled. The others gathered around the window, craning to see. They forgot they were prisoners. All that mattered now was the view.

In the foreground the saucer's rim spun as evenly as a well-thrown top. Beyond it, mirroring its curve, was the brightly lit rim of Planet Earth. The sun rose. Pink and gold clouds spread across the horizon like a flock of puffy sheep. Below the clouds the shadowy contours of the land were purple in the early dawn.

"Holy cow," whispered Jack. He saw the coastline and the great ocean beyond. The night receded, and Earth became a bright, sapphire ball cloaked with whipped-cream swirls of cloud. Until now, the farthest he'd been from home was a trip to Monroe, New Jersey, to visit his Uncle Sid in prison. "Where do you think we're going?" he asked.

"Where are we going? We're going straight to *Mars*!" Sergeant Webb's eyes were wild. He pounded a fist into the curved inner wall, then shook it as the wall bounced back with a rubbery twang. *Bam! Bam!* He struck again and again, throwing his wide body into the effort, while the wall, pliant as a beach ball, repelled every blow. Isadora was reminded of a lab rat scrabbling at the side of its cage.

"Really, Sergeant," Dr. Shumway scolded, "you will exhaust yourself. Even if you could get out, what would you do? To escape with Earth already receding from view would be utterly pointless."

"Oh, yeah?" he huffed, struggling to catch his breath. "Well, I don't see *you* doing anything."

She raised her chin. "I accept your criticism."

"But what *do* we do?" Isadora asked again.

"We analyze the situation, of course." If Dr. Shumway was surprised by the situation, she didn't show it. "Of particular interest to me," she said, "is the role of Mr. Creedle's machine in all this. I couldn't help noticing the space creatures seemed very excited by it."

"Hold on," said Bud. "I'm not sure I like where you're going with this."

Sergeant Webb's red face darkened. "I'm not sure I like where *we're* going, either! Which, in case you haven't noticed, is *outer space!*"

The saucer's spinning disk made Grady queasy. "I want to go home!" he moaned.

Dr. Shumway returned her attention to Bud. "It is not my intention to be judgmental," she said. "I am merely making observations. The aliens were eager to have your machine. Do you deny it?"

"No." He slumped into the wall, which stretched to hold him. His energy drained like air from a punctured tire. "No, I noticed it, too. I was hoping I was wrong. I was hoping they didn't know what they had." He looked to the others for sympathy. "I've been swindled, if you want to know the truth. A *million bucks*, gone like that!" He snapped his fingers. "I should have known they wouldn't play fair. It's the same all over. The little guy never gets a break."

Dr. Shumway was incredulous. "Are you saying you *know* these aliens? Were you *negotiating* with them?"

"Hah!" Sergeant Webb cried. "So you're in cahoots with the monsters?"

"No, that's not it. Screw your ears on, Webb. I never seen these spiders in my life. I was about to sell my invention to a client in New York City. A *legitimate* client." Bud slumped even lower. "How the aliens got wind of the deal, I don't know, but they must have—or how could they have known to grab the thing? Sure, I was worried that was what they came for, but it was just a hunch. If that head of yours was more than a doorstop, Webb, you'd know better. You'd know if we *were* in cahoots, the last place I'd be right now was in a cell with you."

"So who is this client in New York?" asked Dr. Shumway, still in shock.

"I don't know. I never met the man. Call him Mr. X. He was interested in my *destabilizer* concept—and he put his money where his mouth was. Mr. X staked me for most of my materials and gave me some cash to get started."

"Some cash."

"Think of it as a research grant."

"Indeed. And what, may I ask, is a *destabilizer?*"

Bud hesitated. "I guess I might as well tell you. That machine we're carrying is a *dimensional field destabilizer*—the only one of its kind, as far as I know. It wasn't much use to me, frankly, which is why I didn't mind selling it. It makes disruptions in the fourth dimension."

Isadora gaped at him in amazement. "A time machine?"

"Space-time. Which is why it wasn't much use to me. It requires a rocket ship if you're going to do anything with it."

"Impossible," Dr. Shumway said dismissively. "Such technology is decades away, perhaps centuries. We barely understand the principles! Even if we did, we don't have a proper energy source."

"What do you mean '*we*'?" Uncle Bud snorted. "*I'm* the one who figured out the principles. As for energy, she runs on quantum foam."

"Quantum foam?" Isadora asked. "What's that?"

"It's thought to be a characteristic of space-time itself," her mother explained, scrutinizing Bud with intensity. "It may be created by virtual particles of very high energy, which annihilate one another in violent reactions."

"Sort of a matter-antimatter thing," said Bud. "So you've heard of it."

"I'm familiar with the Casimir Effect as part of my research into friction-free locomotion. In short, I am satisfied that vacuum energy exists."

"I'm satisfied, too," Bud chuckled. "A million bucks' worth of satisfied. Quantum foam is the secret to the destabilizer, and I'm the only one who's ever figured out how to use it."

"Fascinating," muttered Dr. Shumway. "So the theory is true."

"I think I'm missing something," said Jack.

"Course you are!" grunted his uncle. "With that half-Creedle brain of yours! Listen, you know about space-time don't you? And the theory of relativity?"

"Sure," Jack lied. "I mean, sort of."

"I do," Isadora said eagerly. Relativity was her favorite subject. Einstein's theory explained, among other things, that time moved differently in different places, huddling around some planets while speeding past others. During the course of a single drowsy morning on one world, thousands or even millions of years might pass on another. Time was like a great river, full of swift currents and plunging rapids, as well as steady, quiet places and gently swirling backwaters. At least that was how she pictured it. "Your machine disrupts space-time? How? And *why?*"

"It makes holes." He gave them all a significant look. "That's what you need to travel in space: holes that will take you *through* to wherever you need to go, so's you don't have to waste your *time* going *around*."

Isadora didn't like the image. It was different from her own. She had never liked small spaces or holes. "Wouldn't it make more sense to think in terms of *currents*—of making fast currents in space-time?"

"Holes," Uncle Bud insisted. "Space is just as holey as Swiss cheese."

. . .

14. INSTA-KOOL

FINALLY XAAFUUN could relax. She adjusted the ship's gravity to one skreepish unit, unhitched her webbed harness, and leaned back in her captain's chair while she watched *Uurth* disappear from view. Back in space, back to proper gravity—she felt the comfortable lightness in her joints. The Special Item sat in front of her, compact and *Uurth*-ugly, but marvelous just the same. "You'll know it when you see it," the Queen had insisted, and it was true. Xaafuun did know it, intuitively. She wondered if she could intuit what it *did*. So far, she hadn't even opened it. Suppose it was fragile or even dangerous? The truth was, alien technologies made her nervous.

She turned to Mellis. "Where is Phoony?"

"The last I saw him, Madame, he was in the officer's mess."

"The officer's mess! I'm not surprised! No doubt he's telling everyone how he saved the expedition." She knew it was true. The thought of her Finder stepping on board with the machine on his back and a little string of slaves trailing behind him was so annoying.

Six *ooman bings*! Why *six*? All she needed was the Item's inventor. That *was* important. Without the inventor, a tremendous amount of time would be wasted trying to figure it out, if that was even possible. There were warehouses on Skreepia full of unexplained alien gewgaws. Clearly the Special Item must not become one of them. She had not traveled 153 light-years to collect a trinket that couldn't be used. But six *ooman bings*? *Six*? And three of them mere hatchlings! Surely a hatchling had not invented the Special Item?

"Can't you see?" she hissed. "He's trying to upstage me."

Mellis bowed slightly. "I'm sure you are right, Madame."

"Of course I am. Phoony is greedy for attention—attention and glory. The wretch!" He was *showy*, that's what he was. Xaafuun hated showiness. *Ooman bings* were more than rare on Skreepia. In fact she only knew of one. Bringing home *six* was bound to create a stir. "He means to present himself as the expedition's savior. Phoony the hero! Phoony the savior! If he convinces enough people, where will I be?"

"I see your point, Madame."

"Obviously. This expedition can only have one savior, and that savior is *me*."

"Madame?" Bambo interrupted. Xaafuun regained her composure. "Yes?"

"It's just that I've seen things like this Special Item before."

"Have you, Bambo?"

"Yes, Madame." He licked the top of his lip nervously. "I saw them in every *Uurth* habitat I entered. They are quite common, I think. They are called *refrigerators*."

"*Are* they?"

"Yes, Madame. They cause cooling. *Ooman bings* favor cooling very much."

She smiled at him. Such an idiot. And yet his foolishness might serve her very well. She lifted her communicator and ordered Phoony to the bridge.

•   •   •

A SHINY NEW uniform clung to Phoony's torso. He struggled unsuccessfully to suppress a grin. *So delighted with himself!* Xaafuun regarded him sourly, allowing the silence to grow between them. Phoony's grin became uncertain, faltered, and died.

Xaafuun pointed an accusing finger at the Special Item. "Ensign Phoony, would you please explain the meaning of *this*?"

Relief struggled with confusion on his face. "Madame Commander, it is the *Special Item*."

"Is it?" Her voice was low and harsh. "Apparently the Special Item is not so *special* after all! Apparently it is a common *Uurthish* appliance. Do you know what a *refrigerator* is, Ensign Phoony?"

"No. I mean, yes! But this is not one of those!"

"A refrigerator is a device used by *ooman bings* for *cooling*. Did you know that? *Ooman bings* are much in favor of cooling. They cool with ritualistic fervor."

Phoony sputtered. "I . . . I . . . I assure you, Madame, this one is different!"

"Is it? Then perhaps you will explain to me exactly what it does, if it does not cool?"

Phoony gaped at her, working his mouth soundlessly. "It is the *Item*," he finally choked.

"Are you an expert in *Uurthish* technology, then?" Xaafuun persisted. She leaned closer to him, her eyes taking on a carnivorous gleam. "Perhaps you can explain these symbols on the machine's outer skin. To me they seem to say '*Insta-Kool.*' I have deciphered many of the *ooman bing* languages, you see. But I must not be an *expert* like you, Phoony! What do you suppose it could mean? Surely nothing to do with a *refrigerator*? Surely nothing to do with the *ooman bings*' odd passion for lowered temperatures? So, Ensign, please explain my error, my *misinterpretation.*"

She waited. The silence became dreadful. Across the bridge nothing moved.

"When I give a direct order for you to return to the ship," Xaafuun said slowly, "I expect to be obeyed. And when I ask you to find an Item, I expect the *proper* Item, not some common dreck. You have failed me, Ensign Phoony. And now you must be punished."

With lightning speed she grabbed his top left arm above the second joint. He stared in horror and screamed as she gave it a wrenching twist. It snapped and broke free.

Phoony staggered backward, clutching at his broken stump. Thick, black liquid squirted onto the floor.

"That is for disobeying a direct order," said Xaafuun crisply. She raised the severed limb to her mouth and casually bit a chunk off the end. After chewing it thoroughly, she swallowed,

then spoke again. "For your sake, let us hope this is indeed the Special Item." She took another bite while he stared at her miserably. "I have not yet made my final determination. If it is, you may be spared further discipline. If not, you may expect your dismemberment to continue, in a more complete fashion."

She tore another bite from the arm, then altered her voice to a motherly tone. "It's all for your own good, Phoony. Nobody likes a showy Finder." She swallowed. "Now go away, and don't let me hear from you again."

Xaafuun leaned back in her chair and regarded the Special Item once more. She yawned. "What do you think, Mellis? I wonder what we *really* have here, don't you? Perhaps I should interrogate the *ooman bings*."

"Whatever you wish, Madame."

She nodded, absentmindedly tracing her scar with one claw. Holding Phoony's arm like a scepter, she glanced at her screens. The ship was moving beyond the system's fourth planet. It wouldn't be long before they reached the Medwig Gulp.

. . .

"I WOULD LIKE to know more about your research," said Dr. Shumway. Outside their cell, Mars drifted past.

Bud looked to the others for support, and found none. "I may as well start from the beginning," he said finally. "I always thought space was the only way for a fella to make a fortune. On Earth it seems like everything worth having is already owned by somebody. That means if you want something, you gotta *take* it." He gave Sergeant Webb a significant look. "You all know the trouble with *that*. Space, on the other hand, is wide open! Nobody's laid a claim on *any* of it yet, so the first one up there is gonna make a killing, right? The only trouble is getting there. I figured it was all about rockets, so I started building. Made some pretty good ones, too, until I realized I was barking up the wrong tree."

"Also, the Feds caught you," Jack reminded him.

"That was later." Uncle Bud dismissed him with a wave of his hand. "If you think about space travel for—oh—five minutes, you run into a basic problem. I ask you, what's the nearest star?"

"Proxima Centauri," said Isadora, turning from the window. "It's approximately four light-years from Earth."

"Bingo. So here's the question. How do you get across four *years'* worth of space? And mind you, that's traveling at the speed of light—which you can't. And even if you got that far, what would you find? Lotta nothing, most likely! So you'd have to go on—a few *more* light-years, and maybe some more after that." He laughed. "The whole thing is like a bad joke."

"I'm sure my colleagues in the department of astrophysics would appreciate your humor," Dr. Shumway said drily.

"No offense, ma'am, but if you scientists are the geniuses you think you are, you didn't need me to point this out."

"We are somewhat vexed," she admitted.

"So was I. Almost threw in the towel. Then I started hearing about flying saucers. Course, a lot of it was pure hokum. But some of them stories were not so easily explained. So I set out to investigate.

"Now, I won't deny I've had my brushes with the law"—he glanced at Sergeant Webb again—"but some folks on the other side of the *legal divide* are a good deal freer in their thinking than your average Joe. When I told *those* folks I was interested in saucers, nobody laughed, nobody got up on a high horse. Instead they gave me my information—for a price—and sent me in the right direction."

"What direction?" asked Jack. "Did they tell you where you could look at some saucers?"

"*Looking* at 'em wasn't the point, sonny boy! The point was this: *How did they do it?* I mean, *how did they travel so gosh darn far?* It took me a while, but I finally got my answer. *Holes.*"

Jack nodded. "You said that before."

"Holes. Nobody on Earth even knew they were out there!"

"That isn't quite accurate," Dr. Shumway said. "Last year the calculations of my colleague, Dr. Lorentz, proved the possibility—in theory."

"Theory, nothing!" snorted Uncle Bud. "These aliens didn't fly here in a *theory*. Nope, they came through *holes*—naturally occurring holes in space-time. Of course, once I knew that, it only raised more questions. What are these holes? How do you find 'em? What do they look like? If you go in, how do you know where you're gonna come out—and *when*? I was right back to my rockets. But word was out on the street now: Old Bud was interested in space travel. So by and by I got the message: Forget about your rockets. Concentrate on those *holes*."

"Who gave you the message?" Jack and Isadora asked at the same time.

Uncle Bud brushed their question aside. "The important thing is that the holes are not only the key to space travel, they're also the biggest problem. They ain't *reliable*. Sometimes they shift or collapse. Sometimes they won't take you where you want to go. The aliens—they're always worried about it. And so are *some* folks on Earth. Folks who are willing to *pay* to solve the problem."

Dr. Shumway said disdainfully, "Like your *Mr. X*."

"Exactly. He put up the cash. Seems he'd been studying

aliens and space travel for *years*. So he helped me—indirectly, mind you—with a few technical problems. Then he found me some of the more . . . *exotic* ingredients."

"Such as quantum foam."

"No, ma'am." Uncle Bud was emphatic. "That was my own doing, the part that made the whole thing work." He gave her a sly smile. "The secret ingredient, if you will. You see, if you want to cause the kind of destabilization I'm talking about, you need to put some *pop* in your gas tank."

"To make holes in the fourth dimension," murmured Isadora. "Shortcuts through space."

"And *time*. With my machine you can really *move*."

"And now the aliens have it," said Dr. Shumway. "I really have to wonder what you were thinking."

"Hold on, now!" he objected, raising his hands. "How was I supposed to know these spiders'd show up?"

"Hah!" scoffed Sergeant Webb. "If you *wasn't* in on it from the beginning, then you're just plain stupid! I'm guessing it was the *aliens* who dangled that million bucks in front of you. Called themselves Mr. X. You bit, and after that, all they had to do was reel you in."

"See what it's like?" Uncle Bud complained to Dr. Shumway. "My whole life I'm surrounded by fatheads who don't understand *science*."

"Who are you calling a fathead?" Webb growled. Grady perked up, the prospect of a fight animating his sullen face.

Dr. Shumway stepped between them. "Do not be foolish, either of you." She addressed Uncle Bud. "Now, how do we know this machine of yours actually *works*, Mr. Creedle?"

"Oh, it works, all right." He eyed Webb cautiously. "I've tested it."

"But you've told us it requires a spaceship in order to function."

"Sure. Like a V-8 requires a set of wheels. But that don't mean you can't fire it up."

"I see. And it made—holes?"

"Little ones." He held his thumb and forefinger an inch apart. "I kept the energy levels as low as I could. But I could feel it—time destabilizing, just a little. Shook things up for as long as it lasted."

"I remember that!" Jack exclaimed. "Down at the garage. I said something screwy was going on, and you told me it was the loose screws in my own thick head."

Uncle Bud chuckled. "I couldn't exactly tell you the truth, could I? Anyway, having the machine don't mean those monsters know how to *use* it. I'd guess they don't, or they would have turned it on by now."

"That is some consolation," said Dr. Shumway. "But one thing is absolutely certain: You must not share your knowledge with these creatures." Her expression was so fierce he was forced to look away. "Are we clear on that point, Mr. Creedle?"

"Sure. What do you take me for?"

She ignored the question. "They may try all manner of persuasion to get you to talk. Some of it could be rather unpleasant."

His face paled. "They'll figure it out themselves eventually. I don't imagine they're *stupid*."

"Knowledge is power, Mr. Creedle. And right now it is the only power we have. Your behavior has been reckless, selfish, and grossly irresponsible. Because of your invention, the entire Earth is imperiled. You have a duty to your *species* to undo the damage you have caused."

"That's a pretty tall order," said Jack.

"Do you really think it's that bad?" asked Isadora.

"I do. Imagine an alien fleet equipped with destabilizers. Such a fleet could go virtually anywhere in the universe at will. If their intentions were hostile—and we must assume they are—the aliens would have an insurmountable advantage over any opponent."

"Now hold on," Uncle Bud whined. "I didn't cause any damage. I just built my invention—a darn good one, too—and then I tried to sell it. That ain't crime, that's business!" He looked at the others. "You ain't against *business*, are you?"

"Mr. Creedle, you have given our captors the means to conquer the entire galaxy. You—*we*—must either stop them or die trying. Our first challenge is to find a way out of this cell."

"Oh, ho!" sniggered Sergeant Webb. "So now it's a *good* idea! I thought you said there wasn't any point in trying to escape."

"Escape? Of course there's no point. We're millions, perhaps billions, of kilometers from Earth. Where would you escape *to*? However, finding the machine is another matter. Mr. Creedle, can we disable it?"

"Sure," he replied, somewhat sulkily. "That is, *I* could."

"I bet I could, too," said Jack. "I'm pretty handy with machines."

"It ain't an old Chevy, you know!" snapped his uncle. "It's a sensitive instrument. You'd be smart to keep your mitts off it."

"Nevertheless," said Dr. Shumway, "we must seize any opportunity. The destabilizer must be destroyed."

As she spoke, a small opening appeared in the wall. It expanded rapidly like a burn hole in nylon. An alien face appeared. When the doorway was fully opened, the monster stepped inside.

Isadora bit off a scream. She pressed herself against the opposite wall. The others packed themselves around her, but there was no place to hide. Sticky cable shot from the monster's abdomen. In seconds, each adult's wrists and ankles were bound.

Uncle Bud was the first to be yanked into the hallway. Sergeant Webb followed.

"Remember what I said," Dr. Shumway advised her daughter coolly. "Any opportunity." Then the alien lifted her by the waist and carried her out. The hole vanished, and the wall became featureless once again. Jack, Isadora, and Grady were left alone.

Grady slumped down with his head between his knees. "I think I'm going to be sick."

Isadora stood in shock. What would they do to her mother? She ran her fingers over the surface where the doorway had been. "How does it open and close?" she thought aloud. "The entire wall seems to dissolve and then somehow reconstitute itself at the molecular level."

Grady watched her with bleary, resentful eyes. "What are you, anyway, some kind of freak?"

Isadora ignored him. She was busy thinking.

• • •

15. KREBS

WHILE SHE WAITED for the *ooman bings*, Xaafuun wondered about the Special Item. What machine was worth a journey of 153 light-years? Answer: an *illegal* one. That could

mean only one thing. And it made sense! Her stomach sizzled
with acid and excitement. "If you had to guess, Mellis, what
would you say this Item is?"

"I really couldn't say, Madame."

"Of course you can't. But what would you *guess*, knowing
the Queen has elaborate plans for *Uurth*, plans that necessitate
an extremely *risky* voyage involving a great number of ships?"

"Might it have something to do with transportation then,
Madame?"

She gurgled. "It might. It might have something to do with
making long voyages safe." She paused. "Not that the Medwig
hasn't been reliable." She thought about the Queen, the very
devious Queen. It would be just like her to enlist the *ooman
bings* as accomplices in their own doom. Besides, where else
could an illegal machine be constructed unnoticed, except
on a backwater planet? New technology always came from
the lower orders. Look at the ship. Foreign creatures had built
almost everything in it. Skreeps didn't invent, they *took*.

The commander bit off another chunk of Phoony's arm
and chewed thoughtfully. A space tunneler would change
everything. But as she thought about it, her stomach began
to churn. She looked at Phoony's arm accusingly and belched.
She shouldn't have eaten so much of it. Fear must have soured
the meat.

"The *ooman bings* are here, Madame Commander," Mellis
announced.

Uncle Bud, Dr. Shumway, and Sergeant Webb huddled
together behind Groot, the dungeon keeper. *So repulsive!*
Xaafuun thought. How she hated them all. She remembered a
flash of steel and searing pain as the light went out in her leftmost eye. Her stomach lurched again.

"Allow me to introduce myself," she said finally, in the *ooman bings*' own language. "I am Xaafuun, commander of this ship, the *Feast of Happiness*. I serve at the pleasure of Her Exalted Majesty, Queen Bureekasaskaphuun, Ruler of All Skreepia, Empress of the Near Spiral Arm, Thirteenth Hatchling in the Dynasty of Saskaphuun—and so forth. It is her image that you see projected above you." She waved a hand at the hologram. "To what do I owe this great pleasure?" She gave them a look containing no pleasure whatsoever, and yawned.

To her surprise, one of the *Uurthlings*, the female, immediately stepped forward. "We were captured by your crew," said Dr. Shumway. "Perhaps we were mistaken for soldiers. But we are civilians. We wish to be returned to Earth immediately."

Xaafuun leaned back. This was almost amusing. "I imagine you would," she said languidly. "But you see, there are certain *time* constraints."

"Constraints?"

"Oh, yes. The unavoidable difficulties of space travel. You primitive *Uurthlings* know *something* about it, don't you?"

"I am a scientist by training, so I do understand certain principles. My name is Dr. Shumway. My companions are Mr. Creedle and Mr. Webb."

"A scientist! I *love* scientists! So *reasonable*." Xaafuun leered at the female. Surely this was her inventor. The other two were males and unimpressive. "I have a question for you, *Scientist* Shumway. It pertains to this machine." She pointed with Phoony's half-eaten arm at the destabilizer. Her deck officers strained at their consoles, listening closely. "Ensign Phoony tells me it was in your *kaar*. Why did Phoony borrow the machine? I cannot say. But here it is, and it puzzles me. Please, I am curious by nature! Can you tell me what it is?"

"It is a refrigerator, a machine used for cooling food. Now, about our return to Earth—"

"Cooling, yes!" Xaafuun showed her fangs. "Cooling is so vital. And yet, I wonder if this *particular* refrigerator does even more than that—"

The sound of a heavy bag sliding across the floor interrupted her. Her concentration faltered. *Krebs!* Why was that wretched garbage collector always underfoot? And did she have to be so *noisy?*

Krebs scooped up a pile of weechee bones and opened her sack. The smell was revolting. Xaafuun gagged. With a flash of anger she threw Phoony's arm at her. It bounced off her head with a meaty *thunk.*

Krebs didn't even flinch. She merely plucked the arm off the deck and dropped it into her sack along with the bones.

Then she bowed slightly in the captain's direction and shuffled away.

"Filthy thing," muttered Xaafuun. Her stomach gurgled. With effort, she turned her attention back to the *ooman bing.* "Now then, Scientist Shumway, where were we?"

"Madame Commander?" Bambo, the navigator, twisted around in his seat. He was clearly frightened.

"What is it?"

"Something is terribly wrong with the Medwig Gulp! The energy levels are nowhere near what they should be. The transaxial is elevated, and the transverse is depressed."

Xaafuun's stomach flipped all the way over.

•   •   •

KREBS SHUFFLED belowdecks, humming along to the durbo music. The song was called "Seven Kinds of Sweet."

I've got to tell you, darling,
You're seven kinds of sweet!
Promise me, hon, you'll be the one
To make my dreams complete!

You've got the taste I'm after.
You're seven kinds of sweet!
Tell me, dear, you'll stay right here.
You're just my kind of meat!

Nice, that durbo music. She passed a portrait of the Queen. Twenty-five long cycles in power! This was her jubilee year. Krebs winked at the hologram, then dropped down to the prison deck.

Her bag dragged behind her. Over many cycles its halter had worn a permanent groove in her neck.

The prison deck made her wonder about the *ooman bings*. It was rumored that hatchlings were in one of the cells. She had never seen *ooman bing* hatchlings before. Were their skins transparent? Did they have limbs? Maybe they were mere larvae: legless, voracious, and blind.

Most crew members didn't care, but Krebs liked to look in on the prisoners, especially the new ones. They were often lively and full of schemes. The old ones lost their liveliness, and after a while, they became one more thing to haul away. But *ooman bing* hatchlings! That *was* interesting!

She came to the cell. When the scanner read her finger's imprint, the wall dilated open. Krebs dragged her bag inside and closed the door. The hatchlings pushed against one another to get away from her. They were disappointing—like the adults, only smaller.

"Krebs I am," she said and wiggled her fingers beside one eye. She could see the gesture meant nothing to them. What bulgy little eyes! "I talk *ooman bing*, tiny bit," she explained. (Wouldn't the commander be surprised by *that*!) "We talk sometime mebbe, hum?"

"O-okay."

The one who spoke was female. Krebs had seen *ooman bings* before, and she knew the difference. "I pikkup traash."

"Thank you." It was the little female again—nice and polite.

Krebs scanned the room. No traash. She hadn't really expected any. The hatchlings watched as she touched the wall and the door opened. When she stepped out, garbage spilled from her bag.

"What do you suppose that was about?" asked Isadora, once the portal had closed.

"Beats me," said Jack.

"It wasn't about anything!" snapped Grady. "Can't you morons figure that out? The spiders are just messing with us."

"It spoke English, though. I find that intriguing."

"*'I find that intriguing!'*" Grady mocked. "What's with your *girlfriend*, Creedle? She talks like an egghead."

Jack ignored him. He began inspecting what had fallen from the alien's sack. Steam rose from the pile, and some of the chunks glowed. The smell was horrific. One piece looked like a tree limb, with small branches sprouting from it. He picked it up.

"Don't touch that!" cried Isadora. "You have no idea what it is! It could be teeming with alien microbes!"

"Microbes," burped Grady. He closed his eyes again.

"But I do know what it is," Jack said, holding it up for her to see. "Look! It's a spider arm!"

•　•　•

16. THE MEDWIG GULP

XAAFUUN SCRAMBLED across the bridge to look at the monitors. Less than one temporal unit away from the Medwig Gulp, and now this! She cursed. It was just her luck. Bambo was correct—the numbers were all wrong.

Blemmix! Everyone said it couldn't happen. The Medwig Gulp was the easiest space-time passage ever discovered. And up until now, it was the most stable. But she had never really trusted it. She knew better.

With luck they could still get through, but the numbers were frightening.

"How long before we reach the opening, Droobit?"

"Thirty-seven subunits, Madame."

Thirty-seven! If only the Medwig could hold up that long. If it didn't, there were ways to survive the long slog across 153 light-years, but none of them were pleasant.

Suddenly the ship hit turbulence and shuddered sideways. "What was *that*?"

Bambo's voice was paper-thin. "Radiation, Madame! A big spike of it, from the center of the Gulp."

Xaafuun swallowed. "Can we still get inside?"

The navigator hesitated. "The entrance is there, but I can't say how long it will last."

"Of course you can't *say*." Xaafuun's temper flared. She had been through a collapse years ago while serving under the legendary Commander Kuurfka-Huzeen. They had been gathering fighting beasts from Krimlops when it happened. Kuurfka had been lucky. Instead of being crushed, they were fired like a photon missile right back home. The time effect was so dramatic they came within a nanosecond of passing themselves coming the other way. They were back on Skreepia an astonishing seven minutes after they left—to the joy of their investors, who profited handsomely from the early return.

It hadn't hurt old Kuurfka's reputation, either. Everyone liked a lucky commander. She received plum assignments after that, and would have been very rich by now if she hadn't been vaporized in a *yarmuk* ambush.

"Madame, the entrance has shifted. The Gulp has moved a third of a helion from galactic center."

"New coordinates, then, Bambo," she said sharply. "We don't care *where* it is, as long as it's there."

"It's behaving strangely, though. Lots of crosscurrents—"

"It's *space*, you fool! It moves. Stop your bellyaching, and fix those coordinates!"

Scuttling back to her dais she noticed Groot. What was he doing here? She remembered only when she saw the *ooman bings* gathered around the jailor like a collection of hideous pets. *The Special Item.* Of course! If her hunch was right, she must find out about it now, before she risked losing her ship inside a faulty passageway.

Xaafuun focused on the female *Uurthling*. "Scientist Shumway," she said, her voice low and dangerous. "I must know the truth. Tell me what this Item is and how to activate it."

Dr. Shumway fixed her with a level stare. "I have no idea."

With some difficulty Xaafuun held back her anger. "You do not understand, *ooman*. We are in great danger! The time tunnel we must pass through is on the brink of collapse."

"Twenty-three subunits," said Droobit.

The captain suppressed a groan. Even if the Item could be activated immediately, it was still almost impossible. "Tell me about this machine, Scientist Shumway!"

"I'm afraid I can't answer your question. I am not an expert in *refrigeration*."

Rage bubbled in Xaafuun's poison glands, scorching her esophagus, sizzling behind her eyes. Such insolence! The female was mocking her! She wanted to sink her fangs into the creature's soft flesh and watch the poison do its slow, cruel work! *Later*, she thought. *Right now all that matters is the Special Item.*

She dragged her attention away from Scientist Shumway. Her eyes settled on the lesser male. Was that a twitch? A nervous twitch? "You!" she snarled. "You have been silent so far. Tell me what *you* know about the machine."

Uncle Bud looked at the floor. "Can't say as I know too much," he mumbled.

Liar! Xaafuun could practically smell the deceit. She would make him talk.

"Seventeen subunits," said Droobit.

Time was running out. Soon the Medwig's sucking vortex would drag them in. "Tell me!" Xaafuun hissed. "Tell me, or I will *make* you tell me!"

"I don't know what you're talking about."

"But you *do* know! Do you think I can't read your feeble mind?" Xaafuun steadied her voice. "You have three minutes. The tunnel we are entering is about to collapse! If it does, we are *dead*. Three minutes! Now *talk*!"

Bud's knees began to shake. He glanced at Dr. Shumway, then up at the captain. "You gotta turn back!"

"No! Tell me how to work the machine." She leaned forward menacingly.

"Maybe we *should* turn back," Bambo suggested quietly in Skreepish.

"Stay out of this!" hissed Xaafuun.

"There isn't enough time—" Bud began. Dr. Shumway silenced him with a sharp kick. His pleading eyes moved from her to the destabilizer. "I mean, not that I even know what this thing is. . . . "

"If we're going to turn back," whispered Droobit anxiously, "we need to do it soon. The vortex is beginning to suck us in."

"We are not turning back! Can't you see? At this distance the shock wave outside the tunnel will be as deadly as the one inside." Xaafuun leaned toward Uncle Bud. "Tell me!"

"I can't, not in three minutes. You *have* to turn back. It's the only way—"

Dr. Shumway rammed a sharp elbow into his ribs. He gasped. Sergeant Webb sneered. "Lousy Creedle."

"Come on," Bud wheedled. "You heard the spider! We're about to *die*!"

"Twelve subunits," said Droobit.

"Two minutes," Xaafuun translated.

"You promised you wouldn't talk, you *worm*," growled Sergeant Webb.

"You can't hold me to that. Not with things the way they are."

"Eleven," said Droobit.

"Your last chance," said Xaafuun coldly.

"You gotta understand," Bud pleaded, "I ain't lying. There ain't enough time."

"Nine subunits, Madame." Droobit's voice was shrill. "The vortex has us. It looks like we're going in."

Going in. Xaafuun exhaled. *Blemmix!* She had finally found the Special Item, determined what it was, and located its inventor. Now this! They were about to enter a collapsing time tunnel with the only device in the galaxy that could save them on board—and it was too late!

She felt another powerful urge to kill them all. Hot bile rose in her throat, but she choked it down. If they did get through the Medwig, she might still need them.

"Take the *ooman bings* back to the dungeon, Groot," she said thickly. *Treacherous monsters.* She hoped she lived long enough to destroy them in a leisurely, painful way.

"Five subunits!" shrieked Droobit.

The stars began to wobble. Xaafuun secured the straps on her captain's chair. Her officers strapped in, too.

"Two subunits!"

Straight ahead the Medwig loomed as pure emptiness. The stars around its rim appeared to bounce.

"One subunit!"

The stars pinwheeled. The ship bucked, then rolled over.

"Zero!" Droobit squeaked.

•   •   •

ISADORA HAD an idea. "Let me see that spider arm, Jack."

He had been examining it closely. The fingers were long and hard as sticks. The wrist was covered with thick, black bristles. He imagined showing it to Smedley Trowbridge. Maybe the arm was garbage here in outer space, but back in Vern Hollow it would be the greatest thing ever! He could make a fortune charging kids to see it.

"Come on, Jack—it's important."

He held on to the arm.

"Give it to *me*," Grady demanded, weakly raising himself from the floor. Jack backed away. Even sick, Grady was still big.

"I said, give it."

"We can use it to get out of here," Isadora insisted. "Don't you see? That Krebs monster was showing us how."

"Shut up, braino," sniped Grady. "Creedle, you give me that thing before I jam it up your nose."

This, thought Jack, *is exactly why I hate Grady Webb*. Whenever anything good happened, there he was, with his flat face and his piggy eyes and his fat, grabby hands.

"You can't have it," he whispered.

Grady looked at him in disbelief. "What did you say?" He staggered forward.

"I said, you can't have it."

Grady held out his hand, palm up. It was damp with sweat. "Last chance, Creedle."

"Please," Isadora repeated. Her voice was urgent. "I need the arm, Jack, the arm."

"I can't." If he gave it to her, he would take a beating, probably a bad one. Grady moved a step closer. The last thing Jack needed was another beating. Reluctantly he held out the arm. Grady smirked and reached to grab it.

•   •   •

WHEN HE THOUGHT about it later, Jack figured it was the smirk that did it. There was nothing he hated more than a Grady Webb smirk. As soon as he saw it, he changed his mind. Just as Grady's hand was closing on the arm, with a flick of his wrist, Jack tossed it to Isadora.

Grady couldn't believe his eyes. He lunged, but nausea slowed him. Jack rolled sideways and popped to his feet on the other side of the cell. Grady turned, breathing heavily. "You really screwed up this time, dorko. Maybe you didn't notice, but there's no place for you to run."

"I noticed," Jack said miserably.

"For heaven's sake," Isadora muttered, without looking up. "Leave him alone." She examined the arm, paying particular attention to the fingers. Now, if she could just find the proper spot on the wall . . .

Grady sneered. "You think your *girlfriend* is going to save you?"

"I doubt it."

Grady lurched forward. Isadora, preoccupied, stepped out of the way. She adjusted the lifeless hand so only the first finger pointed. Then she faced the interior wall. There were no visible clues. When she found the approximate spot where the doorway had opened for Krebs, she passed her hand lightly across its surface. Nothing, nothing, nothing . . . *wait*!

Grady pounced. Jack skittered away.

Isadora tried to ignore the distraction. She moved her palm back across the spot and felt a slight tingle. Exactly as she suspected! An energy field! She pointed the spider finger at the spot and gave it a firm poke.

Jack saw the punch coming. He ducked, and Grady's fist slammed into the porthole. Unlike the rest of the cell, the window was hard as steel. Grady screamed and bent over. Jack dove between his legs. Looking up he saw Isadora in front of him with her back turned. He felt vaguely insulted. She might at least have been *interested*.

Suddenly the wall in front of her melted. She stepped through the open doorway.

"Wait!" Jack scrambled forward on hands and knees. Grady tackled him.

"Come *on*!" Isadora said impatiently.

He wriggled forward, dragging Grady with him.

"Oh, for heaven's sake," she said and swatted Grady's mashed hand. He howled with pain and lost his grip. Jack pitched forward, straight through the opening.

Isadora placed the alien finger against the edge of the doorway. Instantly the hole began to shrink.

"No!" screamed Grady. The hole narrowed. "Stop!" He threw himself at the opening, but it was too small. Only his hand came through. Quickly he yanked it back. The hole closed.

"There's a scanner in the wall," Isadora explained. "An energy field. It responds to the pattern of an alien's index finger. That, in turn, triggers a molecular reaction, which causes the wall to dematerialize. After the doorway has opened, the process can be reversed by another touch along its edge. Fascinating, don't you think?"

"Nifty." From the other side of the wall they could hear Grady's muffled threats and the pounding of his one good hand.

"I regret having to leave him," said Isadora. "But I'm afraid he's too violent."

Jack stood up, rubbing the back of his neck. "He's a clod."

• • •

17. TIME TANGLE

THEY STOOD IN a dim hallway that curved off in both directions.

"What do we do now?" asked Jack.

"We need to find the destabilizer—which may be difficult."

"It'll be tricky, all right. Look at this place. No doors, no windows." Something scurried past their feet. It had more than a dozen legs.

"Well, we can't just stand here."

They started down the corridor, and when the passageway forked, they veered to the right. The hall divided again. This time they went left.

Trash piled in dark corners like drifting leaves. "That Krebs isn't much of a garbageman, is he?" said Jack.

"Funny, I had the impression Krebs was *female*. At any rate, I don't think she came to collect garbage. She came to give us this arm."

"*Give* us? You've got to be kidding. Why would she do that?"

"I have no idea. But you don't think she dropped it by accident, do you?"

In fact, that was exactly what he thought. "Let's go that way," he said. Jangly music began to come at them from all sides. It wasn't exactly pleasant, but at least it masked the sounds of their movement.

The ship's gravity was light; it surprised Jack how easily he bounced along the rubbery floor. He noticed the ceiling was transparent, exposing a fish-gut tangle of tubes and wires in the space above it. "Hold on, Isadora!" he whispered. "Look up!"

"What of it? All I see is a mess."

"No, over there." Beyond the ceiling's clear membrane was a wide tube, like an elevator shaft. "How do you suppose we get into it?"

"Why would we *want* to?"

"Well, we can't stay down here forever. We're probably at

the bottom level of the ship. If we want to see the good stuff, we'll have to figure out a way to go up."

"*Good* stuff?" Isadora nearly choked. The dark, damp, trash-strewn hallway was disgusting. "What *good* stuff could there possibly be on this ship?" She had no desire to crawl into any holes. But worse, it annoyed her that Jack was probably right. Their path to the cell had been *down*. To find Bud Creedle's machine, they almost certainly needed to go up. On the other hand, what would they do on a floor that was teeming with skreeps?

"I'm thinking there must be a hidden button around here," said Jack, rubbing his hand on the wall. "You know, one we could poke with that dead finger."

"What, do you expect an escalator to drop down?"

"Well, there has to be *some* way to get to the next floor."

"All right," Isadora grumbled. "You take that wall, and I'll take this one."

They passed their hands across the smooth, rubbery surface. "What exactly are we looking for anyway?"

"You feel a little tingle. Now be quiet. I have to concentrate." As if honoring her request, the crazy music stopped.

In the silence that followed, they heard a heavy *tap, tap, tap.* Footsteps! Something big was moving on more than one set of feet.

"Hurry!" whispered Jack.

Tap, tap, tap. The footsteps grew louder. Isadora tried to block them out. She concentrated on her fingertips. *Tap, tap, tap.* Suddenly the ship's music came back on, loud and cheerful and slightly mad.

"Isadora, let's get out of here!"

She shook her head impatiently. Her fingers drifted upward.

Tingle. There it was, slight but unmistakable—the spot that would open a hidden door. She raised the dead arm. Just as she placed its finger on the spot, a skreep skittered forward. Its pale eyes glowed. Its mouth dropped open, revealing sharp fangs. It hissed.

Whoosh! A loud sucking noise drowned out the music. Isadora's frizzled ponytail lifted up, followed by her jacket and purse. Jack's hunting cap sailed away, never to be seen again. As he looked up at the newly formed hole, his feet left the floor.

They flew into the shaft and an instant later flew out, spit from the tube like watermelon seeds. Scrambling to their feet, they found themselves in a wide hallway, bigger than the passage below. Broken bits of spiderweb dangled from the ceiling.

Windows lined the corridor. Jack and Isadora bolted from passage to passage, careening left, right, left in quick succession, sure they were being chased.

After the fourth turn, they skidded to a stop. The dim, narrow hallway ended abruptly. A clear pipe ran from floor to ceiling. Yellow fluid gurgled inside it.

"Where are we?" Jack panted.

"How could I possibly know?"

He stretched onto tiptoes to peek through a small round window. "Holy crap!" He popped back down.

"What is it?" Isadora looked, and gasped. "What in the world—?"

The creature inside the cell was enormous. Its round head looked like a cracked boulder, with sharp teeth jutting from the crack. Huge hands and feet ended in curved claws, and its long, clubbed tail bristled with spikes. The monster lay in a heap, its eyes closed, its sides heaving.

"What is it?" Jack whispered.

"I'm flattered you think I know." Isadora turned her head. "I wonder if there are more of them."

Jack crossed the hall and pulled himself up to another high window. "There are more, all right. Take a look at this one."

She joined him. The second beast was dramatically different, with alligator jaws and three slitted eyes. Its hard-shelled body was red splotched and shiny as wet paint. It was bigger than an elephant. "Do you think this is some kind of a zoo?"

"Yeah, the *worst* kind."

From the end of the hallway two skreeps came toward them, deep in conversation.

"Quick," Isadora hissed. "We need a place to hide."

"How about that?" A huge potted plant stood against the far wall. Its purple leaves were as thick as sausages. Curling tentacles twined like snakes.

"Do you think it's safe?"

"It's better than getting caught."

"But those tentacles—"

The skreeps were nearly upon them.

"Come on!" said Jack. He squeezed behind the plant.

Isadora followed, eyes closed, holding her breath.

The skreeps passed, still jabbering. She exhaled and rubbed her neck where she'd been expecting the tentacles to grab her.

"Look at this!" Jack's right arm passed completely through one of the leaves. He did it again. "I think some of this alien stuff ain't even here."

"It's a hologram!"

"A what?"

"A hologram. You're right, the plant isn't real. It's a three-dimensional projection, an illusion."

Jack walked all the way around it, inspecting it carefully. "You'd never guess it was a fake, would you? I wonder what else around here isn't real. Do you think those big monsters were? Say, what if this whole thing's phony—the aliens, the ship, all of it?"

"I think that's too much to hope for."

He sighed. "Yeah, I guess."

"Anyway, our objective remains unchanged. We have to find your uncle's invention and disable it."

"This is one of those needle-in-a-haystack deals, isn't it? Let's try the next level."

"And get sucked through another tube? I don't think so."

"But we don't want to get caught down here in the monster zoo! The spiders might throw us in with one of 'em, just for a laugh."

Isadora shivered. "Okay, you win. We'll look for a tube."

• • •

WHEN THEY found one, Isadora raised the dead arm.

"Wait. Do you hear that?"

She listened. A loud squawk broke through the alien music. More squawks followed like a string of curses.

"Hot dog!" said Jack. "That's Milo!"

"What are you talking about?"

"My rooster! Wait a second while I go get him."

"Don't be ridiculous," Isadora began, but Jack was already gone. Down the hallway she heard a loud screech, and seconds later he came running back with a very indignant rooster pinned to his chest.

"Hurry!" he shouted. "Push the button!"

Two angry skreeps scrambled behind him, their long legs clawing the floor. As Jack and Milo skidded into her, Isadora poked the wall. The ceiling opened. They shot like rockets into the air.

• • •

"WE'RE GOING IN!" cried Bambo. He bore down on the vacuum thrusters. The ship teetered on the edge, then spun into the gaping Medwig Gulp. It fell in a tightening spiral.

Xaafuun's stomach turned with it. She braced herself for the familiar woozy sensation of destabilized time.

It never came. Instead, the ship bucked. The current shifted backward. Time curled like a great wave. "It's breaking up!" shouted Bambo. The ship slewed sideways. Zin Zin squeaked. Droobit covered his eyes. Two other officers crawled beneath their consoles.

Above them all, the great image of the Queen flickered. Outside, stars whirled like sparks rising from a bonfire. Xaafuun felt a thin scream rise inside her. The ship tumbled. The wave broke. Time and space shattered.

• • •

JACK AND ISADORA were halfway up the tube when time came undone. They stuttered, then stopped, suspended in midair. An instant later the ship lurched, and they shot up again. Then time reversed, and they were back down at the bottom of the tube.

The ship tumbled completely over. They shot up again,

stopped, and looked at each other, utterly confused. Outside, the Medwig Gulp had begun to collapse. Inside, Jack and Isadora were suspended between decks in a clear tube. Before them was a scene of frozen chaos.

Through the tube they could see the ship's colossal engine. It was a machine of vast proportions and stunning complexity. Jack stared at it greedily, his eyes taking in pipes and hoses, glowing reactors, huge rotors, pumps, and coils, along with a dizzying array of valves, gauges, monitors, and video screens.

The engine room had been shaken like a toy. A massive computer was about to pitch forward onto the deck, while a black hose, thick as a man's arm, sprayed a frozen jet of yellow steam into the air. The now-motionless crew had clearly begun to panic. Two of the giant spiders were suspended in the air, mouths twisted in terror. Two more stood like statues inside a doorway as they tried to escape. Another skreep had been crushed beneath a bank of computers. Only its legs were visible, flailed out at weird angles across the deck.

Time restarted. Everything jolted into motion again. Jack and Isadora shot upward past more crashing equipment and struggling spiders. An instant later they were spewed out of the tube onto an open deck. Time froze again.

They found themselves in a great domed room ringed with windows; each one revealed endless starry space. Lining the circular walls were brightly lit consoles, and beside them, a dozen or more aliens had been frozen in positions of distress. Some were in the process of diving beneath their monitors, while others sprawled across the deck. A bubble-topped machine tipped crazily to one side, interrupted in midfall. Next to it, a heavier machine had already crashed. Green smoke hovered over it.

In the middle of the deck, on a thronelike chair, sat the

largest spider the children had seen yet. It was curled over, and its mouth was locked in a scream. In front of it, apparently unharmed, stood Uncle Bud's refrigerator.

Time lurched forward again. Milo flew free of Jack's arms, flapping and screeching as the ship rolled over. The bubble-topped machine hit the deck and shattered. The big monster screamed. Outside, stars swarmed like angry bees.

The ship rolled, unrolled, and then rolled back again. *Squawk!* Milo flew backward. The bubble-topped machine un-shattered. Then it smashed again.

Isadora stood up. *Wham!* She toppled backward onto the floor and tried to stand. Instead, she flew. Braced for a hard landing, she suddenly found herself suspended again, but before she could relax—*whomp!*—she crashed. The big monster screamed.

She saw Jack standing beside the destabilizer. The big alien screamed the same scream, and once more Isadora was in mid-air. Milo flew by. What was going on?

Jack rocketed out of the tube, sat up, and disappeared inside the tube again. Then he flew out and crashed.

The monster screamed.

Isadora flopped down beside Jack, and Milo flew backward. *Squawk!* Nothing made *any* sense. Slowly, carefully, Isadora and Jack crawled to a porthole. At first they only saw a speck of emerald light, but then the light grew. An orange star expanded behind it. Now the emerald light became a planet. The star lit the room, then disappeared.

Isadora felt her mind slipping. Completely overwhelmed, she tried to pull herself out of the mental tangle.

The green planet reappeared, then disappeared again. Once more, Jack stood beside the destabilizer, and the monster screamed. Milo flew by.

Isadora tried to remember what she had been thinking. The planet returned, even bigger now, reflecting the light of the orange star in rainbow swirls. It came dangerously close, receded, and came back.

"Jack," she began, wanting to ask if he thought they would crash, but he was gone. So was the planet. Isadora struggled to focus, but her mind was drowning. She struggled harder but forgot what she was struggling about.

A great weariness settled over her. She knew they were crashing. They had been crashing forever. The planet was back again, green as poison. She saw Jack, slammed into a wall, and crumpled. Milo flew away. The bubble-topped machine shattered.

Milo flew backward. The green planet became enormous, filling every window. The monster screamed.

Milo scrambled across the deck, wings flapping. Jack turned to Isadora. The ship tumbled, end over end.

Then the planet rose up and swatted them like a fly.

• • •

18. HELLEBEEZIA

"I GUESS WE'RE dead," said Jack.

An endless green plain stretched before them, flat as a table and covered with short grass. Each blade was ruler-straight. The only feature on the grassy landscape was the saucer. It crouched, nose down, like a dog sniffing at a hole.

"We aren't dead. If we were dead, we wouldn't be talking."

"It must feel like death, though," said a small creature. It perched on Jack's shoulder. "To you whose lives are so thoroughly bound by time." It was furry and yellow, with a pointed face and patient brown eyes.

"Do I know you?" Jack regarded it quizzically. "Who are you again?"

"You never remember," it chided, "at least in this scene. I am Pungo, and this is my planet: Hellebeezia."

A few feet away, Milo pecked the ground. The rooster kicked his feet, raising a small fountain of grass and soil, but as he moved on, the landscape restored itself, particle by particle. An instant later, the grass was again unblemished.

"I remember coming here on that ship," Isadora said. "We were captured by alien spiders."

"Skreeps," said Pungo. "They haven't moved. Everyone is inside the ship but you."

"So why are we out here?" asked Jack.

"I don't know, but you always are."

"We crashed," Isadora persisted. "I remember it. We were trying to escape. We had an alien arm with fingers that opened doorways." She paused, examining her own hands. "I don't know what happened to it."

"Darn!" said Jack. "I really wanted that thing."

"The point is, we were running away. We were sucked up to the top of the ship, and then time stopped making sense. Everything that happened kept repeating. Then we saw this planet in the window, but the next instant it was gone. After that it was huge, but it disappeared again. I thought my mind was being tied up in knots."

"I remember that, too," said Jack. "We were up there so long, it felt like we were always there." He frowned. "I feel the same way now—like I've always been *here*. I have, too." He shook his head. "That doesn't make any sense, does it?"

"You were caught in the tangle warp," said Pungo. "It can't make sense to you, and neither can Hellebeezia. Such places were not made for you, nor you for them."

"At least it's calm here," said Isadora.

"Yes, you always seem calm here."

Jack's mind wandered. When he came back to the present, he felt as if he had been standing in the same place for thousands of years.

"Where did you say we are?" he asked with some effort.

"Hellebeezia, inside the tangle warp. This is the calm place in the eye of the storm. I find you both extremely entertaining."

"How long have we been here?" asked Jack.

"You are *always* here. And we always converse."

"This isn't getting us anywhere!" Isadora said in frustration. "Please, Pungo, can you help us get back to Earth?"

"I always do."

"The ship is wrecked," said Jack. "Just look at it! We won't get anywhere until it's fixed."

"Do you remember how to fix it?" Pungo asked.

"Me? I can't fix it. I'm just a kid! That's an alien spaceship. I don't know the first thing about how it works."

"And yet you always tell me you are a great mechanic. You fix things routinely."

"Sure. Cars. But not flying saucers."

"Then you choose to be stuck here. We will converse more."

"No we won't," Isadora said impatiently. "We have to get out of here. Jack, you have to try to fix the ship. That's why we came outside—to see what we could do."

"You made that up! Anyway, I could *never* fix that ship. Look at the size of it! All I know is we crashed, and we couldn't have survived it. So we must be dead."

"I don't care," Isadora said stubbornly. "We *did* survive, because I say so. And we came out here to look at the damage so we could fix the ship and go back home. Do you have a better explanation?"

"No."

Pungo nodded. "I think she is right. If you wish to leave Hellebeezia, you must make up a story about how you got here and how you will depart. Without a story, you will stand here forever, in the calm center of a tangle warp. Stories are what make you time creatures move. I have grown very fond of them. They are like little bubbles. They make my head fizz. So make up another story—about ships, and repairs, and desperate struggles." He paused, and the moment drifted on. "A word of advice, though. In stories there is time, and in time, consequences. Be careful, then, that you create your story well."

Isadora nodded, her expression serious. "That makes sense."

"It does not!" Jack scoffed. "It's completely loony."

"So," she said, ignoring him, "this is our story. We left the ship to see if we could fix it. That's when we met Pungo, and he agreed to help us. Didn't you agree, Pungo?"

"I always agree. I am very agreeable."

Jack gazed across the even plain. The air was mild and absolutely still. He took a deep breath. It felt good. He wondered if he had been breathing all along. "I guess I might find tools inside the ship."

"I seem to recall that's where you find them," said Pungo.

• • •

THE SHIP had been frozen in midcrash. Huge chunks of Hellebeezian sod hung in the air around it like strange ornaments. Jack led them inside with Pungo on his shoulder. Isadora followed, a step ahead of Milo, who was unwilling to be left alone on the strange planet.

They made their way through wide corridors and dark, narrow tubes. Though she despised closed spaces, Isadora moved doggedly, trying to shake the feeling that eternity might freeze her in place and seal her inside forever. Meanwhile Jack moved with confidence, guided by some fundamental instinct about engines and where to find them.

They slid down some passages and worked laboriously up

others. On the way, they passed piles of broken equipment and dozens of skreeps, all of them stuck in the positions they'd been in when the ship crashed.

Finally they dropped through a hatch into the engine room. It was in even worse shape now. Many of the mechanisms were smashed, and others had toppled. The reactors had been extinguished.

They walked among broken cables, twisted pipes, and dangling webs. The contorted position of one skreep suggested a violent death, while two others were merely stuck in place, eyes wide, mouths locked in grimaces of fear. A fourth lay pinned beneath machinery.

Jack took it all in. "It's the greatest thing I ever saw!"

"I'm glad you like it," Isadora said drily. "But can you *fix* it?"

He walked around an enormous turbine that had been pulled loose from its moorings. "I guess so," he said finally, sizing up the colossal machine. "But it's going to take time."

Pungo chuckled. "I always love it when you say that."

• • •

THE ALIEN tools were strange, ugly devices, designed for alien fingers. Jack organized them by size, then by shape. He boxed them up and carried them around the engine room until gradually he began to understand the purpose of each one. Then he examined the engine in minute detail, going slowly from section to section. It may have taken days, or years, or centuries. On Hellebeezia, there simply was no time.

Isadora watched, sometimes fascinated, but often bored. For relief she asked Pungo questions, never sure that she hadn't asked them before. Once, she saw Jack's face exactly as she had seen it on that first day in Vern Hollow, and she realized that the déjà vu she had felt then had been a memory of the eternity she was spending now. Today, tomorrow, and yesterday had all merged into one. In a world without time, they were all the same thing.

She mulled it over and then asked Pungo the question that had been troubling her. "Why is it always just *us* here? Why are we the only ones talking and thinking and moving around? What about the others?" She worked up her courage to ask the most horrible question of all. "Mother isn't dead, is she? They aren't all dead?"

Pungo cocked his head. "This thought always troubles you. She is not dead, nor are any of the others, as far as I know. They simply *are*, as they have always been."

"Then why aren't they *here* now? Why isn't anyone helping us fix the ship?"

Jack climbed down a ladder and joined them. "I've been wondering about that myself."

"Ah," said Pungo, "I see what you ask. Think of it as a difference in your perceptions of time. For you, eternity is impossibly long, and timelessness goes on forever. Others see it differently. For them, eternity is no time at all, the space between nanoseconds. Both are correct. The mystery is why you choose to experience the same thing so differently."

Isadora turned the idea over in her mind. "I think I understand," she said.

"I don't." Jack climbed up the ladder and went back to work.

Isadora tried to be helpful, but she never understood the engine or how it worked. She was amazed at the way Jack went about his job, patient as a detective. When he found a damaged mechanism, he always knew what it was and which strange tool would be most effective at fixing it.

"How do you know what you're doing?" she finally asked.

"It speaks to me," Jack said softly. "At first I could barely hear it, because it was injured in the crash. But it's healing now, and that makes it easier to understand."

She scowled. "What do you mean, it speaks to you? Are you talking about the ship? I don't hear anything."

"I know it sounds weird," he said, slightly embarrassed. "But it's true. It's like a voice in my head, telling me what to do. Not that it uses words or anything. It just—I don't know." He shrugged and went back to work.

She turned to Pungo. "Is that true?"

The creature nodded. "He always says so."

. . .

19. A DILEMMA

FINALLY THE work was done. The engine looked like new, the ship stood upright, and Jack was certain every bit of damage had been repaired. They stood on the open plain and regarded his handiwork with satisfaction.

"We still need to figure out how to launch it."

Isadora rubbed the bridge of her nose beneath her glasses. "Right. But there's another problem. If we take off, won't we fly back into the tangle warp?"

"I didn't think of that. What if we get stuck up there? I'm not sure I could stand it."

They stood absolutely still. Pungo glanced from one to the other. "Perhaps you need another story."

"Another story?" Hellebeezia still made Isadora slightly

dizzy. "Another story. Of course—something that will help us get off this planet and back to ordinary time."

"To your own universe," Pungo agreed. "A place ruled by clocks." He made a ticking sound with his tongue. "It is where you belong, so you must go back there. I would miss you except that you are always here."

"You lost me again," said Jack.

Isadora was deep in thought. "Our next story has to be about learning to fly the ship."

Jack's face brightened. "Maybe if we figure that out, we can fly all the way home!"

"That certainly is a story," Pungo observed.

"Let's not get ahead of ourselves," said Isadora. "Leaving Hellebeezia is going to be tricky enough. For one thing, we have no idea where we are. Your uncle spoke of holes through space-time. I think we just went through one. Which means that even if we escape the tangle warp, we might end up almost anywhere. We'll have no idea how to get back home. And as soon as time starts up, everyone on the ship will revive—including the skreeps."

"Which will put us right back in the same old mess. Hey, I have an idea. Why don't we just leave them here? We can unload them from the ship while they're asleep, or whatever it is they are, and take off without them!" He cackled.

"It cannot be done," said Pungo. "The skreeps are never here on Hellebeezia, except as they are now—insensate and inside their ship. Whereas you two are always here and always not here."

Jack squeezed his eyes shut. "I hate it when you say stuff like that."

"We have two options," Isadora said thoughtfully. "We can

figure out how to launch the ship and take our chances with the tangle warp. In that case we will still be prisoners, and the skreeps will probably treat us badly, but at least we'll have some chance of going home." She paused. "Or we can stay here."

"We should definitely stay here."

"I didn't say that. The other thing to consider is the destabilizer. We could be anywhere in the universe by now, so it may be our only real hope of getting home. But that leaves us with an even bigger problem, because in all likelihood the skreeps will take the destabilizer as soon as we try to use it. In that case we'll still be doomed, but even worse, Earth will be doomed as well. And it will all be *our* fault."

"Yeah. I liked it better when it was Uncle Bud's fault."

Isadora took a deep breath. "Which means there's no point in Mother's plan to wreck the destabilizer. We either take our chances that we can steal it back somehow, or we stay right here."

"In that case," said Pungo, "your dilemma is solved."

"It is?"

"Certainly. You are always here, but you are always not here. That means that you must leave, because otherwise you would not always not be here." He gave them a satisfied look.

Isadora sighed. Jack rubbed his head.

"It is simple logic," added Pungo, "which you taught me, by the way."

• • •

ON THE BRIDGE everything remained as it had been at the point of impact. The captain sat harnessed to her seat, her body curled into a tight ball. Isadora climbed onto the dais

and inserted herself with some delicacy between Xaafuun
and the ship's instruments. She touched the central monitor.
Something faint, like a pulse, stirred in her fingertips.

She thought about how the ship had communicated to Jack
in the engine room. She wondered if it was speaking to her
now. Patiently she stroked the monitor. To her amazement it
gradually came to life, purring in a way that was part mechanical, part organic. It spoke to her. At first she didn't understand
a single thing it said. Frustration rose inside her, but the purring continued, and she drifted into a long trance.

"The ship thinks we're different," she finally said in a dreamy voice.

Jack looked up from Bambo's charts, not sure if she was talking to him. "Different from what?"

"The skreeps. They aren't curious like we are."

"They aren't?"

"Not at all. They never ask the ship any questions. They don't try to learn anything just for the sake of knowing. The ship says they have no curiosity, only appetite." She paused. "I'm learning a lot."

"Are you learning how to fly this thing?"

She seemed surprised by the question. "Oh, yes, I learned that ages ago."

•   •   •

THEY STOOD in the field again, looking at the ship. Emerald grass spread in all directions, unruffled and unbent. Isadora sighed. "I suppose we must go."

"It's time," Jack agreed. "Or *something.*"

Pungo, perched on his shoulder, patted his ear. "I am sad that you are always gone. Yet I am happy because you are always here."

Isadora looked at the creature earnestly. "Do you think we're doing the right thing? I mean, by leaving?"

"You are doing the *fated* thing," said Pungo. "Beyond that, I cannot say. It seems too busy to me, this life of time, but it is your life, after all." He hopped down to the grass. Using a sharp claw, he cut out a perfect square of sod. "For you," he said and handed it up to Isadora.

It smelled sweet, in a quiet way, like clover back home. But she was puzzled.

"I always give you this gift when you depart."

"Thank you." Isadora placed it gently in her purse.

"What's it for?" asked Jack.

"Who knows? Here in Hellebeezia, outside of time, there is no illness, no disease, no suffering. Maybe this will protect you, or cure you if you are ill. Maybe it will do nothing at all. Maybe it will simply remind you that you are always here."

"I still don't get that," Jack confessed. "I don't see how we can leave and still be here."

"It is so simple," Pungo replied. "Hellebeezia is eternal, and you are part of it."

"Well, sure." Jack raised an eyebrow.

"Don't you see? A thing cannot be eternal for just *a little while*. Therefore you are always here. Eternally."

Isadora nodded. "I see what you mean."

"Surely being here eternally will help you where you are going."

"I'm sure it will," Isadora said politely.

"I guess so," muttered Jack.

• • •

JACK AND ISADORA stood on the bridge, looking out at the flat horizon.

"The ship knows what to do," said Isadora, "and so do I. Just be ready, and I'll tell you which buttons to push."

"All right," said Jack. Milo let out a low grumble.

"Okay, the green one. And then the blinking red one just above it. Now pull down that switch on the right."

He did what she told him.

"Okay, the two overhead switches now."

A vibration ran through the soles of their feet. The saucer's rim began to turn.

Isadora swallowed hard. *I'm still making up a story*, she thought, yet she could feel time pulling her back into its own narrative. "We'll be thrown free of the tangle warp as soon as we launch," she told Jack. "The ship says so. It tells me we would have been thrown free anyway, except the planet Hellebeezia got in the way."

"And then what happens?"

"Who knows? As soon as time starts up again, everything will change."

The saucer lifted off the ground.

Time snapped back into place. The planet was gone. The cold darkness of space replaced Hellebeezia's mild afternoon. Everything that had been frozen came to life. Screams and shouts sounded from every corner of the ship.

On the bridge, Commander Xaafuun began to uncurl. Her yellow eyes peered out at Isadora.

"What are you doing at my console?" she hissed.

. . .

20. DUNGEONS

XAAFUUN STARED at the two *Uurth* hatchlings and the richly feathered *buurd*. Her mind was muddled. She understood the Medwig had collapsed and shattered the ordinary sequence of time. But she did not understand why *Uurthish* hatchlings—and a *buurd*—were on her bridge.

Old stories about *ooman bing* sorcery came to mind. She brushed them aside. But the creatures' talent for escape was no myth. "What are you doing here?" she hissed again.

The hatchlings stared at her mutely. She examined them.

They were stranger than the others. She sensed secret knowledge, maybe even power. It made her uneasy.

"It's hard to explain," the male hatchling finally said. "But so's you know, we saved the ship."

"Saved it!" Xaafuun felt a rising wave of fury. The sheer insolence of the creatures astonished her. "I saw you on the bridge before the collapse," she snarled. "You were not *saving* the ship then, were you?"

"Well, not then."

"I saw you! You were trying to *destroy* the ship! And you nearly succeeded! Saboteurs!" She allowed righteous anger to eclipse her knowledge that the Medwig's collapse had nothing to do with them. She didn't care. They had obviously done *something*. And anger was comforting. She addressed Droobit. "Send Groot up here."

Moments later, the dungeon keeper popped through the floor. "You called me, Madame Commander?"

Xaafuun shoved the hatchlings forward. "I believe these are yours," she said coldly. Her face was composed, but the guard understood the danger he was in.

"I don't know how they escaped, Madame. It isn't possible, really. That is, unless the crash—"

"Take them to the lowest dungeon, fool. Double lock it—with chains. If they get out again, you will be dismembered and fed to the beasts. Do you understand? And take this *buurd*, too."

"Yes, Madame Commander." Groot bound the children roughly, and with great difficulty managed to capture the rooster. The bird continued to attack him as he carried them away.

Now it was time for Xaafuun to face bigger problems. She let out a slow breath. "Bambo," she said, "where are we?"

The navigator had been working furiously since they emerged from the tangle warp. His lips trembled. "I don't know," he whispered. "I don't have a single reference point! Not one of these stars is familiar."

"Then probe deeper, you imbecile!" Xaafuun slumped in her chair, nervously tapping her console with one claw. Outside, the strange stars winked at her brazenly. They could be literally anywhere in the universe! She tried to calculate their odds of survival. There weren't any! Nobody ever came back from such a collapse. They should all be dead.

Fear swept through her like a cold wind. Her eyes darted across the room, finally settling on the mysterious *Uurth* machine, the thing that was *not* a refrigerator. Of course! The Special Item! It was their only chance.

She lifted her communicator. "Groot!" she barked. "After you put those hatchlings in their cell, grab the other *ooman bing*, the inventor, and bring him to me! Quickly! You know the one."

"The female, Madame?"

"No, idiot! Don't you ever pay attention? The *male*! The scrawny, odious little male!" She clicked the communicator shut. *Things are not hopeless,* she told herself. *Surely the Special Item will save me.*

• • •

"I WISH ONE of you eggheads would tell me what just happened!" Sergeant Webb sat on the floor next to Grady, opening and closing his fists. His face was haggard, and sweat soaked through his khaki shirt.

Dr. Shumway stood at the window. The stars had resumed their fixed positions within the wide firmament, but what stars! She could not identify a single one. "I, too, feel sorely agitated," she said. "Clearly the natural order of things has been overturned. I expect we have experienced the collapse that the skreepish captain warned us about. However, I am most concerned about my daughter—and the Creedle boy, of course." She turned to Grady. "Please tell me again where they went."

"How should I know? I told you, they bugged out on me."

"Which doesn't surprise me a bit," grumbled his father. "That's the way it is with Creedles. Always pulling something. Right, Grady? Snuck off when you weren't looking, didn't they?"

"I was *sick*. And I hurt my hand. Otherwise I would have had 'em, honest. Besides, I think they're in cahoots with the spiders."

"That's what I said all along, son. This whole thing stinks to

high heck. Just remember they're still on this ship somewhere. We'll get 'em soon enough."

"I would appreciate it," Dr. Shumway said in an icy voice, "if you would refrain from speaking about these children as if they were criminals. My daughter is a gifted student and a promising young scientist. The boy is—well, he's a boy."

"And for the record, he's half Murchison," Bud interjected.

Dr. Shumway shot him a poisonous look.

"I'm just saying you can't pin everything on the Creedles."

"At any rate," she continued, "if they truly left of their own volition—which I believe they did"—she raised an eyebrow at Grady—"I think we can assume they were attempting to locate and destroy Mr. Creedle's troublesome machine. Which leads me to another question. I wonder, Mr. Creedle, if what we have experienced conforms in any way to your understanding of destabilized space-time? To the 'holes' you were describing?"

"This don't conform to my understanding of *anything*. All of that forward-backward-forward stuff was bad enough, but that ain't the worst of it." He chewed his lip. "Right at the end, the herky-jerky stopped, and time went normal again. Do you *remember*?" His voice cracked. "The saucer was falling end over end like a flipped nickel."

"Which means?" Dr. Shumway asked.

"The thing is, we *crashed*," he said quietly. "That green planet in the window was too close to miss. All I saw was grass. I figured it was the last thing I'd ever see." He stroked his mustache. "Only now—somehow—I'm here."

Dr. Shumway had seen the same thing. "I can't explain it, either."

The Webbs glared at both of them with red-faced hostility.

"I guess we *could* be dead now," Bud muttered, "but this ain't exactly my idea of heaven."

Ffftt. The cell doorway suddenly melted open, and a skreep stepped in. Grady whimpered, and the others crowded around him. Dr. Shumway braced herself, expecting to be snatched away again. But this time the monster skittered past her, seizing Bud by both arms. Sticky cables shot from its abdomen and bound him like a mummy.

"What about the others?" Bud squealed. "What did *I* do?"

"You know exactly what you did." Dr. Shumway lowered her voice to a harsh whisper. "You as much as told them you invented the machine. So now you need to keep your mouth *shut* for a change. Your conduct must be above reproach! The fate of our planet depends on it."

Groot lifted Bud and shoved him under one arm.

"That's easy for you to say!" Bud screamed as they passed through the door.

"I regret your predicament, Mr. Creedle," she called after him, "but please remember what is at stake here!"

. . .

21. A HARD BARGAIN

COMMANDER XAAFUUN looked down at the terrified *Uurthling* from the height of her dais. She disliked how tightly he had been bound. It suggested a fear on Groot's part that the *ooman bings* could escape at will. Could they? She pushed aside her own doubts. "Please release the creature, Groot. This is a *reasonable Uurthling*. We will have a reasonable conversation."

Soon Bud stood in a pile of sticky cords, trying to rub the goo off his arms and legs. His suit was badly rumpled, and his hat had been smashed. He looked as if he'd crawled out of a garbage truck.

"I will be frank, *ooman*," Xaafuun began. "We have undergone a great disaster. Until now, an enormous time tunnel has made travel between our planets possible. You may not know this, since *ooman bings* are not space-faring creatures, but—excuse me, I do not know what you are called—"

"Bud Creedle, Your Honor."

"*Bug Greedle*. As I was saying, I perceive that you, Bug Greedle, know something about time tunnels."

He looked up at her doubtfully. "I wouldn't necessarily say *that*, no."

"We mustn't be coy with each other, Bug Greedle. The time for such playfulness has passed. This tunnel I speak of, this Medwig Gulp, has collapsed. I think you know that. The event was dramatic, was it not? It was only through my skillful piloting that we survived."

"Thank you, Your Honor! I thought we were dead when I saw that green planet. Say, how *did* we get out of there?"

Uncertainty flickered in the captain's eyes, but she quickly suppressed it. "What is more important is this. The force of such an event—the collapse of a major time tunnel—is tremendous, almost inconceivable. We have been thrown a great distance—an *extraordinarily* great distance—off course. We can scarcely hope to overcome it by *ordinary* means. Do you understand?"

Bud swallowed and nodded. "I guess you'll be looking for another one of them holes."

"Precisely." Xaafuun gave him a keen look. She let him simmer in an uncomfortable silence. When she spoke again her voice was calm, almost soothing. "There are many *natural* holes in space, Bug Greedle, but relatively few are useful. Some are too narrow, some too dangerous. Some lead to dimensions that are not fit to receive us. Some discharge into radiation fields, or the blast zones from quasars and nebulae. Most lead nowhere at all, to more and more empty, dismal space." She allowed her words to sink in. "The point is, Bug Greedle, that a ship enters an unknown time tunnel only at great peril. No explorer, however desperate, would *ever* attempt to escape uncharted space by following uncharted tunnels. The chance of success in such a venture is nonexistent."

"It's a pickle, all right," said Bud.

Xaafuun paused at the word. "Yes, a *pickle*. A monstrous, ugly pickle. The *Feast of Happiness* is lost. Bambo, my navigator, searches his charts and finds nothing, not a single familiar reference point. Therefore, we wander. What will happen as the ship exhausts its supplies? *Food*, for instance."

"Food." Bud's left eyelid began to twitch uncontrollably.

"Food. After all, my crew must eat *something*." The commander's many eyes glowed. "I do not *threaten*, I merely explain. Truly I would prefer any other outcome." Her gravelly voice lowered. "If only there was some other way."

"You know there is," Bud muttered, almost inaudibly.

"Yes, I believe there is. Please, Bug Greedle, explain this device."

"The thing is," he began unhappily, "I know this is not important to *you*, but I was supposed to get *paid* for it. A million bucks, which ain't chicken feed."

"Paid?" A gurgling sound escaped the commander's throat. Some of her officers gurgled, too. "You are concerned about *money*? We are hundreds of light-years into untracked space, and this is your concern? You are an interesting *ooman*, Bug

Greedle. So greedy! I almost admire it!" She laughed, stretching her arms wide. "Rest assured, if we make it back to either of our planets, you will be amply rewarded."

"Well, that's part of it, Your Honor. The other thing is . . ." He gulped nervously. "Some of my friends are worried that once you know how to operate this here machine . . . well . . . you might decide to use it against us. Earth, I mean."

"Use it against *you*!" Xaafuun leered, as if savoring the absurdity. "Bug Greedle, we shall be great friends, you and I. Skreeps are always good to our friends. And skreeps always keep promises. I promise, Bug Greedle, that the Special Item will never be used in any way to harm *Uurth*."

Bud smiled tightly. "Well, I guess that's all I can ask."

"You have driven a hard bargain, Bug Greedle. Very hard, very clever. Now, will you please show me how to use this wonderful machine? *Do we have a deal?*"

"A deal." Bud stepped over to the refrigerator and patted its enameled top. "What we have here," he continued with a note of pride, "is a dimensional field destabilizer. You guessed that, didn't you? What she does is this: She makes fourth-dimensional tunnels. Anytime, anywhere. Course, I ain't tested her in space, not having the opportunity until now. But I expect she'll get us out of this fix." He gave Xaafuun another tight smile. "Just give me some time to hook her up."

The commander struggled to hide her elation. She had been right about the Special Item and about its inventor, too. The pathetic little wretch! She watched him closely as he pressed a lock and opened the Item's door. Inside was a tangled mass of multicolored wires. Normally it would have galled her to be asked to promise good faith and undying friendship—but really, the lie was so outrageous it was amusing. And Bug Greedle trusted her. She eyed him with satisfaction.

After all, threats only went so far. Some situations called for diplomacy.

• • •

IT WAS COLD in the dungeon and getting colder. Jack and Isadora blew on their hands and stuffed them into their armpits. After a while, reluctantly, they leaned against each other. Back to back, they shared what little body heat they had.

Milo finally quit complaining and hunkered down on Jack's lap. The stars rode beneath them, visible through a great, curved window at their feet. They were the only inhabitants of the ship's lowest level, a small cave accessible only by a metal grate many feet overhead. The cell was locked in the conventional way, with heavy chains and dull hardware.

"I wish I had my picks," said Jack.

"Why? Would you like to get us into *more* trouble?"

The dungeon was dank and awful. Even the air felt worn out, as if it had been breathed too many times. Jack stuffed his hands into his coat pockets. His fingers stumbled across something small and furry. "Did I ever show you this?" he asked, holding it up in the near darkness. "It's my lucky rabbit's foot."

"No, you didn't show me. Anyway, I think it's barbaric."

"It isn't like I killed the rabbit. They had a whole bin full of 'em at Healy's Five and Dime. I took this green one, because green is the color of luck."

"It certainly isn't the color of rabbits."

"No." Jack hadn't thought about that. "I guess it's just food coloring. They stuck a key chain on it, too."

"Well, I can't imagine that a stolen object could be lucky."

"Who says I stole it?" He *had* stolen it, but still . . . He rubbed the foot again, then put it back in his pocket. "We could use some luck right now, is all I'm saying." He decided to change the subject. "You know, I noticed something when that guard was hauling us down here."

Isadora blew on her hands. "What?"

"Remember when we first escaped from Grady, before the crash? Those crazy hallways upstairs were full of all kinds of stuff—statues, fountains, plants. But now all that stuff is gone."

"It is?"

"Yeah. So I'm thinking maybe all that stuff was hollowgrabbers—and it blew out in the crash."

"*Holograms*, Jack. And I don't think they could *blow out*. But now that you mention it, I don't remember seeing any of them when the ship was on Hellebeezia, either."

Jack stroked Milo's feathers, and the rooster bit his hand. "I'll tell you one thing. I wish we were back there now."

"We *are* there, according to Pungo." Isadora shivered from the cold. "It's something to consider, though."

"What?"

"Holograms are optical illusions. The objects aren't really there. It would make sense if you couldn't see them once time stopped, because they're basically tricks of light and motion. I'm guessing when time stops, you can only see what's real."

"Maybe. But that wouldn't explain why we can't see them now."

"No," she said. "I guess it wouldn't."

• • •

"HOW LONG is this going to take?" Xaafuun asked impatiently. A tangle of wires now ran from the back of the refrigerator to the base of Bambo's workstation.

"It'll take however long it takes," Uncle Bud muttered. "It ain't like I've done this before, you know."

"But you're certain it will work?"

"Well, I wouldn't say *certain*. I've tested it, if that's what you mean."

Xaafuun drummed on the console menacingly.

"You know, even when I start her up, it's going to be tricky finding our way back. I mean, we'll be popping our heads up like gophers until we can get a good read on where we are."

"Govers?" The commander regarded him sternly. "There will be no *govers* on my ship, and no head popping."

"You misunderstand. What I mean is, we can't fly blind. And as I understand it, there's no way to fix coordinates from inside a time tunnel. So we'll have to come out and look around until we know where we are."

"Yes, of course." Xaafuun waved at him with one of her arms. Navigation bored her. She went back to drumming. A durbo song came through the speakers: "Plump and Juicy." She hummed along.

Many songs later Uncle Bud finally stood up. Inside the cabinet, Xaafuun caught another glimpse of spinning wheels, colored wires, and glowing tubes. Bud jiggled something, then closed the door again. "I think she's ready."

Xaafuun dropped down from the dais. The crew stopped to watch the small *Uurthling* and his odd machine. "Turn it on!"

Uncle Bud nodded to Bambo. The navigator tapped his keyboard, then reached for his overhead console. He threw a series of switches.

Uncle Bud stepped back. The destabilizer began to hum.

Xaafuun stared from the device to its inventor. "When will it start working?"

"Give it a second. It has to warm up."

Suddenly the ship began to vibrate. A steady purr ran along the deck. Outside, the stars wobbled. Then they began to twirl.

Xaafuun's stomach lurched as the hole opened, and the flying saucer shot inside. It was a familiar sensation, slipping the bonds of ordinary time. She had experienced it not only in grand tunnels like the Krablops Chasm and the Medwig Gulp, but in dozens of smaller passageways, too. Yet this sensation was something new. Even the Medwig in its prime had been a dirt road by comparison. So even! So smooth! It was glorious.

She returned to her captain's chair and leaned back with a happy sigh.

• • •

22: UURTH KING

THE GUARD came by from time to time, mostly to poke at them or to taunt them with words they didn't understand. His name was Groot—they got that much. He was foul, even by skreepish standards.

Groot made it clear that their earlier escape was a personal insult. On his third visit, he dumped a bucket of icy water on their heads. After that they were twice as cold, but at least they weren't so thirsty. Water pooled in the curved window at their feet, and they twisted around to suck some of it up. Milo drank, too.

Hours passed before the monster brought them food: a foot-long, sausage-shaped tube with a valve at one end. Jack squeezed a thin drizzle of white paste onto the back of his hand. He sniffed it, then gave it a delicate lick. He made a face. "Tastes like old socks."

"Doesn't it concern you that you haven't the faintest idea what it is?"

He licked his hand clean, then squirted more of the stuff directly into his mouth. He shrugged. "You gotta eat sometime."

"I don't have to eat *yet*."

Footsteps pattered overhead, and they braced themselves for another bucket of water. But this time the monster wasn't the guard, it was the garbage collector, Krebs. She wiggled her fingers at them. "You like that food, hum?"

Jack swallowed another glob of paste. "It's okay."

"It not kill you, mebbe. And you get *wadder*, too? Dat good.

Ooman bings like wadder. Insides as soggy as fishes probly."
She pointed at the heavy lock and chain. "Dat arm I gib you
no good down here, hum?"

"I told you she did it on purpose," whispered Isadora, elbow-
ing Jack. She addressed Krebs. "We lost it, but thank you."

"Sure. Krebs plenty good friend to *oomans*." She looked
around. "Don't tell nobody, hum?"

"We won't tell." Isadora smiled. "You speak our language
very well."

"Sure. Krebs plenty good wit landwitches." She lowered
her voice to a conspiratorial whisper. "Krebs know the *rebel*
landwitches most, mebbe."

Jack and Isadora looked at her uncertainly. "Rebel?" they
whispered back.

"Suure! *Yarmuk, gareen, buska-mow-mow.* All dem
rebels." She lowered her voice even more. "Mebbe *ooman
bings* rebels, too, hum?" She raised a single finger to the
corner of her leftmost eye and fluttered her other fingers
like a butterfly. Then she pushed away from the grate, and
disappeared.

"Do you have any idea what that was about?" Jack
whispered.

"Not a clue."

A tremor ran through the floor, up their legs, and into their
heads. The ship began to vibrate. Stars bounced like Ping-Pong
balls.

Their stomachs turned. A sleepy feeling followed, and the
cold cell warmed up. "I wonder if your uncle's machine is
doing that?"

"Wouldn't surprise me a bit," said Jack. He gave his rabbit's
foot another rub.

• • •

IT WAS NEVER clear how long the ship wandered, or how far. Time and space were meaningless inside the tunnels, and they traveled almost randomly. They only popped up to fix coordinates. In this way they obliterated hundreds of light-years, and yet remained utterly lost.

Eventually the skreeps let Uncle Bud sit down. They brought him an ordinary plaid armchair, most likely pilfered from some house in Vern Hollow.

Looking down at the *Uurthling*, Xaafuun wished she had placed the destabilizer elsewhere. It was unsettling to have the little beast situated so nearby. Yet boredom always plagued her, and growing bored, she began to think of the *ooman bing* as an ugly pet, a creature so unworthy she could speak to him without concern. "It won't really matter if we make it back to Skreepia now," she confided during a quiet moment when her officers were busy.

Uncle Bud looked up, startled. "No?"

"Not for my career. I'm finished. Ruined." She sighed. "The Queen will have a field day with this adventure. 'Wrong Way Xaafuun' and all that."

Bud leaned forward in his armchair. "It wasn't your fault the tunnel collapsed."

"Nobody likes an unlucky commander, Bug Greedle. And we'll almost certainly miss the Jubilee, which in itself would be enough to ruin me. Even if we don't, I may not have enough beasts left to fight."

"You lost me. What jubilee are you talking about?"

The captain chuckled. "Really, you *ooman bings* are so ignorant! This long cycle—if we are still in it!—marks the Queen's twenty-fifth anniversary in power—her Fabulous

Jubilee. It's the biggest event in the universe. The highlight will be the games in the Grand Arena. Her captains have traveled all over the empire to gather the most ferocious beasts alive. Ten for each captain. They'll fight match after match." Her eyes gleamed, thinking about it—the wonderful pageantry, the excitement, the smell of death. "It goes on for weeks. The winning captain will receive a fortune, enough to retire with honors to the court!"

"What about the losers?" asked Bud.

She shrugged. "The losers get fed to the winning beast."

"Tough tournament."

"It will provide amusement. If I could make it back in time, I believe I could win. I have good beasts, gathered from the most notorious planets." She scowled. "All except for one. And that one has proven to be a menace to all the others."

"You don't say? A bad beast?"

"Beast Eleven! I'm sorry I ever captured the evil brute. It came from Gelm, which should have told me something. Horrible planet, Gelm. Nothing but poisonous vegetation and *oomalids*. We trade with the *oomalids* from time to time, and they make reasonably good slaves, but they are so primitive. I was negotiating with their chief when he told me about the beast. He called it 'Lord of the Wild' or some such nonsense. He went on and on about its strength, its speed, and its ferocity. Said it was the master of all creatures, a god. So I sent a team out with photon guns, and we caught it. I was impressed. It killed nine of my crew before the tranquilizers brought it down."

"Nine?"

She let out a hiss of frustration. "By the way, you probably think we were treated like heroes when we freed the *oomalids* from their most fearsome enemy. But no, that was not the case. I will tell you something I've learned from hard experience, Bug Greedle: Savages are never satisfied! When we returned, they rioted. Imagine that! All Beast Eleven ever did was rip them to pieces, but they wanted the vicious thing *back*! That's barbarians for you. They claimed the monster made them *free*. I should have let them keep it. Beast Eleven has been nothing but trouble since it came on board."

"I wonder," said Uncle Bud. "It sounds like a fighter. You might want to put some money on that one."

"You haven't seen it. Neither had I, until after we left Gelm. If I had, I might have thrown it back. It's murderous, to be sure, but it isn't particularly big, and it isn't armored or poisonous. It doesn't have any weapons beyond teeth and claws. In the arena, that is never enough."

"Why not kill it, then?"

"Do you think I haven't tried? We fed it enough poison to destroy an army. It only overslept and then woke up in a bad mood. Firing weapons on the ship is out of the question, and the crew is terrified. Every now and then it's gotten loose and killed one of my other fighters."

"Well, don't give up," said Bud, giving the destabilizer a pat. "We're bound to find a way out of this mess before too long."

. . .

BUT TIME passed, however randomly, and the odd, hopscotch journey continued. Whenever they emerged from a time tunnel, Bambo studied his star charts, made notes, and then simply guessed the best way to proceed. Xaafuun settled into a deepening funk. "Ruined, ruined," she muttered.

"I've been thinking about your situation," Bud said the next time they were alone.

Xaafuun eyed him with predatory intensity. He squeezed

the arms of his chair and stumbled on. "I think you need to *sell* this thing a little."

"*Sell?*" She looked around. "Sell *what?*"

"This trip we're on. If we make it back to your planet, you'll want to sell the idea that your mission wasn't a big screwup."

"But it is. It's the worst navigational blunder ever."

"Not if you look at it the right way. You flew farther, *faster* than anyone in history. How many hundreds of light-years have you gone? Nobody even knows! And you did it in a totally new way, making your own passages. Think about it. You're a trailblazer! A pioneer!"

She remained skeptical. "Perhaps."

"Perhaps *nothing*!" He leaned forward, emphasizing with his hands. "And get this—you didn't just *find* the destabilizer, you *captured* it."

"Captured?"

"In battle! With me, the Wizard King of all Earth. Bombs exploding, rockets—you name it. You and your crew were surrounded by hordes of hostile Earthlings. And me—I don't know, I was casting spells. Wizard stuff. But you conquered me anyway!"

She scoffed. "The Queen knows that isn't true. It was her idea to have you build the destabilizer in the first place. You're no king, you're just an inventor. And me? She merely sent me to collect it."

"So the *Queen* is *Mr. X*? *She's* the one who got me to build the destabilizer?" Bud shook his head. "I might have known."

"The Exalted One has knowledge of every planet in her Empire, and her plans are deep." Xaafuun lowered her voice. "Still she is often hazy about details. For instance, she had no clear idea where the Special Item was hidden."

"I shouldn't have panicked," said Bud disgustedly. "You

never would have found it. But that's beside the point now. The point is, the Queen will love my story. Why? Because it makes her look *good*. Everyone likes to look good! Imagine when she tells your planet about her victory. They'll *all* like it, you know why? Because it makes *everybody* look good."

Xaafuun smirked. "You, especially."

"Okay. But think about it. What makes a better story? Capturing a garage mechanic or a *king*?"

She let it sink in. Finally she drew back her lips, revealing the tips of her fangs. "You *are* devious."

• • •

JACK AND ISADORA were dozing when the grate rattled. Groot jammed a bony arm through the bars and poked at them. "Here come *Uurth* King," he grunted, then opened the door and withdrew. Two seconds later Uncle Bud plopped into the cell. His appearance was shocking. A string of chunky jewels circled his neck, and his head and body were decorated with bright red, green, and yellow feathers. His glasses glittered, his cheeks were rouged, and his mustache had been dyed black.

"Uncle Bud," said Jack reproachfully, "what are you *doing*?"

"Making myself a king, is what I'm doing!" he snapped. "It's a little complicated," he added in a milder tone. "I'm taking care of our *problem*. Being a king gives me bargaining power."

"So are we going back to Earth?"

"Sure, eventually. Listen, this is how it's gonna work. I'm a king, but I'm also a wizard. You two are my spies. You're junior wizards or something. I don't know, make it up. That's how you managed to get loose back there."

"But that isn't true," said Isadora. "Anyway, how does being a spy make things better?"

"Because you work for *me*, the king. And I'm important."

"But we aren't spies. Why did you tell them that?"

Uncle Bud threw his hands up in exasperation. "I had to tell them *something*, didn't I? And you didn't give me a lot to work with. I mean, they caught you sneaking around on the bridge. You can't deny that. Who knows what you were doing there? I'll tell you one thing, the captain is mighty bent out of shape about it. Told me she might feed you to the monsters. Says you messed with her instruments, threw the ship off course."

"We did not!" cried Jack.

"I'm just telling you what *she* says. Listen, once we get back to Skreepia, I'll sort this out. I'll go right to the Queen. See how that works? She'll listen to me because I'm a *king*."

"But you aren't, Uncle Bud. You know that, don't you?"

"Sure I know." He stroked his feathers. "What do you take me for?"

"Well, Your Highness, can you at least get us out of here?"

"Ixnay. Right now you sit tight. I came here to tell you so you don't screw up my plans. You got that?" He lowered his voice. "And knock off the escape tricks. It's hard enough being the king without you two messing things up." He banged on the bars. "Groot!" he commanded. "Let me out immediately."

Groot scrambled to the door, and then Uncle Bud was gone. They listened to his footsteps recede.

Jack looked at Isadora. "We're in big trouble," he said.

part
two...
arboria

. . .

23: PUDLEYS AND HOO-HOOS

Bud switched off the destabilizer and listened as it whirred down to silence. Outside, the stars stopped dancing.

"I suppose we should have another look," Xaafuun said in a despondent voice. "See anything familiar, Bambo?"

The navigator punched numbers into his console. He plotted coordinates of all visible stars, then searched the computer data that spewed back at him. The process dragged on.

Xaafuun regarded him impatiently. Navigation was such a

bore! And now that her life depended on it, it interested her even less. She wanted her problems solved. *How* they were solved hardly mattered. "Well?" she demanded.

Bambo remained silent, furiously scanning chart after chart. Finally he magnified a field of stars on the screen overhead. A yellow circle highlighted a single bright dot. "Madame," he said, looking up excitedly, "I think I know where we are."

Xaafuun hopped down from her dais. "Where? Where are we?"

"Here!" Bambo pointed at the dot. "The Gromelik star cluster."

"Gromelik? Never heard of it. What's there?"

"Nothing, Madame, just stars. But once you're in Gromelik, the Krespid system is only a light-year away. You remember the planet Arboria? It's one of our outposts."

Arboria! How in the cosmos had they ended up *there*? Xaafuun's stomach lurched. Everyone knew the place. Horrible, wide deserts, vicious natives, an unending border war. It was the kind of planet where officers were sent as punishment. Still, they were running low on key supplies. "It has hydrogen, I believe?"

"Liquid water, Madame."

"Can we get in and out without being noticed?" *Or attacked?* "I can't tolerate delays."

"There *is* one landing place. Quite isolated, but it's within skreepish territory. And it has water."

"Set a course, then." Suddenly the captain's legs felt wobbly with relief. She climbed back onto her dais. "And be quick about it."

With the destabilizer, it was a short journey. When they popped out of their new time tunnel, Arboria appeared as a bright star straight ahead. Bud adjusted his chair so he could watch their arrival.

Xaafuun gave him an indulgent smile. She liked him better now that he was a king. If nothing else, the feathers improved his appearance. "Your first visit to an alien world, Bug Greedle?"

"You know it is." Hellebeezia had already faded from his memory. "Will we be getting out?"

"Not us! Arboria is a terrible place. We will offload garbage and take on hydrogen, nothing more. But I have been thinking. Perhaps this is the opportunity to dispose of Beast Eleven! The monster could be tranquilized and carried out with the trash." A gleeful rumble escaped from her throat. "An amusing idea, *hmm*?"

"I guess. But why not keep it? A monster like that must be worth *something*, and we're close to Skreepia now."

"So now you consider sixty-three light-years *close*?" She gurgled again, but then her voice became serious. "No, it is too risky. I just received word that Beast Eleven *ate* Number Four. That leaves me with only one reserve beast. I must get rid of Eleven."

"Suit yourself." Bud focused his attention on the windows as Arboria's sun, the star Krespid, rose into view. The deck was flooded with light. Quickly Droobit banked the ship, hiding Krespid from view. Even so, Bud saw it. It was a double star, yellow as a daffodil.

．　．　．

JACK AND ISADORA sat side by side, shivering as they choked down the white stuff they now called skreep paste.

Isadora gagged with every mouthful. Milo refused to even try. Instead the rooster ate a steady supply of small, multilegged creatures that strayed into the dungeon. He was pecking at one now.

Jack pulled his head inside his jacket like a turtle. "Tell me about your dad," he said.

"What do you want to know?"

"Where is he? Is he a scientist like your mom? How come you were traveling without him?"

"If you must know, my father died seven years ago in a plane crash. And he wasn't a scientist. He was a famous jazz musician. Jimmy Shumway. He played the piano."

"Never heard of him," said Jack. "I figured he'd be some foreign science genius. But a musician? How about that! He was, um, *dark-skinned*, I guess?"

"Of course he was dark-skinned. What an idiotic question." She squeezed another dab of paste into her mouth. "Mother taught me to expect such remarks. She said the world is seething with racial prejudice."

"I wouldn't say I'm *prejudiced*. At least, not so's you'd notice. Anyhow, I'm not one to judge. My pop was a grifter and a flimflam man. He ran off when I was a baby."

"I'm sorry to hear that."

"So what I'm saying is, that's worse than being a musician! I mean, at least your dad wasn't a crook, as far as I know."

"Of course he wasn't a crook! He was an extremely talented artist. I miss him very much."

"I probably should have heard of him." Jack put some more paste in his mouth and smacked his lips. "You'd be surprised at the stuff I don't know."

Isadora decided not to comment. "Look," she said. A star

was growing brighter outside. "Do you think we're getting near Skreepia?"

"I don't think it's Earth." The star divided into two suns linked together by a curtain of fire. A planet drifted past, cloaked in pink clouds as fuzzy as a cashmere sweater.

Another planet closed in. When the grate rattled, they cringed, expecting Groot, but it was Krebs again.

"Dis your chance to get out," she whispered. "We land on dat planet. Arboria it called. I take you out wit de traash. Nobody notice."

"Get *out*?" Isadora peered at the shadowy world with alarm. "Why would we want to get out?"

"Crazy idea, hum? Arboria plenty dangery planet. You mebbe not make it. But Skreepia worse. You got *no* chance dere. See?"

"But my uncle Bud said he would help us."

"King not help. Him make plenty ub trouble for you. You *spies*. Spies get fed to beasts." Krebs's tone became urgent.

"Dey's rebels on Arboria. You find 'em and tell 'em 'bout *machine*. Make big plan, start big fight. Save de universe."

"You make it sound easy," Jack said.

"Suure, *sound* easy."

"But what about my mother?" Isadora asked. "I can't just abandon her while I go hunting for rebels."

"It's a dumb idea," Jack agreed. "We'll be stranded on some weird planet for the rest of our lives. Besides, what can a couple of kids do out there?"

"Bad plan, mebbe—but *only* plan, so dat's dat. Krebs gib hatchlings food, wadder, udder stupp. You gotta walk long way, mebbe, right ober mountains. Krebs gib you map. Rebels on udder side."

"We've got to climb mountains on an alien planet we've never even seen before—and that's the *only plan*?"

"Only plan dat keep you *alive*. But you waatch out. Some creatures not so friendish. Where we land are podlings. Dem little, but mean. Hoolies bigger, meaner." The way she waggled her fingers indicated that hoolies might be something like crabs, or snakes, or even giant spiders like herself. "Night greelies bad, too," she added as an afterthought.

"Krebs, we can't do this!" Isadora insisted.

"Yeah!" Jack squeaked. "Those pudleys and hoo-hoos are probably dying to eat us."

"*Shhhh.* I find you weapons, mebbe. Meantime, you not talk so much, hum?" Her voice trailed away. Suddenly she grinned. "Krebs almost forgets *biiiig* surprise."

"What is it?"

"It *surprise*. Not safe to say, eben now, but you gonna like. Gib you plenty help, mebbe."

After she left, Arboria's nighttime face expanded to fill

their window. Isadora's hair began to swirl, then rose in a frizzled mass above her head. Soon her whole body left the floor. She floated to the grated ceiling, surprised and strangely elated.

Milo flapped past, squawking.

"What gives?" Jack paddled up beside her.

"Gravity! The skreeps must have been controlling the force field somehow. I guess they turned it off so Arboria's own gravity can take over. But we're still too far out to feel the effect."

Jack performed a slow somersault. "I wish Smedley could see this. He always wanted to fly." He pumped his arms and jetted past, making a propeller noise. Milo soared, majestic as an eagle. They drifted around the cell until Arboria's gravity strengthened. Then they sank like spent balloons.

As the planet came closer, the hazy atmosphere above its rim glowed dark blue, then turquoise. Milo crowed. As if on cue, the double sun lifted above the horizon, and the rooster cackled smugly.

The saucer struck the planet's upper atmosphere like the head of a match. Sparks swirled. The cell warmed nicely, then became extremely hot. Rivers of flame flowed over the ship's belly. Jack and Isadora hopped like barefoot tourists on a summer sidewalk.

"We're going to be burned alive!" Jack screeched, but the flames went out as the saucer ducked into the planet's stratosphere. Cold returned, and the sky turned Prussian blue. Flat-topped clouds, salmon pink, rose to meet them.

Below the clouds stretched a barren landscape of rocky peaks and wide valleys. Copper-green bands swirled against layers of red iron. Here and there ebony spires poked straight up, sharp as rose thorns. Isadora wondered if her mother was watching.

The planet made Jack think about his mother, too. She had always worried that he would wander off like his father, and now he had wandered farther than either of them could ever have imagined. It was a lonesome thought.

"Where are the trees?" asked Isadora.

"What trees?" As far as Jack could tell, Arboria consisted of nothing but rocks. He watched the planet moodily. "I don't know why you would expect trees. The planet could be made of marshmallows, for all we know."

"But the name is misleading. 'Arboria' suggests 'arboreal'—of, or relating to, trees."

"Well, sure, there's *that*. But I don't know why *else*."

Off in the distance she saw snowcapped mountains. She hoped for a closer look, but instead the ship flew out over featureless desert. They passed craters with ice clinging to their insides like crescent moons, then a long, dry riverbed. "Look!" Isadora exclaimed. A road ran alongside the riverbed until it disappeared under drifts of sand. "That proves there's intelligent life here!"

"Krebs told us that. Rebels, remember?"

"But I'm so glad to see proof of it! If there are roads, there must be vehicles. Which means trade, and towns, and maybe even cities."

But if there was civilization on Arboria, they seemed to be flying away from it. The desert went on and on. Now and then, Isadora saw shapes that might have been houses, but only their broken walls remained.

"It's a pretty cruddy-looking place," said Jack.

"It can't *all* be like this." But as Isadora spoke, the landscape became even less hospitable. An enormous crack appeared in the distance. It stretched from one horizon to the other, a Grand Canyon of Arboria. When the saucer reached the chasm's widest point, it slowed to a hover, high above what appeared to be a bottomless pit. Sheer cliffs fell away into darkness. They began to descend.

Isadora groaned. "Why do we always have to go into holes?"

Once, when she was four, she had accidentally locked herself inside a utility closet. Trapped in the darkness, the mops, brooms, and vacuum cleaner had been terrifying. When her mother finally found her, Isadora had been hysterical.

"Look at these things that frightened you," Dr. Shumway had told her sternly. "Remember, fear thrives in the darkness of ignorance but flees before the light of reason. When you see things for what they really are, you will not be afraid." It had been a good lesson, except for the nightmares—and for times like now, when seeing things in the light of reason was no help at all.

They dipped below the rim into darkness. "Skreeps sure don't like daylight, do they?" Jack said. "It must hurt those big eyes of theirs."

The ship continued to descend, *down, down, down.* Isadora tried to estimate the depth of the hole, but she gave up after a thousand feet slid past. The bottom was still invisible far below.

"Oh, no," Jack groaned. Something big, with tentacles like an octopus, was stuffing itself into a crack in the rocks.

Isadora was torn between scientific curiosity and stark ter-ror. "Perhaps it's one of those creatures Krebs told us about," she said in her bravest voice. "A podling, or a hoolie."

"Hoolie," Jack croaked. "Pudleys are *small*."

A cloud of brown dust swirled around the saucer as they dropped to the canyon floor. When the ship landed, it settled slowly to the ground.

"Water," Isadora said. They perched above a wide mud puddle.

"It looks filthy."

A transparent tube descended from the saucer's belly. It inserted itself into the puddle and sucked. When the water was gone, the tube slurped like a straw at the bottom of a chocolate shake.

Something brown and wet flopped beside it, then burrowed into the mud.

"Welcome to Arboria," muttered Jack.

• • •

24. OLD ACQUAINTANCE

A DULL WHIRRING signaled that a ramp was being low-ered. The ship's turquoise light flooded the canyon floor and made it look like the bottom of an aquarium. Skreeps scuttled down the ramp, their many arms wrapped around bags and boxes. Some dragged heavy sacks like the one Krebs wore around her neck.

Where was *the garbage collector?* Isadora and Jack won-dered. They finally saw her stagger by, overloaded with awkward lumps of broken machinery. When Krebs returned, she passed beneath their window and wiggled her fingers discreetly.

Eight skreeps stumbled down the ramp, dragging something bigger than a truck. They hauled the massive bundle away from the ship and out of sight, skittering sideways like fiddler crabs. Minutes later a thin scream cut through the silence. Six skreeps came charging back, empty-handed and wild-eyed. They scrambled up the ramp.

"What was that about?" asked Isadora.

"I have no idea. But I'm pretty sure I don't want to get off the ship here."

Krebs appeared, grinning through the barred door. "No worry," she whispered. "I drop tings off for you. Ebryting fine. You not get scaredy now."

Oh, I'm scaredy, Jack wanted to say, but the words wouldn't come. Krebs sprang the locks and lifted the chain without making a sound. She opened the grate with one hand and pulled the children out with two others. Jack held Milo, cradled like a grumpy baby, against his chest. Miraculously the rooster stayed quiet and didn't bite. Frozen with fear, they huddled in a dank corridor while Krebs opened her sack. A foul stench wafted out. "You get in bag now. Quicky-quick. Ebryting set. I leeb supplies, you find 'em in traash."

"What about my mother?" said Isadora. "Can't she come?"

"Can't get mudder. Hatchlings find rebels, make plenty ub trouble, den find mudder, hum? Now, quicky-quick." She pushed the open bag at Isadora and pointed. Reluctantly both Isadora and Jack crawled inside. When they were crammed in the bottom, Krebs hoisted the sack off the ground and scuttled away.

It was an awful ride. Inside the bag was a disgusting mess of nauseating trash, some of it sharp and pointed, some of it revoltingly soft. All of it sloshed and slammed and smashed against them as they pounded into each other. Milo struggled in Jack's arms, kicking and biting as Jack tried to keep him quiet. But the worst part was the stench. It was horrific, appalling, and inescapable.

Finally Krebs opened the bag and dumped them onto a great heap of refuse. Immediately she covered them with more debris. "You stay hid till we go," she whispered. "Krebs see you some udder time, mebbe."

Squelch. Squelch. Squelch. They heard her footsteps in the mud, and then the saucer began to hum. The Wiffle-ball sound rose to a loud whistle. Poking their heads out of the pile, they watched the ship lift off. Dust and sand whipped their faces, and they were forced to duck down again.

By the time the cloud settled, the spaceship was long gone. Jack and Isadora crawled out of the pile, half sliding until they reached the ground. Milo jumped free, bit Jack's leg, then trotted across the sand. Jack wiped a layer of grit from his eyes.

"Well, it's hard to feel good about this," he said, taking in the emptiness of the canyon. The place was absolutely barren. Not even a dry weed rose from the ground.

"I suppose we'd better find those supplies," Isadora said in a shaky voice. Her mother was still in that spaceship, and who knew if they'd ever see each other again? She swallowed hard and began to dig through the garbage.

"Need a hand there?"

Isadora stopped digging. The voice seemed to come from inside the pile.

"What was that?" Jack squeaked.

The trash began to stir. A head popped out of the mess, concealed by a battered hat shoved down over its ears. Slowly the figure rose from the heap, unbending like a bean sprout. The man brushed trash from the sleeves of his threadbare jacket and carefully patted his hat back into shape.

"Joe?" said Jack incredulously. It seemed like a lifetime since he'd first met the hobo in his dining room.

"They was throwing out trash, so I figured it was time for *me* to go." Joe smiled and climbed down the pile. "Glad you two could join me. It's always nice to see familiar faces in a strange place." He peered up at the cavernous walls. "I guess this qualifies as a strange place."

"But what are you doing here?" asked Isadora.

"Same as you, I reckon. That night at the Pines, I told you I was interested in the saucer—and so I was. I've had my fill of it now, though."

"We had no idea you were on board."

"I figured it was best that way. I came on as a stowaway in Vern Hollow. Old Krebs kept me hid the entire time. She told me about you. Kept me informed generally. She's the eyes and ears of the ship, that monster." He wiped his forehead with a faded bandanna. "So what's the plan?"

"I was hoping you had one," said Isadora. "Krebs left some supplies in the pile there, but that's all we know."

"Well, that's where we start, then."

They dug through the heap and carried out two transparent crates. One was filled with skreep paste and flexible canteens of water. The other held some shiny blankets, a long coil of shimmering cord, a hand-drawn map, and three billy clubs that glowed with green light when twisted. They spread the contents on the sandy ground. "Is that it?" asked Jack.

Isadora sniffed the water and took a sip. "Were you expecting something else?"

"I was hoping for a ray gun."

"I see your point." Joe briefly scanned the dreary landscape, then turned his attention to the map. He studied it carefully. "Looks like we got some walking to do."

"Climbing, too," said Isadora.

He looked up at the cliffs. "That *is* a climb, ain't it?"

Jack choked on some skreep paste. It hadn't occurred to him that they would *climb* out. The canyon walls went up and up and up. "Wait," he said, a note of panic in his voice. "We can't climb *that*."

"Seems unlikely, don't it?" said Joe. "But at least we got some rope." He held up a coil of skreep cord. "Although," he added, looking at the map again, "there could be a problem."

"What problem?"

"This map don't have any directions on it. Not that skreeps use north and south like we do. But which side of this hole do we crawl out on? If we guess wrong, it's a long walk around."

Isadora crouched beside him. The map was crudely drawn, with symbols she could not decipher. The chasm was clear enough, though. She remembered its shape, like a wide, unsmiling mouth, from the air. "Okay," she said, a bit relieved. "We climb out on the opposite side from where we flew in. East, I guess you'd call it, since we were going toward the sunrise."

"East it is, then." Joe grinned at her. But looking up, his smile faded. The narrow slice of sky gave no clue about directions. "Do either of you remember which way we flew in?"

They exchanged glances. The ride inside Krebs's sack had left them completely disoriented. Isadora walked slowly in a circle, observing the chasm carefully. In each direction, the gorge narrowed quickly. An avalanche of boulders blocked one side; the other was a nasty, open corridor leading into inky shadows. She scanned the cliffs. They rose to unearthly heights, great broken chimneys of reddish stone separated by clefts that sometimes widened into deep crevasses and often narrowed into knife-edged vertical cracks. The near side of the gorge was awful; the far wall seemed utterly impossible.

"It would be easier to go up this side," she said at last. "But the other side is *right*."

"What do you mean?" Jack cried. "That's crazy!"

"Maybe so, but it's what we have to do."

He appealed to Joe. "Tell her she's being crazy."

"I reckon I'd better find out first. You being crazy?"

"No. I have a feeling about this. . . ."

Jack scoffed. "A feeling!"

"Nothing wrong with feelings," Joe said seriously. "Sometimes that's all you got. Anyway, we best get moving. I don't want to linger too long in this ant hole." He gathered scraps of skreep cord from the trash heap and sat down in the sand.

It soon became clear that Joe was very clever with knots. In less than an hour, he fashioned three backpacks with deep pouches, drawstrings, and braided shoulder straps. "We'll carry our stuff in these."

They went back to the crates and were horrified to find them swarming with softball-sized, formless white blobs.

"Pudleys," said Jack.

"Podlings," Isadora corrected. "Krebs told us they could be dangerous."

Joe patted Jack's shoulder. "Hand me that billy club, will you, son?"

He held the baton loosely, then stepped closer
to the crate. When he was about six feet
away, one of the podlings lunged at
him with startling speed. Joe cocked
the club as the podling flew in like
a low pitch, and then he swung
sharply. It connected with a
squishy *thunk*, and the podling
soared away. When it struck the
chasm wall it clung there for
a minute before sliding to the
ground. "Home run," said Joe.

The others podlings
scattered across the sand.
When they reached the
cliff, they vanished into
a nest of cracks.

Joe picked up one of the
crates. Judging by the jagged
hole in its side, the podlings had
sharp teeth. "Lucky this skreep
food ain't worth eating, or them
critters would've cleaned us out."

They filled the packs with food,
blankets, and their coats. Jack tried to coax
Milo into his, but the rooster hissed and scampered away. "Stay
here, then. See how well those pudleys treat *you*."

Isadora analyzed their route. "If we follow the crack over
there to where it breaks up, we can work across that ledge. To
the right there's a ramp, and then another crack goes straight
up. I can't tell after that."

"I see it," said Joe, following the course with his eyes. "After that it gets a little sketchy, don't it?" He hoisted his pack onto his shoulders. "Just a little sketchy."

"We can always improvise."

"That's all I ever do."

• • •

25. THE CLIMB

THEY CROSSED the chasm floor, skirting one of the stagnant pools. Something wriggled beneath its surface. They hurried on. When they reached the wall, Joe stopped and tied one end of the rope around his waist. He secured Isadora to the middle and Jack to the far end.

"I guess it ain't proper mountaineering, but at least it'll keep us together." He put a foot into the crack and hoisted himself up. As he climbed, the line slowly played out, coil after coil.

Jack adjusted his pack. "I never told you this," he whispered to Isadora, "but I'm not crazy about heights."

"How do you feel about being eaten by podlings?"

"Not crazy about that, either."

The rope tugged at Isadora's waist. "My turn," she said and started up. After a few feet she fell into an even rhythm. For her the wall was an easy puzzle. She moved from one handhold to another all the way up to where Joe sat.

Far below, Jack stood next to his rooster. "Come on, Milo," he coaxed. "Hop into the backpack. You know you don't want to stay down here."

The rooster strutted away. The rope straightened until it

dragged Jack to the base of the cliff. "Listen, this is your last chance."

Milo hissed.

Jack lunged, but the bird danced away. By now the rope was as tight as a guitar string.

"Come *on!*" Isadora called from above.

"All right, Milo, I guess this is it. So long." Jack hoisted himself up. "If it makes you feel better, I'm probably going to fall."

Milo walked away.

Jack tried to ignore him. Climbing would require all of his concentration. He was about fifteen feet off the ground when his right foot slipped, and he fell backward. Just before he hit the sand, the rope caught him. He dangled with arms and legs flailing like a capsized turtle. Milo ran in frenzied circles beneath him, jumping up to peck the back of his neck.

Finally Jack caught hold of the rock and pulled himself upright. As if it had been his intention all along, Milo hopped onto his shoulder.

Jack barely noticed. The terror of falling made his feet move like pistons, and he raced up the rock. He had almost reached Isadora when his mind finally snapped awake. He froze, arms and legs splayed against the wall. Milo pecked the top of his head.

"What are you *doing?*" Isadora asked impatiently.

"What does it look like I'm doing?"

"You have to keep moving, Jack. You'll fall if you just stand there."

"I'll fall if I move."

"Go ahead and fall if you want," Joe called down. "We'll haul you up. Unless that rope breaks, of course."

Fear surged inside him, and Jack launched himself blindly upward. Suddenly he tipped diagonally. He remembered a movie he'd seen once, not a good movie, in which the leading man danced up the sides of walls. He had wondered out loud how it was done. "Ropes," said Smedley Trowbridge. "They use ropes, and then later they erase them from the film so you can't see 'em." It made sense. If you wanted to do something really stupid on a wall, you needed ropes. He hung with his feet lodged inside a crack and his hands scrabbling uselessly across the stone, while Joe pulled him nearly vertical. Finally he found the ledge and hauled himself up. He sat beside the other two on the stone bench, his eyes closed tight. Milo bit his ear.

"That wasn't too bad," said Joe. "For starters." He turned gingerly to face the wall. "Reckon it's my turn again."

They climbed until they were far up the side of the gorge. Joe moved with the patience of a professional wanderer; Isadora was bold and graceful. But Jack remained terrified, arriving at the end of each ascent with bleary relief, only to be overcome with renewed dread as Isadora climbed away, tightening the rope between them.

While Joe climbed, Isadora lounged on even the tiniest ledge as if it were an easy chair. After a few hours she reported that the canyon floor was no longer visible in the shadows. Jack groaned.

"Cheer up. That means we're climbing out of it." By now the daylight had ripened to the mellow tones of late afternoon, while the cliffs still rose to nearly unimaginable heights above them. She wondered how cold the night would be, and how long.

Joe sang railroad songs as he climbed, "The Wreck of the

Old '97" and "The Ballad of John Henry," in which the world's strongest railroad man races a steam drill and dies. Jack wondered what a steam drill was.

They began to tire, especially Jack, who was using a lot of energy on sheer fright. The discouraging thing was how far overhead the cliffs still loomed. Jack rubbed his rabbit's foot furiously. Joe squinted upward. "A couple more climbs and we'll need to find a place to spend the night."

"I'm not sleeping on this cliff."

Milo clucked, as if in agreement.

"We'll find a big shelf or a cave," Joe promised. "It won't be half bad." He headed up, singing "The Night of the Johnstown Flood."

Isadora stopped. Had she heard something moving below them? When she looked down, she found that even for her the height had become unsettling. Columns of twisting rock faded into the abyss. She thought she saw movement, but when she blinked, all was still.

On the next pitch she began to notice her own weariness. It would be dangerous to go much farther. She stood on a stone chimney between deep crevasses, catching her breath.

"Hey!" Joe shouted from somewhere farther up. "You're going to like this. I—" His words broke off, and Isadora heard a heavy thump. "Hey!" A shower of gravel rained down beside her. The small stones fell silently into the depths below. Without thinking, she jumped from the chimney onto open rock and began to climb.

The rope stopped her.

"Wait a minute!" Jack shouted indignantly from below.

She tugged impatiently. "Hurry, Jack. Joe's in trouble!" From above came grunts, shuffling footsteps, an occasional loud crash.

"I'm hurrying, I'm hurrying!" Then, amazingly, he was. The rope went limp, and Isadora took up the slack. She scrambled another fifteen feet before she had to stop again.

"That's it, Jack! You're doing it!"

The rope went slack again. "Something's after me!" he screamed.

She peered down but couldn't see him. The view made her head swim.

The situation was maddening. Joe was fighting above her, while Jack was being chased from below. She was stuck in the middle, useless.

"It's big!" Panic rose in Jack's voice.

Isadora didn't know what to do. She couldn't go down, and what good would it do to wait for him? She had only one option. "Keep going!" she called and headed up.

• • •

"I HAVE SOMETHING bad to report, Madame Commander." Groot bit his blubbery bottom lip and bowed almost to the floor.

"What is it?"

His ugly face was miserable. "The hatchlings have escaped."

"*Escaped?* What do you mean, they've *escaped?*"

"Locks undone, chain gone, cell wide open. I searched all over. I asked the other *ooman bings*, too. Nobody knows anything." He trembled. "I have a theory, though."

"A *theory*. No doubt you'll want to share it."

"I think they left the ship when we landed."

"On *Arboria?* Why would they do that?" She turned in her seat. "Bug Greedle!"

"Ma'am?" He brushed a feather away from his glasses.

"My dungeon keeper says your *spies* have escaped. Would they have left the ship on *Arboria*?"

"Not a chance! Even the boy ain't *that* dumb. They'll turn up sooner or later."

Xaafuun considered the situation. Groot was finished. But what about the hatchlings? How had they escaped—*again*? And what could they be up to?

"Madame?" Bambo spoke softly. "If they *are* on the planet, they won't last long. Remember, Beast Eleven is there."

True. But it was still sloppy. What would the Queen say? A thing like this would leave a bad taste. Xaafuun had enough problems. It would be best if the Queen never knew about this one. "Groot," she ordered. "Bring me the other *ooman bings*." One way or another, the hatchlings must be found.

. . .

26. FIGHTING BEASTS

THE BOWIE KNIFE was very, very sharp. On long train rides Joe sometimes spent hours honing its blade. He'd owned it so long its shape had changed; its edge had a slight inversion now, and the hilt had worn to fit the grooves of his hand. For years he'd called the knife his "rabbit skinner." Now he called it his "bug sticker." Nobody ever asked why, and he didn't say. Drifters kept their secrets.

He had been watching the ledge hopefully as he climbed. When he reached it, he was relieved to find a broad, rocky platform stretching back into a cave. The spot seemed made to order, a level, sheltered camp where they could spend the night in relative comfort. And just in time. The last glow of daylight played along the rim of the chasm.

Joe rested a few minutes, breathing quietly. Then he got up and stretched his back. It felt good to stand upright after so many hours of clinging, monkey style, to the rock. He smiled. This would do. They could have some water, a bite to eat, a good night's sleep, then tackle the rest of the cliff in the morning. He returned to the ledge. "Hey," he shouted down, "you're going to like this! I . . . "

Something grabbed his ankles. It had tentacles like an octopus, only pebbled with bits of sand and stone. And it was *big*. In two seconds the thing was upon him. His right hand moved in a seamless motion, like a magic trick, and came away holding the knife. A second tentacle reached for his neck. The blade flashed, and the tentacle parted neatly. Dark blood spurted from its stump.

In the same instant another tentacle closed around his waist. Another wrapped around his thighs. He hacked them away with four deep cuts, then ducked as a haymaker blow whooshed above his head. He remained in a crouch, blocking with his left hand, slashing with his right.

A tentacle coiled around his ankles. Another grabbed his knees. His legs buckled, but somehow he managed not to fall. He ducked, parried, slashed. Severed tentacles twisted on the ground like wounded snakes. Joe fought patiently, marshaling his strength. The thing was dragging him into the cave.

For a moment he saw wide, unblinking eyes. Then the tentacles spun him until he faced outward, toward the gorge. He caught a glimpse of sky. Maybe it would be his last. A tentacle twisted around his neck. When he reached to cut it, another seized his arm. The knife clattered on stones. The noose tightened. His vision blurred.

. . .

JACK SCREAMED. Isadora spotted him on a ledge far below. Milo roosted on his pack. Jack screamed again, and another figure entered the scene. It flowed like smoke from a chimney, dark, silent, and huge. Jack tried to flee up the wall but failed. His feet churned the air. Milo cursed.

The dark thing moved toward them, bigger than a grizzly bear, sleek as a panther. Isadora was unable to make out legs, head, or body—just a wave of motion that rose up beneath Jack and Milo and then, unexpectedly, passed them by. It came up quickly, without a sound. Before it reached her, Isadora felt scalding breath and saw the flash of eyes. They were bright gold and unspeakably wild.

She ducked her head and squeezed against the stone. The creature's musky smell surrounded her. Then it was gone. She opened her eyes and watched the dark shape roll over the ledge above her. A terrible roar shook the air.

She hugged the stone and shut her eyes. Incredibly, Jack pulled himself up beside her. His knuckles were bleeding, and his face was drained of all color. "Are you okay?" she whispered hoarsely.

"Don't know. What was *that*?"

A roar from above silenced them both.

• • •

JOE WAS ON his last breath. The tentacle had already shut his windpipe and was still drawing tighter. Soon, bones would snap. His vision flickered around the edges like a silent movie. His spirit drifted a short distance away.

By the time the monster came over the ledge, Joe was beyond surprise. He had no doubt that it was his own dark fate coming to claim him. Not to worry: He hadn't been expecting a choir of angels. Still, it was interesting that Death had teeth, and claws, and golden eyes.

The beast charged. Joe braced himself, but the impact never came. Instead the grip around his neck loosened, and air flowed into his lungs. Bright explosions flashed before his eyes. He hit the ground hard and lay on his side.

Each gulp brought fresh explosions, as if the air was combustible. When his vision settled, he saw the beast, black as a moonless night, plunging into the cave. Dark blood sprayed. Broken bits of tentacle flew out. Something shrieked. He closed his eyes.

When he opened them, it was because cool water had found its way into his mouth. Isadora's serious face hovered over him. The boy was behind her, looking worried. "Don't get up," she whispered. "I haven't had a chance to examine your wounds."

"I ain't wounded." His words came out slurred.

"Don't try to speak, either."

He slumped back. Overhead, the sky had turned purple. It was evening on Arboria.

"We have to get out of here," Jack whispered urgently. Inside the cave, teeth ripped flesh. The dark creature was feasting.

"We can't. Joe's in no condition to move. And you don't want to climb in the dark, do you?"

"We have to! It's only a matter of time before that thing comes out and . . . you know." He couldn't bring himself to say the words.

"We'll have to take that chance. Anyway, it doesn't look like the creature means to harm us. It had every opportunity if it wanted to, but it didn't."

"It saved my life," Joe croaked.

"You think it followed us all the way up here just to leave us alone?"

"I don't know, Jack." Isadora was too tired to worry about monsters or anything else. Warm air rose from the gorge and swirled gently around them. "Why don't we eat some dinner?"

They ate skreep paste and washed it down with a small amount of water. Jack kept a nervous eye on the cave. Night settled in. They wrapped themselves in the silvery blankets and huddled together. Milo perched on top of them, his small head raised like a periscope. After a while they dozed.

Buuurp! Isadora opened her eyes. A foul odor wafted from the cave. Overhead the sky was full of strange stars. A jagged shadow marked the top of the chasm's far wall. While she watched, something flapped, batlike, away from the cliff, circled across the stars, and returned.

Another belch, this one softer, floated from the cave. Her eyelids grew heavy, and she drifted back to sleep.

When she woke again the sky was a creamy gray. She sat up, feeling stiff and cold. Jack lay with his arms around Milo. Joe seemed not to have moved. Heavy breathing came from inside the cave, along with a growing stench. There was a loud rumble, and the smell sharpened. Jack opened his eyes.

"Ugh! What is that?" He pinched his nose. "You think it's from eating that hoolie?"

"How should I know? Maybe it always smells that way."

"Reminds me of the morning after the Great Chili Cook-off," Joe rasped. "Topeka, 1939. Only worse."

With another explosive belch, the beast dragged itself out of the cave. Milo ran in tight circles, screaming.

Jack might have screamed, too, but the monster collapsed and lay motionless upon the sand. "Look at that!" The huge body was so black it was as if the cave had disgorged a chunk of its own darkness.

"Maybe hoolies are poisonous," Isadora mused. "But it should know that. It must have eaten them before."

"Not if it ain't from around here," Joe said softly. "I bet this monster's no more native than we are."

"What makes you think that?"

"Just a feeling. I get 'em, too, you know."

"Well, here's *my* feeling," said Jack. "I'm feeling we should get out of here, pronto."

"I'm sorry," said Isadora, "but we can't. The creature saved our lives, and now it's ill. We have a duty to help it."

"*Saved* us? Maybe it's just saving us for dessert!"

"Nevertheless." Isadora rummaged through her backpack.

"What are you doing?"

"Remember when Pungo gave us the turf? He said it might cure sickness."

When she opened her purse a summery aroma wafted out. She lifted the hunk of sod. Amazingly, it was exactly as it had been when Pungo cut it, with each blade of grass standing straight and true.

Very gently Isadora tore off a piece of grass and returned the rest to her purse. She stood directly in front of the beast. Then she knelt down and held the grass before her.

The ailing monster opened its murky eyes. Isadora extended her hand and held it, trembling, for the creature to see. Except for the eyes, no other features were visible beneath its sleek fur. The slitted pupils focused, traveling from the outstretched hand to Isadora's eyes. She looked away, and in that instant the great mouth opened like a trap. White teeth flashed.

Isadora yanked her hand away. The grass was gone. The golden eyes closed.

She rejoined the others and sat down, trembling. Joe put a hand on her shoulder. "I reckon I'll be telling *that* story for a while."

Blaaarp! An enormous belch erupted from deep inside the beast. The smell was horrific. Jack's eyes watered. "Now we're *all* going to be sick!"

The odor drifted away. The beast heaved a great sigh and opened its eyes. They were livelier now, and they fixed on Isadora. Then they closed again.

The morning brightened. The beast slept. The humans ate a silent breakfast of skreep paste.

"It must need water, too," said Isadora.

"You must be crazy," said Jack.

"I'm not, though. All living things need water." She opened a canteen.

Jack appealed to Joe. "Can't you stop her?"

"There's no stopping kindness, son."

Isadora placed the water before the beast and quickly retreated. It opened its eyes, looked at her, then devoured the entire canteen.

"You can see why it has digestive problems," said Joe.

Suddenly the beast moved. It raised itself with the same unsettling fluidity they had seen the evening before, as if it were all joints, like a snake, or no joints at all. Isadora closed her eyes.

When she opened them, the monster loomed over her. It pressed its snout against the front of her sweater and sniffed noisily, watching her all the while. She held her breath, and it sprang back, agile as a house cat. From the ledge it looked at her again, then plunged over the side.

"I could be wrong," said Joe. "But I get the impression you just made a friend."

Cautiously she slipped to the edge and peered over. Below her was bare rock and air. "It's gone," she murmured. "It disappeared!"

• • •

27. UP AND OVER

GROOT LAID the *Uurthlings* beneath the captain's dais like freshly caught trout. He stepped back, bowing low. They were wrapped in skreep cord from neck to ankle. "Release them, idiot," Xaafuun said impatiently. "They can't go anywhere *now*."

Groot sliced the cords. One by one the humans stood, rubbing their limbs. Awkward in his feathers, Bud rose from his armchair and tried to help Dr. Shumway to her feet, but she shook him off.

"I would like to know what this is all about," she said.

"I would like to know, too," said Xaafuun. "You *Uurth* creatures have been causing mischief since you came on board." She held up a hand. "Do not deny it. Now two of your hatchlings are missing. It has been suggested they escaped onto the planet Arboria."

"I told her that weren't possible," Bud muttered to Dr. Shumway. "Those kids wouldn't just run off onto some strange planet."

Dr. Shumway considered his feathers, then addressed Xaafuun. "One of those '*hatchlings*' is my daughter, Captain. Therefore, what you say concerns me deeply. Do you have evidence to support your claim?"

"I was hoping you might give that to me. Arboria is an extremely dangerous place, Scientist Shumway. Your hatchling is not safe there. If she was *encouraged* to go for any reason—to meet with rebel forces, for instance—it was very bad advice. Tell me what you know, and I will return for her—and the other one. Like you, I am concerned for their safety."

"No doubt," said Dr. Shumway.

For a while, nobody spoke. Glowing orbs swirled inside the bubble-topped machine.

Sergeant Webb's small eyes took in every detail of Bud's costume.

"Now I've seen it all."

Xaafuun turned to him. "What have you seen, Mister—?"

"Webb. *Sergeant* Webb." He hoisted his trousers. "I can find those delinquents for you. Me and my boy, Grady, can. The Creedles always run off, and the Webbs always bring 'em back. That's just the way it is."

"You are a Finder?" said Xaafuun.

"You could say that."

"And the hatchlings are on Arboria?"

"That'd be my guess."

"We will go there then."

"My daughter is *not* a delinquent," snapped Dr. Shumway. "But if there is a search party, I will go."

"You will *stay*," said Xaafuun. "Finder Webb will search. Also Hatchling Webb. But do not worry, Scientist Shumway. *Ooman bings* are too feeble to climb, so the hatchlings cannot have gone far. The Finders will return them to me quickly—for their own safety, of course."

• • •

THERE WAS nothing to do but climb. With the rope tied around his waist, Joe started up, singing "Streets of Laredo." Isadora followed. Jack went last. He thought about nothing but the rock in front of him, and in that way made it from one pitch to the next. Between climbs he stood like a convict facing a firing squad, while Isadora sat next to him, calmly dangling her feet over the edge.

Gradually the cliff became less steep. By midmorning the top of the canyon was just a few hundred feet above them. The far side of the gorge was honeycombed with caves. "Reckon anything's living in there?"

Until that moment Isadora had forgotten about the bat-creature she'd seen the night before. She told the others.

"Night greelies," said Jack.

"Whatever they are," said Joe, "I reckon we'd be smart to get out of here. I've had enough of the local critters."

They climbed quickly after that. The caves had an ominous look, like eye sockets in a skull. They couldn't shake the feeling that they were being watched.

"You were right to choose this side," Joe told Isadora. "Over there, we would have run into them caves and been on the wrong side, to boot."

She smiled modestly. "It was just luck."

"Intuition ain't luck."

Joe was the first to crawl over the rim. He glanced at the wide desert, then sat and began to pull Isadora up on the rope. Her face was dirty and her frizzy hair bedraggled. Jack rolled over the ledge, and Milo darted away.

The world beyond the gorge was an unbroken plain of red sand and twisted yellow boulders. The rocks seemed as evenly spaced as tines on a hairbrush. Far away, sand met sky in a flat horizon. Cool air whispered quietly among the stones.

"Now what do we do?"

"We'll need some luck, that's for sure." Joe retrieved Krebs's map. "She wasn't too clear on the details, was she? But there's a little circle here above the gorge, and it looks like our path should take us right by it."

"You think it could be water?" As soon as Jack said it, they all realized how thirsty they were, how little was left in their canteens, and how dry the desert was all around them.

"It might be best not to talk about water too much." Joe pointed to a low ridge. "Maybe when we get up on that hump we'll see where to go."

They fell into their familiar order, with Joe in front, Isadora behind him, and Jack a little farther back. Milo ran in erratic bursts, sometimes charging ahead, sometimes straggling behind. Occasionally he rushed in to give Jack a peck on the ankle.

They were all happy to be out of the gorge, but there was something unspeakably grim about Arboria. It was more lifeless than any place Isadora had ever been. Her breath rasped in the dry air. Her tongue felt like a sock stuffed inside her mouth.

She set her mind on reaching the small ridge. It became her only goal. But when they finally stopped to rest, after hours of travel, the ridge seemed as far away as ever. Joe took a very small sip of water from his canteen and handed it to Jack with a gesture indicating that he must limit himself to a single swallow. Jack drank, then passed it to Isadora with a look of deep regret. Only a gulp remained, sloshing enticingly at the bottom. She savored the cool liquid as it swirled over her tongue. Then it was gone.

Joe put away the empty canteen and started walking again.

The planet's strange sun, like a double-yolked egg, began to dip behind them. Isadora became aware that she was moving uphill. The slope ahead had taken on a fiery glow. She put her head down, willing herself not to look again. The ridge seemed as elusive as a rainbow, retreating maddeningly as they walked.

Jack nudged her. A spiky, blood-red plant nestled in the shadow of a nearby rock. It was not much bigger than her hand, but it was the first scrap of vegetation she had seen. She lurched toward it, and it spun like a drill, kicking up a shower of sand. It disappeared beneath the surface. She pressed on, too exhausted to investigate further.

More of the plants appeared and disappeared. Soon they covered the ground like a carpet of sea urchins. They fled in a whirling panic each time the Earthlings approached, only to reemerge when danger passed. The plants grew larger the higher up the slope they went. Before long, some were as big as watermelons. The biggest ones made a furious buzzing as they dug into the ground and did not submerge themselves entirely. Patches of their sharp spikes remained visible above the surface, and it became difficult finding a path between them. Only Milo managed the obstacle course without faltering. The rooster became enraged with the plants and pecked at them furiously until they retreated. In this way he created a path the others followed. When Milo finally halted, they stopped in a line, like commuters waiting for a bus.

Joe was the first to notice. He croaked a single word. "Look!"

They stood on a rim that curved away in both directions to complete a perfect circle—an enormous crater. The groundcover below was like thick moss, and beyond it were violet mounds and a grove of white trees with foliage that swirled like silken veils.

As fascinating as she might have found the view at any other time, Isadora skimmed over every detail and settled on the only one that mattered. In the very center of the valley, shimmering like a silver tray, was a small, round pond.

They scrambled down the rocky slope and across the green field, blind to their surroundings.

Isadora had never really smelled water before, but she smelled it now, long before she reached the pond. Its scent was maddening. She trotted, then ran. Behind her, Jack and Joe ran, too.

When she tripped a few feet from the bank she crawled the rest of the way. She caught a brief, shocking view of her face reflected in the still water—shrunken cheeks, cracked lips, eyes burned down to dark holes. Then she plunged her head in and drank.

• • •

28. JOE'S STORY

ISADORA LIFTED her head from the pond, sputtering, then drank more. The water soaked her to her waist.

"Easy," slurred Joe, water spewing from his mouth. "Don't drink too quick."

She tried to stop and failed. When she'd swallowed all she could hold, she rolled over. Her stomach clenched. Much of the water came back up.

Jack threw up, too. "You don't think it's poisonous, do you?"

"If it is, it's a little late to worry about it."

"The water is good," said Joe. "Leastways, I've drunk worse. All the same, we weren't thinking too clearly just now. It'll be dark and cold soon, and we got our clothes all wet." He sat up. "I hate to build a fire when I don't even know if any of this stuff'll burn, but I think we'd better try, or it's going to be a long night." He ambled away.

No longer blinded by thirst, Isadora was filled with wonder. Trees like purple cigars surrounded them, mingling with a variety of smaller plants and bushes. Some distance away, the veil trees stood aloof, as graceful as brides.

"Here's some branches," Jack said. Isadora watched him pick up a long stick, but as he straightened, it turned in his hand with a violent twist and knocked him sideways. He sat down hard, and the stick rapped him on the head, then retreated into the rocks.

"Are you all right?"

"It *looked* like a stick."

"I guess we'll have to be careful what we pick up. And what we try to burn."

"Does this place feel funny to you?" he asked suddenly.

"What do you mean by 'funny'? It's alien, but you could hardly expect otherwise."

"I don't know. I get the feeling it knows we're here—and it's trying to decide what to do with us."

The idea was unsettling. "That's anthropomorphism. You're ascribing your own emotions to our surroundings. The vegetation here is only vegetation."

"If you say so. But I never got whacked by a vegetation before."

They came to a patch of low, silvery bushes, growing in

geometrical precision like a honeycomb. Beneath the thicket, the ground was covered with dried sticks.

"That wood looks okay," Isadora said uncertainly. The temperature was beginning to fall. Her wet blouse felt cold against her skin.

"Sure, until it *bites* you," said Jack.

Joe walked past with a load of firewood in his arms. "Gather up some of that kindling there," he called.

The sticks turned out to be ordinary, and they added them to Joe's big pile. He built a tepee of small twigs within a ring of stones. "If this stuff'll burn without killing us, we'll be in good shape." He produced a box of matches and lit one by flicking its head with a thumbnail. Soon a small fire was crackling cheerfully.

The wood gave remarkable heat but almost no smoke. As the evening cooled, they leaned over the fire. The stars came out, so numerous it was like being back in space. Isadora nudged Jack. Across the valley the veil trees had begun to glow from within. Their silken finery gave off flashes of pink and turquoise.

After a dinner of skreep paste, Joe fetched a harmonica from his pocket. He sang a song about a mill fire, a song about a mine collapse, and a song called "Jim Blake, Your Wife Is Dying."

"Don't you know any happy songs?" asked Jack.

"Even them sad ones cheer me up somehow." Joe tapped the harmonica against his knee. "You know, we've been so busy up to now, I've barely had a chance to ask a question. I know a little bit about the machine your uncle made, but I couldn't say how you two got mixed up in all of this, or what you're doing here now."

"It's the craziest story you ever heard," said Jack.

Joe looked at them expectantly, and they began to tell it, going all the way back to Vern Hollow. They took turns, interrupting each other frequently. Twice Joe had them repeat the part about Pungo and Hellebeezia. After the second time, Isadora showed him the hunk of sod again. Strangely, it appeared to have mended itself.

"You're right. It's the craziest story I ever heard." Joe placed another log on the fire.

"What about you?" asked Isadora. "How did you get here?"

"Well, the answer to that goes back a ways." He lifted his hat and scratched his head. "Professional tramps such as myself have known about flying saucers for years. Ain't no surprise, when you think about it. Who else spends so much time outdoors, particularly at night? And who else spends so much time sitting around fires like this one, telling stories? But I think there's more to it than that. I think the space aliens keep an eye out for hoboes as much as we keep an eye out for them. We *suit* them, if you know what I mean. We got no homes or families; nobody cares much what we say. If we disappear we're hardly ever missed, and we can almost always be found in places other folks avoid, far from city lights.

"When I was a young'un I started hearing stories from fellas who'd been picked up by spaceships. Didn't necessarily believe 'em. Tramps'll say almost anything to pass the time. But I heard it more and more. I learned there wasn't just one kind of space alien or one kind of ship. Some are harmless, like the *gillimeeds*, or the *skurls*, who ain't much bigger'n a bug and fly around in these little bitty saucers that look like trash can lids." He spread his arms to indicate the size of the ships. "That ain't the only difference, neither. Some of them aliens are so smart and wise and, I don't know, *above* it all, that nobody can get a handle on *what* they're doing, like the *felimars* and the *bora'sonts*. But let me tell you, the one outfit nobody likes is the *skreeps*. I mean, nobody can stand 'em! You can see why. They have this big empire, and they're always stealing from everyone else and catching folks as slaves. They're greedy as tycoons, and they wreck just about everything they put their hands on. In fact, the skreeps just generally cause trouble, to the point where a lot of the other aliens spend all their time fighting 'em. That's the rebels. They include aliens like *yarmuks* and *gingaboo* and *buska-mow-mow*. But anyone can be a rebel if he wants to. Even human beings."

He stirred the fire with a stick. "Me, I had no real interest in the idea. I heard about it all secondhand and figured it wasn't any of my business. Like most folks, I had my own problems to worry about, like staying away from train-yard bulls, or finding a place to lie down on a snowy night. Then one day my old partner, fella named Hognose, who'd been bumming around with me for years, got snatched up right in front of my eyes by a ship that might have been the sister of the one that brought us here—if it wasn't the very same! Right in broad daylight on the South Dakota prairie. That changed my thinking some. And it got worse. A week later I heard that old Hognose's body had been found, withered up like a dead leaf. Folks who saw it said they believed that all the juice had been sucked right out of him.

"Well, nobody pays too much attention to a dead hobo, and I've seen more than a couple of 'em myself, but still, it didn't sit right with me the way them skreeps did that. Just sucked him dry like a bottle of soda pop and chucked him out again. And it didn't seem right for me to just walk away, neither. So I went to see some fellas who'd been muttering about aliens for years, and they asked me if I'd heard about the rebels. I said I had, a little, but just campfire bull. I said if they was fighting the same bugs that took my buddy, though, they could count me in. They said they'd be in touch.

"That was all I heard for a while. I almost forgot about it. Not Hognose—that still bothered me—but these fellas with their talk about rebellion. There's plenty of hoboes who like to talk, you understand. I thought maybe they'd been pulling my leg. Then one night a fella showed up at my campfire—just stepped out of the dark and sat down. Kind of spooked me, to tell you the truth. I still don't know who he was, or how he found me, but he said that in three days there would be a special meeting in a place we both knew, down around Amarillo. A gathering of rebels, he said, and then he was gone—just disappeared as quiet as he come.

"I hopped six freights in three days to get from New York to Texas. The meeting place was just a field way beyond the outskirts of town. I got there right on time and figured I'd been tricked—not a soul around. The next thing I know, this big gray saucer comes swooping down out of the sky, a hatch opens, and I'm sucked up quicker'n a dollar at a banker's convention. I thought I was done for, of course, but it wasn't bad at all. Not at all. The aliens were mostly *yarmuks* from the planet Fempis, but there were some others there, too, *gingaboo* and *burgon*, as well as folks from different parts of Earth, and even a couple more hoboes like myself. The *yarmuks* gave us all a space ride, not a long trip, just a spin around the neighborhood, so to speak—Mars, Jupiter—enough to convince us they were serious. And while we were still flying, they filled us in.

"They told us about the skreepish empire, what a sorry thing it is, and how the planets inside it suffer and sometimes die out altogether." Joe stirred the fire with his stick. "I caught an earful that night. But the main thing I learned, the thing that scared me most, was that the skreeps want to make Earth one of their colonies." He paused. "They might even want to make it the new Skreepia."

"New *Skreepia*?" Jack scrunched over, with Milo nestled in his lap. "What does that mean?"

"They say the skreeps are on at least their second planet! Everyone says the first one is so wrecked there's no way to live there anymore. And from what I hear, the current one ain't a whole lot better. These monsters go through planets the way a hog goes through a bucket of slop. So now they're eyeball-ing Earth. The only problem—from their point of view—is it's a long haul from where they are now, and the passage ain't exactly reliable. And from what I hear, the skreepish Queen don't like to take chances. You can see why, after the way that tunnel collapsed on us. She could've lost her whole fleet in something like that."

"Which is where Mr. Creedle's destabilizer comes in," said Isadora.

"You got it. And that's where I come in, too, in a way. The rebels had an idea the skreeps might be working on something like that and a notion they might try to have it made on Earth. The skreeps think we're savages, but according to Krebs, they think we might have special powers, too."

"Special powers?" asked Isadora.

"That's what they think."

"Is Krebs a rebel?" asked Jack.

"I don't know exactly. All I can say is, she's a skreep who

doesn't like her own empire. She says there are others like her. They don't want to move to Earth. They want to fix their own planet. Some even want to go back to the first Skreepia. They say that's where they belong. They say living in other places has made them forget who they are. Who knows?" He poked the fire so that it flared up, bathing their faces in red light.

"But how did you find out about the destabilizer?" asked Isadora.

"I was getting to that. All the rebels wanted me to do—wanted any of us humans to do—was keep our eyes open for anything the skreeps might be up to. So I did—and in nearly a year I learned precisely nothing. Then I heard a rumor. A rocket had landed in Mexico. It didn't sound like skreeps—"

"Nope," said Jack. "That was Uncle Bud."

Joe pointed a finger at him. "I found that out later. At the time I was wandering through Arizona, so it made some sense to have a look. By the time I reached the site where the thing came down, the Americans were gone and the *federales* were just leaving. But it turned out the skreeps were still interested. They surprised me by showing up right after I got there. I was nosing around among some cactus, and the next thing I know, one of them spiders had me by the neck. Lucky for me, she wasn't paying attention. In fact, she was busy doing about five other things, collecting bits of rocket junk, reading instruments, and talking into her communicator. I guess they don't expect humans to fight back, and I don't guess I would have, neither, if I hadn't remembered what they did to old Hognose. Well, I managed to grab my knife, and when she was leaning over to get a better look at me, I poked her in the eye. It must have hurt, too, because she dropped me like a hot iron, and somehow or other I managed to get away."

"The commander!" Isadora cried. "She's blind in one eye and has a scar running down the side of her face." She pantomimed the mark with her finger.

"So I hear. It's one of the reasons I decided to jump ship. I was already taking some chances as a stowaway, but with her as the captain, my prospects were looking downright gloomy. The main thing, though, is we need to get word out to the rebels. I was working on that before the saucer left Vern Hollow, but nobody was close enough to respond. Which is why I hopped on board. And now that the time tunnel has collapsed, I don't know if they could reach us anyway. We need to find the *local* resistance here on Arboria and hope they can see the danger in that machine."

"But how did you know the skreeps would come to Vern Hollow?" asked Jack. "And how did you find out about the destabilizer?"

"Detective work, mostly," said Joe, with a touch of pride. "In a roundabout way, that rocket led me back to your uncle. I was as surprised as anyone at first. Folks figured it was the government that did it, the army or the air force. Nobody could believe it was just some fella working out of his garage. But I was able to get close, on account of the boardinghouse you live in. Nobody at the Pines paid me the slightest attention. Did you even know I stayed there five times in the past couple of years?"

"I guess not," Jack admitted.

"I ain't offended. I'm just making a point. Nobody notices a hobo." Joe put another log on the fire and picked up his harmonica.

"Speaking of drifters," said Jack sleepily, "I don't suppose you ever heard of a fellow named Stanley Murchison?"

Joe thought for a while. "No, son, I don't believe I have. Why?"

"No reason." Jack curled up, pulling the blanket tight around his neck.

The fire crackled. Joe played songs about faded love.

. . .

29. THE VEIL TREES

ISADORA OPENED her eyes to a dazzle of sparks. She heard a shout and stumbled to her feet. Something heavy knocked her down. Bright coals blazed around her. Their red light reflected in Jack's wide eyes. "What's going on?"

An enormous bat-creature clung to Joe's shoulders. It bullied him to the ground. Its leathery wings fanned the fire.

"I don't know!"

The bat-creature flapped into the air. Joe got up, gripping a heavy branch in both hands. When the monster plunged again, he swung. *Whuump!* The monster jerked up as if pulled by a string. Another monster swooped down. Isadora ducked. Its claws brushed the top of her head.

"Come to me!" Joe shouted. Jack and Isadora followed him out of the firelight. "They're gathering. Five or six of 'em. We need to find shelter quick."

The veil trees still glowed softly in the darkness. "Maybe we could hide in one of those," said Jack.

"I can't think of a better idea." They gathered their packs and ran toward the grove. Overhead the bat-creatures shrieked and circled. Joe swung his club, and they bobbed over him like marionettes.

"Go on!" he shouted, and they ran ahead. The ground soft-ened. White sand glowed like a moonlit beach. Gentle shad-ows swirled around them, shaped by the movement of the veils. The children slowed, walking as if in a trance toward the heart of the grove. Joe stumbled up behind them. Straight ahead, in a small clearing, was the largest of the trees.

With a shriek, one of the bat-creatures flopped to the ground behind them. Its eyes bulged. Its down-turned mouth, hinged like a fish's, contained rows of sharp teeth. Another of the creatures landed behind it, then another. They shambled forward, the tips of their bald wings carving patterns in the sand.

"Night greelies!" Jack spat.

"We'd better see if we can get inside that tree," said Joe. A gap opened, and they charged in. The veils drifted in front of their eyes and slid across their bodies. Their touch was both feather-soft and oddly insistent. Jack tripped over Isadora, who stumbled into Joe, and they all shuffled sideways like shoppers caught inside a revolving door. The veils parted, and they stood outside the tree once again. Two more greelies plopped down.

"What just happened?" whispered Isadora.

"I can't figure it out," said Joe.

"Maybe if we go *under* them—" Jack tried crawling. The veils closed around him briefly, then spit him out. The greelies cackled.

"I think they're afraid of the trees," said Isadora. "Otherwise they would have attacked by now."

"It's a standoff," Joe agreed. "But I have the feeling they're up to something." Abruptly the creatures parted ranks. Heavy wings flapped, and the biggest night greelie of all swooped down. Its jaws were as wide as a shark's.

"Get down!" shouted Joe. He stepped forward, swinging his stick. The greelies hissed. Their leader grabbed the club in its teeth and flung it away.

Suddenly Milo ran in from the darkness. Kicking sand in Jack's face as he passed, he disappeared inside the veils.

The monster paused, and Joe flung two fistfuls of sand into its eyes. It screamed and staggered backward. The humans pressed against the tree.

"How do you suppose Milo got in?" Isadora wondered.

"I don't know," said Jack. "Maybe the tree likes chickens."

"I think it's more than that. I think there's some kind of defense mechanism here. Apparently the tree doesn't regard Milo as a threat."

"It doesn't know him very well."

Joe took a deep breath. "I think you're onto something. Everyone just relax. We gotta show the tree we don't mean it no harm."

"You may not have noticed," said Jack, "but we're surrounded by angry bat-creatures."

"Joe is right. You have to be calm." Isadora breathed unsteadily.

"We can't just stand here! It's crazy!"

"It's our only hope. They're afraid of the trees, so we need the trees to let us in."

"Maybe they know something we don't! Maybe we should be afraid, too."

"I don't think so." A veil caressed her cheek. Another passed over Joe.

"This is one of your *feelings*, isn't it?"

"Just relax, Jack." The veils enveloped her.

Jack stood on the outside, breathing hard. The big monster, still half blind, lunged at him. Jack stepped back, turned his heel, and toppled over, striking his head on the ground. He lay still. The veils drifted over him.

Isadora lost her sense of time. She could still hear the greelies outside, but their shrieks now seemed far away. The glow from the tree reminded her of summer moonlight: gentle, warm, and pure. She felt as if she were floating inside a dream.

The final layer of curtains parted, and she found herself in a circular room. A massive silver column corkscrewed from the ground at its center and rose in loosening spirals to a crown of arched branches high overhead. There a small, round window opened on to the starry sky.

The air was fresh and strangely homey, though its scent was nothing she had ever smelled before. The floor was a beach of soft white sand. Joe sat beside Milo in the middle of the room, gazing at the great trunk. About ten feet up was a circular hole that seemed to have been packed with rocks and mud. She walked over. Joe's expression was strange.

"Do ya hear it?"

She listened. It was not so much an external sound as a strange music in her head, lonely, like the whisper of wind through a valley. *It's telling us something*, she thought, but the meaning escaped her.

"What's up?"

Jack stood beside her, rubbing the back of his head. Raising a finger to her lips, she turned back to the tree, but the spell was broken. The music drifted away. Suddenly she felt tired, as if she had sprung a leak. Her eyelids drooped. She stumbled to the edge of the room and stretched out on the sand.

• • •

HER EYES fluttered open. The sky overhead was creamy. She stretched and felt the sand shift around her. Jack was curled up

with Milo a few feet away. Joe squatted beside the wide trunk.
Two gnarled lumps of stone and clay sat with him. The lumps
were bound together with roots. They had eyes like pebbles
and mouths like cracked cement. The scene was strange but
not at all frightening. Joe walked over to her. He held Pungo's
gift in his weathered hands. "I hope you don't mind me bor-
rowing this. Our hosts were curious to see it."

"Not at all." She returned the turf to her purse. "Who *are*
our hosts?"

"Root people. Least, that's as near as I can translate it. They
crawled out of the hole in that tree trunk after you and the boy
fell asleep. Been talking all night."

"How do you know what they're saying?"

"They talk directly into your head. It takes some getting used to."

Jack crawled over. Joe filled him in.

"Are they friendly?"

"Sure. That is, they seem to like *me* fine. With you two it's a little different."

"Why? What did we do?"

"It's not what you *did*, it's who you *are*. It seems you're part of a local prophecy, and that makes them a little, well, *shy*."

"A *prophecy*?" asked Isadora. "What are you talking about?"

"The root people watch over the veil trees, and in return the trees give them wisdom. One thing they've been predicting is the coming of children—*saplings*, they say—from a place beyond time. Odd, ain't it? You're supposed to have special powers that'll help save Arboria from the skreeps."

"We don't have special powers!" laughed Isadora.

"You don't have to *shout* it," whispered Jack. "If they want to think we have special powers, why not let 'em?"

"Because it isn't true."

"It *might* be true," said Joe. "Not that you can bend spoons with your eyeballs or anything, but *something* is going on here. This power—I ain't too sure it *belongs* to you, but it seems to be following you around. You keep getting out of scrapes when it don't seem possible. And the time you spent—that's the wrong term, ain't it?—on Hellebeezia, well, that was a little *different*. I was there, too, if you recall, but all the same I *wasn't* there, and I'm not there now, if I follow the logic. Somehow, while the rest of us was caught in time, you two stepped right *out* of it. I don't know if that's special power, but it's enough to make you think."

"It makes *me* dizzy," said Jack.

The hobo yawned. "You know, these trees ain't generally kind to strangers. Most folks who step into the veils never find their way out. They just wander on and on, looking for an exit, till they collapse. The root people told me about it. That could have happened to us, too. This crater is a sacred place to all Arboria, and the grove of veils is the most sacred place of all. Strangers ain't allowed. Even the skreeps avoid it.

"Then we come along, splashing in the pond, building fires, scuffling with them greelies. The trees didn't care for any of that. Luckily Isadora had the good sense to settle down, let the trees get a feel for us. That did the trick. Because when they felt you, they felt Hellebeezia, too. All the trees know that place. It's the reason they let us in."

. . .

30. THE ROOT PEOPLE

IT WAS ODD being part of a prophecy. Isadora hated it. Jack thought it was great. Their presence made the root people extremely shy. Seeing the children approach, the creatures scrambled up the trunk and disappeared into their hole. Once hidden, they began to sing. After a while Isadora understood the words, but the song was so full of flattery it made her cringe with embarrassment. She tugged Jack's sleeve. "Come on. Let's go to the pond."

"Wait! This is good stuff."

"Jack!" She tugged again, and reluctantly he followed.

Joe, worn out from his sleepless night, lay on the sand with his hat pulled over his eyes, snoring. Isadora and Jack passed easily through the veils and stepped outside into the light of a clear morning. Milo, who had wandered out before them, crowed.

They drank from the pond and then, stripping down to their underwear, went for a long swim. When they finally got out, they felt truly clean for the first time in ages. They sat down on flat rocks and let the warm sunlight dry them.

Later, Joe walked up. In his hat he carried what appeared to be a collection of yellow stones. "Breakfast," he explained. "Also lunch and dinner, from what I hear." The food consisted of something dense and brown stuffed inside a wrapper of sticky leaves. "The root people make 'em. They say just a little will fill you up."

Jack sniffed one suspiciously. "It's like a potato made out of dirt."

"It couldn't be any worse than that skreep paste." Isadora took a careful bite. At first she thought Jack was right, that what she was eating was nothing more than mud. Then the flavor emerged. She swallowed, and a warm tingle ran through her. "You know? It really isn't bad."

Jack burped.

"The root people are making a bunch of these for our trip," said Joe. "Which starts tomorrow morning, in case you was wondering."

"Maybe we should stick around for a couple of days." Jack stretched in the sun.

"I don't think so. The root people say the skreeps will be coming soon. The greelies may have already told 'em we're here. Besides, it's a long walk to where the rebels are." Joe put the rest of his potato in a coat pocket and leaned back on the rock. "You can rest up today, though. We'll sleep inside the tree again tonight."

•   •   •

THE NEXt morning as they prepared to leave, a root person approached them shyly. It was bigger than the others and seemed older somehow. It spoke in the telepathic language they all used, but was more formal than the others. "You have honored us with your presence, *saplings*." It bowed, and its roots creaked. "We thank you. The *trees* thank you."

"We didn't really do anything," said Isadora.

"You're welcome," said Jack.

"You come from the Eternal Place. You carry the wisdom of that place with you."

"Earth?"

"Hellebeezia!" said Isadora, poking Jack with an elbow.

"Yes. The place of endless forests—"

"Actually—" Jack interrupted, but Isadora elbowed him again.

"—*Our* trees see you there, standing still. It is how they know you are saplings, even though on this world you skitter about so frantically."

"That's really how we are," said Isadora.

"You are saplings," insisted the root creature. "Even though you are timeless, you are young. And you have been sent to help Arboria. You may not know it, but it is true. She has been badly wounded. Once this world was covered with forests from sea to sea. Then the skreeps came. Now most of the trees are gone. But even now the roots remain. The roots link everything together. They bind this planet so that it does not come apart. The wounds are temporary, but the roots are eternal.

You have reminded the trees of
this. You remind them of the
life that is buried beneath
our soil." The root creature
bowed again. They watched
it climb back into the tree.

"That was weird," said Jack.

Joe hoisted his pack onto his
shoulders. "Some parts of this
story ain't gonna be so easy
to tell."

A crowd of root people
followed them across the crater. They stopped at the edge of
the pebbly moss. "I reckon this is good-bye, then," said Joe.

"Thank you for your help," said Isadora.

Jack waved. Milo bit him. As they started up the slope, the
creatures began to sing. The song was like a warm breeze.
When they reached the rim, the humans looked back. The veil
trees shimmered like jewels in the early light.

• • •

THE SAUCER spun to a stop. Dust settled around it. When the
hatch opened and the ramp lowered, Sergeant Webb was the
first to step out. Grady followed, stumbling when Groot gave
him a shove from behind. Last of all came Phoony. A new hand
had begun to grow from the stump of his forearm, but it was
small and not yet properly formed.

They had returned to the exact same landing site. The
gloomy walls of the gorge surrounded them once again.

"Ebryone got talkers, hm?" said Phoony in broken English,
holding up his communicator. The others raised theirs, too.

"Good. Find hatchlings, den you talk." He held the communicator to his wide mouth and pantomimed a conversation. The humans nodded. Groot looked bored. "Meet back here quicky time."

Phoony pulled Groot aside and spoke quietly in Skreepish. "Careful where you go. That Beast Eleven is down here somewhere."

"What?"

"Captain didn't tell you that part, did she? She didn't tell me, either, but I'm a Finder—I found out. She dumped the beast when we came here last time."

"So what are we doing? If the beast is here, it must have eaten those hatchlings by now."

"You catch on quick. I get the feeling the captain just wants proof they were here, so she can stop worrying. I figure she put these new *ooman bings* out as bait. Maybe we're bait, too. She isn't too fond of us, either, the witch."

"You can't call her that!"

"Dry up. You'll be lucky if she doesn't have you dismembered. Did you forget the hatchlings were *your* prisoners? Like I say, we just need to find some proof they were here. Some hair, maybe, or a bone. That's probably all that's left of them anyway."

Phoony chuckled to himself as he wandered into the gorge. As expected, Groot lingered by the open hatch. If the jailor was too scared to help, Phoony didn't mind. Finding was solitary work, and Groot was an ass.

• • •

SERGEANT WEBB showed Grady a sneaker print in the mud. "That's Creedle, right there."

Grady found another one. "Look, Pop! The girl was here, too."

"Good work, son. That proves both of 'em were down here. Now we just have to figure out where they went."

They moved slowly across the sand. On the edge of a puddle, Grady found another shoe print. It was unmistakably human, but much too large for Jack or Isadora.

"Hey, Pop. Come here."

Webb examined the print. "Well, that's something, ain't it?"

"What does it mean?"

"I don't know, son. I'll have to think about it."

• • •

GROOT WATCHED them from the ship's ramp. *Bait*, he thought. Suddenly his communicator buzzed. When he opened it, Phoony was practically shouting.

"They went up the cliffs! I didn't think they could, but they did. The beast was here, too! Come quick."

"But—"

"Now!" said Phoony and clicked off.

• • •

"STAY," GROOT told the Webbs, as if they were a pair of dogs. He scurried up the cliff as easily as a spider on Earth might run up a wall.

Sergeant Webb clicked open his communicator. "What gives?" he asked peevishly.

Phoony's harsh voice responded. "We find hatchlings. *You* stay." He clicked off.

The sergeant stared at the communicator, then put it away. "So much for teamwork."

"Now what do we do?" asked Grady.

"We do what cops always do," answered his father. "We wait."

They waited. After a while they dozed. A dark shadow detached itself from the canyon wall and drifted past them like a cloud of smoke. It moved silently to the ship.

. . .

31. WALKING

BEYOND THE crater the land wrinkled like a furrowed brow. Wiry plants huddled in the gullies, while the ridges remained rocky and bare. Occasionally an ancient tree stump appeared, flat topped or toppled so that its roots clawed the sky. The travelers went up and down, up and down.

"Ain't exactly cheerful, is it?" said Joe.

They stood on top of a ridge. In one direction, thorny spires, black as onyx, stabbed the sky. In another stood a series of gray-green domes, creased and convoluted like massive brains. Straight ahead, the landscape shattered in a rocky jumble. "You sure we're going the right way?" asked Jack.

"*Sure* would be a pretty strong word for it. The root people call these the 'dead lands.' They say we'd best get across 'em before nightfall."

"Or what?"

"They mentioned a critter that sounded like a giant scorpion—not to be alarming."

"Not at all," muttered Isadora.

From the top of the next ridge they looked down on a valley pocked with dark holes and twisted chimneys of calcified stone. Colored gases rose from the chimneys, while steaming goop bubbled from the vents. Occasionally a geyser spattered green or orange mud high into the air.

"There it is," said Joe with satisfaction. "The root people told me about this place, and Krebs drew it on her map. There's fresh water on the far side of this valley. We can camp there."

Jack started down the hill.

"I don't believe I'd do that," the hobo called after him.

"Didn't you say that's where we're going?"

"Sure, but you'll never reach it that way. The gases from those vents'll kill you like a cockroach. This is one of those times when it's best to go *around*."

In the blue distance the ridge curved to form the valley's far wall. "What a cruddy planet," Jack muttered. They began to walk.

. . .

LATER HE lay on a flat rock and listened to the tinkling of water as it dripped into a tiny pool. Dinner, such as it was, had already been eaten; Isadora sat a few feet away, writing notes in her journal. Joe built a fire. Gases from the poisoned valley glowed in the fading light.

"You believe what that creature said about roots binding this world together?" asked Jack.

Isadora put down her pen. "I have no idea what to believe."

"It doesn't work like that on Earth, does it—with the roots?"

"Certainly not."

"On Earth we use rubber bands," said Joe. The fire crackled. He took out his harmonica and played "Leaving Cheyenne." Jack got up and put on his coat.

•   •   •

XAAFUUN TAPPED her console. "You are certain they escaped?" Time had played a subtle trick. Though the ship had returned to Arboria as soon as she discovered the hatchlings were missing, already several Arborian days had passed.

"Positive," said Phoony. "They killed a hoolie halfway up the wall—"

"Killed a *hoolie*?"

"I was surprised, too!" He had already decided not to mention that the beast had played a part, or that there was another *ooman bing*, a full-grown one, with the hatchlings. Those were facts he couldn't explain—facts, therefore, that could be used against him. "The greelies followed them, but something went wrong—they wouldn't say *what*—and the hatchlings got away."

"Clever, aren't they?" Xaafuun leered. Phoony was hiding something. In fact, ever since she'd disciplined him, the Finder had been different: sullen, and worse than that—*untrustworthy*. Perhaps more discipline was needed. A plan began to take shape in her mind. "You wish to catch these *Uurthlings*, don't you, Ensign Phoony?"

"Of course, Madame."

"*Of course.* You were stationed on this planet once, weren't you?"

"Yes, Madame. The base at Kraakeria." It had been his job to track Arborian spies as they ran messages across the border. Knowing the planet didn't mean he liked it, though—in fact, just the opposite.

"I'm pleased you're so eager to do your duty! So pleased I will not only grant your wish, I will give you extra help! Groot will accompany you and the *ooman bing* Finders, too. Working together, you should have little difficulty capturing the fugitives."

"But, Madame," Phoony sputtered. "You can't—"

"*Can't I?*" She could almost hear her little trap snapping shut. Groot and the *Uurthlings* would be a terrible burden on poor Phoony. They would slow him down unbearably. He would still complete his task. He was a competent Finder, and the fugitives *were* just hatchlings. But he would look ridiculous—and more important, the search would drag on, while she returned to Skreepia without him—and without his self-serving, self-congratulating, *officially untrue* account of how the Special Item was captured! "You may gather whatever provisions you need. But be quick about it. Time drags on. Oh, and Phoony?"

"Yes, Madame?"

"Enjoy your journey!"

. . .

"'ENJOY YOUR journey!'" Phoony stared at the desert. Its bright light was painful to his eyes. The saucer was gone, and with it, his anticipation of a return to Skreepia, his anticipation of the moment when he could finally let it be known who had located the Special Item and saved the expedition. Unfortunately Xaafuun had anticipated the moment, too. *Sneaky witch!*

He scanned the horizon, his eyes unconsciously skipping over the big crater. Two things spurred him on. First was the job itself. Tracking three *ooman bings* across an alien desert—*that* would test his skills! But second, and even more important, was *revenge*. He would complete his mission so that he could return home. He would return to Skreepia so that one night he could twist Xaafuun's neck just as she had twisted his arm. Yes, that was enough to keep him going. "Grab those slaves, Groot," he ordered. "We're heading east."

• • •

FOR DAYS the hobo, the children, and the chicken traveled over hard country. None of it was as barren as the landscape surrounding the gorge, but it was all harsh, windswept terrain full of narrow ravines and spiny ridges. The trees were mostly what the root creatures had described as *krek*, short, stubby things with trunks like stacked inner tubes and wispy crowns that offered little in the way of shade. Occasionally they came across more impressive, purple-skinned trees with spreading branches and yellow leaves that spiraled like rams' horns. The purple trees provided decent firewood, if you were careful about thorns—and if you were even more careful, a safe place to shelter overnight. There were also thousands, maybe millions, of closely cropped tree stumps. The desolate landscape had once been a vast forest.

Joe spoke little, preferring to sing, but the children could tell he was uneasy. Some evenings he doused the campfire with sand before it was fully dark; other times he chose to lead them across difficult country, even though easier passages could be seen in the valleys. "They're following us," he said simply, when Isadora asked about it, but he would not say who was following or how he knew.

One day they came to a ghost town filled with the ruins of houses like the ones Jack and Isadora had seen from the air. Some had been mere huts, but others were far more elaborate, with curving walls and the shattered remains of big windows and great wooden doors. Joe pointed out the signs of battle, from deep craters to pockmarked walls where time had reduced the black starbursts of impact to a whispery gray. On the road they found the unmistakable three-toed footprints of skreeps. Joe brushed away their own prints with a handful of twigs, and they hurried back to the hills.

The next morning as they were striking camp they heard a stifled yelp and, stepping into a clearing between several small pink trees, saw a wolf-sized animal with dozens of legs thrashing madly on the sandy ground. It took a moment for them to realize that the beast had been snared by a tree root, which had wrapped itself around its head in a series of tightening coils like a boa constrictor. Soon another root shot out of the sand and grabbed the animal around its middle, while another rose to take it by the tail. When the victim was completely bound, the sand underneath it subsided. It disappeared with a slurp. After that they avoided pink trees.

Sometimes at night Joe told them what he had learned about Arboria from the root people. "There's easier country to the north of here," he explained, tucking his harmonica into a coat pocket and leaning back on one elbow. They were camped beneath one of the purple trees. "But I don't dare take us that way, because skreepish roads run right through it. Skreeps control this whole part of the planet—which is to say, most of it. The rebels have just a little strip along the coastline. From what I gather, the skreeps don't like water too much. But what really stopped them was that they got whipped by the natives when they tried to cross the mountains. So that's the way it stands. They keep threatening to finish the job, but for now they just guard the border and wait."

"Wait for what?" asked Jack.

"Troops. From the sound of things, the skreeps are spread pretty thin."

"If they're guarding the border, does that mean we have to sneak past them?" asked Isadora. "How are we going to do that?"

"There's a pass, way up where it's snowy all the time. The skreeps don't like the place, and they don't guard it very well." Joe leaned against the trunk, pulling his blanket over him. He tilted his battered hat down so that the brim rested on his nose. "At least that's what we gotta hope."

. . .

32. HUNTED

XAAFUUN REGARDED Bug Greedle sourly. "Why is it not working?"

"How should I know?" He peered into the refrigerator cabinet as if searching for a midnight snack. "I'm still working out the *bugs*—so to speak. It's complicated."

The commander leaned back in her chair. *She would make his* life *complicated, the brute!* It pleased her to think about all the ways in which she might destroy him when the time came, but in truth, she had come to accept a certain amount of insolence from Bug Greedle. The alien was a *king*, after all.

She no longer questioned his royalty, which fit so neatly with her own ambitions. Truth, after all, was whatever important people like herself said it was. Still, something about the story bothered her. Perhaps she was simply irritated because the destabilizer wasn't working. Or perhaps it was Beast Eleven. Evidently the monster had found its way back on board when the idiot Groot left the hatch open on Arboria. She would skin Groot alive if he ever found his way back to Skreepia. But that wasn't what was bothering her.

Of course—it was obvious! The problem was the king. Bug

Greedle *by himself* made no sense! Who'd ever heard of a *male* ruler, a king without a queen? The idea was unnatural, even on a backward planet like *Uurth*. Only queens were fit to rule. As soon as the thought came to her, she relaxed. She couldn't imagine how she'd missed it.

And look, there was the proof! While Bug Greedle labored like a common slave on his invention, the queen, *Uurth's real ruler*, sat quietly in her private cell. Xaafuun thought about Scientist Shumway. Hadn't she seen it right away, the odd dignity, the poise? Only the stress of their voyage had distracted her from the truth. "Bug Greedle," she said quietly. "You have been hiding your queen from me."

He pulled his head out of the refrigerator. "What?"

Xaafuun gurgled. *The Exalted One would be pleased!* A conquered *Uurth* Queen would make a fine addition to her Fabulous Jubilee. "Never mind," she said, "just fix the machine."

"You got it." Bud went back to work.

. . .

PHOONY RARELY slept now beyond a catnap. He didn't trust Groot or the *ooman bings*. But more than anything, he didn't trust the planet. Arboria was a shifty sort of place, too much sunlight during the day, too much stirring below the surface at night. He felt he was being watched. Worse than that, he felt he was being *hated*. How he wished he could proceed directly to Kraakeria, with its illusion screens and smell chambers and durbo music. But the trail he followed led relentlessly away from civilization, and anyway, he did not wish to alert the Kraakerian skreeps about his mission. The swine! They would be only too willing to catch the *ooman bings* themselves and steal his glory.

Big Webb dozed beneath a baanakaas tree. Groot was on the other side of the ridge, pretending to keep watch. No doubt he was dozing, too. The hatchling, Little Webb, was asleep on a rock. It was late afternoon. A snapper approached Big Webb, waving its claws in the air. He thought about letting it do its work. But no, that would only give Xaafuun more ammunition to use against him. He must keep the aliens alive, at least for now. He snatched the spiny beast and held it in front of his face. As its poisonous fangs bit the air, he crunched it loudly and tossed the carcass into his mouth.

Webb opened his eyes. "What was that?"

"Snapper. Very poisony. I save your life." Phoony yawned. The double sun slipped toward the horizon. "I hear you big Finder, on *Uurth*."

"I'm not a *Finder*, whatever *that* is. I'm a cop."

"Same ting. So, *kaap*, what you find?"

"All right, have it your way. I find bad guys. I find 'em, and I lock 'em up."

"Ah, *lokkemup*. So, some *ooman bings* are *baadgize*?"

"That's right." Webb sat up. "The boy is, for sure. All the Creedles are rotten to the core. As for the other two, you tell me. Just the fact that they're running around with this Creedle character says a lot. And look at 'em! You got a black girl from Boston who claims to be a scientist. You ever hear of such a thing? Me neither. And the other one—who knows? So, yeah, I guess you could say they're *bad guys*."

Phoony yawned again. Big Webb bored him. "Phoony," he said, pointing to himself, "is *great* Finder. Spies, treasure, slaves, Phoony finds ebryting." He described the time he found fourteen escaped rebels hiding in the Mist Swamp on Trenchen Five, and the time he discovered the Great Jewel of Asmarkop hidden in the Well of Whispers on Veeng. But he had the feeling Big Webb wasn't listening.

"It's the Creedles who caused all this, you know." Webb's gesture took in all of Arboria, if not the entire, flawed universe. "They're the reason we're out here. And I'm not going to let them get away with it. Not this time."

Grady joined them. "You talking about the Creedles?"

"You bet I am. The boy especially. That kid'll be the worst of the lot, someday. Wanna know why?" He answered his own question. *"Blood."*

"Blood!" Phoony licked his lips.

"That's right. He's not just a Creedle, you see. He's a *Murchison*! That's on account of his father, Stanley Murchison. Talk about crooks! This Murchison blew into town one day, all full of schemes. Gold mines, copper mines, hair tonics. Man could sell anything. Sold Ogden Parnell a share in an undersea oil well, sight unseen."

"He got Pop with the hair tonic," said Grady.

"Never mind that," said his father.

"Turned his scalp red for two months!"

"That's not the point. The point is, these schemes of his

were all hot air. Everything he sold was a fake. The man is dangerous—or at least he was. One day he just disappeared without a trace. By then even the Creedles knew he was a bum. The mother wouldn't even keep his name. In fact, the only thing he left behind was the boy. But that's bad enough. You see? Murchison was a criminal, and he married a Creedle. So what does that make?"

"Don' know," said Phoony.

"What's crooked times crooked?"

The Finder recalled a mathematical principle about multiplying negatives. "Straight?"

"Wrong! It's *double* crooked! That's what Jack Creedle is: double crooked! And that's why we need to catch him. We need to stop him before he grows up!"

. . .

BY THE SIXTH day the travelers could see mountains rising far to the east. When Joe began pointing at what he called a pass, Isadora suddenly realized she had been staring at them all morning. What she had imagined to be white clouds on the horizon were in fact snowy peaks. "We have to go across *that*?" she asked, horrified.

"Unless you can find a way around it."

They stood on a rocky ledge surrounded by a bed of the orange succulents they had come to call "kissing plants" due to their disconcerting habit of nibbling hands and legs. "There's a place off to the left that doesn't look *so* awful. Do you see it?"

"Sure do. Unfortunately that's Battle Gap. The root people told me all about it. That's where the Arborians finally stopped the skreeps. It's the one place we have to avoid at all costs, since the skreepish base is just below it. The spot I'm talking about is way on down to the right, between those peaks that look like rabbit ears."

"You've got to be kidding," said Jack.

"I ain't. The natives call that one 'Fool's Gap.' I believe the skreeps came to grief there once. According to the root people, they avoid it now. Looks a bit tricky, don't it?"

Four days later the mountains were much closer. They formed an immense barricade across the whole horizon. Battle Gap was far to the north. Isadora could no longer find the narrow slot of Fool's Gap, though Joe assured her she was staring right at it. "That's the way with mountains," he said. "They always look bad from below."

"You think they'll look better when we get up there?" Jack asked hopefully.

"I didn't say that. We'll be up to our necks in snow, most likely, and that's if we don't fall off." He smiled. "On the other hand, at least we're traveling light."

"Traveling light" meant they had nearly run out of food and water. The dirt potatoes were almost gone now. Their canteens, filled three days earlier from a sulfurous pool, were nearly empty. And they were now certain they were being followed.

Because the mountains made him nervous, Jack had adopted the habit of turning his back on them whenever they stopped to rest. One day, as he sat on a rock, he noticed four figures moving slowly across the valley below. "Hey!" he whispered. "Who's that?"

Squinting through her glasses, Isadora could only make out indistinct specks, but Joe, whose eyesight was keen, saw two skreeps. "As for the other two—if I thought I could believe it, I'd say they was human."

"It's the Webbs!" Jack said disgustedly. "I'll bet you a million bucks the little ugly one is Grady!"

• • •

ALL THE EVIDENCE said one thing: The *Uurthlings* were heading for the mountains. Phoony wrinkled his lips. He *hated* the mountains. It wasn't so much the towering cliffs—such obstacles were trivial to a skreep. No, it was the *snow*. Cold, awful, wet snow! Skreeps were not made for it. Their legs plunged through its surface like pushpins, while their heavy bodies quickly became mired. Still, *ooman bings* could not be much better. Did the hatchlings really think they could get across such a divide? Or were they tricking him somehow?

He had seen little sign of his quarry since the second day. And no wonder. The planet was working against him! He was certain the *Uurthlings*' footsteps were being brushed away, just for spite, by the wasteland's miserable, stumpish trees.

But Phoony didn't need footprints. He didn't need clues. He had instinct, which was better. He moved to the lowlands where travel was easier, and headed east. When the Webbs faltered, he carried them under his arms. When Groot complained, he kicked him. Time was everything. He had to find the hatchlings before they reached those awful peaks. He had to cut them off.

When the Webbs needed a rest, Phoony gave it to them. He wasn't sentimental; he simply knew they would die. What would Xaafuun do to him if *that* happened? It was a clever trap she had set. If he went too fast, his *Uurthlings* would die, and if he went too slow, the other *Uurthlings* would get away.

Then there was Groot, the wretch. Phoony kicked him again. "Get up. You need to call Kraakeria."

The jailor's face was filthy from the long trek, his bodysuit torn. His antennae hung from his head like broken wings. "Me? Why should *I* call?"

"Because they *know* me on this planet. They know I'm a Finder. If I tell them I'm here, they'll know I'm looking for something valuable. I don't want them to know that. I want them to think it is just you, a stinking jailor, sent to find prisoners." His eyes glinted dangerously. "Listen. I want them to send patrols down the mountain road to head off the *Uurthlings*. I want them to *scare* the *ooman bings*, but I don't want them to *find* the *ooman bings*. That part we will do ourselves."

"So what if they find 'em? The sooner they do, the sooner we can all go home."

"Idiot! Do you want to go back to Skreepia empty-handed? Do you want to tell Xaafuun how you walked all the way from Grand Gorge to the mountains and *didn't* catch those *ooman bings*? What do you think she'd do to you then?"

"All right! You don't have to *yell* at me." Groot flicked open his communicator.

•   •   •

Dr. Shumway hoped she had been using her time wisely, but the journey had been full of distractions and frankly, *foolishness*. She ignored the feathered crown perched on her worktable, though the matching cloak had practical value. Since feathers were efficient insulators, she had laid it on her bed. Her new quarters were commodious and clean. Still, there was that underlying absurdity. Did they really think she was a *queen*?

She opened the electronic scroll. For some time she had been attempting to learn the skreeps' written language. Now she was uncertain whether such a thing was possible with only two eyes. When the doorway opened she switched it off. Bud Creedle appeared, accompanied by the captain's footservant, Mellis.

"Mr. Creedle," she said, then addressed the servant. "Mellis, I wonder if you would give us a moment of privacy?" She had been practicing the Skreepish tongue.

"Certainly, Exalted One!" Mellis nearly tripped over himself backing out the door.

Bud plopped down on one of the pillowy seats that had been provided for Dr. Shumway's comfort. "Nice digs," he said with a hint of jealousy. His head was still crowned with feathers, but he had fewer jewels than the last time she'd seen him.

"I assume *you* are responsible." The richly furnished cabin featured two portholes. Outside, the stars had begun to twirl. That and a wooziness in her stomach told her they were once again traveling through destabilized space.

"In a way I am. But you being queen—that was the captain's idea. They have a thing for *females*, you see. It seems I've been demoted to second banana."

"The situation is absurd, Mr. Creedle. You do see that, don't you?"

"Well, sure. *I* know you ain't really a queen, if that's what you're getting at. But the skreeps? They believe it! The truth is, they'll believe whatever makes them look good. And this royalty thing does that." He took off his crown and fluffed its feathers.

"So your deception worked. You must be very proud."

"As a matter of fact I am. We can use this thing as a bargaining chip. Who knows what they might do for a king and queen? Who knows what they might give us? You could get your daughter back, for one thing—once those Webbs find her. Maybe I can get my destabilizer back, too. I bet if we play it right, they'll even return us to Earth." He chuckled. "Heck, maybe we'll really *be* king and queen by the time this is done!"

"Has it not occurred to you, Mr. Creedle, that you are as ensnared in these lies as they are? Really, it's grotesque."

"Well, it ain't like I *planned* it. In this life you play the cards that's dealt you." He replaced the crown on his head. One of its feathers wobbled in front of his nose. "Being king and queen gives us *power*. And a little insurance that nothing bad happens to us. Think about it. Would the Queen of Skreepia hurt the Queen of Earth? You're practically related, in the royalty sense."

"Your reasoning is faulty, Mr. Creedle. The situation remains what it has been since we were captured. The Earth is in grave danger, and delusions of grandeur will not save us. As the destabilizer's inventor, you have both the ability, and the moral obligation, to destroy it. You *will* do that, won't you?"

"I think you're missing the point. We can sort this thing out, you and me, but we need to be smart. And no offense, but getting hysterical ain't gonna help. Now, you keep talking about destroying the destabilizer. Don't it occur to you that we *need* the destabilizer to get home?"

"It is not my intention to go home, if we are to be accompanied by a skreepish invasion fleet."

"Now see? There you go again, getting emotional." Bud paced to the nearest window. "All I'm saying is, let's not do something we'll regret later. We still have options. You don't want to throw away your options, do you? Now, if it comes to the point where there really isn't any other way, why then, I'll take care of the destabilizer, just like you want."

"Is that a promise, Mr. Creedle?"

"Sure. But meanwhile, I need to know I can depend on you." He removed his glasses and wiped them on his feathers. "Please, ma'am. You gotta act like a real queen. Will you do that for me? Will you finally start acting like a *queen*?"

. . .

33. FOOL'S GAP

THE DOUBLE sun lowered toward the horizon, and the looming mountains wore a mantle of glowing red. The travelers

crouched among jumbled boulders, looking into a valley filled
with deep shadows and swirling mists. Jack rubbed his rabbit's foot. "What do you think it is?"

"I ain't quite sure," said Joe. The valley followed the base
of the mountains in both directions. Silvery trees scattered
across it; their fronds curled at the ends like party hooters. A
gravel road ran up the valley's center. In the distance, something moved up the road.

"Do you think it's them?" whispered Isadora.

"No, but I'll bet it's some of their friends."

The thing approached swiftly. "Oh, man! Look at that," Jack
cried, his enthusiasm for fast vehicles overcoming his fear. It
ran on two legs like a mechanical ostrich, though smaller legs,
acting as stabilizers, pawed the ground in front of it. A transparent cabin, curved at both ends like a kidney bean, rode on
top. Inside the cabin were skreeps.

"Better get down," said Joe. "These boulders are the best
place for us, if we gotta fight." He considered the idea. "I guess
if it comes to it, we can throw rocks."

"I got a paper route," said Jack. "So I'm pretty good at
throwing."

Isadora stuffed stones into her coat pockets, trying not to
think about how useless they would be if it came to a show-
down. Jack gathered stones as well.

The machine slowed to a trot. By the time it was a few hundred feet away, it was walking. Joe slipped his bowie knife
from its sheath and allowed the blade to dangle between his
knees. The skreeps were now clearly visible inside the cabin.
Milo clucked. Jack put a hand up to stop him, and the rooster
bit it. "I can't stand this waiting."

"Just think about old Mother Earth," Joe suggested in a voice

as soft as breathing. "It ain't so bad to go down fighting, long as you know what you're fighting for."

The vehicle stopped, and its legs folded underneath it. When the cabin popped open, crazy music blared out. Four skreeps lowered themselves from the cockpit; the last one out turned off the music. They gathered for a minute, and when the conference ended, they headed off in different directions. One approached the humans. It moved slowly up the bouldered slope, stopping occasionally to taste the air with its tongue.

Isadora crouched lower. Surely the monster would smell them. They had been days without a bath. She lifted a stone from her pocket, her elbow tingling in anticipation, but Joe put a hand on her wrist. The skreep stopped. Its eyes darted. It pulled a ray gun from its utility belt and swung it slowly from side to side. A faint breeze swirled among the rocks. The monster stepped forward, so close now that Isadora could see its nostrils twitch. Jack put a hand over Milo's beak. They held their breath.

From the bottom of the slope, one of the other spiders called out, waving its arms emphatically. The skreep in front of them stopped, turned its head, and yelled back. The first skreep shouted again, gesturing toward the vehicle. The others began to return.

Jack's stomach gurgled. The skreep turned quickly, leveling its ray gun. For a moment it seemed to stare straight at them. Joe raised his knife. The skreep sniffed, and its tongue darted across its lips.

The other skreeps shouted, then climbed back into the vehicle. *"Blemmix."* The monster lowered its gun and scurried down the hill.

The crazy music resumed, and the monster climbed in. When the pod closed, the music abruptly cut off. The machine stood up on its ostrich legs and loped away, gaining speed as it went. Silence returned to the valley.

Isadora let out her breath in a long, ragged stream. Jack rubbed his face.

"Did ya see that?" said Joe. "It's like the root people said. Them monsters are scared."

"They're scared!"

"Sure they are. They couldn't wait to get back to that pod of theirs. This place has 'em spooked. They set out to kill Arboria, but they botched the job. Now they've got a war that won't

end, and a planet that hates 'em, and they ain't too sure what
to do about it. Come on," he said, hoisting his pack. "We'll
camp in the mountains tonight."

● ● ●

GROOT PUT down his communicator. "The patrol found
nothing. They're on their way back."

"On their way back?" cried Phoony. "What about my
instructions?"

"They stopped where you said. They didn't find anything."

"Idiots! They weren't supposed to *find* anything! They were
supposed to *stay* so the *Uurthlings* couldn't get into the mountains." Phoony knew *exactly* where the *ooman bings* were
heading. He could *feel* it. And that was the problem. Because
where they were heading was snow: deep, deep snow.

If only the fools from Kraakeria had listened to his instructions! Now everything would be difficult, and he would have
to reveal a lot more about his mission than he wanted. But
Phoony knew one thing—he wasn't going into the mountains
alone, or with only Groot and the Webbs, which was worse
than alone. No, if he had to approach that evil pass, he would
have company. He would have as many soldiers as he could
find.

There was still time. One thing about *ooman bings*,
they were slow. If he hurried, he could have his own force
pulled together by noon. That should give him just enough
time to catch the *Uurthlings* before they reached the snow.
He picked up his communicator. "Yes, air base. Phoony the
Finder. You remember me! I'm here under *special orders from
the Exalted One herself*, and I'm in a hurry. I need your best
patrol."

. . .

IN THE MORNING the travelers broke camp without speaking, shouldered their packs, and headed up a steep ravine. This was the final day. They would either get across the pass, or they wouldn't. Isadora shoved aside the mental image of a spider running up a wall.

The air thinned; the slopes steepened. They climbed relentlessly, stopping only twice to catch their breath. Dark cliffs towered overhead. By midmorning they came to a faint path, which led into the first real forest they had seen on Arboria. The trees had trunks like braided rope, and their boughs marched upward like steps on a spiral staircase. Instead of leaves, the branches were carpeted with shaggy fur that changed color in patterns that moved from tree to tree like clouds across a windswept sky.

The forest was so thick, and its foliage so dense, that the path leading into it was like a cave disappearing into darkness. "Maybe we should try a different way," said Isadora. "I mean, we won't be able to *see* in there. Besides, won't the skreeps be watching this path?"

"Could be," said Joe. "But this is the trail to Fool's Gap, and what we need now is *speed*."

"We got flashlights," said Jack, fishing one of the clubs out of his pack.

Isadora could think of nothing else to say except she was scared, and she wasn't about to say *that*. She found her own light, and they headed in.

The trail wove between tree trunks. Soon the darkness was complete, except for the glow of their clubs. An odd sort of undergrowth slithered around them like colorless worms.

Where the vines crossed the trail, they stepped over them. When a heavier tangle blocked their way, they jumped. When the path became even more overgrown, they followed Milo, who, out of boldness or stupidity, had elected to take the lead, pecking savagely at the tendrils as he went.

The trail began to climb. Pale trunks hovered like ghosts. The air was soggy, yet depleted, as if the trees had captured all of its oxygen. Their legs wearied; their chests heaved. The vines squished beneath their feet. Drops rained on them from overhead.

Suddenly something else began to fall, something hard. Isadora thought of acorns, but she could not see the things clearly. One struck her shoulder and caromed off. Another hit her head. Jack got pelted, and she heard him curse. The things began to fall steadily, like hailstones. They looked like hailstones, too, round and milky white. Joe raised his collar and lowered his hat brim. Milo squawked. Isadora lifted her hands to protect her head. One of the things hit her wrist, then scurried down her arm. She stifled a scream.

They came down in a torrent. Most bounced away, but some hung on. "We'd best be leaving!" shouted Joe. He grabbed Isadora with one hand and Jack with the other. They ran.

Soon the trail was covered with squirming blobs like a living carpet. Some stood up defiantly, snapping at the travelers with tweezerlike claws. Many crunched under their shoes. A baseball-sized creature struck Jack's head, and he fell to his knees. Others swarmed onto him. Joe scooped him up by the collar and dragged him away.

It became harder and harder to maintain any sense of direction. They swatted at the blobs with their flashlights and followed Milo. Nobody questioned his leadership. There was no light, except for their batons, and almost no air.

Slowly the storm lifted. The hail of monster balls (as Jack would later call them) diminished to scattered drops. The path cleared. Points of light appeared like stars in the darkness, and they ran for them. The stars grew into patches, then erupted into bright daylight.

Isadora staggered onto open ground. Momentum carried her a few more paces before she was forced to bend over with her head down and her hands pressed against her knees. She gasped for air, and it filled her lungs, thin and mountain fresh.

The first thing she saw when she looked up was snow. Enormous peaks rose all around, buried in deep white powder. The next thing she saw was Jack, then Joe. Her companions were covered, absolutely covered, with clinging blobs.

She realized that she was covered, too. She batted her head and neck, shook her arms, kicked her legs. The creatures flew off in every direction. After a while Joe came over and swatted more away with his hat. When she turned to thank him she saw that his face was streaked with blood. Jack's face was bloody, too, and very pale. "Suckers!" he said with horror.

Isadora wiped her brow. Her hand came away red. "Are they all gone?"

"Far as I can tell," said Joe. He plucked one of the monster balls off the ground. Its underside was ringed with spiny legs. Its mouth snapped open, revealing triangular teeth.

Despite her disgust, Isadora regarded the thing with interest. "Its bite must contain some kind of anesthetic. I didn't feel a thing."

Jack kicked one of the creatures toward the woods. "That don't make me *like* 'em any better."

"At least we made good time," said Joe. "Nothing like a scare to get you moving."

The way ahead was easy, but only for a while. The meadow

they stood in gave way to rocky slopes, and the rocks gave way to snowfields, rising on all sides to enormous peaks. Icy clouds drifted from the summits like white flags. The only break in the ridgeline was a notch so narrow it might have been struck by an ax.

"There it is," said Joe. "Fool's Gap."

"Ever wonder how it got that name?" Jack grumbled.

Before long they had crossed the meadow and were heading up the rocks. At the top of the ridge they found a pond of milky blue water, where they filled their canteens. Beyond the pool, the rocks ended, and the snow began.

"Here goes." Joe kicked a foothold and started up. Isadora followed. Milo fluttered onto Jack's shoulder, as if by mutual agreement.

Climbing the snow proved to be slow work. They marched in single file. Isadora followed Joe, placing her feet inside his prints, while Jack struggled along behind, still complaining about "Martian monster balls." Joe sang "Streets of Laredo," sometimes merely humming the tune while fighting for breath in the thinning air. As the slope steepened, the climb became more treacherous. Occasionally the hobo's steps gave way, and he slid, grabbing handfuls of snow until he stopped. "See what I did there?" he asked Isadora. "Don't do that."

They reached the top of the slope. Jack had assumed the pass would be straight ahead. Instead, an even higher ridge rose before them.

"Look!" Isadora pointed back down the valley. It seemed as if all of Arboria had been laid out beneath them. Beyond the mountains were the smaller ridges they had crossed in recent days, and beyond that, stretching to a dusty horizon, was the vast, barren desert. But what seized their attention was movement at the edge of the forest. Suddenly a group of skreeps emerged from the trees. They ran from the woods, swatting their backs and performing odd, panicky dances.

"You had to figure they'd show up sooner or later," said Joe.

"At least those bloodsuckers got 'em," said Jack.

"We left footprints right up the snowbank," Isadora cried. "They'll see exactly where we went!"

"They weren't fooled anyway. Now it's just a race to the top." Joe didn't say who he thought would win.

The higher they climbed, the more difficult it became to breathe. In the shadows of the peaks, the snow was hard and treacherous. In other places they found themselves plowing through thigh-high drifts. The temperature dropped. Their hands and feet stung from constant contact with the ice. Their wet clothes began to freeze. After a while, toes and fingers grew numb. A cruel wind whipped against them. Still they climbed.

Joe stopped singing. He hummed ragged snatches of "The Wabash Cannonball" and moved relentlessly. The children struggled to keep up. Anytime Isadora thought about stopping she remembered the skreeps and was spurred to take another step, and another. Her head swam. She glanced back. The skreeps were closer now. They had topped the first ridge and were heading up.

"All . . . we're . . . doing," Joe gulped, "is . . . breaking . . . trail for 'em."

"What choice . . . do we have?"

He took another step. "None."

Jack looked at the pass, still hundreds of feet overhead. It was completely blocked by a huge cornice of snow that jutted out in a giant wedge. "How do we get over that?"

"No idea. We'll be lucky if it don't fall on our heads."

"Should we fight 'em then?" Just saying the words made Jack's stomach churn.

"Not yet." Joe grinned. "Spoken like a hero—but not yet. We ain't done yet." He swung his foot into the snow like a hammer and hoisted himself up.

The skreeps came fast. Jack saw them every time he turned his head, a string of dark blotches on a white field. The Webbs were there, too. Grady was the smallest speck of all.

They were in a steep chute heading for the pass, but Joe had begun to angle to one side, where enormous cliffs erupted from the snow. He reached the rock and turned around, his head swaying dizzily as he tried to catch his breath. The children struggled up behind him. They wedged themselves into the rock and stood there, unable to go on. The pass was just overhead but was hopelessly blocked by the jutting shelf of snow and ice.

"I guess this is it," said Joe.

A voice called up. Not a skreepish voice, but a familiar, irritated human one. "All right!" yelled Sergeant Webb. "Get down from there. All of you. The game is up."

"Nuts!" shouted Joe.

"Don't make us come get you!"

Another, higher voice chimed in. "That means you, Creedle!"

"Get lost, Grady!" Jack hollered.

"Don't shout," said Isadora. "It only encourages them."

"No, do!" Joe's eyes held a sudden intensity. "*Do* shout. Like this." He cupped his hands around his mouth and faced the pass. "AVALANCHE!" The word echoed from the surrounding peaks.

Jack, who had been expecting a prime insult, was disappointed. "*Avalanche*'? What's that supposed to mean?"

"Just what it says!" cried Isadora. "Sound vibrations can trigger avalanches."

"You don't scare us!" shouted Grady.

"We should," said Jack, grinning at the others.

Isadora cupped her hands as Joe had done and shouted, "Avalanche!"

Jack shouted, too, and was surprised to see the skreeps begin to scatter. As they strayed from the broken path, they floundered in the deep snow. He saw Grady's angry, upturned face. Then his father grabbed him by the collar and started dragging him across the field. Jack placed his hands around his mouth. This time they all shouted at once. Their voices were ragged but loud. "AVALANCHE!"

The word echoed away. For a moment, all was silent.

SCRAAAAAK! The sound was like tearing paper, only huge. The snow cornice broke. For a moment it tilted crazily. Its leading edge pointed down like an accusing finger. Then, with a hollow blast, it broke free. It fell straight down, fifty feet to the ice field below. The mountain began to slide. It came down in a great whooshing torrent. The skreeps in the middle of the chute were the first to go, buried by the onrushing tide. Those who had reached the edges hung on a moment longer before being swept away.

Joe, Jack, Isadora, and Milo watched from their perch among the rocks. Finally a cloud of powdery snow shot up, blocking their view. The sound echoed down the valley. The cloud swirled away. Below them was nothing but snow. The mountainside had been swept clean. "Avalanche," said Joe.

Isadora considered what they'd done. "It's horrible."

"I won't say it ain't."

"Don't be so gloomy," said Jack, pointing to the open gap where the cornice had been. "Look! The pass is clear!"

• • •

34. ALIEN HOSPITALITY

THEY CAMPED in a valley beside a rushing stream. The plants on this side of the range were different from what they had seen so far, and there were more of them. Flat-topped yellow trees competed for space with waxy-skinned red giants bearing pods as big as streetlights. There were flowers for the first time, little pink bells and others that exploded blue confetti whenever a blundering foot came too close.

While their clothes dried on rocks, Joe, Jack, and Isadora huddled over a campfire, wrapped in shiny skreep blankets but still shivering. Isadora distracted herself from the terrible events at the pass by making notes in her journal, Joe played his harmonica, and Jack poked the fire with a stick. Milo scratched for bugs, which left him hungry and annoyed.

Food had become their greatest problem. That evening they shared the last of the dirt potatoes and fell asleep with their stomachs grumbling. In the morning they started downstream, hungry and wet, as a thin drizzle stiffened to cold rain. Leaving the muddy, swollen stream, Joe led them to a shallow cave. There they built a fire and sat down to wait out the storm. When the rain slackened, Joe headed back out. He returned with a hatful of pale yellow berries, which they shared for dinner.

That night they fantasized about food. "You know what I'd like?" said Jack, breaking a long silence. When nobody answered, he finished his thought. "Chicken pot pie. I've always liked chicken pot pie."

"Sweet-and-sour pork," said Isadora. "There's a Chinese restaurant in my neighborhood in Boston. Sometimes when Mother is too busy to cook, we go there. I always get sweet-and-sour pork and fried dumplings."

Jack had never tasted sweet-and-sour pork, but he wanted it now. "Mom's meat loaf," he said, raising his eyebrows suggestively. "What do you think of that?"

"Mmm," Isadora replied, forgetting her earlier impression of the dish.

Next morning they returned to the stream and walked slowly, foraging for food. After a number of unpleasant experiments they discovered a patch of broad-leafed plants with tubers like small, bitter carrots. That night they tried roasting the tubers on sticks, but they were still bitter. Even so, there wasn't enough to eat.

The next day, rain swept across the countryside in sudden downpours. They came to a path and followed it through open country. The path led to a broader trail, which led to a bald hill. On top of the hill stood a collection of clear domes, interlocking like bubbles in a bath.

"You reckon that's a house?" said Joe.

"It *has* to be." Isadora had been dreaming of finding a house, *any* house, for days.

"You wait here, then." He straightened the lapels on his frayed coat. "If nobody eats me, I'll whistle for ya."

"No," she insisted. "We'll stick together."

Jack eyed the bubbles uncertainly. "Yeah, that's right."

As they came close, they saw a figure in front of the main dome. The creature wasn't much bigger than an average-sized dog. Its skin was pale green with brown freckles, and rubbery like a salamander's. Round eyes perched on top of two stalks. It wore a shimmering green tunic.

When the creature saw them it squealed and bolted through a hole in the round, clear wall. The portal slammed shut; the wall darkened to an opaque blue.

"Now what do we do?" said Jack.

"I guess we wait."

Suddenly the portal opened, and a much larger creature stepped out. It held something at its waist that looked like a tommy gun. When it spoke, a stream of hard-edged syllables poured out.

Joe held up his hands. Isadora and Jack did the same. "Would you mind repeating that last part, brother? I didn't quite catch your meaning."

Catch your meaning? thought Isadora. *How could he? And how did he expect the alien to understand him, either?* But even as the thought occurred to her, she realized that Joe had not spoken English. He had used the monster's own language. It wasn't possible, but it was true.

The alien lowered its weapon. "I asked you who you are, and what you are doing here. We don't receive many visitors in this country."

"Hey, I understood that!" Jack blurted.

"Me, too," said Isadora.

"Odd, ain't it?" said Joe.

The creature's expression softened. "They are children."

"They are at that." Joe smiled like a proud parent. "We've traveled a long way, these young'uns and me. We mean you no harm. Our quarrel is with the skreeps."

"They are our enemies, too." The creature bowed. "I am Zelum. I share this home with Belwan and our children. There have been rumors of your coming, but I was not sure. Forgive me. You are welcome here."

"Glad of it. But can you tell us how we understand your language? I never heard it spoke before. None of us have. Now we're chatting like we was born here."

"You have been eating queechy root!" Zelum declared. "It grows wild in these hills. It is called 'the ambassador' because it promotes understanding among creatures of all planets."

"You don't say? We ate lots of roots on our way here, and that's a fact. How long does it keep working?"

"It is permanent, as far as I know." Zelum switched effortlessly to English. "Queechy root makes Arborians very good with languages, as you see."

"Amazing," said Isadora.

"Wait'll Smedley Trowbridge hears about this," said Jack.

The portal opened, and another creature stepped out. It was shorter than Zelum but stouter. Its spotted skin was yellower. "Zelum! Where are your manners? Did I hear you say they've been eating queechy root? They must be starving! Nobody can live on *queechy root*!" It wagged its eyestalks at the humans. "Hello, travelers. I am Belwan. To think that you should come right to our door! We are honored. Welcome!"

The domes cleared, revealing six more creatures, ranging in size from about five feet tall down to a cat-sized infant. The one they had first seen stood in the middle. The largest held the baby. All of them gaped, openmouthed, at their visitors.

"Don't stare, children," scolded Belwan. "These monsters are our guests."

• • •

THE TECHNICIAN held up the injector, which was loaded with a swirling pink liquid.

"Give it to them," Phoony growled.

She approached the *ooman bings* cautiously, but they didn't move. Even after she injected them they didn't move.

"Why—?" she began, but Phoony cut her off, holding up the capsule containing Xaafuun's orders.

"My orders come directly from the Queen," he lied. "You needn't question me. These *Uurthlings* are mine. The mission is secret."

She left the room. Phoony regarded his *ooman bings* with annoyance. He'd gone to the trouble of saving them; they owed him the courtesy of not dying.

"You lied," said Groot. "Those aren't the Queen's orders."

"So what if I did? You think they'd help me if I didn't push them around?" Skreeps were like that, he thought: selfish. None of them cared about his problems.

But Phoony cared. The matter was personal now. The runaway *Uurthlings* had tried to *kill* him! Just thinking about the collapsing, suffocating mountain of snow made him shiver, despite the extreme heat of the Warming Room. Such a simple, stupid trick, but that was the way savages operated. There was nothing more savage, he now saw, than an *ooman bing*.

As soon as they had started shouting, he'd understood. But snow made such an evil trap! He had been unable to make it to safety before the mountain came down. Big Webb had seen it coming, too. That was why he and Little Webb made it to the far side of the chute. It was why they were not buried as deep as the others.

The effort had probably saved their lives, as it had saved Phoony. He remembered tumbling end over end. When he'd stopped, he couldn't see or hear or breathe; he could only feel frozen wetness pressing in all around him. It had been his Finder's sense of direction that allowed him to get out.

Once he was on top of the snow, he'd used his communicator to locate the Webbs. Then he called Kraakeria to demand help.

While he waited, he found Groot and another skreep named Fleem. Fleem died, along with the others. Digging up Groot had been his mistake. Sometimes being a Finder got the best of him. Groot was a nuisance he should have left buried.

"What do we do now?" asked the jailor.

"For the millionth time, we wait. The fugitive *Uurthlings* will go to the spaceport in Parnadan. It's their only option. We'll nab them there."

"We can't go there! It's enemy territory!"

"Would you rather take your chances with Xaafuun? We'll catch 'em at the spaceport. But first, we need to revive these Webbs."

"Why not leave 'em here?"

"Now there's a brilliant idea! Why not just leave the Webbs here to be eaten by all these other skreeps as soon as we turn our backs!"

"I was thinking," said Groot. "You could leave me here, too—to guard 'em."

"Sure I could. If I was an *idiot*! And as soon as I was gone, you could sell 'em and run off to one of the outer colonies. No, you're sticking with me."

He turned his attention back to the *Uurthlings*. After four injections of nerve igniter they still looked bad. But even as he watched, beads of sweat broke out on Little Webb's forehead. More sweat formed on Big Webb's bald dome and ran in snaky trickles down his chest. Little Webb stirred. He said something. Phoony leaned closer, listening. He said it again: *"Creedle."* Phoony smiled. Vicious little beast!

• • •

CLEAR WALLS sparkled in the sunlight, and silky curtains hung from the domed ceilings. The floors were polished blue stone. A fountain bubbled gently against one wall. Isadora, Jack, and Joe felt very grubby.

"Strangers in this land are often unfriendly," said Zelum, "and not always what they seem to be. The roots sent messages, but I could not be sure."

"Really, Zelum, who else could it have been? A group of other-worlders wandering half starved through the forest?" Belwan urged the humans farther inside. "You must excuse Zelum. Since the skreeps came we all live in isolation and fear. Tell me, did you see Arborians on the other side of the mountains?"

"Not a one," said Joe.

She sighed. "Our kind lived all over Arboria once, but the skreeps killed most of us."

Isadora thought of the ruined houses they had seen, and how different they had been from this tidy home.

It was embarrassing to be so dirty. She slipped off her shoes, but her socks were just as bad. She pulled those off, too, and was left staring at filthy feet.

"You are wearing the honest soil of Arboria," said Belwan

kindly. "But we are poor hosts! Perhaps you would like to bathe before we eat?"

The bath was glorious. Isadora swam in a stone pool formed by natural hot springs and spiced with minerals that made her skin tingle. She might have stayed there for hours, but the smell of cooking finally coaxed her from the tub. Jack took the next bath, followed by Joe.

When they were clean and clothed, Zelum led them to a wide stone table, set no more than a foot above the floor. Elaborate dishes had been placed there. A few might have given the travelers pause, had they not been so hungry. "Eat what appeals to you," laughed Belwan, observing their reaction. "If any of it does."

In the end nearly all of it did. They ate without plates or utensils, washing their hands frequently from a little stream of clean water that flowed around a depression in the table's edge. More water was provided in wide bowls for drinking, subtly flavored with herbs that were at once minty and tart. The Arborian children were fascinated by Milo, who hissed at them rudely until they gave him food.

"Try these black things," said Jack, giving Isadora a nudge. "They're as good as steak and taters all rolled into one."

"It is good you like our food," said Zelum. "The skreeps claim everything Arborian poisons them. I hope it's true."

"Of course it's true," said Belwan. "After what the skreeps have done to Arboria, why wouldn't the planet poison them? But you are different. Arboria has *adopted* you. The roots say you come from a land beyond time."

"I come from Vern Hollow, New York," said Jack.

"That may not be the place she's talking about," whispered Joe.

"It's called Hellebeezia," said Isadora.

They told the whole story, beginning on Earth and continuing through their escape at Fool's Gap. By the time they were finished, dinner was over.

Everyone moved to the living room, where they sat on cushions around a pit of bubbling lava. Milo dozed on Jack's lap. Joe played his harmonica and sang "Leaving Cheyenne" and "Oh My Darling, Clementine." Outside, trees rustled in a gentle breeze. The Arborian sky sparkled with stars.

35. TO THE COAST

IN THE MORNING the travelers ate a huge breakfast, and Joe taught Duween, the oldest child, how to play "Red River Valley." They were interrupted when Zelum brought out a clear-bodied wagon with eight spokeless wheels. "We must be leaving soon," he said.

Belwan objected. "They need more feeding. Look at them—they're starving!"

"Time is precious. You heard: The skreeps are up to worse mischief than ever. We must get to Parnadan as quickly as possible."

"You're going with us?" asked Joe.

Zelum bowed. "It is the fastest way."

It was difficult saying good-bye. When Joe sat down in the wagon, he handed his harmonica to Duween. "With a little practice you'll be the best harmonica player on Arboria."

"Why'd you do that?" asked Jack. An odd version of "Red River Valley" serenaded them down the hill.

"Because she liked it."

"But *you* liked it. You played it all the time."

"That's what a gift is, son. If you don't care about it, it ain't worth giving." He adjusted his hat. "Anyway, I can always pick up a new one in town."

Jack was fascinated by the wagon. It moved at a sedate speed, making no sound other than the hum of its wheels. He scanned its clear body but couldn't see what powered it. "Where's the engine?'

Zelum raised a finger. "The Twins are the engine for everything."

"You mean the sun?"

"*Suns.* Yes." He seemed surprised by the question. "Where else would energy come from?"

Jack thought about gasoline, and the virtues of a big V-8, but decided to keep it to himself. "It runs real smooth, for a wagon. How fast will it go?"

Again the question seemed to puzzle Zelum. "As fast as it wants."

The journey to the coast took two days. In Jack's opinion, the wagon never achieved real speed, but it was quicker than walking and much easier. Sometimes they did get out to stretch their legs, and the carriage trailed behind them like an obedient dog.

It was hard to believe Arboria was a ruined planet, but Zelum saw signs of distress everywhere, in green trees that should have been yellow, in a spiky ground cover that had spread across meadows where it did not belong, in the silence of skies which were once crowded with birdlike creatures called *skrel*. "Arboria will come back," he sighed, "but she will never be the same."

"We were told to find the rebels," said Joe. "Are they at the coast?"

"Many of us are rebels. Each of us has sacrificed much for the cause."

"Well, ain't I the fool for saying it like that? What I meant was: Is there a *ship* we can use? That machine we're chasing will be most of the way to Skreepia by now. We need someone who can take us there. Someone who don't mind a scrap."

"There are many ships in Parnadan, but it is a lawless place. Among the foreigners there are more pirates than rebels. And very few would go willingly to Skreepia! Still, we will visit the spaceport and hope for the best."

Jack had a sudden, alarming thought. "Won't the skreeps be looking for us there? I mean, they must know that's where we're headed."

"I've been wondering about that myself," Joe said, "ever since we crossed the mountains. What's to stop them from just hopping over in one of their saucers and scooping us up?"

"We are not as feeble as you imagine," said Zelum. "The skreeps are afraid to provoke a battle and restart the war. They aren't ready for that—*yet*. But beware: They have agents everywhere, even among my people. War does that. It ruins more than trees and houses."

As they neared the coast they passed through settlements, small towns with bubble houses and towers like melted candles. Some of the Arborians greeted them with curiosity, some with fear. One or two cast hostile glances. But a surprising number seemed not to notice them at all.

"An effect of the veil trees," Zelum explained. "Those who

have been concealed, remain concealed, at least partially. It is a subtle thing, but it may help you."

The road zigzagged up a grassy ridge. From its top, gentle slopes descended many miles to a ragged coastline. The sea beyond was milky green; its surface sparkled with afternoon light.

A portion of the coast was taken up by a city that stretched from point to point around a wide bay. Bubble palaces hugged the coastline at either end.

"Parnadan," said Zelum. "It's the only free city remaining on Arboria." As they took in the sight, a breeze rose to meet them, crisp and salty. Closing her eyes, Isadora imagined she was near the shore at Cape Cod rather than at an alien coastline trillions of miles away.

Parnadan was not as orderly as it appeared from a distance. Many of the buildings were run-down, and blast marks gave evidence of past warfare. They saw Arborians, but also other creatures, which Zelum named: *karasul*, *amazak*, *genis*, *belau*. The aliens came in a variety of shapes and sizes, but many had sharp teeth and cruel eyes. Zelum pulled out his tommy gun and laid it across his knees.

As they passed, a creature with a domed head watched them from an alley. It stepped into the shadows, lifted an object to its mouth, and whispered.

• • •

PHOONY LIFTED his communicator. His eyes brightened. "Are there any ships in port?" His mouth stretched into a humorless grin.

"That was one of our spies," he told Groot. "The *ooman bings* have been spotted on their way to the port. But here's the best part: Once they reach it, they'll be stuck! After all that running, the only ship in the crater is a broken-down hulk—a wreck of a *crannek* pirate ship. It limped in a couple of weeks ago and hasn't moved since. And that's it! Not a rebel in sight." He chortled. "They're trapped!"

"Good!" Groot flopped on his stomach. "Then we can slow down."

"*Slow down!* You sniveling wretch! We're not slowing down, we're *speeding up*!"

They had passed through Battle Gap two nights earlier. By now the Webbs lay nearly lifeless at his feet. They would have to be carried.

"Pick up Big Webb," he ordered Groot. "I'll take Little Webb. If we hurry we can make it to Parnadan by tomorrow evening. You know, I can already feel my fingers around those *Uurthlings'* necks."

Groot grabbed the sergeant roughly and hoisted him off the ground. "Why do *I* always have to carry Big Webb?"

. . .

BEYOND THE city, the travelers came to a wide, shallow crater. On its far side, perched on four spindly legs, stood a smallish flying saucer. Its dull body was as charred as an old coffeepot. There were no other ships in port.

"Pirates," said Zelum, giving the saucer an appraising look. "That won't do you any good. But with luck a rebel cruiser will come in a few days."

"I don't think we *have* a few days," said Joe. "Not with the skreeps after us, and the destabilizer in their hands."

"Perhaps the station agent can help us." Tucked into the crater's near slope was a small building with a curved metal roof. Warm light gleamed from its portholes. "We will ask if any ships are scheduled."

When they knocked on the door, a musical note chimed inside. They heard footsteps.

"Just a moment, please!"

The voice was human.

. . .

36. THE STATION AGENT

WHEN THE DOOR swung open, a tall, thin man stood before them. His face was narrow, with a long nose and a pointed

chin. Red hair rose in an unruly mass on top of his head. A silver jumpsuit covered his body. In his hands was a plastic folder stuffed with documents. "Well now," he said. "This *is* a surprise."

"*Surprise* don't hardly cover it," said Joe.

"No indeed. How many Earth expeditions even come to Arboria anymore? I can't think of the last one. Have you been here a very long time? You must have been; there are no records of recent arrivals." He shook his folder. "Not that there are any *proper* records at all, recent or otherwise. The station is a shocking mess. I've only been here a fortnight myself, but I can scarcely make heads or tails of it. Nigel Dimplewhite."

He stuck out a hand and dropped the folder. Papers scattered across the doorway. Isadora helped pick them up.

"Really," he said. "You're too kind. Won't you come in? You *are* from Earth, aren't you?" He saw Zelum. "*You* aren't! Fine Arborian fellow! Nigel Dimplewhite, at your service."

"Of course we're from Earth." Isadora handed him his papers. "We're from America. We were kidnapped by skreeps and brought here on one of their ships."

"Kidnapped, were you? You'll want to fill out a form. Please, come in."

The room they stepped into was very much like an office on Earth.

Dimplewhite settled behind a big desk, and everyone took a seat. "You'll join me for dinner? It would be lovely to hear news from dear old Earth. I don't suppose you have documents of any kind? Passports, visas, that sort of thing?"

"We were kidnapped," Isadora reminded him.

"You said that before, didn't you? One rarely hears of such things anymore, though perhaps I shouldn't be surprised, judging by conditions in Parnadan. I'd been expecting more, hadn't you? The brochures are grossly misleading."

Milo jumped from Jack's arms and began to run in circles. Jack leaned toward Joe. "Do you know what he's talking about?"

"Not a word."

"Lovely rooster," said Dimplewhite. "I was told I was to be the agent at a thriving commercial port, with a large staff, in a cosmopolitan city. You see the true conditions. The only ship to land here since I arrived is the vessel across the crater. It is badly broken—and the crew is quite hostile." He spread his arms. "But you have your own problems to worry about! No doubt you were looking for the Earth Embassy. Would you believe it? There doesn't appear to be one!"

"We've been out of touch for a while," said Joe, "but to the best of my knowledge, Earth don't have any embassies on other planets."

"No embassies! How do you imagine we maintain diplomatic ties?"

"There again, my impression would be that we don't *have* diplomatic ties. My impression would be that folks on Earth just *stay* on Earth—except maybe for a situation like this'n, which as far as I know is something of a rarity."

"What an amazing notion—!" Dimplewhite stopped suddenly. "Oh, my."

"What is it?" asked Isadora.

"I just noticed your clothing. Extraordinary! Like pieces from a museum! Do you mind telling me what *year* it was when you left Earth?"

"The year? Nineteen fifty-six. October, 1956."

"Nineteen fifty-six!" He slapped his desk. "Well, that explains a good deal, doesn't it?"

"Don't explain *nothing* to me," said Joe.

"Well, it explains my confusion! It explains why there are no records here, and no embassy. It explains why the only vessel in port is an ancient wreck of a pirate ship. You see, I left Earth in the year 2207."

"Twenty-two oh seven! That's more than 250 years into the future!" cried Isadora.

"From *your* point of view, yes."

"But that's awful! If it's the year 2207, then we'll *never* see Earth again. At least, not any Earth we would recognize."

"Don't jump to conclusions, my dear. Who's to say it's 2207?"

"*You* just did!"

"I said it was 2207 for *me*, when *I* left. I never said what year it was for *you*. For you it could be anytime—but shouldn't we assume it's still 1956?"

"But how could it be 1956 if it's already 2207? You aren't claiming to have gone back in time, are you?"

"Clearly I have. That is, I've gone back in *Arborian* time. The evidence is overwhelming. As for *Earth* time, who can say? But as we know, people *tend* to remain bound to their own time. Can you imagine the chaos if we didn't?"

"Not really," said Jack. An idea occurred to him. "Say, how *is* the future anyway? I mean, how do things turn out? We're having a pretty bad time with the skreeps, here in 1956. I guess you've heard of them. My uncle made a machine he shouldn't have, and the skreeps swiped it. The way things look, Earth could be in real trouble. So maybe you can tell us. Do the skreeps get the destabilizer? Do they conquer Earth?"

Dimplewhite was shocked. "Well, of course I couldn't tell you! It would be quite inappropriate."

"You don't have to tell us details. Just give us a general idea."

"Absolutely not! Don't you see my words could have a dangerous effect on settled history? Think of the causality violations."

"Causality violations?" asked Isadora.

"Besides which, my information would likely be false, from your point of view, as explained by the Theory of Residual Anomalies—"

"—and Enigmas!" Isadora finished. "Of course! The non-linearity of time. Our future and your past might not line up, and both may be somewhat malleable. Mother explained it to me. She showed me the calculations, but I never really believed it."

"Extraordinary mother. Yes, she is quite right. You might be changing *my* past even as we speak, or you may belong to a *different* past, one that leads not to my world but to some alternate reality. There's no way of knowing! In other words, your future and my past may have nothing to do with each other." He clapped his hands, as if putting the matter to rest. "But come! You must be famished."

They ate in his small apartment. Dinner consisted of pre-packaged, self-heating steak-and-kidney pie. The station agent spoke of his own journey to Arboria, speculating about what led to his unexpected time travel. "Of course it's more common to be thrown *forward* in time, but I wouldn't say what happened to me is unprecedented. Not at all, though it may require a bit of complex navigation to get me back." He patted his mouth with a cloth napkin. "However, one expects difficulties when one enters the foreign service."

"Don't I know it," said Joe. "We got difficulties, too. Those kidnappers are still chasing us. Meanwhile, the destabilizer machine the boy mentioned is on its way to Skreepia. I reckon it's up to us to get it back. A tall order, and the clock is ticking. So here's my question: Do you know when a rebel ship might come in? Because we need a ride out of here in a hurry."

"I quite see your point." Dimplewhite cleared the table. "The problem is, there simply *are* no ships—rebel or otherwise." He returned with tea and biscuits.

Zelum sniffed one of the biscuits suspiciously. Jack added spoonful after spoonful of sugar to his tea.

"What about that pirate ship?" asked Joe. "Any chance they might give us a lift?"

"I'm afraid not. It's a *crannek* vessel. The *crannek* may be—*historically*, of course—hostile to the Skreepish Empire, but it appears they are equally belligerent toward *all* creatures. The fact that they can't get their saucer working seems to enrage them." He sipped his tea thoughtfully. "I suppose it's understandable. For a pirate, a functional ship is an absolute necessity."

"I can fix spaceships," said Jack, adding more sugar to his tea.

Dimplewhite put down his cup. "Did you just say you can *fix* spaceships?"

"Well, yeah."

"It's true!" Isadora cried. "I should have thought of it myself. Jack fixed a really big flying saucer once, one that was horribly damaged."

"That *is* extraordinary. But I can't imagine the *crannek* would accept your help. They are very proud—not to mention short-tempered and prone to criminality."

"That don't bother me," said Jack. "My family's the same way."

• • •

ISADORA WOKE to a strange whistling. At first she thought it was a ship coming in, but soon realized it was just the teapot. She got dressed and put on her glasses. A title on Dimplewhite's bookshelf caught her eye: *Space Travel, The First 200 Years*. There were others: *A Brief History of the Skreepish Empire, Exercises in Cross-dimensional Thinking, Krasnikov Tubes—And You!, 40 Wilderness Journeys in the Upper Radeetz Sector, The Mystery of Xarbok 9*, and *Perceptual Limitations in 21st-Century Thought*. As she read, her sleepiness fell away. These books had not even been written yet! The idea was nearly as dazzling as the books themselves.

Her hand strayed to *A Brief History of the Skreepish Empire*. As Dimplewhite had been quick to point out, the history might be false, from her point of view. Then again, it might not. A glance at the index might tell her all she needed to know. *Did they succeed in their quest or fail? Did Earth become a skreepish colony? Was the destabilizer used?*

No, she wouldn't look. As a consolation, she picked up *Perceptual Limitations in 21st-Century Thought*. What she read there puzzled her all day.

• • •

37. THE CRANNEK

AFTER BREAKFAST they said good-bye to Zelum. Isadora gave him her stuffed dog, Foo Foo. "A gift for your children."

Jack considered handing over his rabbit's foot, but it was getting shabby, and he still needed all the luck he could get.

"The hope of Arboria travels with you," Zelum said formally. "Remember, you carry the power of the Eternal Place." The wagon disappeared over the lip of the crater.

"Guess we should see about bumming a ride," said Joe.

The *crannek* saucer gleamed dully in the morning sunlight.

"Right, then," said Dimplewhite, and they set off.

Jack's confidence began to fade. Just because he'd fixed the skreepish ship didn't mean he'd be able to fix this one.

"Be careful how you offer to help," the station agent advised them. "*Crannek* are very, very touchy."

"You focus on fixing that engine, son, and I'll do the talking," said Joe.

Up close the saucer looked even worse than it did at a distance, with lots of dents and several patches on its charred skin. Its size was only a fraction of the skreepish ship's. Instead of a molecularly recombinant doorway, a simple metal ladder led to an open hatch. Below the ladder was a tarp, across which were scattered engine parts. Jack examined them with professional interest. They were unfamiliar but not *entirely* unfamiliar. Memories of Hellebeezia came back to him. The skreepish saucer's infinitely complex engine began to reassemble itself in his mind.

His thoughts were interrupted by a brusque voice. "What is it?"

He was about to answer when he realized the language was foreign, and the words were not intended for him. A second voice answered. "It's that swine of a station agent. And some more just like him. *Oom'n beans.* Should I run 'em off?"

Isadora winced. Joe tapped his ear and whispered, "*Queechy root.*"

"No," barked the first voice. "I'll do it. You keep working on that engine." The alien slid down the ladder rails and landed among the humans with a thud.

"I told you we don't have any documents! Now beat it."

The pirate was no more than four feet tall, but it was nearly as wide. Tusks protruded from the corners of its heavy mouth. A single tuft of bright blue hair swirled like soft ice cream from the crown of its head. Bandoliers, studded with weapons, crisscrossed its chest. A small cannon rested on one broad shoulder.

"I've been studying your language," said Dimplewhite apologetically. "But I'm afraid I don't *have* it yet." He stammered out a single *crannek* phrase, which translated as "Do you have a passport?"

"I just told ya I din't!" roared the alien.

"Whoa, now," said Joe, speaking mildly in *crannek*. "This fella's just having some trouble with your language. He don't mean nothing by it."

The alien looked at him suspiciously. "Who are *you*?"

"Travelers—me and the young'uns, that is. And the bird. Got caught up in some trouble with skreeps. Now we're doing our best to get away."

"Ha! It was skreeps that wrecked my ship! I hate 'em. I'll *kill* the next one I see."

"That's how we feel, too. And since we buried a bunch of 'em up at Fool's Gap, they ain't too fond of us, neither."

The pirate narrowed its eyes. "Buried? What do you mean, *buried*?"

Joe described the chase to Fool's Gap and the avalanche that ended it. "They don't like snow, skreeps. It's a cold way to die."

"Dommit, Furgok, Blim!" shouted the alien. "Come down here! You'll want to hear what these *oom'ns* did up in the hills!"

The other three *crannek* looked much like the first one, who was the captain, and whose name was Skrank. Skrank, Dommit, and Blim were all female. Furgok, the grease-stained mechanic, was male. Skrank had Joe repeat his story.

"Buried alive!" cheered Dommit. "Ha!"

"As soon as we fix this pockmarked, potbellied, dented disgrace of a flying machine," said Skrank, "we're going to do a little *skreep hunting* of our own."

Joe tipped his hat. "We'd be happy to help out, if you'd take us along."

"We don't take *passengers*," Skrank said flatly. "Even skreep killers. And we don't need any help. A single *crannek* is worth *ten* skreeps. A *crannek* with a blaster is worth *forty*! Give us a decent vessel, and we'd take on the whole, worm-eaten empire!" She glared at the humans. "Problem is, the ship isn't working."

"That's part of what we come here to talk about," said Joe. "You see, I wasn't asking you to give us a ride for *free*. It's more of a *business* proposition. The boy here is handy with engines—"

"*Him?*" Skrank's eyes flashed dangerously. "Don't waste my time!"

"When I say handy," Joe continued, "I mean *unbelievably* handy. He's worked on much bigger saucers than this'n. So the proposition is, the boy fixes the ship, and you take us where we need to go."

His words caused an uproar.

"Hold on," said the captain. "Can't you see it's just a *bet*? This *oom'n* is a *gambler*! Well, I'm a gambler, too. So what do *I* get if the boy fails?"

"Never happen. I'm telling you, the youngster is good."

"If he fails," said the captain, "you and me will fight." She plucked a stone off the ground and crushed it, then threw away the pebbles. "Furgok is the best mechanic on this side of the spiral arm. He's been working on this engine since we got here. So I'll give you one last chance: Wanna change the bet?"

"I reckon not."

"Furgok," said Skrank. "Show the boy the engine."

Joe tipped his hat. "Jack," he said, still smiling, "I sure hope you're as good as you say."

• • •

PHOONY PRESSED on, through the night and into the next day. Sometimes he and Groot carried the Webbs, and sometimes they forced them to march. Here in enemy territory, Arboria was positively vicious. Vines grabbed them, and stinging thorns poked through the soles of their tough feet. Twice they had to detour around impassable swamps.

Phoony called his spy. When he returned the communicator to his belt his face was troubled. "Come on, we have to go."

"But we just got here," Groot whined.

"Remember how I told you the only ship in Parnadan was a broken-down hulk? Well, they're working on it right now."

"So, what did you expect them to do?"

"I'm not talking about the *crannek*, idiot! It's the *ooman bings*. They're the ones working on it."

Groot opened one eye. "Why would *Uurthlings* help the *crannek*? And why would the *crannek let* them?"

"I don't know!" shouted Phoony. "All I know is we'd better get to that spaceport. *Now.*"

.   .   .

"I DON'T KNOW what the captain was thinking, letting you up here!" said the alien. "Furgok is a better mechanic than you'll ever be."

Jack nodded.

"Furgok has fixed more ships than a fuzzy-headed, half-pint grease monkey like you has even *seen.*"

Jack removed a coil from a gap between two pipes and set it on his knee. "Hey, can you hand me that nubbly thing with the two prongs?"

Furgok passed him the tool. "It's an insult to Furgok. It dishonors Furgok before the rest of the crew."

Jack remembered similar conversations with Uncle Dwayne under the hood of his '48 Oldsmobile. "Can I see the doohickey with the little plunky valve on it?"

Furgok found the part and handed it up. *"Oom'n beans can't* be mechanics."

"Now that little squidgy thing." They were in a tight space, and Jack could barely see. He groped for the tool with one hand.

"It isn't natural. *Oom'n beans* don't even have *ships.*"

"I *wish* I did! Can you picture me buzzing over Vern Hollow in one of these babies?"

"Oom'n beans should not mess with things they don't understand!"

"I don't understand this whatchamacallit. The way it wraps all the way around. Wouldn't it be simpler if it went straight up? Hey, hand me that pinchy thing with the zapper on one end."

He raised the tool into the gap. Something glowed green, and sparks rained down.

"What are you doing?" cried Furgok.

"Don't worry, it's just a shortcut, fusing those things together. It's what you would've done if you had skinny arms like me."

"I would *not*! Furgok would not have done that! If those wires overheat, both thrusters could go at once!"

"Not *now*, they won't. Remember? I separated them other goobers so's they *can't* overheat."

Furgok climbed through the hatch and down the ladder.

"How goes the repair, Furgok?" asked the captain. "Is the *oom'n* any good?"

"*Good?* Oh-ho! He's a gem! You'll be lucky if you have a ship at all, once he's done." The mechanic stormed off, raising clouds of dust with every step.

Skrank looked up at the open hatch. Joe whistled "Streets of Laredo" and sharpened his knife on a stone.

• • •

38. REPAIRS

JACK WORKED through the afternoon, until all the parts were back in the engine, and nothing remained on the tarp. The suns were low on the horizon when he climbed down one last time.

"Give up?" asked Skrank.

"No, the engine's pretty much fixed, but I need Furgok. Know where he went?"

The captain pointed. "Be careful what you say."

Furgok stood near the crater's slope, target practicing with his ray gun. Thirty feet away a pile of stones glowed bright red. "What is it?"

"Ship's about done. I need some help with that thingy, though. It keeps sticking every time I unspool it."

"That *thingy* is a *spraggle*. What kind of mechanic doesn't even know the parts of an engine?"

"I hear that a lot. Anyway, it's jammed."

Furgok holstered his ray gun. "Fixed it, did ya?"

"Except for the thingy—the *spraggle*."

"Stupid part has never worked like it's supposed to. Best you can do is jimmy it by hand, then stick it in half spooled. Once we start, the vibration will pick up the slack."

"I could use some help."

"It isn't natural, you being able to fix ships like that. But Furgok will not complain. Furgok is not some whiny, wet-nosed baby-brat who runs off when a thing doesn't go his way. You don't think Furgok is one of *those*, do you?"

"No," said Jack sincerely. "I don't."

"Furgok is still the mechanic on this ship. Furgok can still teach *oom'n beans* a thing or two."

"You could teach me how to wrap that *spraggle*."

"Darn right I can. So, how did you learn to work on saucers, anyway?"

"It's a long story."

"They always are," grumbled Furgok.

Jack smiled. The alien even looked like Uncle Dwayne, in a way.

• • •

COMING OVER the ridge, Phoony saw Parnadan spread out beneath him. His eyes were wild, his bodysuit tattered. Blood oozed from a dozen cuts on his abdomen. Groot shuffled up behind him.

Beyond the city was a crater. Phoony could just make out the *crannek* ship. Tiny figures moved around it. They were still there!

"We have them, Groot! You see? They weren't able to fix it! All we have to do now is scoop them up."

"*Scoop them up?* Those are *crannek* down there!"

"Pah! They're *pirates*. We'll bribe 'em—double whatever the *oomans* are paying. But we'd better hurry. I've seen too many *Uurthish* tricks."

Grady stumbled over the ridge. Like the Finder, his clothes were torn. "Where is he?" he demanded. "Where's Creedle?"

• • •

FURGOK CRAWLED out of the hatch. His eyes locked on the other *crannek* defiantly. "What are you gawping at? It's done. The ship is fixed."

They looked away. So did the humans. Jack didn't say a word.

"The *crannek* keep their promises," Skrank said grumpily. "So where do you want to go? You never told us."

"*Skreepia,*" Joe said quietly. "We need a lift to Skreepia."

Skrank looked at him in disbelief. *"Skreepia?"*

"We have business there. The skreeps stole something that belongs to us."

"You don't know what you're asking, *oom'n. Nobody* goes to Skreepia, except as a prisoner or a slave. Give me a new destination."

"Fair enough," said Joe. "Fly us as close as you can. We'll find someone else to take us the rest of the way."

The captain's toadlike eyes narrowed. "You don't understand, *oom'n*. The *crannek* aren't *afraid* to go. The *crannek* fear nothing. I'm telling you for your own sake. Skreepia is a suicide mission. Getting there is one of the worst journeys in the spiral arm. And if you do make it past the police cruisers and satellites, the best you can hope for is a speedy death. Otherwise they'll torture you or throw you in the mines! Trust me, you don't want to see the mines of Kaarkuul. Worst place in the galaxy. They say some *crannek* are there, but nobody will rescue them. Kaarkuul is that bad."

"It's a long shot," Joe admitted. "All the same, I reckon that's where we're going. You're welcome to come if you like."

"What do you mean *'welcome to come'*? Are you blind stupid, or pigheaded, or just plain crazy? Call it off! If you don't, then the *crannek have* to come. You leave us no choice."

"That ain't true. I gave you a choice. You can drop us off on the nearest friendly planet and go on your way."

"And you will go to Skreepia?"

"Yes'm. That's our plan."

Skrank faced her crew, eyes blazing. "You see what he does? He tries to *shame* us! He knows we agreed to the bet, and the *oom'ns won* the bet. Now *we* must take these *oom'ns* wherever they want to go. Clear enough! But now he says, 'Oh, no, if you *crannek* are such low-down, slab-sided, yellow-bellied cowards that you won't go to Skreepia, I *understand*. Me and my *children* will find someone *brave* to take us there instead!'"

"Hey, that ain't what I said at all."

"Oh, but you did! So let me tell you one more time, mate: The *crannek* aren't afraid of *anything*!" The captain stood next to her crew. "If *you're* going to Skreepia, *we're* going to Skreepia!"

"Well," said Joe, "in that case, we're much obliged."

• • •

"I'M NOT at all clear what happened there," said Dimplewhite. They had returned to gather their belongings.

"Joe got 'em to take us to Skreepia," Jack said gleefully, "even though they don't want to."

"You must be very persuasive."

"I never thought so. Seems like they persuaded themselves."

Dimplewhite said good-bye at his front door. "You know how risky this is. I won't belabor the point. Nevertheless, I almost envy you. You are actors on an enormous stage. The fate of worlds hinges on what you do."

"I'd rather not think of it like that," said Isadora.

• • •

THEY CLIMBED aboard the ship. Blim sealed the hatch, and Dommit started the engine, which rumbled to life in a healthy way. Jack held Milo on his lap. Space inside the small saucer was tight, and the mood was tense. Nobody said a word as Skrank initiated the liftoff sequence.

• • •

PHOONY SPED up the side of the crater. In the last light of day he became an inky silhouette perched on its rim. Already the saucer had begun to turn, faster, faster.

"No!" he panted. "No, you can't do this to me!"

Sergeant Webb tottered up behind him. "Stop them! They're getting away!"

Phoony felt a surge of rage. *Big Webb was right!* So what if Xaafuun wanted the *Uurthlings* returned alive? He'd bring them to her in a bag and say they died in an accident! He tried to aim his ray gun, but his thorax was still heaving, and his arm shook wildly. He steadied it with two more hands and turned the energy level up to maximum. That much power could knock down a building! The saucer lifted off. Phoony fired.

The strength of the blast pitched him backward off the crater. He fell forty feet and lay stunned as the *crannek* ship rose above him like a dark moon. The saucer hovered, spinning lazily. Then it whisked away.

part
three...
skreepia

. . .

39. THE JABANEER DREAM TUNNEL

THE PIRATES approached their journey in a professional manner. The fact that it was the result of a lost bet, and would likely kill them, rarely came up. "The good thing about the *crannek*," Jack told Isadora as he gnawed on a hard biscuit, "is they don't hold a grudge."

Furgok banged on the engine room ladder with a wrench. "Creedle, you halfwit! Where did you put my *bimily* clamp?"

Jack wiped his mouth on his wrist. "Well, I guess I'd better get back to work."

The ship was a simple vehicle, as flying saucers go, with metal hatches, swinging hammocks, and ladders leading between decks. Its main deficiency, beyond its appearance, was that it was slow. Jack couldn't stop talking about it.

"You'll never change her," said Furgok. "She is what she is."

The long night of outer space wore on. Joe played a table game called Smash with Dommit and Blim and lost eleven straight rounds. He was on his way to losing a twelfth when Furgok ran up the galley ladder, swinging a club.

"Where is he? Where is that little vandal?"

Jack crouched behind the captain, wiping his hands on a rag.

"You!" screamed Furgok. "You ruined it!"

"What did he do?" demanded Skrank.

"You won't believe it, Cap'n! The hooligan rerouted the *trinik* coil through the *glick* chamber and rigged up six new barrel valves where the bucket surger used to be! I don't even know how to fix it!"

"Explain yourself, *oom'n*."

"That's why I came up here. You see, the old bucket surger wasn't cutting it—"

"Skip the details. What did you *do*?"

"I souped her up a little."

"Souped her up?"

"I made her faster!" His voice lowered to a husky whisper. *"By about a bazillion miles an hour!* If you open up the throttle, you'll see."

"Shumway!" barked the captain. "Code the thrusters. Initiate a five-point sequence. We'll take her to level two for now."

Isadora, now the captain's assistant, tapped on a keyboard, then pressed a glowing green button. A deep rumble ran through the ship. She read the monitor aloud. "Eighteen thousand helions—and climbing."

"At level two? Impossible!" Skrank checked the numbers. "Try level three."

She tapped again. "Forty-six thousand!"

At level four the ship hit 62,000 helions per standard unit without so much as a body rattle. "That's enough," said the captain breathlessly. "Take her back to three, and leave her there."

"I don't believe it," Furgok whispered. "All of a sudden, this old rowboat is the fastest raider in the spiral arm!"

Skrank turned to Jack. "Do you have any idea what you've done? With speed like this we could outrun any saucer in the skreepish fleet."

"You'll be winning races all over the galaxy," Jack assured them. "Nobody will expect the old jalopy to move so fast."

• • •

THEY SPED THROUGH the Krespid system faster than Skrank had ever believed possible. "Shumway, you've set the coordinates?"

"Yes."

"Then you've heard about it? The route we're taking?"

"Only what the crew is saying."

"The Jabaneer Dream Tunnel is the only way to Skreepia from here. You won't find a nastier passage. Sailors say it's haunted—haunted by all the ships that went in and never came out. Do you understand? They're still in there, every one. Not that the crews are dead, mind you—they're stuck in time. And they *talk*. If you listen, they'll suck you in, too. Make one false move and *bam!*—you're lost in time *and* space."

Isadora's stomach fluttered, and her palms dampened.

"Only the skreeps manage to get through the Jabaneer without trouble," the captain continued. "Filthy brutes. Nobody knows how they do it."

Her fear of closed spaces was unreasonable, Isadora told herself. The Jabaneer was not really a hole; it was a disruption, an anomaly in space-time. She took deep breaths and rubbed her hands on her skirt. "We're almost there," she told the captain. Within a narrow field ahead, the stars began to wobble.

Entering the Dream Tunnel was like stumbling into the basement of an old house. The saucer slewed sideways, then fell. Skrank and Dommit struggled to get it back on course.

Something swirled in front of them—a colossal, twisting clot of blackness.

"Dive! Dive! Dive!" The captain yanked on her joystick. The ship rolled over. "Dive, you miserable scow!" The saucer slowed as if sticky fingers were holding it back.

Skrank clung to the stick with both hands. Furgok cursed, and Milo cursed back, flapping his wings.

Suddenly they broke free. The saucer plunged.

"What *was* that thing?" Isadora squeaked.

"Time trap," muttered Skrank, tapping furiously on one of the keyboards. "When time turns back on itself, and the loop closes, that's what happens. Get caught in one of those things, you stay there forever. Worse than death, if you ask me."

Isadora watched the clot recede from view. Hellebeezia had been timeless, but not like *that*. Were there different kinds of eternity?

"Look out!" screamed Dommit. A saucer hurtled toward them, blazing light from every porthole.

"Hard port!" cried Skrank.

The gap narrowed. The image wavered. "Wait!" said Isadora. "It isn't real."

"We're going to hit!" shrieked Dommit.

"It isn't real," Isadora repeated.

The pirates closed their eyes and waited for the final, sickening crunch. It never came. The big saucer plowed into them, and then it vanished.

Skrank studied Isadora. "How did you know?"

"It's hard to explain." Isadora thought about the holograms, and how she had been unable to see them after their visit to Hellebeezia. "I just don't see illusions anymore. That is, I saw it, but only for a moment. Jack's the same way, aren't you, Jack?"

"Yeah. But that was still kind of scary."

"Illusions," said Skrank. "The old skreepish game. So that's how they use this tunnel without wrecking! They must turn 'em off when they come through."

They passed another saucer, hanging in midair like a moth on a screen. "Is that an illusion, too?" asked Blim.

"I think it's real," Jack told her.

"Stuck in time," said Skrank. "They made a wrong turn. Now they can't get out."

"Can't we help them?"

"Not without getting stuck ourselves. They've been there awhile, by the looks of things. Nobody's built ships like that in fifteen lifetimes."

The tunnel twisted, dipped, and dove into inky pits. Side tunnels beckoned, but Skrank, using charts and instinct, held steady to the course. Twice more they passed ancient vessels mired in invisible traps. Once, screaming voices filled the bridge, broadcast through open channels on their communicators. They turned the devices off. Jack rubbed his rabbit's foot down to the skin.

A jagged hunk of metal zipped overhead. "That was real," said Jack, "in case you were wondering."

"This lousy hole's full of junk like that," said Skrank as another hunk whizzed by. "Bits and pieces of old ships would be my guess. If a big one hits us—*splat!*—then there'll be more bits and pieces."

The journey went on and on. "How long have we been in here?" Isadora asked wearily.

"It seems like forever," said Jack. "I don't even know why we're still kids."

Then, so suddenly they couldn't even feel it, they were out. The stars stopped dancing, and emptiness opened all around.

"Oh, thank goodness," Isadora sighed.

"Don't relax too much," said the captain. "We're deep inside skreepish territory now. Every ship will be an enemy. Spy satellites, security patrols, and big floating eyeballs are watching everything that passes in and out. Skreeps don't like intruders. Their empire is a fortress."

• • •

PHOONY BULLIED his way through security at Kraakeria, sometimes waving his orders, often simply snarling demands in a tone that defied opposition. Nobody stood up to him. He was too strange, with his tattered uniform, scarred limbs, and glowing, half-crazy eyes.

He demanded a ship, a fast one, and got it.

"Take it!" said the agent. Arboria was full of diseases; the Finder could be contagious. "Just go."

They left. The planet became a disk, then a bright star, then a pinprick. The saucer *was* fast. Phoony pushed it hard.

"How do you know where they went?" Grady asked grumpily. His Skreepish was improving, but not his mood.

"They're going to Skreepia."

"But how do you *know*? Why couldn't they go to Earth, or Mars, or anywhere?"

"They *could*, but they won't. I know. I'm a *Finder*. They'll try to get to Skreepia, but they'll fail. Their ship is old and slow. They'll get stuck in the Dream Tunnel, and that's where I'll catch them."

The ship was crowded. Sergeant Webb snored. Groot rubbed a nasty-smelling ointment on his wounds. "This is the worst trip ever," said Grady.

. . .

40. RIIBEENX

"UGLY ONE!" said the Queen.

Xaafuun jumped in her chair. This was not the canned image but the Exalted One's actual visage. The giant face leered, its jewels sparkled, and its feathers floated, ghostlike in the still atmosphere of the bridge.

"Finally you return! It must have been a lovely vacation for you, away so long! Did you bring me my Item?"

"I did, Exalted One."

"You have taken the liberty of using it, I think. Should I not be *very* angry?"

"I hope you will not be, Highness. Everything I have done has been for you—and for the glory of your empire."

"A pretty lie. Go on."

Xaafuun quickly explained the Medwig's collapse, and how the Special Item had saved them from ruin. "I have other gifts for you as well, Highness: the *Uurth Queen* and her consort, conquered in battle."

"*Uurth Queen*? This lie is not so pretty! Do you mean to *amuse* me?"

"I had hoped it would *please* you, Highness. As you know, the rabble are always impressed to see a conquered ruler with their own eyes. It gives them confidence. I thought if the *Uurth* creatures were carried in a victory parade at your Jubilee—and then executed, of course!—it might make the colonization of *Uurth* more appealing."

"I hardly need to flatter my swinish subjects, Ugly One. They do what I say under pain of death—as do you, I might add."

"Certainly, Highness!" Xaafuun bowed so low she nearly kissed the seat of her chair.

"Nevertheless," said the Exalted One, "I see what you have in mind: a *spectacle*. Those *can* be charming. Now that your looks are gone, Ugly One, you have decided to be *clever*! An *Uurth* Queen, is it? Death in the Grand Arena?"

"Yes, Highness. Death, certainly."

"The idea grows on me," said the Queen. Her eyes narrowed. "I will accept your cleverness—for now."

"Thank you, Exalted One," Xaafuun said uncertainly.

The Queen's head flickered. Soon only her canned image remained, hovering over Xaafuun like a bad dream.

• • •

"W E ' R E   B E I N G followed," said Dommit.

The captain scanned her monitors. "What makes you say that?"

"I can *feel* it. The *oom'n* feels it, too."

"I feel *something*," said Joe. "Been nervy as a cat for a while."

"You must tell me about this *cat* sometime." She faced her crew. "So what do we do, fight?"

"Outrun 'em," said Furgok. "We've got the speed."

The captain thought about the situation. "We can run. But that'll just draw more attention. What we need is a place to *hide*."

"Here's the place," said Dommit. The navigator pointed to a spot on her monitor. "It's a planet called Riibeenx. Decent air, lots of room, and it's wet."

"We could use the water. But what kind of place can it be, this close to Skreepia?"

"Deserted, but I don't know why. The computer doesn't say anything."

"A paradise, no doubt." Skrank checked her monitors again. "Okay, we'll try it. Let's have some speed so we can lose whatever's behind us."

They set the thrusters at level four, then sped toward Riibeenx at 56,000 helions per standard unit.

.   .   .

SKREEPIA HUNG outside Dr. Shumway's twin portholes like a lead weight. The planet had rings—not the colorful bands of a Saturn, but dozens of crisscrossing spiderwebs in low orbit above its outer atmosphere. On closer inspection, the clouds were not uniformly gray but were mixed with shades of brown and creamy white, swirled like batter in a mixing bowl.

The door winked open. "Come in," she said, without turning. "I am observing Skreepia."

Bud joined her at the window. "So what do you think?"

"The cloud cover is heavy, so I have not been able to see much. But it is my impression that there is little in the way of ocean or water bodies of any kind. Perhaps there are aquifers underground. According to the crew, much of the planet is urban sprawl."

"That's my impression, too—lots of cities. Imagine a whole planet full of those spiders! Makes your skin crawl, don't it?" He scratched himself under his feathers. "We're heading for the capital, by the way—place called Qurya. Listen, I hate to keep harping on this, but will you wear the robe—maybe the crown, too? From what I hear, we're going straight to the Queen's palace. And you know what they say about first impressions."

"That they are often false? That they represent a triumph of prejudice over critical thought?"

"No, that they're important. We really want to *wow* this skreepish Queen, win her over, get her on our side."

"Honestly, Mr. Creedle, doesn't that seem unlikely? We have been kidnapped by hostile aliens and dragged across the galaxy. Along the way, Isadora and Jack have escaped onto a foreign world where they may be trying to enlist the help of sympathetic rebels. That is where our hopes lie—not in making a favorable impression on the skreepish Queen!"

"Well, sure. I give those kids credit. They showed real spunk, even my nephew. But that don't mean we can't do *our* part, too."

"Our part, Mr. Creedle, is to destroy your fiendish invention, not to playact the role of foreign dignitaries."

"Well, that's where we disagree. These skreeps, they don't think it *is* playacting. They think it's real! So all's I'm asking is for you to put on them feathers and *pretend*. It couldn't hurt, and it just might help."

"And all I ask of you, Mr. Creedle, is to remember your promise."

"All right!" he said irritably. "Just don't crowd me. It's a tricky situation."

"On the contrary, it is a simple question of courage and moral clarity."

"Listen, I'm all for that stuff—courage and moral whatever—I'm just saying we should try to fix this mess without *killing* ourselves. Is that so horrible?" He cleaned his glasses on his feathers. "I hate to criticize, but for a brainy scientist you take an awfully narrow-minded view of things."

The saucer descended rapidly toward the planet. Up close, Skreepia's rings were revealed to be nothing more than clumps of orbiting garbage. A gooey wad of orange trash splattered against one of the portholes. Dr. Shumway recoiled in disgust.

"Very well," she muttered. "I'll put on the robe."

"That's the spirit," said Bud.

Dr. Shumway was buttoning her collar when an immense cable arched up from the planet's surface, and the saucer hovered beside it. "A space elevator," she said. "It hoists vessels in and out of orbit. Dr. Furnstadt, one of my colleagues, has been studying the concept. How fascinated he would be."

"I saw the same thing once in a comic book," said Bud.

The saucer, securely harnessed, began its descent.

• • •

THE *CRANNEK* saucer zipped over Riibeenx. A vast, army-green forest seemed to cover the entire planet, interrupted only by mossy lakes and wide green seas. Even then Isadora could almost imagine the trees marching on underwater.

"The question," said Skrank, "is where do we land?"

That *was* the question. From a hundred feet up, the jungle appeared impenetrable. The canopy was practically a solid surface. Herds of round-bodied, rabbit-sized creatures bounded across it. The ship swung over a lake. "Maybe there's a place along the shoreline," suggested Dommit. "We need to be close to water anyway."

"What shoreline?" Skrank asked. The trees extended far into the water. *Or maybe,* thought Isadora, *the whole planet is flooded.* But as they flew closer, nothing astonished her more than the *size* of the trees. They were *enormous*. Straight as Roman columns, they rose hundreds—perhaps thousands—of feet to their crowns.

Finally Drommit spied a small break in the canopy. The opening wasn't large, but it was big enough for the ship to pass through. "Another hole," Isadora muttered as they began their descent.

The saucer spun to a stop. "All right, you swabs," growled Skrank. "Let's have a look around."

They popped the hatch and were blasted by hot air so thick it almost seemed liquid—a putrifying soup, rich with decay.

"Oh, man!" Jack pinched his nose. "We gotta go out in *that*?"

"The Creedle can *stay*," said Furgok, "if he is so weak and useless and fainthearted. But the *crannek* will collect water."

"Take it easy. I just meant it was *stinky*."

"I'll go," Isadora volunteered.

"Count me in, too," said Joe.

In the end only Milo remained in the ship, watching from the top of the ladder as they carried empty barrels across the landing site.

The clearing was not a natural feature. Scattered among

colossal stumps were the enormous machines that had cut them. The forest edge was strewn with litter—cans, crates, and bottles, some of it partially burned.

"We're a lot of geniuses!" said Furgok. "Hiding from the skreeps in one of their own filthy camps!"

"Don't go wobbly," Skrank grunted. "The camp is abandoned. I bet there hasn't been a skreep here in a long cycle, at least."

"I wonder why?" asked Blim. "If they were after lumber, they couldn't do better than this."

"Who knows? This place has a funny feeling. You want my advice, I say we gather our water quick and get out."

They carried their barrels into the jungle, moving easily in the planet's weak gravity. The forest canopy was so high that thin clouds formed beneath it. Flying creatures swooped between the trunks.

After hiking some distance through the underbrush, they found themselves knee-deep in gooey muck. The *crannek* plowed ahead, and the humans followed. A fallen tree created a bridge to the lake, and they scrambled onto it. The trunk was twenty feet across, creating a wide pathway, which they followed single file.

Finally the lake spread out before them. Their bridge became a dock. When they came to the end, Furgok knelt and stirred the water. His nostrils twitched at the smell.

"Drink this filth, and we'll all be sick."

"Go on," said Skrank. "Fill the barrels. We'll zap 'em with chemicals when we get back to the ship."

The stagnant water gasped when it poured into the casks, as if startled from an unhealthy dream.

"Can you believe the size of these trees?" Jack asked Isadora.

"I counted my footsteps. This one was almost three thousand feet tall!"

"That's a long way to run if we have to leave in a hurry." The jungle planet made Isadora uneasy. "Let's finish up and get out of here."

Jack discovered that water behaved strangely in the light gravity. When it splashed, blobs of it floated several feet before shattering into tiny droplets. The blobs could be made to glide along the water's surface. He became so engrossed in his splashing that he barely noticed the *crannek* heading back, full barrels braced across their shoulders.

Splooosh!

"What was that?" asked Isadora.

"What?"

"It sounded like something jumping out of the water."

They peered into the mist. As Joe finished filling the barrel, a low wave rolled in. The log lifted, then dropped, just as a second wave arrived. It lifted again.

"Whatever that was, I reckon it was *big*." A third wave splashed their feet. They struggled to raise the barrel and started back down the log.

SPLOOSH!

"How bad do we need this water?" asked Jack.

"It's starting to seem less important, ain't it?"

A huge shape rose from the lake's surface a thousand yards away.

"Run!" shouted Isadora.

They dropped the barrel and sprinted for shore. In the feeble gravity, each stride became a ten-foot leap. Even so, they couldn't move fast enough. Another splash came right behind them.

"Run!" Isadora screamed again when she came upon the *crannek*, plodding under their heavy loads. They pitched the casks aside and bolted for the ship. Many years later, in the kind of dreams no one wants, Isadora would still see the hideous thing rise from the lake.

Its bullet-shaped head and round body were as brown as the muck it came from. Its oval mouth held rows of yellow teeth.

The head plunged beneath the surface with another massive splash, and its body slid in behind it.

They ran. The log ended, and they were back in the muck, but that barely slowed them. They splashed and bounded, slime draining from their hands.

Skrank reached solid ground and roared to the others, "Come on, you lumbering slugs! You miserable belly-flopping, slop-sliding mud-rats! Step lively, or you'll all be worm meat!"

They ran for the ship with all the energy they had left.

"Get inside!" shouted Furgok. They stumbled past the rusting hulks of skreepish machinery and crowded under the saucer. They groped for the ladder.

It wasn't there.

The hatch was closed.

. . .

41. THE PRINCESS

"THIS IS MORE like it!" said Bud. He sat beside Dr. Shumway in a huge walking vehicle that lumbered through the crowded streets of Qurya. Happy spiders in festive costumes gathered along the route, waving silken banners and cheering lustily. Flowering trees with pink leaves bloomed along the roadside. Huge skyscrapers climbed to unbelievable heights. They were mushroom-capped in silver, gold, pink, and green. Shimmering webs stretched among them, obscuring the roiling sky.

From above, the city—indeed the entire planet—had seemed a gloomy place, but on the ground the air was bright, if not exactly sunny. The cheering crowds were lit to perfection. "It's something, isn't it?" Bud said, taking it all in.

"It's an elaborate fraud," said Dr. Shumway. "Just as there were illusions on the ship—fountains, sculptures, and potted plants—here we see golden streets, shiny buildings, and cheering natives—the whole thing is ridiculous!"

"Well, maybe it *is* phony," Bud admitted. "The point is, we're getting the royal treatment, same as I predicted."

"We're being served on a platter. Be realistic, Mr. Creedle.

Flattering illusions will not benefit us any more than they have benefited the skreeps."

"Begging your pardon, ma'am, but the skreeps seem to be doing fine."

"They aren't, though. You saw the reality from the air. The planet's atmosphere has been poisoned, its landscape ruined. If the skreeps face the truth, they might yet save themselves—*and* this desolate world. But from what I see, their prospects are poor. A culture that subsists on fakery is doomed."

• • •

"SOMEONE MUST'VE got inside!" panted Furgok.

"Well, they'd better open up in a hurry," said Joe. "That monster ain't waiting."

"HEY!" shouted Skrank. "Whoever you are! Open this door!"

"The creature's at the edge of the clearing!" shouted Blim.

"Shoot it, then!"

Blim unholstered a shiny weapon. When the monster's head emerged from the jungle, she fired. *Zzzzap!* A yellow ray crack-sizzled from the gun's nozzle, slamming the creature on its bulbous snout. It recoiled. A putrid smell of charred flesh filled the air.

"Look out!" shouted Isadora. "It's coming back!"

This time Dommit and Blim shot together. The bolts connected, and more flesh sizzled. The monster retreated.

"I'll let you in," said a muffled voice, "if you promise to take me away from here."

"Skreepish!" muttered Skrank. "Why am I not surprised?"

The monster came back, and Furgok shot it twice. "It just keeps coming!"

The creature writhed into the clearing. "All right!" the captain shouted to the voice inside the ship. "I'll take you with us. But you'd better move fast and open this door!"

"We aren't stopping it, Captain," said Furgok. "We're barely slowing it down."

The creature lunged at them. Skreepish equipment shattered. Suddenly the hatch swung open. The ladder came down.

"Everyone!" yelled Skrank. "Inside! On the double!" She pulled two heavy pistols from her bandoliers and stepped into the clearing.

The monster rose, preparing to strike. Its body curled like a question mark. Its wide mouth dropped open. Skrank fired. Two bursts of lightning disappeared down the monster's gullet. The blasts blew twin exit holes through its slimy body. Its head jerked backward. Its body convulsed. The ship's crew scrambled up the ladder.

"It's a matter of timing," Skrank grumbled, to nobody in particular. The creature's tail swung in a dying spasm. When it struck the ship, the sound was like the tolling of a bell.

•   •   •

PHOONY'S SHIP rocketed out of the Jabaneer Dream Tunnel. The Finder relaxed. They were inside skreepish territory now. He stretched his new arm, which had grown to almost full length. He was becoming himself again. The wounds from Arboria were healing. Only his eyes had changed, his eyes and the cruel line of his mouth.

He scanned his monitors for any sign of the alien craft. It was an awkward old tub and wouldn't be hard to find. He signaled every satellite he could reach, offering money in exchange for information. An odd story came back. A ship had been spotted, but by the time an interceptor was dispatched, it was gone.

Anxiety, usually buried, stirred within the Finder. They should have overtaken the *crannek* ship by now. Unless he'd guessed wrong. He poked Big Webb. "If you were one of those *Uurthlings*—the *baad Uurthlings*—where would *you* go?"

"Home," interrupted Grady.

"Now hold on, son," said his father. "You gotta think like a cop. Those Creedles are looking for a payday. And home ain't the place to find it."

"So what do you think, Big Webb?"

"Skreepia," said the sergeant. "That's what I think. They're headed for *your* planet."

Phoony's anxiety disappeared. Big Webb was right. The answer was so simple, even an *Uurthling* could figure it out. Now all he had to do was catch the runaways before someone else did.

• • •

THE SKREEP crouched at the back of the deck. Her legs were drawn up around her, and a robe of bedraggled feathers clung to her back. Her yellow eyes were filled with panic.

Furgok unholstered his ray gun.

"Easy," said the captain. "Nobody's shooting anyone until I say so."

"She could've got us killed."

"True, but so could your lousy aim." Skrank turned her attention to the skreep. "Okay, who are you? And what are you doing on my ship?"

"Please," hissed the stowaway. "Take me away from here. I am very wealthy. I can pay whatever you wish."

"I like you better already. But you didn't answer my question. I asked you who you are, and what you're doing here."

"My story goes beyond anything you could imagine." The skreep's voice gained confidence, even a touch of arrogance. "I am the Princess Troonidar, Fourteenth Hatchling in the Dynasty of Saskaphuun." She waited for the magnitude of her words to sink in. "I am, in short, the rightful heir to the skreepish throne."

"I guess that makes me the King of Velvoon," said Furgok.

"Hold on," said Skrank. "Give the spider a chance to tell her story."

"I was exiled here by my aunt, the Queen. She is a jealous, wicked hag. She fears and despises me because I am so loved by the skreepish people. The story is long and sordid, but you can see for yourself: I was left to die. Just take me to Fangoo Seven. My relatives there will reward you handsomely."

"You can stow that idea," said Skrank. "We're not going to Fangoo anything. We're going to Skreepia. Still want to come?"

"You mustn't do that!" pleaded the Princess. "You will die. *I* will die! Please, Fangoo is much better for you, too. They are very lenient toward riffraff there."

Skrank spoke to the others in *crannek*. "What am I to make of this spider? Any suggestions?"

"I'll take her out and shoot her," Furgok offered.

"That would be cold-blooded murder!" cried Isadora. "Besides, you made a deal."

"She does *act* like a princess," said Joe, rubbing his chin. "All snotty and full of herself. And she's got them feathers . . . "

"If she *is* a princess," Skrank said, "she could be valuable."

"We could use her to get onto the planet."

"Or to put our heads in a noose!" scoffed Blim. "It doesn't sound like she's popular with the Queen."

"We're facing nooses or worse either way." Skrank switched to Skreepish. "Princess, can you get us onto Skreepia without getting caught? We have business there."

"You don't *understand*. I don't wish to go to *Skreepia*. The Queen is my aunt, and she *despises* me. I wish to go to Fangoo Seven."

"Yes, Your Highness, but that won't happen. It's Skreepia or nothing. If you want, I'll leave you here. Wanna think it over?"

"I don't like you," she said, pouting. She held the pose a moment, then sighed. "Very well. I'll take you to Skreepia. But you'll get no reward, and if you are captured, I will do nothing to save you."

Skrank said, "It's a deal."

• • •

"I GROW IMPATIENT," said the Exalted One. The great hall in which she sat was intricately carved from black and yellow stone, festooned with feathers and glittering gems. Golden columns rose in lazy spirals to a vaulted ceiling, where artificial insects buzzed and chattered, or struggled comically to free themselves from webs. Behind the Queen, a tapestry depicted a ghastly picnic, in which dozens of bejeweled spiders gorged on creatures with red fur and terrified eyes. "Impatient," she repeated, "with you, with the *Uurthlings*, with the fools who call themselves my technicians. Tell me again why the Special Item has not been replicated."

"We *have* made progress, Your Highness." Xaafuun bowed until her antennae brushed the buzzle-stone floor. Slaves scurried about, and kimili pods opened like giant clams to bathe the scene in turquoise light.

"*Progress*, Ugly One? I see no sign of progress! My invasion fleet must be fully equipped by the start of the next long cycle."

"We have made hundreds of cabinets, Exalted One, just like the original."

"Cabinets! I cannot traverse 153 light-years of ruined, untunneled space using *cabinets*. I cannot colonize *Uurth* using *cabinets*. Again! Why has the machine not been replicated?"

"There is a difficulty with the energy source, Highness. The male *Uurthling* asks for rare ingredients and outlandish equipment—"

"Give him whatever he needs."

"Yes, Your Highness. But Your Highness—?"

"What is it, Ugly One?"

"Your Highness, the male *Uurthling* is a creature of dubious character. It may be that he is stalling—"

The Queen held up a single claw. "Do not bore me with details. The *ooman bing* will be *made* to talk, if need be. He is not a creature of consequence. Meanwhile, give him his supplies and watch him closely. Have the technicians replicate every element of the Item faithfully, and install the copies in every ship we have. Once the energy source is isolated, we'll install that, too."

"Yes, Your Highness."

"The Fabulous Jubilee starts in two short cycles, Ugly One. The tournament begins in three. Following the preliminary matches will be my victory parade. We will rid our-selves of our royal guests at that time. By then, this matter must be resolved."

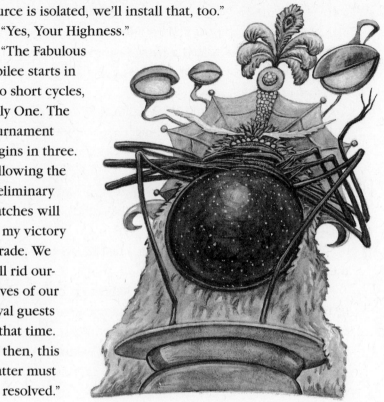

• • •

42. QUANTUM FOAM

"DO NOT ASK me about that horrid planet," said the Prin-cess. "I never want to think about it again."

"I was just wondering where the rest of you went," said

Jack. "I mean, it looked like there was a bunch of skreeps there at one time."

"There is no rest of *me*. I am the Princess. As for slaves and prisoners, hundreds passed through that camp, perhaps thousands. Outposts like it are all over the planet, so you can imagine how many died. Nevertheless, all of that happened before *I* was left there." She paused dramatically. "*I* was alone."

"Why did they all die?" asked Isadora. She sat beside Jack in the ship's galley. The Princess yawned, showing her fangs.

"They were slaves. That's what slaves do. Still, you can imagine the expense! My family lost a fortune! When I was a hatchling, Riibeenx was all I heard about—the endless forests and the money that could be made cutting them down. How were we to know those trees are so poisonous?"

"Poisonous?" said Jack. He handed her a hard biscuit.

"You have no idea." She popped it into her mouth. "You could die just *looking* at them."

Isadora gave her another biscuit. "Is that why the site was abandoned?"

"No, but it's why we switched to prisoners. They're much cheaper." Once it would have embarrassed her to speak so freely with aliens, but the loneliness of exile had loosened her tongue. She swallowed the biscuit and held out her hand for another. "But even prisoners cost *something*, and they died as fast as we could plunk them down. Supposedly it was the sawdust that did it. A few breaths and—" She pantomimed a body falling over. "Then the eel-monsters came. They ate their way through camp after camp—which provided wonderful video entertainment, but it ruined the logging industry. Then all the sites were abandoned, by decree of my aunt—the witch. So my family lost gobs of money, and we were all upset."

"And your aunt sent you back there after all that?"

"Can you believe it? It's simply the wickedest thing ever."

"I don't know," said Jack. "Getting all those loggers killed was pretty bad, too."

"Silly!" The Princess ate another biscuit. "They were *slaves*."

"It's unbelievable," said Isadora. "Your own aunt!"

"She could see how popular I was becoming, so naturally she was afraid I'd take her throne. You've heard the old saying, *Queens hatch hungry babies*. She'd become unpopular herself. People were constantly plotting against her. Not just peasants and riffraff, either, but actual *decent* people—there was even a *general*! She was sent to Kaarkuul. Personally, I hate politics, but you can see why the Queen was worried."

"You almost sound sympathetic," Isadora commented.

"Well, she isn't *stupid*. She had to get me out of the way. But *Riibeenx*? It's monstrous!"

"That's a crummy planet, all right," said Jack. "But you still haven't said why she's so unpopular. With regular skreeps, I mean."

"*Regular* skreeps? How should I know? Famine, plague? You have no idea how much peasants like to complain."

"You can't blame them for being upset if they're starving!" said Isadora.

"I can blame them if they're whining at *me*!" Riibeenx was now nothing but a distant green star, surrounded by other stars. "I'm a *princess*, not a *cook*. But the peasants were also upset about *Uurth*, for some reason."

"Earth?" said Jack and Isadora together. "Why?"

"Who knows? Peasants whine about everything. I think they resent the Replacement Planet Program. You'd be surprised

how many skreeps would like to stay on
Skreepia, no matter how worn-out it gets! I
know, you think skreeps are absolutely the
most fabulous, modern, *with-it* creatures in
the universe. Some of us are. Still, there are
a lot of backward thinkers on Skreepia, too."

"But Earth is a terrible place for you!"
cried Jack.

"Really," said Isadora, "you don't want
to go there."

"I forgot, you're *ooman bings*, aren't
you? Anyway, it's my aunt's idea. Truth is, I
couldn't care less about your stupid planet."

•　•　•

X AAFUUN LED her guests onto a wide balcony. Far below
lay the invasion fleet, spread out like a carpet of silvery toad-
stools. Dr. Shumway's breath caught in her throat. "An impressive sight."

"Isn't it? The Exalted One commissioned this fleet for the
Department of Peaceful Exploration. It is her hope that these
ships will soon go forth on journeys of *goodwill* and scientific
inquiry."

"I would be interested to know how you define those
terms," said Dr. Shumway.

"Like all queens you have a suspicious nature." Xaafuun
gurgled approvingly. "But do not worry. Our intentions are
entirely benign."

They left the balcony and stepped into a windowless room.
Durbo music screeched; a spiny plant slumped against one

wall. "The Exalted One is a wonderful diplomat. It is why
skreeps are loved and admired throughout the galaxy. As a
queen yourself, you must understand her wisdom."

"I see her ambitions. She wishes to have destabilizers placed
on each of these vessels?"

"I am glad you mention it! Please, I will show you the project that Bug Greedle and I have been supervising."

An elevator tube sucked them to a lower level. Xaafuun led
them into a transparent pod suspended above a warehouse.
Inside the warehouse stood row upon row of shiny refrigerators. Laboring over them were dozens of skreeps, dark against
the white enamel.

"What is this?" asked Dr. Shumway. Bud looked away.

"It is a project of great importance for both of our planets. I thought you should see how it progresses—or fails to progress. The Exalted One grows impatient. She believes Bug Greedle is stalling. She fears he will not uphold his end of the bargain."

"Well, she's wrong!" he said. "Though for what it's worth, I haven't seen my million bucks yet, either."

"Mr. Creedle!" cried Dr. Shumway. "What have you been doing here?"

"Easy now," he said softly. "It's *negotiation*. The thing is," he continued in a louder voice, "you can build all the destabilizers you want. Without the foam, you've got nothing more than a place to hide a ham sandwich. Which I've explained a hundred times, by the way. The foam is the key, and to make it, I need a lab, and equipment, and that list of ingredients I gave you when we landed."

"Ah, yes. Your famous ingredients," said Xaafuun. "Follow me; I think you will be pleasantly surprised."

"You never *mentioned* you were building a fleet of destabilizers!" Dr. Shumway hissed. They followed the skreep down a corridor. "What is this all about?"

"Diplomacy. Play along, will you?"

Xaafuun switched on an unusually bright light. She winced, shielding her many eyes with a bristled arm. "Is this what you had in mind, Bug Greedle?"

The lab was not so different from his workshop at home, though it was cleaner, and some of the instruments were unrecognizable. Bud picked up small bottles and examined their contents under the glaring light. "This seems to be it, all right."

"Good!" Xaafuun seemed genuinely relieved. "I will leave

you to it, then. You will make great quantities of this *foam*, enough to power the fleet."

"Hold on! This ain't like whipping up a milk shake. A job like this takes time."

"It will not take *too much time*, though, or the Exalted One will be unhappy. Perhaps the *Uurth* Queen will supervise?"

"Indeed I will," said Dr. Shumway. "I only wish I had *supervised* sooner."

"Excellent! The Exalted One has planned a fabulous parade in your honor. It will take place in a few short cycles." Xaafuun scuttled out of the room.

"Really!" said Dr. Shumway as soon as the spider was gone. "Your villainy goes beyond all bounds, Mr. Creedle. And now this! A laboratory perfectly designed for the production of quantum foam."

"I was only buying us some time. Still am, if you haven't noticed."

"*Buying time* has never been the objective. The objective is the destruction of your destabilizer—of *all* destabilizers."

"Well, maybe it ain't as easy as you think."

"I never imagined it would be *easy*! Rather, it is *necessary*."

Bud picked up a bottle, then set it back on the counter. "How much do you know about quantum foam?" he asked seriously.

"It is a form of vacuum energy, akin to antimatter. I believe it is rather volatile. . . . "

He clucked his tongue and pointed at her. "That's the word. *Volatile*. I've been soft-peddling it so as not to alarm you. But do you know what would happen if I tried to take the quantum foam out of the destabilizer? Or if I busted up the machine?"

"I imagine there might be some kind of explosion."

"*Some* kind, yeah."

"Are you saying it would be large?"

"Put it this way: It might not blow this planet to pieces, but it'd crack it pretty good."

For a moment Dr. Shumway was speechless. "You created this substance in your *garage*, then transported it over *dirt roads* in my *station wagon* . . . "

"There's no point in dredging up ancient history—though for the record, I was plenty nervous at the time. The problem is what to do now. I can't figure out how to get the stuff out of there."

Dr. Shumway sat down. "Certainly we cannot risk an entire planet, even one as wretched as Skreepia. Therefore we must find another solution. Meanwhile, Mr. Creedle, you must not make any more quantum foam!"

. . .

43. THE GRAND WILDERNESS

"Let me get this straight," said the captain. "If we use this special frequency, nobody will know we're coming?"

"Quiet!" The Princess struggled to tune a communicator. "I'm trying to find it. Yes, there it is—the Queen's own frequency. Only the Queen is allowed to use it, under pain of death. Which means it will hide us—but only if she isn't listening."

"And how can we know that?"

"*I don't know!*"

"Don't go wobbly, now. I was just wondering. Anyway, it's a fine idea. We'll tune everything we've got to the royal frequency. Even if the Queen spots us, it'll confuse her, and that could give us more time."

"It won't, though! Can't you see? We're doomed! This scheme is madness!"

"It isn't," Skrank insisted calmly. "The garbage idea is brilliant. You'll see. We'll be on Skreepia in no time."

For most of the last cycle they had been hiding in a close orbit around the moon Felmuus. Now they took off, blaring the royal frequency. Skrank pushed the thrusters to level four, and the sudden acceleration pinned them to their seats. Skreepia rose above the moon's horizon. The Princess slunk off to her quarters.

The gray planet swelled before them. "We can't go in this fast!" shouted Dommit. "We'll burn like a cinder!"

"Not to worry," said Skrank. "Be ready to back down hard."

Dommit's fingers were already on the lever. Jack rubbed his rabbit's foot.

"Right—*now*!"

The lever came down. The thrusters wailed. The saucer bucked into a reverse spin. Milo tottered backward, flapping his short wings.

As the ship settled into orbit, small objects began to ping against its sides.

"Garbage," said Skrank. "Dommit, see if you can't find us some cleaner space."

They drifted lower, until the debris no longer pelted them but flashed overhead like shooting stars.

The Princess presented herself on the bridge in her cape and crown. She had done what she could to clean the garments; they looked, if not quite regal, at least better than they had on Riibeenx. She addressed the captain. "You have succeeded, I see."

"So far. We still have to find a way down, but at least we'll be hard to spot in all this trash. If those coordinates you gave me are right, we've got Qurya just below."

"There's a ship approaching," said Dommit. "What do you think—should we shoot or run?"

"Neither. We'll let the Princess talk to 'em."

"No!" she shrieked. "I don't want to! If they see me, they'll tell the Queen."

"If they see *me*, they'll blast us out of the sky!" Skrank's tone grew stern. "You're the *Princess*, remember? You get to order all the other spiders around. Ask them who they are and what they're doing. Bully 'em a little. See if they can help us out."

A skreepish face appeared on the ship's projection screen. "Who are you? What're you doing in the sanitation zone?"

"Scum!" spat the Princess. "Is that the way you address your superiors?"

•　•　•

PERCHED AT THE controls of the launch was a very dirty, very uneasy skreep named Gloorg. Behind him sat the Princess, the humans, the chicken, Furgok, and Skrank. Dommit and Blim had been left to mind the saucer. The seal broke with a pop, and the launch drifted away from the *crannek* ship.

Gloorg looked over his shoulder, first at the humans, then at the Princess, and tried to hide his jitters.

"Stop staring at me, or I'll rip off your eyeballs."

"Pardon me, Your Highness. It's just that they're *ooman bings*!"

"Of course they're *ooman bings*, nitwit. Can't a princess travel with *ooman bings* if she wishes?"

"Forgive me, Your Majesty, I make no judgment."

"A garbage scow. To think I would return to Qurya in a garbage scow."

"The *Blue Morning*," said Gloorg. "There she is now!"

The Princess looked away. The scow floated overhead, gray and square-bodied. As they watched, doors in its belly swung open and a stream of trash spewed out. "Almost empty!" Gloorg exclaimed.

Inside the scow were two more skreeps, Nuunk and Huursk. They seemed, if anything, even more nervous than Gloorg. When the Princess appeared, they threw themselves facedown on the filthy deck. "Forgive us!" they cried.

"Get up," she ordered. "Your groveling disgusts me."

A durbo song, "Paradise of Food," played in the background. Isadora noticed that Huursk was watching her intently. "It's true!" he whispered. "They're *ooman bings*."

"Of course they are," snapped the Princess. "Why shouldn't they be? What's wrong with all of you, carrying on about my *ooman bings*?"

"It's the prophecy! You *do* know the prophecy, don't you, Your Majesty?"

"I'm the *Princess*. I know everything. And I demand that you take me to the surface right now."

"Hold on," said Skrank. "Just so you characters know, this isn't what you'd call a *legal* visit. You'll either come willingly, or as our prisoners, but there'll be no running off to tell the Queen. One sneeze from the Princess and we'll shoot you both."

"No!" They shouted in unison. "We're with you! With the Resistance," said Huursk. "And the Princess. Don't worry, we'll land in the Grand Wilderness before you know it. Then we'll take you to our leaders."

"Grand Wilderness?" said Jack. "I thought we were going to some big city."

"The Grand Wilderness Reclamation Center," Gloorg explained. "It's the largest refuse depository on Skreepia."

An hour later, the *Blue Morning* broke free from its elevator cable and plopped down in a canyon formed by mountains of garbage. Above them the skreepish sun, masked by layers of smog, burned like a wound.

"There are watchers even in the Wilderness," said Gloorg. "When it's clear, we'll take you to the safe house."

The Princess eyed him suspiciously. "What in the world is a *safe house*?"

"A place where the Resistance meets, Your Highness. There's one at the edge of the mire. But we must be careful. You're a dangerous outlaw, a traitor. Everyone knows you're the leader of the Resistance."

"I am not!"

"Of course you are!" Nuunk gurgled. "It's why you were exiled. The Exalted One said so herself."

"Oh!" she huffed. "My aunt is *such* a hag!"

They set off, sheltered by banks of trash. The Grand Wilderness went on and on. They stayed in the valleys, meandering so that Jack and Isadora soon lost whatever sense of direction they might have had. Occasionally one of the skreeps cast a wary glance at the sky. "We'll want to be out of here before the gruzzle starts," said Huursk.

Finally they stepped out of a narrow defile and found themselves beside a stagnant canal. A jumble of squat buildings hugged the far bank. It was evening now, and most of them spilled pale light from their oblong windows. Flares of burning gas illuminated some rooftops, while dirty smokestacks rose from others. One stack belched a steady stream of iridescent green smoke. Another produced a steady *plop-plop* of sticky bubbles, which sometimes drifted out of sight, sometimes exploded, splattering the surrounding buildings with yellow goo. Taller buildings rose in the distance, then taller ones still, climbing in ranks like the ridges of a mountain range. Far in the distance, faded by intervening mists, rose the tallest buildings of all, a panorama of ghostly giants, mushroom-capped skyscrapers on wide, undulating stems.

"Qurya!" exclaimed the Princess. "But how odd to see it like this—from the outside. I hardly recognize it, without the illusion screens. It's so dirty! But look, there's the palace." Far to the left, a collection of garishly lit towers rose to unrivaled heights above a rounded hill.

"Excuse me, Your Highness, but the safe house is below us." Huursk pointed to a small, dark building on the far side of the foul water. "We'd better go quickly. It isn't wise to be out in the open. The Queen's patrols are everywhere. Anyway, it looks like we're due for some gruzzle."

"That *shack*?" said the Princess.

Something wet smacked Isadora on the head. Another glob hit Joe. A blow to the snout made Furgok curse. Then they were all pelted.

"Gruzzle," said Huursk. "We'd better get inside."

A brown clot splattered across Jack's nose. *"Ow!"* he cried. "What the heck is *gruzzle*, anyway?"

"Space garbage. Not everything we carry into orbit stays there. Some of the bigger chunks can be dangerous—which is why we put up nets." They crossed a footbridge. Gruzzle caromed off their bodies and roiled the canal's sickly waters.

They ducked under the shack's webbed canopy. Nuunk pounded on the metal door.

"Yes, yes," said a voice. "I'm coming."

The door swung open, and a skreep peered out. The face was ugly, the body bent. Only her sack was missing. "*Hatchlings,*" said Krebs. "I'm glad you are here!"

. . .

44. SAFE HOUSE

WITH THE HELP of a robotic arm, Dr. Shumway lifted the small, transparent orb and placed it inside the larger, magnetized, vacuum-sealed orb. It hung there in perfect suspension. She rubbed her eyes. "What do you think, Mr. Creedle? Is it a reasonable facsimile?"

Bud peered at the orb. At first glance it seemed to contain only air, but as he leaned closer he perceived a subtle thickening, as if space itself had congealed into transparent foam. "You'd never guess it wasn't the real thing! How'd you do it?"

"I do have *some* education. The substance is related to quantum foam, but it produces a tiny fraction of the particle annihilation. It will have a much lower energy yield, not nearly enough to create dimensional holes—or destroy planets, for that matter."

"*Phony foam!*" Bud chuckled. "Now there's a racket I never thought I'd get into. And it just might work. These spiders don't know half as much as they think they do."

"I hope you're right. But will it work as we discussed? Will we be able to use it to compromise the foam within the existing destabilizer?"

"Lookee here." Bud plucked a tool from the counter and held it up for her to see. The device had metal handgrips, wires, a sharp nose, and a transparent tube attached to a curling stem. "If I can get some of that phony foam in here without breaking the vacuum seal, then I should be able to inject it into the real foam later on. No guarantees, of course, but the dilution might be enough to take the fizz out of the soda pop, so to speak."

"If you mean the machine will be disabled, then I am relieved. Our next challenge is to find the destabilizer. Do you know where it is?"

"They've got it under wraps in a warehouse." Bud's expression darkened. "I hope you've thought this through. I don't mean to scare you, but they'll kill us if they catch us down there."

"Really, Mr. Creedle! They will kill us anyway. I thought you knew that."

∙ ∙ ∙

XAAFUUN LOOKED at herself in the mirror and belched. She felt positively bloated. All she had done since arriving at the palace was eat. She tried arranging the feathers so they obscured her dead eye, but they continued to pop up. "Mellis! Come in here."

The servant arrived. "Yes, Madame Commander?"

"Fix this hat, will you? The feathers won't stay down."

Mellis prodded the hat into shape with expert fingers. "Have you heard about the mystery ship?"

Xaafuun had forgotten the way rumors buzzed through the palace. She smiled. Next to the feasts, the clothing, and the lovely, luxurious surroundings, rumors were one of the things she loved best about being back. "Mystery ship?"

"They say it flew into skreepish airspace last night, absolutely *blaring* the Queen's private frequency! Nobody dared monitor it, of course. Nobody tracked it, and then it was *gone*."

"But that's impossible! The Exalted One was *here* all night. You saw her; she never left the feast."

Mellis placed the hat on her head. "That's the mystery."

"Are you saying someone *stole* the frequency? It's a state secret! Nobody even knows what it is."

The feathers covered her eye, but the hat had lost some of its arresting beauty. Mellis lifted it off again. "An interesting crime, don't you think? Whoever did it will be executed. *If* they are found."

"Of course they will be found." Xaafuun examined her fangs. The left one was a bit stained. "Anyway, another execution will be fun, with all these *marvelous beasts* to choose from."

It pleased her to mention beasts. The games were going well—*very* well. So far she had four victories and *zero* defeats. Beasts Three, Eight, and Nine had all proven unbeatable in their opening matches. None was seriously wounded. Every beast she had was a potential winner, with the possible exception of that cursed Number Eleven. But Beast Seven was the real story, the brute! Not to jinx the matter, but the monster looked like a shoo-in for the championship. With all that armor—and that tail!—what could destroy it? It was too early to start thinking about the *Most Glorious Prize*, but she knew the other captains were jealous, and that was a prize in itself! Two nights ago at another feast she had overheard that whiner Druubel complaining: "If I'd been given planets like Treveline and Zarbinch, *my* beasts would be winning, too."

Xaafuun gurgled. *Boo hoo!* The funniest moment of the tournament so far had been when Druubel's Number Two and

Huumster's Six fought to a draw. A draw! Number Two had its head knocked off just as its venom caused Number Six to keel over dead. How they had all laughed at that one! Except for Druubel, of course, and Huumster.

But even the success of her beasts was not the best news. "Did you know the *ooman bings* have finally produced enough of their secret energy potion to power all the Special Items in the invasion fleet?"

Mellis tried to act surprised. The entire palace had heard the news. "There will be a parade then, Madame?"

"Of course there will be a parade." It annoyed her that Mellis knew so much. "The Exalted One scheduled it for the day after tomorrow."

Mellis applied makeup to Xaafuun's scar. "Another rumor, Madame?"

She couldn't help herself. "Please."

"They say your Beast Seven will almost certainly be chosen to deal with the *Uurthlings*."

"Really?" Xaafuun smiled so wide her makeup cracked. Such a coveted honor! She gurgled, imagining what Druubel would say about *that*.

•   •   •

INSIDE KREBS'S shack a gas lamp flickered on a wooden table. Its light cast a greenish glow on the faces of the figures seated at the table. One was a fox-sized creature with absurdly large ears, the second, an alien with four eyes and a fish's dissatisfied mouth. The third was a skreep, mostly hidden in shadow. Outside, the gruzzle pounded down.

"Good-good," the garbage collector said in her broken

English, stepping aside to let the travelers in. She waggled her fingers beside one eye. "Now tings get interesty."

"It's not just us, Krebs," said Joe. "Or the *crannek*, neither. Look, we brung your princess, too."

"Highness!" Krebs bowed.

The Princess fluffed her feathers and glared imperiously. "Greetings, peasants."

Everyone rose from the table.

"Dis get *berry* interesty!" Krebs whispered.

"I reckon so," said Joe. "Who're your friends?"

"Ho, dem some rebels, like me. Little one called Hroag. Fish Face, him named Gellup. Dem aliens. Skreep you know, mebbe. Him Mellis, capm's servant."

"Xaafuun's servant?" Joe asked. "What's *he* doing here?"

"Him rebel, like I say. Come from palace quicky-quick wit big news. About to say, when you get here." In Skreepish, Krebs asked, "So, what is it?"

Mellis cleared his throat. "The *Uurth* Queen is at the palace—her and that little inventor-king. The Exalted One has been keeping them alive while she builds a fleet equipped with Special Items. The *ooman bings* had to explain the Item and make a batch of the special sauce that fuels it. But that's done now, so the Exalted One doesn't need the *Uurthlings* anymore. So the victory parade will be the day after tomorrow."

"Victory parade?" asked Jack.

"Alien rulers always get a parade before we execute them. It shows how great the Exalted One is. This time it's an even bigger event, because it's the Fabulous Jubilee. Plus, it will help the Queen with her Replacement Planet Program."

"Ugh!" muttered the Princess. "I'd forgotten about the Jubilee."

"So what should we do?" asked Huursk.

"Gather as many rebels as you can," said Mellis, "and attack the parade. You know how important the *Uurth* Queen is."

"The prophecy," said Gloorg.

"Plan no good," interrupted Krebs. She rubbed the back of her grooved neck. "Too riskish. Whole lotta rebels get killed, mebbe. *Ooman bings*, too."

"She's right," said Hroag. "The Queen's servant needs to rescue them himself."

Mellis jumped up. "Not me! I just bring messages. That's my job."

"You're the only rebel inside the palace," said Hroag. "That is, if you *are* a rebel."

"Why would I be here if I wasn't? Please, they'll *kill* me!"

"Jack and I will go get them," said Isadora quietly. "Joe, too, if he wants."

"What?" said Jack.

"It's *my mother* they're talking about, Jack. And your uncle. Of *course* it's up to us to save them."

"Who said anything about your mother? They're talking about the Earth Queen."

"Come on, Jack! Wake up! Who do you think *that* is?"

"I don't know, the Queen of England?"

"What would the Queen of England be doing here, 153 light-years from Earth?"

"I don't know," he said. "What are any of us doing here?"

"Well, I'm in," said Joe. "When do we go?"

"No, no, no," said Krebs. *"Uurtlings* not go! Hroag right: Mellis needs do dis."

"But I can't!" wailed Mellis.

Suddenly the Princess stepped forward. "You are a *servant*, therefore you will *serve*. Bring me the *Uurth* Queen and her consort tomorrow, or I will boil your head." She sat down. "Now, somebody give me food. I'm starved."

. . .

PHOONY WANDERED the dark streets of the inner city. The path was cold, and he was worried. Had he been wrong? Had the *Uurthlings* gone somewhere else? No, it wasn't possible. They were here. He would find them.

At the sound of footsteps he ducked into an alley. Two skreeps passed by, deep in argument. If Xaafuun found out Phoony was here, she would have him dismembered, slowly. But if she knew the *hatchlings* were here, or the Webbs, who knew what she might do? The thought made him shiver uncontrollably.

He had done what he could to conceal the Webbs. Groot was guarding·them in a hidden dungeon. So far Phoony had been able to conceal himself, too. He was a shadow now, a creature of the city's forgotten places.

The shops in this part of town sold weapons, fake documents, or foreign junk. The buildings were either overcrowded or abandoned. On the street were as many aliens as skreeps, and most of the skreeps were soldiers, or security forces, or Finders like himself. Phoony knew some of them. He would have to be careful.

Still, he had to talk to *someone*. He slipped into a small shop where Carbo-Fizz and Grabbasnax were displayed behind a dirty window, and eased through a carefully disguised doorway into a dimly lit back room. He had been in enough shops like it to know there was *always* a dimly lit back room.

The proprietor was an alien, of course, a *buskaan*. She was dismantling a ray gun and barely looked up when he entered. "I already paid this month."

"I'm not collecting," said Phoony. "I'm looking for a weapon."

The *buskaan* fluttered her row of tiny black eyes. "Ray gun or blaster?"

"Neither. I want something *Uurthish.*"

"*Uurthish?* You won't find such weapons around here. That stuff is for collectors only. I sell *practical* arms."

Phoony gave a fake yawn so the alien could see his fangs. "Haven't you heard? There's more *Uurthling* stuff around these days."

"If by *stuff*, you mean actual *Uurthlings*, yeah, I've heard." The alien leaned over her gun. "It's all some folks talk about. The great *Uurth* Queen! Ruler of the *ooman bings*. Blah blah. But I've yet to see any merchandise."

Phoony pretended to be interested in the ray gun. "You got any others like it?"

While the *buskaan* unlocked a drawer in a hidden cabinet, he asked, as if making small talk, "Why would anyone in *alien-town* care if there's an *Uurth* queen up at the palace?"

"I *don't* care." Beneath the drawer's false bottom was an assortment of ray guns, from big shoulder cannons to the tiny pistols known as clapzappers. "But for some it's like a religion.

They've concocted a prophecy about how the *Uurth* Queen will save Skreepia from itself. Lot of fairy-tale nonsense. The Exalted One will have her killed, and that'll be the end of it."

Phoony lifted a medium-sized pistol from the drawer and checked its balance. "I've heard there are other *Uurthlings* in Qurya these days, too. I thought they might be selling weapons. I'd pay good money for an *ooman bing* blaster or even a blade."

"So you *are* a collector."

"I'm a Finder. I just have an interest in *Uurthish* stuff. Even the *ooman bings* themselves interest me. I'd pay for information, if it was helpful."

The *buskaan* locked her cabinet. "I'll let you know if I hear anything."

. . .

45. THE PROPHECY

XAAFUUN SAT IN the Queen's own box watching one bloody contest after another, while the crowd cheered and laughed itself hoarse. She had to share the box with the other captains, several of whom were favorites of the Queen, but no matter. She was still winning. She adjusted the feathers over her dead eye and leaned in to laugh at the Exalted One's joke: "If *bleeding* was what counted, Captain Belveen's Number Twelve would be a champion!"

"True, Your Greatness! How true!" The laugh was not heartfelt. All morning she had been troubled by a niggling sense that something, somewhere, was not right.

At least she knew what was bothering her about the tournament. It was Commander Falkoop's Beast Nine. Oh, what a monster! She had rarely seen its equal: a true giant, powerful, fast-handed, armored, and vicious. Stupid, of course, but what did that matter? The monster was destroying all of its competition. She wondered how her own Number Seven would stand up to such ferocity.

Perhaps she should bribe a handler to poison Number Nine before the next round. That would be expensive and risky, but it might be prudent all the same. She had already tripled the guard on Number Seven so nobody tried the same trick on her.

Belveen's Number Twelve expired in a final shower of blood. The crowd hooted. As attendants rushed to clean up the mess, the Queen addressed Xaafuun. "Have you heard, darling? I have chosen your Number Seven to deal with the *Uurthlings*."

Xaafuun pretended to be surprised. "But that's wonderful!"

"Isn't it? I only worry the beast will kill them too *quickly*. The peasants do like a show."

"If I may, Your Highness," Xaafuun remarked, amazed by her own audacity, "I'm surprised you are holding the parade so quickly. I had thought it would make a fitting *end* to the tournament."

"That is why you are only a captain, whereas I am the Queen. You think the *ooman bings* are important because they are your little pets. Trust me, they do not matter so much to common skreeps. The peasants have seen victory parades before. Do you really think *this* one has special significance?" She clapped as the next pair of monsters entered the ring. "The rabble care about three things, Ugly One: blood, mayhem, and *death*."

•   •   •

KREBS STUCK her head outside. Random pieces of gruzzle continued to fall, but the storm was mostly over. "Urry now. We move quicky-quick before dem patrols come out."

She led the group along the canal until they came to a giant metal pipe protruding from its bank. A trickle of slime drained from the pipe. "In 'ere. Is safest way to city."

"Another tunnel," groaned Isadora.

"Quicky-quick!" Krebs repeated. The tunnel turned and twisted. Isadora winced with every squishing step. If she ever got back to Boston, she would lock her bedroom door, climb under her blankets, and stay there forever.

Krebs stopped where the tunnel forked. "Dat way to palace," she said. "Dis way to safe house nummer two. We go dere, meet udder rebels, make big plan. Mellis go to palace, catch *Uurtlings* quicky-quick, bring 'em to us. Hokay?"

"I'll do what I can." Mellis disappeared into the palace sewer. The others followed Krebs.

•   •   •

THE NIGHT was half over by the time Krebs hoisted herself through a hole into a dark alley. Shoving aside old boxes, she began to pull the others up behind her.

Beyond the alley a wide street glowed with artificial daylight. Skreeps hurried by, singly or in groups, carrying unidentifiable loads upon their shoulders or munching gruesome snacks. Flying machines buzzed overhead on insect wings. The buildings rose to fantastic heights in every direction. Most were capped with the mushroom tops they had seen at a distance.

"No stand dere gawping, *oomans*!" Krebs scolded. "Patrols snatch you plenty quick! Go in, gawp later."

They entered the building through a ventilation duct and found themselves in an empty room. Broken machinery littered the floor.

"What is this place?" asked Joe.

"Nutink, anymore. Embersies before dat."

"*Embassies*? I didn't think skreeps went for that sort of thing."

Hroag squeaked. "You got that right! This was the *yarmuk* embassy. The Exalted One got tired of negotiating, so she sent her soldiers down here. They *ate* everyone."

"True," said Krebs.

"Ever since, the building has been empty. All the aliens left. But the Queen still claims it's full of embassies, because according to her, *everyone* in the galaxy loves skreeps. So she's hidden the place behind illusion walls. Happy aliens in foreign costumes, that kind of thing. Skreeps don't even notice anymore, which is good for us, because it keeps 'em away. Our safe house is in a secret room on the top floor. So far, nobody's bothered us."

By the time they climbed to the 179th floor, Jack and Isadora were exhausted. They plopped through a hidden trapdoor and lay on their backs, gasping.

"Feh," spat the Princess. "Look at this vile pit! To think that the Princess of all Skreepia would be hiding in a safe house with riffraff, traitors, and alien scum."

"Go ahead and call us names," said Skrank. "We're the only chance you got to defeat that aunt of yours."

"*Chance*? There's no chance in *this*, a handful of fools in a small room! The Exalted One will crush you like gnats."

"Not to be ungrateful," said Joe, "but I've been thinking the same thing. What chance do you reckon we have?"

The rebels were silent. It was the creature named Gellup, also called Fish Face, who finally answered. "We have no chance at all, unless we can liberate Kaarkuul. There are a million slaves in the mines. If they join us, we win. If not, we lose."

"Slaves!" scoffed the Princess. "Do you really think such vermin could defeat the Royal Army?"

"A million of anything can do some damage," said Joe. "But what makes you think they'll join us?"

"The Prophet is there. If he can persuade the slaves that the prophecy has come true, they will come."

"Which is why we'd better hope Mellis knows what he's doing," squeaked Hroag. "Without the *Uurth* Queen we've got nothing—no offense to you, Your Highness."

"We keep hearing about this prophecy," said Joe. "But nobody has explained it."

Hroag seemed surprised. "We thought you knew. After all, the Prophet is an *ooman bing*, like yourself."

"Human! That's a twist! Now I'm more confused than ever."

"The Prophet was the first *ooman bing* ever to come to Skreepia. He was captured during the Hiingis Expedition. The Queen believed that if the skreeps saw him, they'd stop fearing *Uurth* and would like her Replacement Planet Program better." Hroag's beady eyes glittered. "But this *Uurthling* was a trickster! They were about to feed him to a fighting beast, but he escaped! Nobody had ever done that. The Queen pretended it was nothing, but it was an embarrassment. Skreeps started talking. What if *all* the *oomans* were tricksters, or wizards, or *demons*? Not that I cared," Hroag continued. "I'm a *klepid*, not a skreep—"

"What's a *klepid*?" asked Isadora.

"A *klepid* is a creature that's *native* to this planet. It was called Klepernon before the skreepish invasion."

"So what happened to the Earthling?" asked Jack.

"After he escaped, search parties were sent out to find him. They never did. He was hiding where you met us this evening—Krebs's shack on the edge of the Grand Wilderness. Would you like to tell them about it?"

"No," said Krebs. "You doon' fine."

"The Prophet was lucky he chose her shack. Most skreeps would have turned him in or *eaten* him. But Krebs is kind. They lived together for many cycles."

"So that's how you learned to speak English!" said Isadora.

"Sure," said Krebs. "Mee'n *oom'n*, we talk aldy-time."

"Krebs introduced the *Uurthling* to the Resistance," said Hroag. "We were just forming at the time. We all thought if we could just treat *this* planet a little better, we wouldn't have to leave."

"*That* fairy tale . . ." The Princess rolled her many eyes.

"Things *are* bad here," Hroag continued, "but they aren't hopeless. The *ooman bing* told us that. He said on *Uurth* it is known that one day a great queen will come from the sky and set everybody free."

Jack nudged Isadora. "You ever hear that?"

"Never."

"He said on that day *Uurth* will become a beautiful paradise, not the smelly lump we hear about from those who have seen it."

"Earth isn't a *smelly lump*!" Jack objected.

"We knew he was a prophet," Hroag continued, "because his story was much like one the *klepids* used to tell, a story of salvation."

"The skreeps had a story like that, too," said Nuunk, "until the Exalted One made it illegal."

"She made it illegal because it's stupid," said the Princess.

Hroag seemed not to hear. "So we asked the *ooman bing* if his prophecy would happen here, too. He said it would. In fact, he said the very same *Uurth* Queen would come to Skreepia one day, and when she did, everything would fall into place, same as on *Uurth.*"

"But how do you know that's a real prophecy?" asked Jack. "I mean, couldn't it be a huge whopper this guy made up?"

"How can you ask that? The *Uurth* Queen is already here, and *you* are here. For that matter, so is the Princess, here to become the new Exalted One."

"Which is why we have to get to Kaarkuul," said Fish Face impatiently. "Once the *Uurth* Queen escapes, she'll need an army. Otherwise the revolution will fail. So who will go to the mines with me?"

"Hold on," said Joe. "Did you say this Prophet fella is a prisoner out there?"

"We think he allowed himself to be captured so he could free the slaves. Freeing the slaves was part of his prophecy— and now the time has finally come."

"Well, I believe I'd like to meet the man," said Joe. "When can we leave?"

"We *must* leave immediately!"

"We're ready," said Jack.

"No, we aren't!" cried Isadora. "I have to be here for Mother when she comes. She's probably worried sick about me. You should be here for your uncle Bud, too."

"*He's* not worried. Anyway, we can all go to the mines *after* we see them. Come on, Joe. We can't split up now!"

"Sorry, son," said the hobo. "I got a feeling about this.

Like maybe I can do some good out there. And time is everything. You and Isadora keep an eye on things. Make sure old Furgok don't shoot anyone. I won't be long." He put his hat on and followed Fish Face to the trapdoor. "Hopefully when we come back, it'll be with about a million new friends."

. . .

46. POISON

GETTING THE *Uurth* King to come wasn't hard. Mellis simply told him he was about to be killed. It was the queen who proved difficult.

"I appreciate your efforts," she said politely. "However, escape is not our priority. We must first disable the machine you call the *Special Item*."

"Too risky, Your Highness! There are guards and patrols in every hallway."

"Nevertheless." She turned to Bud. "You have the disabling mechanism, I trust."

"I got it. But maybe this critter is right. Maybe we *should* escape now, while the getting's good, and worry about the machine later."

"There will be no later, Mr. Creedle. Mellis, please lead us to the destabilizer."

Mellis thought about grabbing the *Uurthlings* and simply carrying them off. But they *were* royalty, after all. "Yes, Exalted One," he said and led them away.

• • •

THEY STOOD at the warehouse's sealed entrance. "There are guards inside," said Mellis. "We need a diversion."

Through a small window in the door, Bud and Dr. Shumway watched two skreeps playing a board game. The destabilizer stood a few feet to one side.

"I know that game," Bud whispered. "It's called Grabbit! The officers used to play on the bridge when Xaafuun was away."

"Everybody knows *that* game," said Mellis.

"Okay. What happens when somebody gets two flops?"

"An argument, usually."

"Bingo! Lots of fighting in Grabbit! What if the guards got so worked up they forgot to do their jobs? Wouldn't that be a diversion?"

"I suppose. But they'd still see us as soon as the door opened."

"What if they got *really* mad?"

"Would they *kill* each other? Is that what you mean?" *Uurthlings* had a reputation for deviousness; Mellis began to see why. "Such things happen when nobody breaks them up. Or when someone steps in at the wrong moment."

"What if *you* were that someone?"

A voice from inside the warehouse yelled, "Flop!"

"It wasn't!" shouted a second voice.

"Was! And you're halfway to your second flop already."

"I'll flop that fat abdomen of yours."

"Stay here," said Mellis.

The guards were so enraged with each other they barely noticed the servant enter.

"What are you doing?" Mellis asked cheerfully.

"*I* ain't doing nothing. As for him, *he's* cheating!"

"*I* am? You know you were still two paces away when you called that flop!"

"Does that look like two paces?" The first guard asked Mellis.

"Well, not from here, it doesn't. It looks like a flop. Actually you've got a second flop if you just drop down a bit."

"*Second* flop?" cried the other guard. "Say, who are you?"

"I work for Xaafuun. She sent me down—"

"You work for *him*, more likely. *Second flop!*"

"That's how it looks from here."

"The servant's right," pronounced the first guard. "I saw it myself, before he got here. I was about to move the piece."

"That's a filthy lie!"

"You're calling *me* a liar? After the stunt you pulled? I'm moving the piece right now!"

"Just try it!"

"You think you're going to stop me?"

"I'll stop *both* of you! You think I don't know he's in on it?"

"I never seen him before in my life. But look, here's your *second flop!*"

He moved his piece, and the other guard jumped on his back. They grappled madly with all their arms. The table tipped over; Grabbit! pieces scattered everywhere. Mellis stepped in quickly, as if to break up the fight, then stepped back. The first guard screamed.

"You bit me!"

"I didn't!"

"With *poison*!" He leaped at the other guard. They fell to the floor, rolling and biting. Mellis retreated a safe distance and watched. Soon the poison took effect. One of the guards got up, staggered, and keeled over. The other lay still.

Mellis opened the door. "Act quickly," he whispered. "You won't have much time."

The destabilizer stood slightly apart from the clutter that filled the giant room. Bud opened it and dropped to his knees. He pulled the container of false quantum foam from a coat pocket and held it to a gap between two spinning disks. "I wish I could see what I'm doing. This spider-light is terrible."

"Allow me to help," said Dr. Shumway. "My eyesight is excellent."

"The thing is, if I do this wrong . . ." He left the thought incomplete.

A few feet away, Mellis examined the guards. Not that he'd really wanted to kill them, but it *had* been neatly done. What would Xaafuun think if she could see him now?

Suddenly he noticed the communicator. It lay on the ground flashing—an open distress signal! He froze. That signal would be blaring in every guard station in the palace! He heard foot-steps, then a shout. The *Uurthlings* heard it, too, a second too late. As the first guard crashed through the door, Mellis dove behind a stack of crates.

. . .

47. KAARKUUL

"So THAT'S what happened," Mellis explained. "I barely got away." The city outside appeared lifeless in the twilight of a skreepish afternoon.

"What do we do now?" asked Isadora.

"We go after 'em," said Skrank.

Hroag's pointy nose twitched. "Yes, but how? They'll be guarded like the Royal Mint all the way to the arena."

"We'll pound 'em as soon as they step out of the palace!" growled Furgok.

"Do you know how hard it is to *find* the palace? The Queen has so many illusion screens, the only way to get there is with special goggles. And only the Royal Guard has those."

"The Exalted One is careful," Gloorg agreed. "It's how she's managed to stay in power so long."

"It's also why you idiots are bound to fail." The Princess was watching a program on the three-dimensional illusion wall. The show called *Be My Slave!* told the story of a beautiful young skreep who tricks a series of admiring males into slavery, then sells them to buy an apartment. "If you want to be useful, why don't you get me something to eat?"

Skrank ignored the remark. "Mellis, why can't *you* lead us to the palace? After all, you live there."

"I could take you *inside*, through the sewers, but you'd be captured by the first patrol. Even I couldn't find the *outside* of the palace from here."

"Wait," said Isadora. "Are illusion screens the only problem?"

"They're a *big* problem. You can get so lost down there, you never get out."

"But illusions don't fool *me*," she said excitedly. "Or Jack, either. We see right through them."

"She's telling the truth," said Skrank. "I've seen it. I bet these *oom'ns* could walk right up to the Queen's front door."

"No," said Krebs. "Hatchlings stay here. Too risky ubberwise."

"It's too risky *not* to," Isadora insisted. "You need us!"

"They're coming," said Skrank. "And that's that."

• • •

EARLY THE next morning they wound their way through the sewers. Mellis was back at the palace, and only Gloorg and the Princess remained in the safe house. The Princess refused to participate in "moronic rabble-rousing" and demanded that Gloorg stay as her servant. Milo stayed behind because nobody knew what else to do with him.

The group surfaced through an iron grate in a filthy alley.

"All right," said Skrank, once they were assembled. "Where are we?"

Grimy buildings squeezed together all around them. Nearby, a single pipe dripped brown goop into an oily puddle.

"Dis place called Old Town," said Krebs. "Palace near here, summare." She led them away. "Riskish to run in open like dis, but ebryting riskish now."

Rounding a corner, Isadora saw the tall spires of the palace rising through the gloom. "Look, Jack! We're almost there." The towers appeared through a billboard advertising Tweener's Trubilo Nuts.

"Dat sign not dere, hum?"

"An illusion," said Isadora.

"Mebbe you go-head now, hokay?"

"Okay," said Jack.

They continued to find openings in what seemed to be solid walls until finally the palace stood before them, somber behind immense metal gates.

"Listen," said Skrank. "Those gates should be opening any time now. We need to be hidden when they do. Wait until the *Uurth* Queen and King are all the way out before we attack. When I give the order, don't hold back. I'll grab the *oom'n beans* myself."

They retreated a safe distance from the street. "Furgok, you take these *Uurthlings* back to that last alley. Stay there and make sure nothing happens to them."

"You want me to *babysit*?"

"I want you to follow orders!"

"Ha! Furgok's worth ten of these spiders! Let *them* babysit!"

"Why can't we stay?" said Isadora. "It's *my* mother we're rescuing."

"And my uncle," said Jack, without much conviction.

"Quiet! This is *war* we're talking about. And you, Furgok— you'll have more fighting than you can stomach before this is over. Now do as you're told!"

Furgok led them back to the alley, cursing bitterly. Dank mist swirled around them.

They waited.

Suddenly a metallic clang broke the silence.

"The gates!" whispered Isadora. Grunts, shouts, and the rumble of machinery followed. Thousands of bony feet marched as the Queen's guard entered the boulevard. Furgok and the children slipped to the edge of the alley. They held their breath.

"Chaaaarge!" Skrank's voice rang like struck iron.

Kabooom! A thunderclap split the air, then a dozen more, until the noise became deafening. Between blasts came screams and curses. Something crashed. Someone moaned. Flames crackled. The flash of ray guns lit up columns of oily smoke.

"Back to the palace!" cried a panicked skreepish voice. Feet slapped the pavement, machinery squealed, heavy guns barked.

"After them!" shouted Skrank.

"Stay here!" Furgok ordered. He lifted his blaster and hurried to the fighting.

"How do you like that?" said Jack. "Now it's just you, me, and the garbage."

"I'm sure he knows what he's doing," said Isadora, not sounding sure at all.

The trash stirred behind them. As Jack turned, a long, bristled arm snaked around the outer wall. Before he could shout, hard fingers clamped over his mouth. A second hand grabbed Isadora. She screamed, but the sound was lost in the roar of battle.

Jack and Isadora wriggled in midair like hooked fish until the cords tightened. The skreep turned them so they could see his grinning face.

"Remember me? It's your old friend Phoony."

• • •

IT WASN'T a bad ride, exactly, hidden under bundles of prison uniforms. His own uniform was itchy, but Joe had been through worse. Still, something about the way the big vehicle walked, rolling with each step, made his stomach uneasy.

He burrowed a gap between two bundles and watched Skreepia go by. It wasn't much of a view. The landscape looked as if a war had passed through at least seven or eight times.

Collapsed buildings and ruined machinery littered the roadside. A few weeds grew through cracks in the pavement. Brambles struggled across blasted fields.

"Not long before we reach Kaarkuul," said Fish Face.

"You think we'll get in without being spotted?"

"Getting *in* is not the problem. Our challenge will be getting *out*."

The walker headed downhill. Rocky bluffs closed in around it. Squirming sideways, Joe saw the tunnel entrance, gaping like an open throat. Guard towers rose on either side, but the walker passed them without even slowing. The tunnel spiraled downward, lit by gas lamps that flickered against stone walls. Far underground, the vehicle finally stopped. Steam hissed from its sides as the cargo pod popped open. Bundled uniforms began to thud to the ground.

"Laundry delivery!" shouted a harsh voice.

A skreepish face loomed above them. "You're here, you crazy buggers!" Fish Face held up a handful of money chips, which the driver quickly snatched. "First time anyone ever paid to get *into* Kaarkuul!"

"I'll give you another fifty if you take us to the Prophet."

The driver pointed at Joe. "You mean the *other* crazy bugger, like this one?" He considered the idea. "I'll take you—for a hundred. But you gotta be chained, like the other slaves. And keep your heads down!"

He led them through a narrow tunnel, uphill, then quickly down. They passed several guards and many prisoners, but nobody took notice of them. Nobody seemed to notice much of *anything*, as they shuffled along, backs bent, eyes dull.

The guards were all skreeps, but the slaves came in many forms, most of which Joe did not recognize. He kept his own eyes lowered and tried not to stare, even when a brute with two heads slumped by, followed by a creature with skin as transparent as a jellyfish.

Tunnels opened on all sides. They heard the metal-on-rock sound of digging tools, the crack of whips, and more than once, a scream. Twice they had to make way for carts hauling stacked corpses.

A big room opened off the main tunnel. The driver poked his head inside.

"You're in luck. Your boy is off duty." He gurgled. "A few more cycles and he'll be off duty *permanently*!"

The low-ceilinged room was a mess hall, full of miners noisily slurping thin gruel from small bowls. The Prophet sat at a small table all to himself. Aside from Joe, he was the only human in the room. His uniform was tattered, his arms mere bones. His spiky hair was as white as snow.

Joe stepped forward, rattling his chains. The other prisoners stared. Silence fell over the room as he stopped at the small table.

"I reckon you must be the Prophet."

When the man looked up his eyes focused, then unfocused again. "I never really liked that title, to tell you the truth." He held out his hand. "Murchison's the name. Stanley Murchison."

. . .

SIRENS WAILED. Ray gun flashes lit the smoky air. Dr. Shumway stepped away from the safe house window. "Why in heaven would you take *children* into a battle?"

"Dey was guides," said Krebs.

"Without them," added Hroag, "we couldn't have found the palace. We might not have rescued you."

"I don't care about *me*! I care about my *daughter*!" She took a deep breath. "And I care about the destabilizer, which, I regret to say, we were unable to destroy."

In the silence that followed, the only sound that could be heard was Furgok's head, rhythmically pounding the wall.

"Your plan was idiotic," said the Princess, "and you're surprised it didn't work?"

Outside, Qurya was in a state of near panic. During the ambush the Queen had retreated into her palace. Now a squadron of very small saucers buzzed around its towers like flies. Bigger saucers patrolled overhead, their hovering bodies visible only as shadows, while battalions of armed police roamed the streets. All across the city, images of Skrank filled holographic screens, some as big as twenty stories tall. The news reported that a minor alien uprising had already been suppressed. There was no mention of the parade, or of the *Uurth* Queen, and no explanation for why that day's games had been postponed.

"You have angered the Exalted One," continued the Princess. "And for what? *Ooman bings*? Now the Queen's forces will hunt you down, every last one of you. And here's the problem: They will hunt *me* down, too! The whole planet will see me consorting with slaves and scum. I will be killed *and* publicly humiliated!"

"Tell me again why you're so popular," Skrank muttered under her breath.

"The Princess is known for her kindness," said Huursk. Two of his arms had been blown off in the fighting, and a nasty gash ripped across his thorax.

Furgok pulled his ray gun from its holster. "Why don't you just say it? It's Furgok's fault the *Uurth* children were captured." When nobody argued, he went on. "That's right, it *is* my fault. So I will get them back." The trapdoor was eight feet above his head. "Somebody give me a boost through that hole!"

"Don't be stupid," snapped Skrank. "You'll stay put, like the rest of us. When Mellis gets here, we'll find out where the children are. Then we'll make a plan."

"I refuse to accept that," said Dr. Shumway. "We must rescue them immediately."

"Listen, *Uurth* Queen," said Skrank. "I know things don't look good, but this war is far from over. Believe me, the skreepish Queen is worried. We caught her by surprise this morning, and we'll surprise her again. And those youngsters—well, there's something very *unusual* about those youngsters. They're a lot tougher than they look."

• • •

48. RULERS OF THE GALAXY

INSIDE THEIR dungeon, Jack and Isadora didn't feel tough. They felt tired, weak, and very frightened. Their cell was a clear pod set inside a larger stone chamber far beneath the palace. Hissing lamps gave the dungeon its only light.

In the adjoining cell, the Webbs simmered. Grady made faces at Jack. "I'll get you, Creedle," he promised, his voice muffled. "I'll get you good as soon as they let me out."

"Oh, like they're gonna do that."

Grady was far down on Jack's list of concerns. In a world full of nine-foot spiders, a fat-headed bully didn't count for much.

"How about it, Groot?" demanded Sergeant Webb. "We're pals, remember? When are you going to turn us loose? *Those* are your prisoners, not us. In case you forgot, we helped you catch 'em! Why, anyone passing through here would think me and Grady were crooks like them!"

"Nobody's going to pass through here."

"That's not the point! The point is, you're treating us like criminals."

"You tell him, Pop," said Grady.

"Shuddup! All of you." Groot pounded the cell wall. "You make my head hurt." In truth, he felt like a prisoner, too. While Phoony was upstairs, sucking up the glory, where was he? In a dungeon, *as usual*. Watching over a passel of filthy *ooman bings*, *as usual*.

He was still seething when the ceiling opened, and Phoony plopped down. The Finder was dressed in a new bodysuit.

His antennae were powdered, and his bristles gleamed with fresh oil. He carried what looked like a sack of feathers under one arm.

"Congratulations, Groot! You managed not to lose them this time!"

"Very funny."

"Don't worry. I put in a good word for you—with the *Exalted One*! Or at least I recommended you not be dismembered—which is more than you deserve." A happy gurgle escaped his throat. Why not? Things were finally going his way.

He turned his attention to Jack and Isadora. "You know, you're *almost* worth the trouble you caused me! The Exalted One is happy—*very* happy—to have you! She lost her *Uurth* Queen this morning, which means she lost her victory parade. Very embarrassing! It might have ruined the Fabulous Jubilee! But what happened instead? Instead, *Phoony* showed up with a *new Uurth* Queen! A new queen and a new little male consort! Which means the parade will go on as planned! Which means the Exalted One is *very* pleased—which means Phoony is now *very* popular!"

"But they're only hatchlings!" Groot objected. "They aren't the *real* queen and king."

"Seriously, Groot. You give stupid a bad name." Phoony pulled the bundles from under his arm and unfurled them, revealing two feathered cloaks and matching crowns. "Do you really think anyone will notice, once we put these costumes on them? How many skreeps would know the difference between a full-grown *ooman bing* and a hatchling, anyway?"

"Well, I don't like it. It ain't right pretending you're a queen when you're not one. You'll see. Something bad will come of it."

"Of course something bad will come of it, you ninny! That's the whole idea. Something *very* bad will come of it for these *Uurthlings*! But it won't be bad for the Exalted One, and it won't be bad for *Phoony*, and if you keep your mouth shut, it won't be bad for you, either." He stepped into the cell. "Come here, little ones! Uncle Phoony has some fancy clothes for you."

• • •

THE SKY churned with streaks of charcoal and mustard. Gruzzle spattered the parade route. A sudden hail of bigger chunks came down, and a few ripped through the canopy of webs and cratered the street below. A smaller missile decapitated a pedestrian. His headless body staggered in woozy circles while the crowd roared with laughter. When he finally toppled, attendants hauled him away.

The Queen's guard marched into view, resplendent in golden bodysuits. While the real spectators cheered halfheartedly, the illusion crowd, stacked into tall grandstands on either side of the boulevard, erupted in a deafening roar. Hundreds of robotic cameras picked up the scene and broadcast it around the planet, where it aired simultaneously on huge projection screens in every city and inside every office, factory, shop, and private domicile.

The Exalted One's victory parades were must-see events, beloved for their pageantry and for the comforting message they sent about the empire's enduring power. But today, many watched for a different reason. They had heard a quiet rumor, never even whispered among the ruling classes, that the *Uurth* Queen carried with her a terrible fate.

For several long cycles the rumor had been spreading. It had traveled without urgency. Skreeps passed it along with a shrug and a nervous giggle—a treasonous thought, to be sure, but mostly just an odd one. Who even knew if there *was* an *Uurth* Queen?

Until now. Now they knew, and they watched with curiosity, to see if any part of the rumor—the *prophecy*—was true.

Had the Exalted One known about the rumor, she might have chosen a different course of action. She might have cut the *Uurthlings'* throats herself, in private, and simply displayed their corpses.

But the Exalted One did *not* know, and the look on her face as she rode into view was both complacent and unsuspecting.

Isadora and Jack wore very different expressions. Sitting inside a transparent bubble mounted on a multilegged walking machine, they were shocked to find themselves the focus of such widespread interest. Beyond that, they were terrified. Isadora, suddenly the most watched creature on the entire planet, sat next to Jack, ticklish under her feathers, and gazed at the parade route with wide eyes. She could see the illusions that had been set up, though to her they seemed ghostly and unreal. The great crowds had a shimmery, ephemeral quality; their hearty cheers seemed muted.

The *real* crowd was uneasy. The street battle of the day before had kept many at home. Some glared at Isadora, while others were hopeful, almost pleading. "Imposters!" shouted one, before his neighbors restrained him.

Banners made from tightly woven webs hung listless in the thick air, though on the illusion screens they danced and shimmered merrily. WE LOVE THE QUEEN! they proclaimed, and SKREEPIA WINS AGAIN! Fat, spidery cherubs perched on the branches of silvery illusion trees, playing sonorous music on instruments designed for multiple arms.

The parade route wound its way between towering skyscrapers before continuing into a part of the city where the buildings were not so grand. To compensate, the illusions became twice as elaborate. More trees appeared, more banners, more cherubs. Multicolored geysers shot high into the air. The route straightened. Like a great serpent, the parade slithered into full view. Long columns of marching soldiers led even longer columns of marching, bubble-topped machines. Two big saucers hovered overhead.

The parade headed toward a single building standing alone on a barren hilltop. The Grand Arena was a round, nearly featureless structure with tall, internally lit green walls. Its near side was flattened and served, as much of Qurya did, as a screen.

Right now the screen was broadcasting the parade. Looking up, Isadora was horrified to see herself magnified to stupendous proportions. Her glasses glinted, and yellow feathers shone bright against her dark skin. Despite the size of the image, she looked small and frightened, like a baby bird plucked from its nest.

A grandstand had been set before the arena. Both the dais and the podium were festooned with feathers. A glowing sign proclaimed HER ROYAL HIGHNESS, THE QUEEN.

The parade broke against the side of the arena like a spent wave. Soldiers, police, and guards fanned out in rigid formation while the vehicles halted in a straight line. Bubble tops sprang open, and skreepish dignitaries climbed out. They filed into the grandstand. Xaafuun was identifiable by her scar, though she had attempted to disguise it with makeup and feathers.

The children's bubble was among the last to open. Skreepish guards in shiny black uniforms lowered Isadora and Jack to the ground, then prodded them toward the dais. The crowd erupted in a chorus of jeers, though many remained silent, and a few even applauded quietly. The illusion crowd's reaction was more uniform—a steady chorus of howls.

Isadora and Jack huddled on the dais as the Queen came forward with her retinue of slaves. She was the largest skreep they had ever seen, and the most frightening. A crown of peacock feathers rose two feet above her enormous, bejeweled head. Her antennae sparkled with glittering stones, and her long, painted fangs glowed silver in the light of a hundred cameras. Red and white feathers erupted from her shoulders and cascaded down her back.

Beside her, Isadora and Jack looked puny and drab, a point that was not lost on the crowd.

When the Queen bowed with mock respect in Jack's direction, then genuflected elaborately before Isadora, they burst out laughing.

"Dearest skreeps!" she shouted. "The glorious victory we celebrate today is not mine alone!" She waited patiently as the cheering swelled, then slowly subsided. "No. It is yours as well! As you know, the skreeps went to *Uurth* as a gesture of goodwill—of kindness!" She paused. "But were the *Uurth* creatures kind to us?"

"NO!" thundered the crowd.

"No," agreed the Queen. "They were not. In fact, even as we tried to *leave*, they attempted to destroy us! This evil one"—she pointed at Isadora—"this *Uurth* Queen—led a great army against us! They outnumbered us by *three thousand to one*! But were we frightened?"

"No," said the crowd, somewhat uncertainly.

"NO! We were not! We fought, as only skreeps can, and we prevailed. And in the process we found this." She gestured toward a short round column that had, until that moment, been hidden by an illusion tree. As the tree faded, bright lights fell on the column and revealed, sitting on its top, Uncle Bud's destabilizer. Surrounded by all that glitter, the white refrigerator cabinet seemed a dull thing, though its chrome handle managed to shine in a feeble way. The crowd chattered.

"It doesn't look like much, does it?" said the Queen.

"Yet with this fiendish device the *ooman bings* planned to conquer the galaxy! Yes, and turn the skreeps into their slaves!"

The crowd gasped. Many jeered.

"What is it, you ask? I will tell you. It is a machine for tunneling through space, a machine to make space travel *as easy as a trip to the kitchen!*"

The crowd continued to chatter.

"I know, this is not what you came for. You came for *justice*, and you shall have it. But before we enter the arena, I ask you to remember this machine, for this machine, this *Special Item*, is your future! With this machine, we will go back to *Uurth*—all of us! With this machine, we will finally realize the great destiny of our race. With this machine, the skreeps shall rule the galaxy!"

The crowd exploded in a prolonged roar of approval. The Queen waited patiently. When the cheering finally subsided, she spoke again. This time her manner was pious. "We shall be *benevolent* rulers, of course. Even the *Uurthlings* will receive our blessing."

Some in the crowd shouted, "No!"

The Queen paused. "Yes, the *ooman bings* are lowly creatures; they are benighted. They are too childish to be more than our slaves. But they will not be made to pay for the folly of their rulers. No, only the rulers themselves shall pay. *These* rulers: the Queen of *Uurth* and her consort, the King. Justice demands that they be punished. And *tradition* demands that they meet their fate here, in the Grand Arena! Follow me, skreeps! Let us watch them meet their doom!"

The crowd screamed and stomped and shouted. Police restrained many from rushing in to seize the children themselves. Others threw gruzzle.

The Queen left the stage. A moment later, two red-cloaked guards plucked Jack and Isadora from the dais and hauled them away.

• • •

ISADORA AND JACK sat together in a metal cage. All around them in the dark tunnel were bigger cages. Though they could barely see, they could hear and smell well enough to know the cages held very large creatures, creatures with hot breath, strange odors, and hostile, glowing eyes. Overhead they heard the scrabble of thousands of bony feet as the stands filled.

"I guess this is it," whispered Jack. "The end of the line."

"It is not!"

"Oh, come on, what are we going to do?"

"I don't know. But I didn't come this far to give up."

"Suit yourself." An idea occurred to him. "Do you think we're still on Hellebeezia?"

Isadora thought for a moment. "We're always on Hellebeezia."

"Well, that's something. All the same, I'd rather not be dead."

A guard emerged from the shadows and unlocked their cage. As they climbed out, he prodded them into a slow walk. Ahead, an oval of light marked the tunnel's end.

"That's the ring," he grumbled. "Try and make it look good."

When they reached the wide opening the children's feet stopped all by themselves. The guard leaned over them, his skreepish breath hot on their necks. "I heard about that prophecy."

They looked at him blankly.

"Well, should I believe it?"

"Why not?" said Jack.

. . .

49. THE GRAND ARENA

THEY STEPPED into the arena. Its floor was soft sand. Its walls were smooth and unscalable, rising at least fifty feet into the air. In many places they were spattered with stains that looked uncomfortably like dried blood. The grandstands were so tall Isadora and Jack had to crane their necks to see the highest tier.

A special canopy had been erected to house the Queen. She perched on a tall throne surrounded by dignitaries. Robotic cameras danced around them like moths.

When the Exalted One's image appeared on the giant screen, Isadora realized with a jolt that the ruler was staring directly at her. The Queen's expression was bright with malice.

An announcer's voice rang out above the chatter of the crowd. "Skreeps!" it shouted. "You see the *Uurth* criminals before you! Soon, their opponent will emerge from the same tunnel."

Gales of laughter followed Jack and Isadora as they sprinted across the ring. The announcer resumed her speech. "The battle you are about to witness will be a fair fight." More laughter rained down.

"I could eat 'em myself in two bites!" someone heckled.

"A fair fight," the announcer insisted. "Remember, these *ooman bings* are mighty sorcerers!"

"Mighty small!" shouted a heckler.

"And so, to fight them, the Queen has chosen the beast she considers the most promising of the entire tournament! This creature comes from the savage planet Kripseed, where it was captured by Her Majesty's ship, *Feast of Happiness*. Skreeps, I present to you Commander Xaafuun's *Beast Number Seven!*"

Jack and Isadora fixed their eyes on the tunnel. Slowly the beast emerged. It was so huge its sides scraped the tunnel walls as it squeezed through, dragging its belly on the ground. Its round head was like a boulder, with small eyes and gaping nostrils. Long spikes protruded from the clubbed end of its tail.

The crowd cheered as spectators on Earth might have cheered a famous prizefighter. Clearly it was familiar to them, a favorite. But Beast Seven was familiar to Jack and Isadora as well. When they first saw it on the ship, it had been sleeping. Now, awake, it was even more frightening. What remained of their courage began to drain away, like water into the sand.

As the crowd went wild, the beast preened, raising a gigantic hand in acknowledgment. It held the pose, then raised its other hand. Making a fist, it gave its rocky chest a hard thump. The children edged back and pinned themselves to the wall.

The monster noticed them for the first time, and some of the cheers turned to laughter. It glanced up at the crowd, then back at the children, as if trying to understand an obscure joke.

"What's the matter?" someone shouted. "Afraid they won't *taste* good?"

The beast snarled, and the crowd went silent. The Exalted One's face appeared on the screen. When the beast saw her, she gave a curt nod. Sitting beside her, Commander Xaafuun looked embarrassed. Her great beast, so fearsome in battle, was revealing a buffoonish side she had not seen before.

Number Seven stepped forward halfheartedly. The children scrambled away. The crowd booed.

Gruzzle began to fall. A few chunks found their way through holes in the webbing and into the stands, causing more laughter. The merriment confused the beast. It made a few sullen attempts to squash the children with its feet, then howled when a big chunk of gruzzle struck it on the head. The crowd laughed again. The monster turned on Jack and Isadora angrily. The children scrambled away. More gruzzle came down. A few small pieces rained onto the sand. Jack hurled one at the monster, but it sailed away harmlessly.

"Nice throw, *sorcerer*!" someone shouted.

"It *slipped*," said Jack.

"That's a good idea, though." Isadora carefully selected a chunk that fit in the palm of her hand. When Beast Seven stepped forward again, she zinged it into its mouth. The monster bellowed. The crowd gasped. Isadora found another projectile and threw again. The object struck the monster's left eye with a loud pop.

Screeching, Beast Seven stumbled backward. The crowd laughed, cheered, and stomped its feet, but gradually fell silent as the creature staggered away, still whimpering.

Things were not going quite right. The killing had begun to drag on. "Boring!" someone shouted. Others booed.

On the screen, the Exalted One whispered to Xaafuun, who looked as if she had been struck by an object, too. The announcer's voice boomed across the arena again. "By order of the Queen, a second beast will enter the ring." The speakers buzzed. "This will be, from the planet Oncredar, Commander Belveen's *Beast Number Three*!"

The crowd came back to life, then quieted as all attention fixed on the tunnel. The beast emerged. It was nearly as big as Seven, but was otherwise entirely different. Its snout was pointed like a wedge of cheese, and its mouth sprouted a thicket of fangs. Red-rimmed eyes nearly circled its domed forehead. It had eight powerful legs and a long, pointed tail. It moved like a crocodile, with its stomach low to the ground.

With two beasts, the arena felt very small. "You think we should throw something?" asked Jack.

"Let's try not to be noticed," whispered Isadora.

Across the ring, Beast Seven dropped its hand from its injured eye and turned to face the newcomer.

If the Queen had expected the monsters to join forces in destroying the *Uurthlings*, she was wrong. Instead, Beasts Seven and Three began to circle each other.

The battle was short and furious. When Beast Three charged, Beast Seven used its tail as a whip. The spikes dug deep, and before Three could recover, Seven flipped it on its back. Sharp claws dug into the exposed belly. Beast Three screamed, struggled, and died. The crowd went wild. On the screen, Commander Xaafuun smiled.

But some in the crowd, and many around the planet, noted that the *Uurthlings* were still unscathed. Some wondered about sorcery. Some recalled the prophecy. Many simply worried and watched.

Newly victorious, Beast Seven marched to the center of the ring. Goo dripped from its injured eye, but it seemed not to care. When it beat its chest, the crowd roared. Some screamed, "*Ooman bings!*" Then more joined in. The words became a chant. *"OO-MAN BINGS! OO-MAN BINGS!"* The beast lumbered back toward Jack and Isadora. The crowd took a collective breath. The monster lashed out with its tail, digging furrows into the sand. The children ran. The beast closed in.

Suddenly the shouting stopped, replaced by an excited murmur. Beast Seven turned around. Jack and Isadora scrambled out of range.

Something stirred inside the tunnel. For an instant the screen flashed on the Exalted One. Her confidence had changed to confusion. The image disappeared, but the crowd had seen it. They shifted uneasily. A black shape drifted silently into the ring, traveling across the ground like smoke.

Isadora saw the familiar golden eyes, and her breath left her in one long *whoosh*. Beast Eleven watched her. Isadora smiled, raised a hand, and waved.

Beast Seven roared. It advanced on the intruder, angrily beating its chest. Beast Eleven waited, absolutely still. It was much smaller than its opponent, but its poise was unnerving. When Number Seven snapped its whiplike tail, Eleven simply drifted out of range. Seven struck again, this time with its claws. But when it reached its target, Eleven was no longer there. The enemies circled. Again and again Seven lunged. Again and again Eleven slipped away. The crowd went silent. Seven moved forward, panting. Eleven watched with slitted eyes.

The big monster attacked with teeth, tail, and claws. It whirled like a hurricane. The smaller beast crouched down. Sand shot into the air. For a moment, Beast Eleven vanished altogether. Jack froze. Isadora stifled a scream. Seven howled in triumph as it plunged in for the kill.

But it plunged into a buzz saw. Furious blows jolted Seven backward. The black shape swarmed. It moved like thought, like light. Seven staggered. Its head jerked back. White teeth flashed, jagged as lightning inside a cloud.

In an instant it was over. The beasts parted. Eleven drifted away.

Silence returned to the arena. The crowd seemed puzzled. Nobody understood what had happened. Seven appeared puzzled, too. The monster moved unsteadily toward its enemy. It stepped once, twice, then stopped. Blood spurted from its neck. The wound widened, then opened like a book. Its boulderous head toppled sideways. Its body tilted. Its legs buckled. It hit the ground like a falling tree.

The crowd watched in stunned silence. For a few seconds, as the image of the collapsing monster flashed across a billion video screens, the entire planet was still. Only Isadora did not watch Seven die. Her attention remained fixed on Beast Eleven. For just an instant the golden eyes returned her gaze. For once, she held them with her own.

Afterward she could never say exactly what passed between them. A shared knowledge, maybe: an understanding. Then the beast turned. She felt its body tense, its powerful muscles contract. She knew with utter certainty what it was about to do.

The beast jumped.

The walls of the Grand Arena had been designed for monsters of immense size and savage temperament; more than a few had tried to scale them. None had ever succeeded. None had even come close.

But none had ever leaped like Beast Eleven. And none had ever been so *fast*. While the crowd continued to gape at the twitching corpse of Number Seven, Eleven plunged into the Royal Box. Too late, the Exalted One screamed.

The crowd, turning in unison, watched it happen. It was nearly impossible *not* to watch. The Queen's terrified, jewel-encrusted face jolted back as the dark shape overwhelmed her.

Her royal arms flew from their sockets, and royal blood, black as motor oil, splashed across her throne.

. . .

50. THE BATTLE OF QURYA

THE ENTIRE planet was stunned. Then panic set in. Screams filled the air. The crowd began to scramble, slowly at first, then in a frenzied surge. Skreeps trampled one another, pushing for the exits. In the Royal Box, Beast Eleven raged, striking down politicians, dignitaries, generals, and ship commanders. Those with their wits about them fled. In no time the stadium was empty.

Isadora and Jack found themselves forgotten, standing alone in the middle of the arena between the bodies of two dead monsters. The tunnel guard ran to them, then threw himself on to the ground. When he lifted his head, sand clung to his lips. "It's true! The prophecy is true!"

"I suppose . . . " said Isadora. She felt numb.

"Never mind! You must leave! It isn't safe here. Please, Exalted One!" The guard got up and scurried away.

"I guess he's right," said Jack. He felt numb, too.

They staggered through the tunnel and out of the arena. The scene was surreal. Though the illusion of cheering crowds remained, a violent reality had begun to emerge. Ray guns flashed, blasters blasted, and broken chunks burst from the sides of buildings. Jack and Isadora tried to make sense of the situation but could not. Were the rebels attacking? There were plenty of soldiers, too, and they were fighting back.

A familiar figure climbed onto the dais where the Queen had given her speech. It was Xaafuun. Her feathers were gone now, but her captain's uniform stood out. As she shouted orders above the uproar of exploding rockets, the Queen's guard began to rally around her. Soon army units arrived as well. Xaafuun directed the soldiers, and they took up positions with their backs to the arena. Other units advanced, crouching, behind a barrage of ray gun fire. The rebels retreated, first in an orderly way, then in a rout.

"What do we do now?" asked Jack.

Isadora threw away her crown of feathers and let her cloak fall. "We do what everyone else is doing. We run!"

Xaafuun poured more troops into the battle. The rebels scattered. Jack and Isadora ran from cover to cover, building to building, and eventually worked their way downtown.

Everywhere was pandemonium. Soldiers marched into rebel ambushes; rebels were pinned down by soldiers. "The empire!" shouted some. "Freedom!" shouted others. Illusion crowds cheered them all. Bombs blasted, and missiles exploded overhead. In the midst of it, more gruzzle began to fall. The children ducked into a dark alley.

"There you are," said Furgok, as if they were late for an appointment. His clothing was torn, and his tuft of blue hair had been reduced to a charred swirl. White smoke danced around the mouth of the blaster he held in one big hand. "Furgok's been trying to get to you since you left the arena. I don't know how you made it. Cameras have been following you practically the whole way. Didn't you see yourselves on the video screens?"

"Um . . . "

"Hold on," he said and stepped into the street. An explosion was followed by smaller blasts. Furgok returned. "That takes care of the cameras. Now follow me. You're wanted at the safe house."

An hour later they were there. It seemed especially dull after the day's excitement. Milo clucked at them while Gloorg peered down at the smoke-filled streets. The Princess watched the battle on the video screen.

"Where's everyone else?" asked Jack.

"At the battle," Gloorg replied. "Or looking for you."

"Rabble!" muttered the Princess. "Fools! What were you thinking? You cannot defeat the Royal Army. See how strong it is? The peasants are driven backward, always backward. Soon there will be no place to run. Then you will all be killed."

Furgok watched the screen. "I don't trust those cameras. They're on the army's side."

"Believe what you want," said the Princess. "You will still die."

"We can go to the roof," Gloorg suggested. "Maybe we'll see better from there."

A few minutes later they stood atop the skyscraper's wide dome. Jack gripped the thin rail that prevented them from slipping off the edge.

Furgok pointed to the Grand Arena, alone on its hill. "That's still the center of things. After the Queen was killed, the Resistance attacked her forces there. It seemed like our big chance, especially since we were up there anyway, trying to save you two.

"We were doing okay, but then that spider Xaafuun took over. She knew what we didn't—that the army would still fight, even without the Queen, as long as they had somebody to lead them. She *became* that somebody. The rebels had to retreat. Then I saw you *oom'ns* on the screen and went after you. Can't say why nobody else picked you up."

"Maybe it was the veil trees," said Isadora. "Zelum said they might hide us."

"I don't know about that. What I do know is things aren't looking good. I hate to say it, but the Princess may be right. We're taking a beating." He walked across the roof to another vantage point, and the others followed. "That's some heavy fighting over there."

"The spaceport," said Gloorg unhappily. "Once the fleet is in the air, we're doomed."

Bursts of ray gun fire lit the streets around the port. Explosions sent columns of debris into the air. Fires raged. Then, as they watched, three saucers left the ground. They hovered over the airfield, then turned toward the city. "It's as I feared," said Gloorg. "Those saucers will blow us all to pieces."

"Time for me to get back to the fight, then," said Furgok.

"We're coming, too." Isadora grabbed Jack by the sleeve.

"Oh, no, you're not! I lost you once, but not again! This time you're staying in the safe house."

A loud explosion interrupted them. One of the saucers spun away like a deflating balloon. The other saucers hovered as a dark ship, scorched like an old coffeepot, plunged from the vaporous sky.

"That'd be Dommit and Blim," said Furgok matter-of-factly. "I was wondering when they'd show up." The pirate ship fired its big guns and pounded the skreepish saucers like a hammer driving nails. One exploded, then the other. In an instant the *crannek* ship vanished.

"Where'd it go?" Gloorg asked in amazement.

"She's *fast*," Jack explained.

The pirate ship returned, destroying two more saucers on the ground. When the Queen's army fired back, it zipped away. Again and again it returned, each time pounding the skreepish fleet before it could get airborne, and always disappearing before the skreeps could mount a proper resistance.

The Queen's forces shot random bursts of antiaircraft fire into empty sky, only to watch the *crannek* return a moment later, from some unexpected direction, to continue their deadly work.

"I'm not sure I understand what's going on here," said Furgok.

"What do you mean?" said Jack. "We're whipping 'em!"

"I mean, where's the rest of the Queen's space force? Dommit and Blim are good pirates, but they aren't *that* good!"

The pattern continued. After the sixth attack, the antiaircraft guns remained silent. The pirates no longer retreated but remained in a low hover above the airfield, methodically destroying the invasion fleet as it sat helpless on the ground.

"This changes things," Gloorg said after the last saucer had been reduced to a charred ruin. The *crannek* ship performed a loop-de-loop and disappeared from view.

"Come here!" shouted Isadora. While the others watched the air show, she'd gone to the far side of the roof.

"What is it?" said Jack.

Skreepia's sun rested like a boiled tomato on the horizon. Below it, hundreds of thousands of pale lights streamed toward them in a ghostly tide.

"Kaarkuul?" asked Furgok.

"Kaarkuul," said Gloorg. "This changes things, too."

• • •

DR. SHUMWAY stood up, brushing dust from the front of her suit. "It's difficult to see through all this smoke, but I believe the destabilizer is still on its column."

"You'd *know* if it got hit," Bud said from his hiding place beneath a collapsed walker. "That is, it'd be the last thing any of us *ever* knew."

"Which is why we must get to it quickly. The planet is in peril as long as that machine of yours remains exposed." A bomb burst nearby.

"Speaking of which," Bud said anxiously, "why don't you get down? You're liable to get blown up standing out there like that."

"Our personal safety is not the issue, Mr. Creedle. Come! Time is of the essence."

"Ixnay! I'm waiting here till things cool down. Besides, we'd never make it. Xaafuun's army controls the whole hilltop."

What he said was true. Furthermore Xaafuun herself stood no more than ten feet from the destabilizer, directing the royal forces. Things were going very well, despite the unexplained difficulties at the airfield. Peasants were no match for trained soldiers.

Though her thoughts focused on the battle, an interesting question had begun to worm its way into Xaafuun's mind. The question was this: With the Exalted One dead, and the Princess in exile, what was to prevent her from seizing the throne herself? Skreepia *needed* her.

She surveyed the battlefield, full of charred wreckage and mangled corpses. After what she'd done today, who could deny it?

Her communicator buzzed, and she picked it up. "Slaves? Why are you bothering me about *slaves*?" She listened to the answer. "How many, did you say?"

• • •

THE SLAVE army entered Qurya like a rising tide. Xaafuun sent in battalions, then brigades, then whole divisions of the Queen's army, but nothing could stop the relentless assault. Where ten miners fell, a hundred rose to take their place, fighting with the desperate intensity of those who have nothing left to lose.

Slaves without guns fought with picks and shovels, and they advanced, always advanced. When the Queen's army retreated they captured weapons by the thousands. Turning them against their former owners, the miners drove deep into the heart of the city.

The slave army was directed by one of the Exalted One's former generals, an officer named Gornbluuk, who had been exiled to the mines for showing insufficient enthusiasm for the Replacement Planet Program. But the army was *led* by a strange, white-haired figure, who rode on a stretcher because he was too weak to walk. Another figure, very similar in appearance, ambled beside him, singing as he went.

Joe sang because it passed the time. Since they'd left Kaarkuul, he'd taught the miners plenty of songs: "Oh My Darling, Clementine," "The Wreck of the Old '97," "Red River Valley," and, as they marched into the city, "San Antonio Rose." It was terrible music, the way the slaves sang it, and it filled the Royal Army with dread.

The Queen's forces retreated, street by street. At the Grand Arena, Xaafuun strode the Exalted One's dais, barking orders, waving her arms, and screaming into her communicator. Rockets exploded overhead. The arena itself, already blackened by a hundred direct hits, trembled under a hundred more.

Because the rebels were winning! The awful truth could no longer be denied. That it could have happened so quickly, when victory was so near, struck Xaafuun as the cruelest twist in a lifetime filled with injustice. And there was nothing she could do to stop it, nothing she could do to turn the tide.

In time, the battle wore its way back to her hilltop, where her army, finally, could no longer retreat. She cursed them, threatened them, aimed sharp kicks at their backs. Already she could hear the slaves in the streets below singing a hideous battle song. Wretched fate! How it taunted her, as the illusion crowd cheered on, banners waved, and cherubs danced in their treetops. Even the Special Item, useless now, mocked her from its decorative column.

She turned away from the machine, and there, inexplicably, was the *Uurth* Queen. Xaafuun had no idea how the scientist had managed to walk right through the battle, to stand, imperious as always, at her feet. Bug Greedle hunched beside her, nervously rubbing his hands.

"Scientist Shumway!" Xaafuun said coolly, as if the meeting pleased her. "*Uurth* Queen. Tell me, why are you here?"

"We have come to propose a cease-fire," the *ooman bing* said calmly. "You may not be aware of it, but the situation here is extremely perilous."

"Oh, but I *am* aware." A rocket exploded overhead. Flaming shrapnel rained down. Xaafuun watched it with apparent calm. "Battlefields are often that way."

One of her officers ran by, on fire, screaming, "Overrun! We're overrun!"

"Indeed," said Dr. Shumway. "But the peril I refer to is of an even greater magnitude. A *much* greater magnitude! You see, within that machine, your *Special Item*, is a substance so volatile, that were it to explode, it could literally destroy this planet."

Xaafuun watched her closely, then looked at the king. "Is this true, Bug Greedle?"

"I wish it weren't."

"Commander!" shouted one of her officers, hobbling up the hill on four broken legs. "We're beaten! The miners have us surrounded. It's nothing but butchery now."

More officers arrived, then common soldiers, crowding back against the walls of the arena. Many were wounded;

all were wild-eyed with fear. Xaafuun looked at the *ooman bings*, then at the Item. Her mind began to work on a new equation.

"We have to surrender!" shouted an officer.

"They'll kill us all!" screamed another.

Xaafuun pulled a ray gun from her utility belt and held it against the destabilizer. "Tell them to stop firing," she ordered.

"They already have!" wailed the officer.

"No, idiot. Tell the *slaves* to stop firing. Tell them to stop firing or I'll *blow them up*! I *can*, you see. Tell them that. Tell them if I pull this trigger I will kill them all! Tell them they must surrender to me, or I'll blow up the entire planet!"

"But that's outrageous!" said Dr. Shumway.

"Indeed it is, *Uurth* Queen."

Shouts rang down the hillside. The firing became sporadic, then stopped. Not understanding what was happening, the Queen's soldiers laid down their arms, picked them up, then laid them down again. Armed slaves gathered around. The illusion crowd cheered. Two figures stepped out of the smoke. One was a very frail, white-haired *ooman bing*. The other was a soldier Xaafuun knew, or had once known, before it became illegal to mention her name.

"General Gornbluuk," Xaafuun said smoothly. "This is *very* great treason, even by your standards."

"What's your game?" asked the general.

Xaafuun stroked the destabilizer lovingly. Her ray gun brushed its enameled side. "You see this machine, General, this *Special Item*? Do you know what it is?"

"Should I?"

"I think you should. You see, this *Uurthish* machine has more power than all the bombs on Skreepia put together."

"So what's your point?"

"This device can *destroy* Skreepia. All of it. And it will, unless that verminous army of yours lays down its weapons."

A ripple went through the crowd. The general said, "You're bluffing."

"Am I? Tell her, *Uurth* Queen."

"I'm afraid it's true."

"And can she really explode it, right here, right now?"

"I believe she can. A ray gun blast would be more than sufficient to ignite the quantum foam in the destabilizer's core. Isn't that right, Mr. Creedle?"

Bud swallowed hard. "The explosion would likely destroy every bit of life on this planet."

"Not a great loss, from my point of view," Xaafuun said cheerfully. "Judging by what I've seen of that life today! Lay down your arms, General. I won't tell you again." She watched the strained faces of her adversaries and realized with a thrill that they were *all* her adversaries now: *every living thing on the planet*! The thought filled her with joy. So this was what it was like to be the Exalted One, to rule an empire, to master them all!

"Do it," croaked General Gornbluuk. "Lay down your arms."

"Very wise." Xaafuun watched benevolently while the slaves did as they were told. For a moment her gaze turned to the Special Item. Lovely Item! In the end, it was worth every bit of trouble it had caused! As her eyes caressed its milky shell, something stirred beside her. She would have seen it, except that it came from her blind side, the side where her scarred eye perched dead upon its stalk. Instead, she merely sensed the movement through some dim instinct.

And that made her a fraction too slow. A sudden pain exploded in her head. Two eyes burned white, then black.

She screamed and was slashed again. This time the blade cut through her arm, her *weapon* arm. Her hand flew off. The ray gun clattered harmlessly to the ground.

For a moment she saw her enemy, saw the face she remembered from so many nightmares. *"You!"* she gasped.

"Me," said Joe, and his blade flashed one last time.

. . .

51. THE FEAST

"OH, GOODY, I've won!" said the Princess when she heard the news. She gazed cheerfully around the safe house at the children, the *crannek*, and the battle-worn general who had come for her. "Don't just stand there gawking at me!" she cried. "Take me to the palace, where I belong."

A victorious throng met her outside the embassy building. They raised her on their shoulders and carried her away, singing "Streets of Laredo" at the top of their lungs. The torch-lit procession was a very different parade from the one that morning. There were no aristocrats, dignitaries, uniformed officers, or relentlessly cheering crowds. Most of Qurya's illusions had been destroyed in the battle. But the way to the palace was now clear, as true night settled on the city for the first time in anyone's memory.

When the Princess arrived, the palace guards flung open the gates. Then, seeing the faces of those who walked with her, they quickly tried to close them again.

"I'd leave 'em open if I were you!" shouted Skrank. "These swabs are hungry and irritable. Anyway that castle of yours could use some airing out."

In the end, the gates stayed open. Later that night, the city's food warehouses were torn open, too. The feasting began, and with it, a new era. There was no electronic durbo music in the streets of Qurya that night, no ads for Dramool's Kimili Pods or Spatz Nutro Juice, no broadcast warnings from the Queen. Instead there were campfires, and laughter, and freedom songs from planets across the spiral arm, a million voices, strong and weak, raised to the boundless heavens.

• • •

AS WITH ALL battles, confusion followed. Some could not be accounted for, while others reappeared unexpectedly. Nobody could say who first remembered the Webbs, stuck in their dungeon deep below the palace, or who finally rescued them. "It wasn't *my* idea," was Jack's only comment.

Nobody had any idea where Phoony went, either. The Finder was lost and could not be found. Groot was gone, too.

It was never known why the royal space patrols failed, at the critical moment, to answer their distress calls, or why the Queen's far-flung armies never came to her aid. Some of her forces fought battles elsewhere around the planet, but most simply dissolved. There was, in the end, a great deal of surprise at how easily the revolution succeeded. It turned out the Exalted One, for all her grandeur, and for all the apparent power of her empire, had enjoyed very little real support.

Perhaps strangest of all, though, was the mystery of Beast Eleven. Following the battle, stories about the creature multiplied. If the tales were to be believed, Beast Eleven had been everywhere that day, wreaking havoc on the Queen's guard, driving off crews before they could fire up their saucers, smashing illusion screens, freeing the other beasts, killing tunnel worms in the mines. Many of the stories were flatly impossible. All that could be said for certain was this: After the battle, Beast Eleven was gone.

Only its memory remained, yet that was a vision of such savagery, power, and grace that it became the stuff of instant legend. Some said that after Beast Eleven disappeared into the hills beyond Qurya, forests began to grow there with amazing speed. Others swore that animals long thought extinct were now coming out of hiding in forgotten places around the globe. These were fanciful tales, no doubt, from creatures who had lived too long behind walls of illusion. But none could dispute that Beast Eleven was out there, *somewhere*. It was an idea full of terror and joy.

•   •   •

THE DAY BEFORE they were to depart, the Earthlings and the *crannek* were honored with a grand feast at the palace. It wasn't an event anyone was eager to attend, especially the new Exalted One, its ostensible host. In fact, the feast was Skrank's idea, and nobody wanted to argue with the captain. "The skreeps need to see their rulers getting along with others," reasoned the pirate. "This way we'll get our Princess started on the right foot."

"I'd like to put *my* foot right up her royal arse," grumbled Furgok.

"So would I," the captain assured him. "But these spiders can't imagine a world without a queen, the sorry buggers, so we may as well put on a good show."

And so they did. In the dim twilight of a skreepish afternoon they gathered around a long table to eat dish after strange dish, while a slew of robotic cameras fluttered around them like bats, broadcasting the event to all of Skreepia.

"These rolls ain't half bad," said Joe, gnawing on what looked like a river stone. In addition to the Earthlings and the *crannek*, the leaders of the Resistance had been invited, including General Gornbluuk, Mellis, Fish Face, and Hroag. Krebs had long since returned to her shack.

The new Exalted One sat at the table's far end, sulking. The former Princess had wanted to cloak the event in the usual illusions, but her tablemates had flatly refused. It was a new era, they said, and in the end agreed to only one illusion, applied to the Queen herself: that of surpassing beauty. She did not feel entirely mollified. Ruling Skreepia, it turned out, was not nearly as much fun as she had imagined. Nobody was terribly *obedient*, for one thing.

At the table's opposite end sat the *Uurth* Queen, Dr. Shumway. It had taken many hours of argument to persuade her to dress in an elaborately feathered crown and cloak. "Really, it is a ridiculous fraud," she complained.

"The skreeps demand it," said Skrank. "And I say, give 'em what they want."

"I think you look dandy," Joe said seriously. "A sight for sore eyes."

"Please!" she said, but smiled.

Isadora and Jack, sitting on either side of her, were similarly attired, as was Uncle Bud. An empty seat next to Jack belonged to Milo, who quickly fled under the table. He was sick of all the attention. Since the victory, the rooster had become easily the most popular of the *Uurthlings*. His image was everywhere. The Queen merely *wears* feathers, went a popular saying, but Milo *grows* them!

Jack shared food with his father, though Stanley Murchison did most of the eating. A few days' rest and some Hellebeezian sod, slipped, at Isadora's suggestion, into his daily gruel, had begun to restore his health. Sergeant Webb sat next to him, sour as ever, and Grady, equally sour, sat next to his father.

"Tell me again how the skreeps caught you," said Jack. He was still having some trouble with the story.

"There ain't so much to tell, son," said Murchison. Though his plate was filled to overflowing, he grabbed a handful of trubilo nuts as the bowl passed by. "Seems they were after your uncle and nabbed me by mistake. When they figured out I *wasn't* the inventor, they decided to keep me anyway. You might say I was in the wrong place at the wrong time."

"Why don't you tell the boy *why* you were in the wrong place?" grumbled Sergeant Webb. "Heading out of town at *ninety miles per hour*?"

"I guess I was having some trouble with the law," he said with his mouth full. "Seems to me some people don't have the *sense of humor* they ought to."

"Now, that's a fact, ain't it?" said Joe. "Hey, Doc, pass me them taters, will you?" Dr. Shumway handed him a bowl of orange, rough-bodied vegetables that didn't look at all like potatoes, and which bled purple juice when poked with a bowie knife. Joe didn't mind. "I can't remember the last time I dined with so much royalty," he said and winked at the nearest camera.

. . .

52. VERN HOLLOW, 1956

THE JOURNEY home was uneventful. The *crannek* ship was uncomfortably tight with so many passengers, but the destabilizer more than made up for it. Uncle Bud's Special Item cut a tunnel that neatly paralleled the old Medwig Gulp, and they zipped across space in literally no time at all.

Skrank was flabbergasted by the technology. "I never saw anything like it," she said. "So these time tunnels you make—do they close up after you go through?"

"You know," said Bud, "I'm not really sure."

"Good heavens!" said Dr. Shumway. "You mean these holes we're making could be *permanent*?"

"Well, it ain't like I've done this before."

Isadora had a different concern. "It looks as if we'll make it back to Earth," she told Jack as they sat on the bridge watching the swirling stars. "The question is, *when*? We may have traveled nearly as far through time as we have through space."

Jack pictured a strange, futuristic Earth, a place without the Pines, without *Sentinel*s or *Courier*s, without Smedley Trowbridge, without his mother. "I'm trying not to think about that," he said quietly and rubbed the last bit of fur from his rabbit's foot.

His father joined them. From time to time Stanley Murchison reminded Jack that they had "a lot of catching up to do." Which was true, though there were still some awkward silences.

"I've been wondering," said Jack. "What was all that prophecy stuff about?"

"I don't know," Murchison said finally. "It seemed like those monsters needed a little *encouragement*—same as people on Earth. Well, on Earth we got stories like the one I told—about a great king coming to cure the sick, feed the hungry, free the prisoners, that sort of thing. You know, somebody who'd generally put things right. I thought a story like that might cheer 'em up."

"But what's that got to do with this *'Earth Queen'* stuff?"

"Son, they don't have any notion of *kings* on Skreepia! So I kind of spiced things up to suit their tastes. That's a lesson you'll need to learn: *Know your audience.* Once you do, you'll know exactly what to tell them."

"Spoken like a true con man," sneered Sergeant Webb.

"The funny thing is," Murchison continued, ignoring him, "after a while I started believing the story myself. Especially once I was down in those mines. By then, *I* was the one needing encouragement. So I decided that one day a queen *would* come from Earth and turn us all loose. I *had* to believe it, you see. It was all I had. I told the other slaves, and a lot of them believed it, too. And then, what do you know? It happened!"

Jack thought about Hellebeezia, where he and Isadora had rescued themselves by making up stories. He wondered how often that sort of thing worked. "I think you got lucky on this one, Pop."

Uncle Bud joined them. "Won't be long now. Dommit's going over the numbers. We'll be back in our own solar system before you know it."

"What will they do with the destabilizer?" asked Isadora.

"Dump it! The *crannek* know a place where it will fall into something they call a *black hole*. And that'll be the end of it. They'll go back to their own planet using natural tunnels." He looked at the destabilizer sadly. "I can't believe they're going to destroy it! The greatest invention since the internal combustion engine, and everyone says it's too dangerous to keep!"

"You'll think of something else," said Jack.

"Maybe. But I'll never see that million bucks. Some folks can't catch a break, and I'm one of 'em."

• • •

MAYOR HANDY, Colonel Miles, and Mrs. Creedle stood on the front porch of the Pines. Perhaps ten minutes had passed since the saucer took off. Since then, a deep silence had settled between them.

"Those were skreeps, all right," the colonel declared, puffing his cigar. "You can tell them from other aliens by the kind of ship they use."

"I certainly hope they don't come back," said the mayor. "Imagine what *that* would do to Vern Hollow's reputation!"

"I hate to say it, but they *might* come back. We're living in the space age now." The colonel removed his cigar and scowled at it. "Anyway, I take full responsibility for this failure."

"What failure?" asked Mrs. Creedle. "They left, didn't they? What more do you want?"

"I came here to fight an enemy. Instead, I let them slip away. That's failure."

"If it makes you feel any better, I didn't expect that much of you in the first place."

Colonel Miles started to answer, but his words were cut off by a low hum from overhead.

Sergeant Price ran in from the darkness of the front yard. "They're coming back, Colonel! Should I give the order to fire?"

Colonel Miles paused, his expression one of fixed concentration. "No," he said finally. "The sound is different. It isn't the same ship." He peered into the sky, puffing.

Suddenly there it was, a small saucer with a blackened body. Its top was ringed with yellow lights.

"It *is* different," said Mayor Handy, his voice full of wonder. "It's a different saucer altogether."

The spaceship came down slowly until it hovered over the spot in Dutch Woods that the other ship had vacated minutes before. A shower of green sparks shot from its belly as it descended into the trees. Then the silence of the town was once again complete.

A cold breeze, full of the promise of winter, whispered down from the north.

"I'll put on some coffee," said Mrs. Creedle. "Something tells me this is going to be a long night."

.   .   .